THE CELEBRATED LETTERS OF JOHN B. KEANE VOL II

LETTERS OF A CIVIC GUARD

LETTERS OF AN IRISH PUBLICAN

LETTERS OF A COUNTRY POSTMAN

LETTERS TO THE BRAIN

MERCIER PRESS

CONTENTS

Letters of a Civic Guard

INTRODUCTION

Leo Molair, chief author of the following letters, is a member of the Garda Siochana, that most respected and distinguished of peacekeeping forces which has almost always succeeded in attracting to its ranks a most superior and dedicated type of individual.

Leo Molair is a man of honour but he is also possessed of a wry and somewhat caustic sense of humour. For reasons best known to himself he never took a wife although it could be said that as years went by he became married to his vocation.

The preservation of peace always was and is his primary function but because the strict enforcement of the code does not always succeed in maintaining order he is often obliged to harness the chariot of the law to the horses of discretion and humanity.

He is the man on the spot and as such knows the value of such effective weapons as tact and delicacy. He also knows the case histories of his clients the way a family doctor knows his patients.

He is always mindful of the evil of wrongdoing but mindful too of many areas of innocence relating thereto and it is here that discretion and insight of a high order are needed if the law is to serve rather than expose the community.

If some of these letters read seamily or sordidly it is not the fault of the author. Rather it is the fault of the community which has been entrusted to his care. If there were not a seamy side to life there would be no necessity for custodians of the peace. Leo Molair's role is one which has been created by the follies and weaknesses of his fellows.

Consequently folly and weakness must, perforce, dominate the greater part of the following correspondence.

We find our man, towards the end of his career, writing to his nephew Ned who is also a civic guard but of a mere two years standing.

Dear Ned

You ask about your new Super. I had a visit four years ago from the same Patcheen Conners who now answers to the call of Superintendant Patrick Conners. We were together in the Depot and afterwards we spent a spell in the same station in Dublin. Patcheen has an accent now like you'd hear from an elocution teacher. On top of that he needlessly indulges in a lot of other grandiose antics. The wife, of course, must shoulder the blame.

Answering to the name of Susie McGee she graduated thirty years ago from a juicy ranch of nine acres in the latter end of Mayo and between cajoling and screeching, nagging and pestering you might say she would be entitled to take full credit for all of Patcheen's promotions. Fair dues to her she was and still is a fine ball of a woman. There are some unkind souls who say she went to bed a half a dozen times with a certain politician, once for sergeant, twice for inspector and three times for superintendent. However, you may take it from me that those who spread such stories come under the general head of hostile witnesses.

Patcheen was all right when I first knew him. He was as easygoing as an in-calf heifer, tough as an ass, fond of a pint and afraid of nothing of God's earth until he was hooked and gaffed by the aforementioned Susie McGee. She was the oldest of seven sisters and neighbours who knew them will give evidence that not one of them drew on a knickers till the day they went into service.

Susie came to Dublin to work as a housemaid for a surgeon named Halligan. She was only barely gone eighteen at the time. She arrived in the city in the middle of March and she married Patcheen Conners in the middle of June. She changed him overnight.

About six months after the marriage I called to see them one evening when I was off-duty. They had their own house in a nice area of Rathmines.

There was Patcheen, made up by the wife like he'd be a magazine model with cardigan and slippers and a fart of a pipe hanging from the side of his mouth. We sat down for a chat. From the minute I took to the chair he never stopped sermonising about the evils of drink and the terrible after-effects of late-night carousing. After a while Susie landed in with three small cups and a tiny teapot you wouldn't put in front of a midget.

There was no mention of drink and I having a head on me like a furnace after a party the night before. After a while Susie says to me:

'How's your handicap?'

I told her it was as good as could be expected thinking she was referring to my private part. I was ruptured earlier in the year making an arrest outside a public house in Henry Street.

'Patrick's,' said she, 'is down to fourteen.'

'Twas then I knew she must be referring to golf. I nearly fell out of the chair because when I first met Patcheen he wouldn't know a golf club from a hockey stick. Susie is one of those strong-willed women who will never latch on to a made man. They prefer to start with their own raw material, no matter how rugged or crude and to mould what they want out of that. The husbands have no say whatsoever in the outcome. She did a fair job on Patcheen. When I knew him he wouldn't track an elephant through six inches of snow. Anyone who could make a superintendent out of Patcheen Conners could make a bonfire out of snowballs. He called here once to see me. He didn't stay with me long. He had an appointment for a four-ball at Muskerry Golf Club. Susie stayed in the car so I came out to say hello to her. You'd hardly expect a woman so high-up in the world to call into a one-man station.

'You'll never marry now,' was the first thing she said to me.

'Not unless you divorce Patcheen,' said I by way of a joke.

'Surely you mean Pawtrick,' she said and she cocked her nose high.

'He'll always be Patcheen to me missus,' said I.

That stung her. What the poor woman keeps forgetting is that the only real difference between myself and Patcheen Conners is the colour of our uniforms. Patcheen himself is all right. You don't have to worry about him. All he wants is to draw his pay, play golf and be seen in his uniform now and again. My fondest regards to Gert and the baby. Find out the names for me of the older guards and sergeants in your division. Chances are I know some of them.

Your fond uncle

Leo

Main Street
Monasterbawn
County Cork

Dear Guard Molair

Sacred heart of Jesus and his divine Mother will you do something about the carry-on at Fie's public house. I am the mother of a family that never put a hard word on no one but the conduct going on there you wouldn't hear of in Soho. At all hours of the morning is the after-hours guzzling of drink going on, single men hobnobbing with married women and vice versa if you please. God alone knows what amount of whoring goes on there. If you don't do your duty and close down this den of iniquity before the whole village is corrupted and scandalised I will write to the minister that you are turning a blind eye on criminal and immoral activity. Margie Fie is worse nor any madam you'd find in a whorehouse with her lips daubed scarlet and the make-up an inch thick and the grey hair dyed blonde. Who does she think she's codding. Hurry up quick and close her down in the name of all that's good and holy.

Devoted Catholic wife and mother of a large family.

Main Street
Monasterbawn

Dear Guard Molair

It is high time someone took the initiative in the stamping out of after-hours drinking and other vices that arise from it. Wives are without money for their shopping and many children in this godforsaken village are hungry and without proper clothing. The money is squandered on drink to buy style for the wives of certain publicans. The most brazen example of after-hours boozing is to be seen at Crutt's public house right here under your very nose in Monasterbawn. On my way from eight o'clock Mass yesterday morning what did I behold outside the front door of Crutt's pub but a rubber object which I took at first to be a finger-stall or some sort of unblown balloon. Casually over breakfast I described the object to my husband. Imagine my horror when he told me that what I had seen was undoubtedly a contraceptive. Hell is a light punishment for the proprietors of Crutt's public house.

Signed

Indignant Housewife

Fallon Street Garda Station
Dublin 13

Dear Uncle Leo

Many thanks for your letter and for the enclosed gift of which there was no need as we have more than enough. We are all very distraught and upset here after the brutal murder of our colleague yesterday. It is incredible that an Irishman should gun down another Irishman in cold blood merely because the victim was doing his duty and upholding the law for the benefit of all the citizens of the state. There is a despairing feeling of futility at the callousness of these extremists who snuff out life without thought for loved ones left behind. I cannot conceive of a more foul and brutal deed. Those who murdered this likeable and loyal member of our force cannot be called men. Yet the arch-criminals who are their superiors walk the streets as free men with smug looks on their faces. God forgive me if I ask Him to wipe these scum from the face of the earth. I'll say no more now as I may say too much. I see the gentle smile on my dead comrade's face and I hear his light laugh fading away forever. It's terrible.

I envy you your peaceful way of life down there, far from the madding crowd and all that and the clean countryside at your doorstep. It is my ambition to move down the country as soon as possible. I'm checking up on the older members of the division to find out who would have been most likely to have served with you. I'll write as soon as I hear from you again. Be thankful for the grand, quiet, peaceful place where you live and for the innocent people in your bailiwick.

Your fond nephew

Ned

PS We are making a collection for the widow.

Ned

Garda Barracks
Monasterbawn

Dear Ned

I enclose a subscription towards the collection for our dead comrade's widow. A horrible business altogether. How should one react when one's brother is murdered, gunned down mercilessly without a chance of any kind and remember that we who wear these uniforms are brothers and comrades in the cause of law and order. All we must endeavour to do is protect our charges, the small boys and girls, the fathers and mothers, the senile and the helpless and to see to the safety of their belongings and their homes. Nothing must come between us and our concern for those in our care. If one of us is brutally murdered our function is to stand fast and to pray for the resolution and courage to carry on with the job. We may ask ourselves how any human being could cut down another in his prime without regard for his young wife and family. We may ask ourselves how such an awful deed can be justified. We may ask if there is any form of punishment on this earth severe enough for these inhuman wretches who spill our life's blood. We may ask and ask Ned but in the end all that matters is the honourable discharge of our duty regardless of all other considerations and this force, in that respect, can look to its record with pride.

Like yourself I will draw the line here and now on this most tragic event. Stick to your post. Be loyal to your superiors and to your comrades and there need be no fears for the future of our country.

In your letter you say to me that I should be thankful for this grand, quiet, peaceful place where I live and also for the innocent people in my bailiwick. Wait till you're as old as I am and you'll find out that there aren't as many innocent people as you think. There is an extract from *Hamlet* which goes like this:

> *I could a tale unfold, whose lightest word*
> *Would harrow up thy soul; freeze thy young blood;*
> *Make thy two eyes, like stars, start from their spheres;*
> *Thy knotted and combined locks to part,*
> *And each particular hair to stand on end,*
> *Like quills upon the fretful porpentine*
> *But this eternal blazon must not be*
> *To ears of flesh and blood.*

I too my dear Ned could a tale unfold, in fact a hundred tales, about this village and no other, that would make the *News of the World* read like a Communion tract but this would achieve no worthwhile end except to do the world of harm and absolutely no good.

If you think Monasterbawn is quiet and peaceful read this account of one particular day in the life of your humble servant, Leo Molair. I rose at seven-thirty and went to eight o'clock mass which I had to serve for the good reason that the altar boy's mother forgot to call him. How could she and she at a wren dance till five in the morning. On my way from Mass I was summoned to a house in Jackass Lane by a gorsoon of eight who informed me that his father was in the process of murdering his mother. From the casual way he spoke I gathered it wasn't his first time murdering her. I arrived at the house to find the poor woman seated on a chair with a bleeding mouth, a swollen right eye and a cut nose. The husband whose name is Mocky Trembles was still giving out when I crossed the threshold. My first instinct was to lay him out but when you're in this game as long as I am you'll find it pays to play cool. I started attempts at reconciliation at quarter to nine and six cups of tea later at precisely eleven o'clock I had the two of them cooing like pigeons and Mocky promising never to lay a finger on her ever again. For her part she knelt and swore that not a nagging word would be heard out of her as long as she lived.

When I left he was bathing her face with a sponge and telling her that she was to keep the next allotment of family allowance money in order to buy some style for herself. Mocky drank the last allotment.

Back at the barracks there was a caller awaiting me. She was the female teacher in the national school down the road, a spinster by the name of Monica Flynn who, if I may say so, has had strong matrimonial designs on yours truly although if you saw her you wouldn't give me any credit. Monica had arrived to make a complaint about a man called the Bugger Moran. She had some difficulty in explaining herself but I gathered that the Bugger had been exposing his population stick, if you'll pardon the expression, opposite the young girls on their way home from school. I promised to look into the matter. Monica refused to proffer charges for fear of embarrassing herself, the school and the children. Rest assured that the Bugger will have a sore posterior shortly.

When Monica departed I had my breakfast and took a skim through the paper. My next chore was to visit the farm of a man called Thade Buckley about five miles up in the mountains. No hope of a lift in that direction so late in the day with all the creamery cars long gone. Nothing for it but the bicycle. I arrived after nearly an hour on the uphill road. Some months previously at a bull inspection the same Thade had a yearling rejected and it was my job to ensure that certain requirements be fulfilled if he was to keep the animal.

'What brought you?' asked Thade with an innocent face and he knowing well what brought me.

'You had a bull for inspection lately?'

'I had a bull,' said Thade.

'And did you castrate that bull,' I asked, 'in compliance with the departmental order?'

'I squeezed that bull myself,' said Thade, 'and you may be sure that he is now a happy bullock grazing the mountain.'

'He must be a very odd sort of a bullock,' said I, 'seeing that he attacked and nearly killed a fowler last Sunday.'

'That's the first I heard of it,' said Thade. I then instructed him to locate the bull for me so he led me across a few wet fields to the base of the mountain where sure enough there were some bullocks grazing. He pointed at the animal in question. I noted that this beast was castrated beyond doubt but when I looked for the rejection mark on his ear which the departmental inspector impresses on all rejects I could find no trace of it. Alongside this animal was another with a wicked-looking pair of bloodshot eyes and he pawing the ground indicating a charge at any minute. Sure enough in his ear was the letter 'R'. The animal was not castrated it was plain to be seen.

'Explain this,' I asked Thade but when I turned he was haring his way down the mountain. The next thing you know I got an almighty thump on the rump and there was the rejected bull coming at me again. I followed Thade's example and scrambled over a gate into a nearby field. Back at the house I confronted Thade.

'I must have squeezed the wrong one,' he explained, 'or else they must have grown there again.' I had enough of this nonsense. I charged him with possession of a reject and refused his offer of whiskey which I strongly suspected was home-made anyway. Three years earlier his house had been searched from top to bottom for poteen but not a drop was found. I discovered later from a friend that under every bed in the house was an enamel chamber pot and every one of these pots was filled to the brim with a liquid which was not urine.

When I arrived back at the barracks it was too late for lunch although there is always a plate kept hot for me at the house where I normally have lunch. There were two visitors awaiting me at the barracks. One was an elderly woman who had just been badly bitten by a dog and the other an unfortunate woman whose husband had suddenly and mysteriously disappeared. I took particulars from both women and went into action. A phone call confirmed what I suspected about the missing man. He had spent the family allowance money the night before in Clonakilty, started a row in a chip shop and wound up in the barracks where he was still being held for refusing to identify himself. The orderly promised to send him home in the patrol car some time that night. As for the cross dog the poor creature is now in the kennels of Heaven.

Three o'clock. The children would now be coming from school. I took up my position in a concealed entrance where I had a good view of the roadway. At three the school bell rang and at five past three our friend the Bugger appeared and pretended to be relieving himself. When the children appeared he exposed himself fully so I moved in and arrested him. I first of all gave him a good rooter in the behind. Then for good measure I let him have two more boosters in the same spot. Then I lugged him to the barracks where I charged him. His pleading not to charge him was piteous. The awful disgrace of it and the effect it would have on his mother, a doting old crone who would hardly know night from day.

I decided to let him go but I warned him if I ever caught him again I would personally belt the daylights out of him and see that he went to jail as well. It wasn't out of pity for him or his mother but the prospect of undesirable publicity for the whole village. At five Jerry Fogg the postman arrived with the morning post. We had an arrangement that if I was missing from the barracks he would hold the post until my return.

There were two letters, one each from the wives of two publicans who have premises at opposite sides of the street. They think I don't know who writes them. I know more about them than they know about themselves. Remember I have been studying these people night and day for twenty-five years since I was transferred here for raiding a politician's public house. Both do good business and are fairly well off but the letters are motivated by jealousy. I dare not take a drink in either house for fear of invoking the enmity of the other. Whenever I feel like a few drinks I slip in the rear door of the Widow Hansel's pub at the northern end of the village. No one sees me come and no one sees me go.

Sometimes I have a game of thirty-one in the kitchen with Jerry the post and a few pals. I'll file the letters and ignore them.

Four-thirty. Time to take a stroll around the village and make sure that everything is all right. Five-thirty, back at the barracks. Boiled two eggs and made a pot of tea. Turned on the television and sat back to relax. Enter a small fat woman whose face is vaguely familiar. She is accompanied by a pimple-faced teenage girl who looks sufficiently like her to be her daughter. She gets down to business right away.

'My child is after being raped,' she says.

'Will you state the particulars missus,' says I as calmly as I could.

'Well,' says she, 'she's in service below at Jamesy Cracken's these past four months and she hasn't had a minute's peace with the same Jamesy chasing her at every hand's turn. Finally he done it. This very evening he raped the child in the henhouse.'

I nodded, awaiting the remainder of the story.

'I don't see you taking any notes,' she said.

'Notes about what?' said I.

'About the rape,' said she.

'And was it you or your daughter was raped missus,' said I.

'My daughter,' said she. That quietened her awhile. I set about finding out what really happened to the daughter. Apparently, Jamesy Cracken, a feeble old lecher of seventy-four, attempted to knock the girl on the floor of the henhouse where she had been sent by Jamesy's sister to collect eggs for the supper. All, it transpired, that Jamesy succeeded in doing was thrusting his hand under her dress, where it trespassed for a second on that most prized and private of all personal properties. The innocent young girl, presuming this to be rape, ran home screeching to her mother who, with a nose for easy money, came first to the barracks before launching on a campaign to milk Jamesy Cracken of some of the thousands he is supposed to have hoarded over the years. I burst the bubble there and then and informed her that the only charge, to my knowledge, of which Jamesy might be guilty was indecent assault and that her best bet, in such a situation, would be an ambitious solicitor.

Do you still think that this is a quiet and peaceful place? Remember that, at the time of writing, it is only eight o'clock and that the ship of night has yet to discharge its mysterious cargo. I'm tired. It's been a long, long day. I think I'll slip up to the Widow Hansel's and chance a few pints.

Love to Gert and the child.

Uncle Leo

Fallon Street Garda Station
Dublin 13

Dear Uncle Leo

Good to hear from you. I suppose I shouldn't complain. I have a nice home, a lovely wife and child and a good job. There are times when I am driven to despair. One night last week I interrupted a smash-and-grab raid in Grafton Street. There were two youths involved. As soon as they saw me they took off in different directions. I followed one and after a chase cornered him in a lane near the Shelbourne Hotel. He produced a knife but I managed to disarm him. What do you think happens? A suspended sentence of six months. The mother arrived at the court to plead for him. I risk my life to arrest him and instead of a jail sentence the judge gives him permission to further his career of crime. Would you blame me if I were to close my eyes the next time I come across a smash-and-grab?

There is an old guard here by the name of Mick Drea who says he was stationed with you in Mayo. He says he could write a book about the times the pair of you had together. Tell me about the raid on that pub and why it was the cause of your being transferred. Young Eddie is grand. Gert sends her love.

Your fond nephew

Ned

Main Street
Monasterbawn

Dear Guard Molair

This is to acquaint you with a terrible disturbance that took place outside Crutt's public house just on midnight on the thirtieth of November while yourself and the Widow Hansel were cavorting and doing what else among the tombstones of Monasterbawn Graveyard. They all but kicked one another to death but who is to blame teenagers if they are given rotten whiskey by Mrs Crutt. They were no more than children the creatures. Well might their poor mothers curse the demon that took their money and threw them out drunk and incapable on the cold street. May the blessed Mother of God forgive her for I cannot. I am writting to Superintendent Fahy since it seems to be a waste of time writing to you.

　Signed

　A devoted wife and Catholic mother of a large family

Garda Station
Monasterbawn

Dear Ned

I can understand your frustration but the last thing any judge wants to be is first to jail a youngster. What that pup needed was a good hiding, a hiding he'd remember every time he'd see a guard, but that's frowned upon now and these days in cities there's little fear and less respect for the uniform and you'll have less still while you have lenient courts and naive judges who play games with the law with their fines of ten and twenty pounds on young bucks who pay more than that on income tax every week. As far as I can see courts are presently no more than places where licenses to commit crimes are issued to snot-nosed whelps who should be flogged and isolated until they show respect for society. I'm all for giving a young fellow a chance but too many chances make a mockery of my job and yours.

I remember Mick Drea well. For many years he was my closest friend. We were stationed in Mayo together in those days when the sight of a guard's uniform enraged the local bucks. Their sole aim was to have it to their credit that they kicked or beat the stuffing out of a guard. Off then to England where they'd be boasting about their exploits in pubs and Irish clubs. Mick and myself were stationed in the tiny village of Keeldown. There were several pubs and several shebeens. Shebeens sprang up overnight. What happened was this. A young navvy would arrive home from England with maybe a hundred or more pounds. Mighty money in those days. In case he might spend it foolishly on drink for others the mother might advise him to invest it and what better way could you invest money than in drink. That was how many shebeens started. Most were quickly found out and closed when reports would be sent to the barracks by the proprietors of other shebeens whose trade had suffered a knock because of the new opposition. The stock of a shebeen consisted mainly of porter and poteen, a few bottles of the very cheapest in sherry and port wines and inevitably a wide range of the most inferior Spanish brandies. These were easily purchased at the nearest fishing port from the crews of trawlers operating out of San Sebastian and Bilbao in the north of Spain. Two shillings a bottle was the going rate and for this you got a pint and a quarter of a concoction powerful enough to fuel a spaceship to the moon. Quite often an overdose of it resulted in permanent mental and physical damage and, on occasion, death.

On very rare occasions there would be legitimate Hennessy's brandy but this was almost always beyond the scope of the regular patrons. Usually it was sold at four-pence a thimbleful to old men and women and those who might be invalided or convalescing. I was witness to several murderous brawls which could be directly attributed to the consumption of a mixture of Spanish brandy and poteen. One night in the height of summer Mick Drea and myself cycled in plain clothes to a shebeen in the north of the county. It was situated near a dance hall. In the kitchen there was one long stool and six chairs all told. There was a table in the centre. The bar was a tea chest on top of which was a biscuit tin which was used as a till. Most of the customers were seated on the floor drinking happily or crooning snatches of songs, some in Gaelic, some in English. The hardest drinkers would be the navvies home on holidays from England. They sat, as I say, on the floor and when Mick and I entered they eyed us with great suspicion and deliberately bumped or fell against us when we made our way to the counter. Those on the floor were drinking their shorts out of eggstands, eggshells, stolen inkwells and saltcellars. They drank porter out of cups, mugs and pannies. There was a brisk trade and I wondered if the local guards knew about the place. Unlikely since it was only a few weeks old. We called and paid for two mugs of porter and surveyed the situation without pretending to do so. After a while a dwarfish fellow with a cap on the side of his head and a crooked smile asked us where we came from. It was easy to see that he was the spokesman for a group of young thugs who sat drinking shorts in the nearest corner.

'Foxford,' we lied.

'And what line of trade does ye be in whilst ye're there?' he asked.

'We're in the bank,' Mick told him.

'Are ye Mayo men itself?' he asked, turning to wink knowingly at his cronies who had meanwhile edged a bit nearer so that they could hear better.

'Indeed we're not,' said we.

'Musha you have the poll of a Galway man whatever,' he told Mick.

'He's from Cork,' said I.

'Musha we have nothing against Corkmen, eh boys,' he addressed his friends.

'Yourself. Where are you from?' he demanded. I was about to say Kerry but since he had declared that they had nothing against Corkmen I decided to opt for that county.

'I don't like one bit of this,' I whispered to Mick. 'Let's move out of here. I can smell trouble.' We finished our drinks and headed for the dance hall. It was crowded. Mick wasn't long in finding himself a partner. She was a beautiful dark-haired girl with a pale face. I took a few turns on the floor but could meet nothing I fancied. The next thing you know Mick comes across to me and announces that he is seeing the girl home. Kathleen is her name and she lives only a half mile up the road.

'You keep an eye on the bikes,' Mick said. 'I won't be gone long.' We arranged to meet at the crossroads below the village. I pushed the cycles in that direction and waited. It was a warm night without a puff of wind. The stars shone in their millions and the moon was full. There was a rich scent of honeysuckle and I thought how peaceful it all was. It was then I heard the footsteps. After a while I made out the shapes. I had no bother in recognising the dwarfish fellow with the slanted cap and undoubtedly the four with him would have to be the four who had been squatting on the floor of the shebeen although I couldn't swear to this. I sensed they were looking for me so I drew away from the roadway and crouched under a convenient whitethorn bush. The next thing I heard was 'Come out you effin Peeler, we know you're there.' I made no move. If only Mick would return, I thought, the two of us might be able for them. Someone in the shebeen must have recognised Mick or myself and spread the word. They were all shouting now. The language was obscene. I crossed myself and started to pray. It was as if I had invoked disaster because at that instant cadhrawns of black turf and fist-sized stones fell in a shower around me. One of the stones landed on my left shoulder and nearly paralysed me. I was forced into coming out but there were only three of them on the roadway. The small man and another seemed to have disappeared.

'What do you want?' I asked fearfully.

'Your effin blood,' said one.

'What harm did I ever do to any one of you?' I asked.

'You're an effin guard,' said the same man and he came for me swinging. I ducked and caught him smartly in the jaw. He went down without a sound. Two to go I thought. The odds have shortened. I braced myself for the other two but they seemed reluctant to mix it. I decided to make a run for it and try to intercept Mick on his way back. It was then I was struck from behind. I remember no more after that. When I came to I was in hospital. I had a fractured jaw, three smashed ribs and a cut on the forehead which required several stitches. I was black and blue all over and the doctor assured me that I was lucky to be alive. The gang had left me for dead for when Mick returned that was his first impression. My attackers went to England the following day. The shebeen was raided and the stock destroyed that night. I spent a fortnight in the hospital and another fortnight at home with my mother. God rest her soul. I went back on duty after that. The incident, terrible and all as it was, taught me one invaluable lesson: a Civic Guard has to watch his every move. If, while off duty, his presence causes antagonism or resentment he should remove himself from the scene at once. It is unfair and unjust I know but the truth is the minute you don the uniform of the guards it's the same as if you pulled a jersey over your head. You are a member of the team of law and order for the rest of your life. You are irrevocably committed. In short, you're a marked man.

Mick went back to the place again the following Sunday night. He had fallen in love with his dark-haired Kathleen. For six successive months he paid her court and then unexpectedly, one Sunday night, she jilted him. He demanded a reason and at first she was reluctant to tell him. He insisted that he was entitled to know so she gave in. That very morning after Mass her father discovered that she was doing a line with a guard. He had overheard it in a pub. When he got home he summoned his daughter up to her bedroom and there he told her that she was never to have anything to do with a man wearing a uniform, no love, no friendship, no nothing be he priest, parson, peeler or trooper. He told her that he would blow her brains out if she did not send Mick Drea packing immediately. When Mick heard this he told her he would resign his position but still she refused.

'My da do maintain,' said she, 'that once tainted is always tainted.'

Give Mick my best regards and my love to your care.

As ever

Your fond uncle

Leo

District Headquarters

Dear Leo

I haven't time to call so you need not expect me for inspection this month. I am enclosing a number of letters received over the past few weeks from anonymous scribes in your quarter of the world. You'll have to do something about these public houses although I remember you telling me once that the wives of the proprietors are the authors of the letters. Nevertheless, you had better give them a reminder one of these Sunday nights. I'll leave the timing et cetera to your own discretion. Just let them know who is boss. One of the letters, as you will see, accuses you of indulging in black magic and other forms of witchcraft with Nance Hansel in Monasterbawn graveyard at the witching hour. Give Nance my regards by the way and tell her she is to stay with us whenever she comes to town.

You know me, Leo. I don't believe a word about this graveyard business but like yourself I also have superiors who may question me about the goings-on in Monasterbawn. All it needs is one bitchy letter or an anonymous phone call to some newspaper and then we're all in trouble. Just let me know the score, Leo. I must know about everything that happens in my district. Not alone must I know everything but I must be the first to know everything. I'll see you as soon as I can. If you have any problem that you cannot put down on paper or talk about over the phone drop in some night and we'll talk it over. That's what we're here for.

Sincerely
Joe Fahy
(Superintendent)

Jackass Lane
Monasterbawn

Dear Guard Molair
Last week my husband gave me none of his wages and I had to tick the groceries. This happens often. He spends the money in

Fie's pub where he goes to play darts every night. I haven't had a decent stitch of clothes in over five years only hand-me-downs my sister sends me from England. All he does is give out whenever I ask for money for the house. My children are often hungry. I'm sure if Fie's were closed at the normal time he would be all right as he does not go there till close on closing time. He is barred from Crutt's and the Widow's over he rising rows. God forbid I should get you into trouble Guard Molair as I know you are a decent man. The truth is if you did your duty there would be no after-hours drinking. I am going to have to write to the minister if you don't get a move on.

Signed

Hungry Home

Garda Station
Monasterbawn

Dear Ned

Sorry for not writing sooner but I've been up to my eyes. This can be a most complicated job at times with so many awkward situations to resolve. Don't mention perjury to me. I have had my bellyful of it over the years. Take note of the following.

Last week I had Thade Buckley up for having seven unlicensed dogs. I had warned him repeatedly but he chose to ignore me. In the court he was asked by the clerk to take the oath.

'Do you,' said the clerk, 'promise to tell the truth, the whole truth and nothing but the truth?'

'I do,' said Thade in a loud voice and then in a whisper he says, 'I do in my arse.' I heard him quite plainly from where I was standing inside the door of the courthouse near the dock. I requested the judge to make him take the oath again. You must know by now Ned that judges have no patience with guards who take up the time of the court. He agreed to my request however. Thade was approached secondly by the clerk who asked the appropriate question.

'I do,' he said in the same loud voice. Then in an almost inaudible whisper, 'I do in my arse.' I knew from the look on the judge's face that another request from me would be turned down flatly. No blame to him. He couldn't be expected to hear Thade's whispers from where he sat. Thade swore on his oath that none of the dogs was his, that they were owned by tinkers and horseblockers while others were strays. The case was dismissed. Perjury used to be a reserved sin in Kerry until recently which means it was common there but believe me it was almost as common everywhere else. I remember that case in Kerry involving a small farmer. His thirteen acres had grown over a year to fourteen. This happened because he kept extending his paling sticks into a neighbouring boggy commonage. He was reported by other users of the commonage. He was asked by the clerk, 'Do you swear to tell the truth, the whole truth and nothing but the truth?'

'I do boy,' he said. 'Oh jaysus I do.' Then to himself he says, 'I do in my hole.'

'What's that?' asked the judge. 'What did you say?'

'I said, "'pon my soul" my lord.'

'There is no need for the embellishments,' said the judge who addressed himself to the clerk and instructed him to ensure that the oath was taken a second time. The clerk repeated the question.

'I do,' said the defendant and then in the weakest of whispers to himself, 'I do in my hole.'

Evidence was heard and the defendant was asked if he had anything to say for himself. He denied extending his boundaries.

'I read in a book once,' he said to the judge, 'that bog does grow.'

'Yes,' said the judge, 'upwards at the rate of an inch or so every ten years but never outwards at the rate of an acre a year like yours.'

He was fined twenty pounds and ordered to draw back his paling sticks. I'll close now but in the next letter I'll tell you about that raid in Mayo. It happened shortly after De Valera's visit to Keeldown during a general election. Those were noisy and troublesome times.

Love to all

Your fond uncle

Leo

Garda Barracks

Monasterbawn

Dear Joe

I am enclosing a letter which I yesterday received from a woman who signs herself Hungry Home. From the contents you will see that she blames Fie's public house for the drinking habits of her husband. If he wants to drink he'll drink anyway and my raiding Fie's won't stop him. He'll get it in any one of ten villages by merely mounting his cycle or thumbing a lift. I will now explain, to your satisfaction, about the alleged witchcraft in Monasterbawn graveyard. I know you're my superintendent but you should know better than to seek an explanation for such a disgraceful and unfounded accusation. It was the last night in November which, as you know, is the month of the Holy Souls. Around ten o'clock I went to the Widow Hansel's for a few pints and a game of thirty-one. The Widow shouted time at about quarter to twelve so we finished our drinks and made for the door. At the door Nance Hansel called me back.

'Leo,' she said, 'would you believe it's the last night of the Holy Souls and I haven't visited Oliver's grave yet.' Oliver

Hansel, as you well know, was her husband.

'Is there any chance,' said she, 'that you'd accompany me till I say a prayer or two over the grave?'

I told her to be sure I would so off we set. It was twelve o'clock when we arrived at the graveyard gate. It was half past twelve and we leaving, it being a fine moonlight night and the Widow having several other relations to pray for, including her mother and father, aunts, uncles and whatnot. While she was praying I used to swing my arms back and forth and jump up and down to keep warm. That is the authentic account of the witchcraft and black magic which took place in Monasterbawn graveyard on the night of November the thirtieth in the year of our Lord nineteen hundred and seventy-five and may the good God perish the craven wretch who penned that infamous letter. I'll raid Fie's on Sunday night next and to keep the score even I will pay a call to Crutt's as well. I won't take names and I won't charge the publicans.

I don't like raiding public houses even when after-hours drinking goes on. Hard-working men and women deserve a drink or two at night if they so desire, provided they can afford it and provided that they do not blackguard their wives and families and leave them short. You're the super. You know as well as I that there are no young people drinking here in Monasterbawn. They go to the towns and the city where they have no problem getting all the gin and vodka they want whether their ages are fourteen or eighteen. The drinkers in Monasterbawn are settled oldsters with those beastly exceptions who drink the weekly dole money and the family allowance and forget about home. The wives would be better off widows. They'd have the widow's pension and no one to take it from them.

When I first came here I foolishly believed that there were all sorts of orgies going on in public houses. I fell for the letters and the phone calls which are the bane of all guards' barracks in this green land. I set about cleaning things up. What a terrible mess I made in my ignorance. Sunday night was and is the best night for public house trade. There's life in the village from an early hour and there is the pleasant sound of music and singing and the deep hum of conversations coming from the doorways of the warm, companionable public houses. It was the one night which made life tolerable when I first came to Monasterbawn.

There was a bustle to the place, Men, woman and children walked the streets and would stand listening outside Crutt's before crossing to Fie's or going further down to Oliver Hansel's. There would be an occasional fight amongst the young bucks. No transport in those days so they were confined to their pleasures in the village. You might get a carload of townies out on a booze or have a window broken or have bicycles stolen but by and large it was a quiet enough place, all things allowed.

Sunday nights then and holy day nights were the only nights that the village permitted itself the luxury of rejoicing. Limited after-hours trading in the three pubs was taken for granted. In the spring, summer and autumn farmers and agricultural workers who lived in the vicinity were unable to come to town before nine or ten o'clock, particularly if the weather was fine. Neither would the villagers frequent the pubs until around the same hour. The man I replaced was an easy-going, popular Meathman who allowed this very lax situation to exist. He never went near the pubs and generally minded his own business unless specifically invited or incited to do otherwise. No doubt the man knew what he was doing. No one spoke ill of him after he left.

I should have followed his example. Instead I started to listen to stories and to believe the contents of the anonymous letters which came regularly, riddled with complaints about after-hours drinking and filled with character assassination and exaggerated accounts of normal, human behaviour. I raided Fie's first. I must say they were astonished. Mrs Fie went so far as to ask me why, as if she didn't know that after-hours drinking was illegal. Most of the customers escaped but I took the names of the others. These consisted mainly of old people or others who were too drunk or too lazy to run.

The following Sunday night I raided Crutt's and the Sunday night after I raided Oliver Hansel's, a premises which had not been raided in two generations. There was no one to shout stop. I was in the right and I knew for certain that many people approved.

The raids had no effect whatsoever on the after-hours trade. Neither had the fines imposed by the judge on the three publicans and their customers. A month later I struck again. I raided and cleared all three pubs on the same Sunday night. Convictions in the court followed. The customers hung around the street disconsolately for hours afterwards. Still they showed no resentment towards me.

The following Sunday night all three premises were at it hammer and tongs as if nothing had happened. I raided again and again and eventually there was no more after-hours trading on Sunday nights. Just to make sure I carried out one final raid. The pubs were closed, however, and my knocking was ignored. They were empty. I could testify to that.

The following Sunday night the village was deserted. Except for a few locals the pubs were deserted, their clientele scattered amongst the many other licensed premises at crossroads and villages not too far distant. A week later I was told that Jack Fie had gone to England to find work and that Crutt's was up for sale. Well they couldn't blame me could they? I was merely doing my duty. I convinced myself that I would be drawing money under false pretences if I did otherwise. Also I was responding to appeals from law-abiding people who felt that the law of the land was being flouted. On top of that I felt a new sense of authority. I must confess I was somewhat frightened by my power. The sad thing was I didn't look forward to Sunday nights anymore. There was no apparent change in the attitude of the village people towards me but at the newsagent's and the post office there was a tight rein on the conversation when I appeared. Then one Sunday night I met Oliver Hansel walking two of his greyhounds along the roadway. The loss of the after-hours trade had no effect whatsoever on him. He was a wealthy man, not dependant on the pub alone. He had a sizeable farm and, by all accounts, lashings of money. He had no family. If anything the closure was an asset because it had given him more time to train his dogs.

I bade him a goodnight. He returned my salute civilly enough or so I thought. I fell into step beside him and we walked out of the village together, not saying anything, just enjoying the mildness of the summer night. I remember every word of our conversation as though it were yesterday. I daresay it was because Oliver was a man of few words and contrived to make these few memorable.

'The village is very dead in itself tonight,' I said in an effort to get conversation going. There was no answer. The dogs were squealing at some scent or other at the time. It was possible that he hadn't heard me.

'The village is very dead tonight,' I repeated.

'I heard you the first time,' he said without feeling of any kind. I decided to say no more after that. Then suddenly he stopped dead in his tracks.

'If the village is dead,' he said without a trace of emotion, 'you're the man who must take the blame. It was you who murdered it.'

A week later Oliver Hansel was dead. He succumbed to a

heart attack just as he was going to bed. He died in his wife's arms. His words stayed with me. Another week passed. Then on a day off I mounted my cycle and proceeded to the village of Derrymullane, nine miles away, to see a friend, one Jim Brick, a civic guard of thirty years standing. We often met in the course of our duty. His would be the nearest barracks to mine. His sergeant was a bit of a recluse who hated his job. Jim did most of the work.

'You know,' Jim said when I entered the day room, 'I was more or less expecting you.' I told him about the raids but he already knew everything. He wouldn't be much of a policeman if he didn't. I told him what Oliver Hansel had said to me.

'He was never a man to say things lightly, the same Oliver,' Jim Brick said.

'Granted,' I replied, 'but you'll have to concede that all I was doing was applying the letter of the law.'

Jim remained silent for awhile, drawing on his pipe. Then, after a long pause he examined it closely and looked me in the eye.

'My dear Leo,' said he, 'applying the letter of the law when you are not a legal expert is like handling a Mill's bomb when you are not a bomb disposal expert. Both can blow up in your face when you least expect it.' I was about to interrupt but he waved his pipe in front of my face and continued.

'When the law does damage to the people it is supposed to benefit then the law has to be re-examined. The people who originally drew up the licensing laws did a fairly good job. They would, of course, have no way of knowing about villages like Monasterbawn or the situation that exists there. The solution, therefore, is to stretch the law as far as it will go. It will not stretch all that far but it nearly always stretches far enough provided we do not expect too much from it. I hope you are paying attention to what I am saying because I am giving you the benefits of thirty years front line experience. I could have been a commissioner if I so desired but my wife always said I was too brainy.

'Remember my dear Leo that, in many ways, the law is like a woman's knickers, full of dynamite and elastic and best left to those who have the legal right and qualifications to handle it properly.'

'So what am I to do?' I asked.

'Do nothing,' he advised. 'All scars heal, all wounds close. You have shown quite clearly that you are in charge of proceedings. Bide your time and do nothing. The drift back to the pubs will start sooner than you think. They'll naturally feel their way for a while but in a few months things will be back to normal. My advice is to leave well alone and keep a close eye on developments.'

I left Jim Brick a relieved man. Things turned out as he predicted. On Sunday nights now the village hums with trade and everyone is happy. In case they get too happy I will do as you suggest and give them a reminder but I would hate to see Monasterbawn returning to that forlorn state which I once created by innocently overplaying my hand.

Best regards to the missus. I'll convey your regards to Nance.

Yours obediently

Garda Leo J. Molair

Toormane Hill
Monasterbawn

Guard Molair

That you might get VD DV.

Signed

A TT

Garda Station
Monasterbawn

My dear Ned

Sorry for the delay. I have before me the shortest letter ever received in these barracks. My guess is that it was sent by Miss Lola Glinn, a shining light in the local branch of the Pioneer Total Abstinence Association. It has her crisp, bitchy style and in addition she passed the graveyard the night the Widow Hansel and myself were visiting it. She is the chief danger to the pubs. She is capable of writing to members of the government and to ministers, not to mention supers, commissioners and assistant commissioners. The chief reason is her father, a harmless poor devil who fancies a few pints on Saturday and Sunday nights. He is, alas, unable to carry more than three pints. After that he has to be helped home but he's not a nuisance and he offends nobody. The villagers always keep an eye out for him. For a while the pubs stopped serving him but they became sorry when they saw the forlorn cut of him and he staring through their windows.

About that raid in Mayo. It's a long time ago now. As I recall it was a fine autumn night. The air was crisp with frost and in the village of Keeldown where Mick Drea and myself were stationed there was an air of tension and excitement. De Valera was expected to speak on behalf of his party's candidate and our sergeant, Matt Bergin, had us on our toes hours before the event. We were to watch out for suspicious characters who might be entertaining notions of assassination and to make sure that the village square was clear of all obstructions. We had the help of three other guards and an inspector who was just after getting promotion. Every window he passed he squinted in to admire his reflection. He was much like a gorsoon after being presented with a new pair of shoes.

At eight o'clock the first of the crowd began to arrive. Dev wasn't due until ten but there were many admirers of his who wanted a good position near the platform where they could be close to him. I never knew a man who could inspire so much genuine love and provoke so much vicious hatred at the same time. Our sergeant hated the sight of him. We would often be sitting happily in the day room when unexpectedly Dev's name would be mentioned on the radio in connection with some statement of policy or visit abroad. Our sergeant would rise and spit out and then leave the room without a word. On the other hand if Dev's name was mentioned while Mike Drea was wearing his cap the cap would come off at once and Mike would hold it across his chest with a radiant look in his eyes. That was Dev, the devil incarnate in the eyes of Matt Bergin and a saint in the eyes of Mick Drea. I won't attempt to analyse him. All I will say is that his visit to Keeldown turned out to be the most colourful event that village ever knew before or since. At nine you couldn't draw a leg in the pubs and by half-past nine the square was thronged. There were several nasty fist fights. There would be a reference to Dev's ancestry and the man who made it would be asked to repeat what he said by some other hothead. Then the clipping started. It gave us all we could do to prevent a minor war. At ten a rumour swept through the crowd that he was in the outskirts but it was unfounded because almost an hour was to pass before he would make his appearance. Finally he arrived. He already had a bodyguard but we took up our positions at either side of his immediate entourage to keep back the crowd. In front of the procession were one hundred men in double file. These carried uplifted four-prong pikes on top of which were blazing sods of turf which had earlier been well steeped in paraffin. The bearers of these torches were grim-faced and military-like men and boys of all ages. Behind them were two score of horsemen and to parody these there were several asses, mules and small ponies mounted by youngsters and drunken farmer's boys. Next came the Keeldown fife and drum bank playing 'O'Donnell Abu.' Then came a brass band playing 'The Legion of the Rearguard.' It was a circus of a kind that would have delighted the heart of Barnum. Dev, the ringmaster, never batted an eyelid. After the brass band came a number of village idiots, local drunkards, bums, characters, clowns and an assortment of other irresponsible wretches to whom an occasion like this is meat and drink. After this contingent came the major attraction, the man himself flanked by local dignitaries, ministers and TDs. He walked with his head erect, body rigid and with no trace of a smile on his pointed face. His dark felt hat and long black overcoat became him as they became no other man I ever saw. He looked as if he carried the whole weight of the country on his shoulders and who am I to say whether he did or not.

'Look at the strut of the hoor,' Matt Bergin whispered, 'and the innocent blood still reeking from his hands.'

'Wash your mouth out,' Mick Drea whispered with suppressed fury. 'He is the saviour of our country, the greatest Irishman since Saint Patrick.'

'But Saint Patrick wasn't an Irishman,' I said innocently.

'Neither is Dev,' Matt whispered triumphantly. The procession continued. Behind the celebrities came the members of the local brigade of the old IRA. They must have numbered two hundred.

'Where in the name of God did they all come from?' Matt asked sarcastically.

'They're good men and true,' said Mick.

'Maybe so,' Matt retaliated, 'but where the hell were they when the Black and Tans were here?'

They marched solemn-faced and sombre without looking to

left or right. Sometimes they were taunted and jeered. Other times they were cheered. They showed no reaction whatsoever. Here, for one night only, were men of action, of steely resolve, men to be reckoned with. Tomorrow the carnival would be over and for several years until Dev's next visit they would revert to their natural roles of small farmer, labourer, clerk, tradesman and unemployed. Tonight was theirs. They were expressing unity and solidarity in the presence of the chief whom they adored and revered as no man was revered since O'Connell or Jesus Christ himself. The old IRA were followed by a throng of ordinary supporters and hundreds of others who came out of curiosity merely to have a glimpse of the Man of Destiny. Hundreds more from the opposition came to scoff and jeer or maybe to engage in a spot of heckling although they would want to ensure that they were out of clouting distance of the more rabid Fianna Fail supporters. As the procession entered the square a great cry arose from the multitude. The Irish people have always been caught short for leaders of quality and when they were presented with De Valera they clung to him for dear life.

He attracted the most extraordinary and contradictory collection of people that ever assembled to pay homage to the same person. There were tycoons, priests, nuns and professional men rubbing shoulders with illiterates, semi-illiterates, halfwits and stunted unfortunates, the personification of utter poverty. Allegiance to Dev or to Cosgrave was often the cause of violent rows and lifelong bitterness between neighbours. Matt Bergin insists that De Valera was alone responsible for the Civil War and its horrific bloodshed.

'He was the cause of it,' Matt insisted, 'because he could have stopped it and failed to do so.'

What Matt overlooked was that Dev certainly gave the poorer elements new life and hope and pride in themselves, a quality lacking in the vast majority of the Irish people for ages. In the square the air reeked of paraffin. The crowd were chanting now as Dev climbed on to the platform. An aged, shawled woman clung to him, kissing his hand. He good-naturedly pushed her to one side. Others wept when they touched his hands or clothes. At the base of the platform were the most vocal of all, a band of craven bums whose loyalty could be bought for a bottle of stout. These were pushed away by stewards to make way for the real supporters. When Dev came forward to speak men and women in the crowd wept openly. Others held infant children aloft that they might get a glimpse of the great man and have it to say to their children that once they saw the Man of Destiny. There was frenzy now in the square as he laid allegation after allegation against the opposition. Emotions were at fever pitch. On the edge of the crowd a fierce fight broke out and we had to draw our batons to prevent its spreading. There were hundreds of wild-eyed, crazed patriots spoiling for mayhem. Fortunately, it ended peacefully. Afterwards the pubs were jammed and throngs of troublemakers infested the lanes and streets. We had a busy time maintaining law and order. At about one o'clock in the morning, long after Dev had departed, the inspector informed us that we were to clear the pubs.

'I want the job done thoroughly,' he said, 'and I want the job done now or there will be repercussions.'

So saying he got into his car and left the dirty work to us. One by one we cleared the pubs of customers until only one remained. This was the property of a local county councillor. I knew it would not be easy to clear the place but justice would have to be seen to be done or the guards would be the talk of the place the following day.

'You do the back,' I told Mick, 'and I'll do the front.'

The sergeant had gone to bed at this stage. We had no intention of prosecuting. Our only aim was to clear the place as peacefully as possible, it being the night it was. I made my way into the thick of the thronged bar and then as loud as I could I made my intentions clear. I could also hear Mick's voice coming from the kitchen. Suddenly the proprietor was fuming by my side.

'What the hell do you think you're doing?' he shouted.

'My duty,' I replied.

'What's the trouble?' The question came from a burly, well-dressed man who I recognised as a TD of considerable prominence and a man who was tipped for a ministry should Dev win the election.

'This fellow wants to clear the house,' the proprietor informed him.

'Eff off out of here fast you Free State shagger,' said the politician, 'or I'll have you transferred to Timbuctoo.'

'I am a Guard on public house duty,' I said as calmly as I could, 'acting on the instructions of my inspector. I am now ordering you to leave these premises.'

'And if I don't go,' he said with menace. There was a deadly silence at this stage with all present clinging to every word. This was a showdown. There could be no backdown. I found Mick Drea standing beside me.

'If you don't leave peacefully I will remove you forcibly,' I told him.

'You blueshirt bastard,' he shouted and he swung a fist at me. I ducked and spun him around and then propelled him out of the pub. Meanwhile Mick had drawn his baton in case some of his supporters decided to take part. Rather than risk prosecution the publican decided to cooperate. The repercussions came at once. The following morning I was visited by the Chief Superintendent who asked me for a full account of what happened. The politician had rung him up first thing that morning demanding my dismissal from the force. The super heard me out.

'Write him a letter of apology,' he suggested. 'It's sure to mollify him.'

'Apology for what?' I asked.

'Please don't be difficult,' said the super.

'I can't apologise for something I didn't do,' I told him.

He rose to go.

'Write that letter today,' he said.

Immediately I rang my own district super and told him the score. I also told him I was a supporter of the Labour Party.

'There's little I can do Leo,' he said, 'except to promise you that I will oppose any move to transfer you.'

Transferred I was, not to Timbuctoo but here to Monasterbawn, less than thirty miles from the place where I was born. Instead of punishing me the politician, in his ignorance, had done me a favour.

Love to Gert and little Eddie. Write soon.

Your fond uncle

Leo

Derrymullane GS

Dear Leo

After you left the last day himself made one of his rare appearances in the day room and asked who the visitor was. I told him it was yourself.

'I am your sergeant,' he said. 'All these matters must be reported.'

He then ordered a full turnout for inspection of every garda in the barracks. I turned out smartly and this seemed to satisfy him. He went back upstairs talking to himself. He has me in a terrible state but he's harmless for the most part. He doesn't do a stroke of work, just goes out to eat and comes back when it suits him. Luckily the work is light and I can manage on my own but one of these days I will have to make a discreet report to Superintendent Fahy (Call-me-Joe). There is always the danger that things might get out of hand and who knows but the locals might start pinking off letters to higher places. I'll keep an eye on him as best I can. If I send for you come running as we don't want a scandal.

Yesterday he was particularly grouchy and warned me that he would not stand for insubordination. Upstairs with him then and on goes the talk. This time there was loud laughter as well and I became worried so I crept upstairs. There were other voices. I could hear them quite plainly. However, when I peeped in the keyhole I could see nobody but himself. He was addressing himself to two imaginary gentlemen who occupied two chairs facing the table where he sat. He would speak for a while and then listen to what the others had to say. When he had digested their remarks he would throw back the head and laugh to his heart's content. It was all quite harmless but the danger was that Mrs Hussey the char might make an appearance requesting instructions. She lives down the street and comes for an hour or two every day.

He poured out imaginary drinks for his two friends and then listened to some news of great import. He nodded his head from time to time and his face grew more serious as the talk went on. When the address was finished he banged the table with his fist and shouted hurrah several times. Then he started to weep but not for long. Manfully he wiped his eyes and rose from his seat. He saluted smartly and shook hands with his two visitors. I crept downstairs again and he started to show them to the door. He led them down and in the hallway there was some more banter and loud laughter. Out on to the street with him then where he shook hands with the pair, embracing both in turn as he did so. He then carefully banged the door of the car and waved goodbye. He was so convincing that I could almost hear the engine running. Luckily it was raining cats and dogs at the time and there was nobody on the street. He came into the day room rubbing his hands. He put his back to the fire and eyed me in a friendly way for the first time in years.

'Why didn't you come up, Jim?' he said.

'Up where?' said I.

'Upstairs to meet the lads,' said he.

'What lads?' said I.

'The assistant commissioner and the minister,' said he.

'I know my place,' said I.

'Ah well now,' he said magnanimously, 'the lads wouldn't have minded. They're just like ourselves, man.'

'Why didn't the commissioner come?' I asked.

'Jealousy, Mick. Jealousy, boy.'

I shook my head sympathetically.

'There's nothing he can do now except scratch himself. My promotion has been sanctioned by the minister.'

'Does this mean I'll be calling you inspector from now on?' I asked.

'You'll be calling me superintendent,' he said proudly. 'Apparently they have heard of my work at headquarters and want me up there with them.'

'When will you be leaving?' I asked.

'That's entirely up to myself. I'll have to straighten out a few things here first before I decide upon a time.'

He remained silent for a long while after this announcement so I returned to my work. The next thing he threw a fiver on the table. 'Get a drink for the lads,' he said, 'and tell them there's no hurry back. I'll hold the fort here.'

He went upstairs and after a short while I heard him pacing to and fro. I took the fiver and had three large whiskies in case I'd go out of my mind. Say nothing about all this to anyone. Just say a prayer that I can handle the situation when the inevitable happens.

As always
Jim Brick

PS You may be wondering if he was always like this. I suppose you could say he was always a little odd. However, for the past year he has been showing signs of going off the head altogether. I don't know what triggered it off. I believe he was let down by a good-looking girl at one time in his youth. That wouldn't be any help to him. What may have got him going was a visit we had from a lady here about a year ago. Her son had broken into the local presbytery and struck the Canon with a timber crucifix he took from the wall. A touch of religious mania. Anyway the Canon who played football for the county in his youth gave the fellow a shot in the gut and put him on the flat of his back. We locked him up, gave him his supper and retired to the day room where we had work in plenty. It was a quiet winter's night as I recall. The wind howled outside but we had a good fire. Suddenly the door burst open and our prisoner's mother stood there with a crazed look in her eye.

'Where's my boy?' she screeched. 'Which one of you two rotten bastards has taken my baby?'

The baby, of course, was twenty-two years of age but it was hardly the time to point this out to her. She was obviously in a demented state and I detected a strong smell of whiskey.

'Give me back my boy,' she screamed at the top of her voice. 'Take me but give me back my son.' With that she ups with the front of her skirt. My eyes nearly popped out of my head. Not a screed of a knickers or bloomers of any kind did she wear. The sergeant was transfixed to his chair like a man who had been struck dumb. She lifted the skirt higher and stood directly in front of the sergeant revealing as fine a brush of jet-black hair as ever sprung from the base of a female belly. He sat transfixed, his mouth opened, utterly shocked out of his wits.

'Release my child,' she cried out in drunken frenzy, 'and do with my body what you will.'

'Missus,' said I, 'go home and have the grace of God about you and we'll put in a good word for your son when the hearing comes up.'

She dropped her skirt. 'Scum,' she screamed. 'Scum in uniform.' In the end I succeeded in getting her out. I locked the door behind her. She screamed and shrieked for a short while and then went off when nobody came to listen to her. When I returned to the day room my man was still in a state of shock from the spectacle he had seen. He must never have seen the likes before, being a bit of a celibate and all that.

I'll have to sign off, Leo. I hear him coming downstairs, no doubt for inspection.

As always
Jim

The life of an unmarried civic guard, solitary custodian of the peace in a remote village, can be lonely in the extreme, yet Leo Molair is not a lonely man. Neither is he a bored man. Regarding the people in his bailiwick he could be a mine of information but he chooses to keep all that is not relevant to law and order closely to himself and is as careful about revealing information concerning his charges as a priest or doctor. He listens and says nothing even when he disbelieves the outrageous concoctions which the villagers invent about each other.

His power lies in his willingness to listen and later to reject or absorb what he has heard. He is perhaps the most respected figure in the area. Of enemies he has his share. He would be a poor policeman if he hadn't. Of friends he has many and of close friends his fair quota. Not since his Dublin days has Leo been intimate with a woman. His relationship with Nance Hansel is a purely platonic one. As far as he is concerned it would never amount to anything more than a cosy chat or a day out with the other regulars. His plans for the future are carefully laid. He owns a site on the mountain road. Here he plans to build a small chalet on his retirement. He is happy in his work and can have no way of knowing that the real crises of his life loom ahead of him. We find him now writing to his superintendent.

Monasterbawn
County Cork

Dear Joe

As usual the crowds arrived into the village on Sunday night last and as usual the pubs started to fill up around ten o'clock which is closing time as you well know. I raided Fie's first and cleared the house of forty-seven customers. Mrs Fie asked me the very same question she asked me when I first raided her nearly twenty years ago.

'Why?'

'Because, missus,' said I, 'it's against the law.'

''Tis a cracked law,' said she, 'that closes the pubs at the very hour the people wants a drink.'

'I didn't make the law, missus,' I reminded her.

'I hope,' said she, 'that you will clear out that brothel across the road.'

I assured her that nobody would be neglected. I also told her that while I continued receiving letters I would continue to raid the pubs. Unable to conceal her astonishment she asked for clarification.

'You must understand, Mrs Fie,' said I, 'that when I get a letter complaining of one pub it means that all have to be raided. For instance if tomorrow I receive a letter complaining about after-hours trade in Crutt's it does not mean that the other pubs are immune. Far from it. My super would expect me to make a clean sweep of all three licensed premises in Monasterbawn so that everybody might see that the law has no favourites.'

This set her thinking. We can only wait and see if it will have the desired effect. Next I raided Crutt's, who hadn't the good sense to clear the house while I was engaged with Fie's. There were seventy-one customers on the premises. All made their escape without difficulty. I explained to Mrs Crutt about the letters. She agreed it was a disgraceful thing entirely for one publican to write in to the barracks complaining about another.

'And they call themselves Christians,' she said with a look of outrage on her face. I left her and proceeded towards the Widow's but that cute creature had taken the hint and cleared the house while Crutt's was being raided. She would have had a few customers, possibly a dozen or so old topers of my own age. It was the company rather than the business that induced her to keep the place open at all. I drank a hasty half-one and a pint before making a final tour of the village for the night.

In Jackass Lane I encountered several courting couples but there is no law against this so I passed them by bidding each pair a goodnight. From Tremble's shack came the sound of discord. Drawing nearer I could hear Mocky's voice raised in anger and the screams of his wife from time to time. I pushed the door open and there was Mocky and he having the poor woman by the throat. The children were huddled in a corner. What a start to life. I broke Mocky's grip on his long-suffering partner and dragged him outside. I slapped his face for a while. There was no other way to sober him up and there was no point in charging him with assault because the wife wouldn't testify against him. I lugged him back to the barracks and locked him in the cell for a while. Later when he would be sober I might allow him home. I continued on my tour of inspection. At the foot of the Mountain Road I saw a figure in front of me. It was none other than Goggles Finn, the local Peeping Tom and the biggest general nuisance in the whole district. This time he was peeping in the window of a house owned by a middle-aged lady whose name was Aggie Boucher. This surprised me somewhat for Aggie has a figure like a sack of spuds and a face to match. When I tiptoed up behind Goggles Finn, Aggie was disrobing for bed. There was a light on in the room and nothing was left to the imagination. She stripped to the skin and took her time about it. I tapped Goggles on the shoulder. He let a scream out of him that could be heard at the other end of the village. Without looking around he ran for his life up the Mountain Road, screeching like a scalded cat.

Aggie Boucher, in a nightdress and coat with her hair in curlers, appeared all of a sudden in her doorway.

'What's going on out there?' she called angrily.

'Goggles Finn,' I explained.

'What about him?' she asked.

'He was peeping at you,' I called back.

'Don't you think I know that you goddam interfering get,' she said. I went away chastened.

I'll close for now.

As ever

Leo

Fallon Street GS
Dublin 13

Dear Uncle Leo

Superintendent Conners arrived this morning and instructed me
to forget about some summonses I was preparing for a gentleman
who parked his car on three different occasions outside a hospital
entrance. I was about to object and to point out the incalculable
amount of trouble this man had caused not to mention all the
cost to the state and all the time involved when he cut me short.

'There are exceptional circumstances involved here,' he said.
'Just do as I say like a good man.'

Ours is not to reason why. Mick Drea says the car owner must
be well-up in the world, probably a member of the same golf
club as Patcheen but my sergeant says it is quite possible that
the man may have been of considerable service to the guards on
occasion and on this account we cannot be too critical. What
do you think? Also tell me about Big Morto McNeal who Mick
Drea says once drank a firkin of porter in the round of a day.
Often too the old boys here talk about a guard called Flash
Muldook and about his fatal charm for women.

Gert and your godson Eddie are grand altogether.

That's all for now

Your fond nephew

Ned

Garda Station
Monasterbawn

Dear Ned

First of all let us look at Patcheen and the summonses. You
would be best advised not to question your super's actions no
matter how provocative or irresponsible they may seem to be.

What the hell bloody use is there in being a super if you can't do a turn for a friend. So long as he doesn't overdo it you have no option but to play along. Take your brothers-in-law now. Wouldn't you be the hard-hearted man if you turned one of them down after he asking you to square the parking summons. Try and put yourself in Patcheen's place. A super has to use discretion and he needs to have the more influential of the public favourably disposed towards the law. Ninety-five per cent of the time our supers go by the book and that's more than can be said for any police force anywhere.

My own super here now is a great character so long as you remember who is boss. He likes to be called by his first name which in his case is Joe. My man is not a squarer of summonses but he will be moved by the plea of a decent man or woman or honest, hard-working parents. When the strict enforcement of the rules is likely to do more harm than good he will know the right move to make. No better man to have a few jars with and no better man to back up those under his command but tell him the truth and don't come the smart alec with him or he'll nail you to the cross. As long as he knows what's going on all is well but when he doesn't know life can be a misery for the whole district. For instance if he hears something second-hand he'll eff and blind all comers indiscriminately until he cools down. However, when you meet a new-made super who's just a natural-born bastard dig in your heels and work to rule. The novelty of his new found authority will wear off after a specified time. Remember that so long as we of the rank and file stick together we are the real bosses no matter what anybody says.

You ask about big Murto McNeal. Of all the uncommon, unlikely, uncivilised, uncouth, unmannerly sons of bitches this was the pure-bred, pedigreed champion. Of course he'd never get into the guards now. He was rammed in after the Economic War by a TD who should have known better. Some say he was the bastard brother of a minister. Murdo was six feet five inches tall and weighed nineteen stone with a big fat red face not unlike a prize boar. He was never seen to spend a single shilling in his entire life. He handed every last penny of his wages over to his wife Minnie. Minnie the Pom she was nicknamed. She was puny, poisonous and bitter. You wouldn't notice her alongside Murto. Neighbours used to say that she slept on top of him lest he suffocate her by accident some night. My first meeting with Big Murto McNeal was at a guards' dance in Mayo. He never paid for the tickets. He just told a publican who was doing a prosperous after-hours trade that he would like two tickets for himself and the Pom. I happened to be sitting at the same table as the pair of them. There were sixteen people to each table. Murto consumed three separate dinners and then he noticed a large plate of buns in the centre of the table. These had been placed there earlier to go with the tea which would be served after the meal. Murton reached across a huge hand and grabbed the plate.

'Christ boys what have ye agin' these?' he asked with a huge smile. With that he placed the plate on his lap and he swallowed every last one of those buns as if they were crumbs. It's true he drank a firkin of porter once. It was at the wake of a well-known publican. The wake lasted all night and since it was a talkative town the guards could not very well be seen to be taking intoxicating drinks while on duty. The publican's son very considerately called Murto aside and told him that he would be placing a tapped firkin of porter especially for the guards in a comfortable outhouse at the rear of the premises.

'The Lord have mercy on the dead,' said Murton. 'There is no guard in this district but won't be praying for your father.'

The barrel was duly taken out by the son and left on a handy perch inside the door with glasses galore and a bottle of good quality whiskey for starters. The first thing Murto did was to go to the outhouse and consume half the whiskey direct from the bottle. Periodically afterwards he would visit the outhouse and lower a few pints preceded, of course, by a snort of the hot stuff. Murto saw to it that no other guard was informed about either the whiskey or the porter. He came off duty at six in the morning. He went immediately to the outhouse where he took off his cap and coat in order to get down to the business of serious drinking. At eleven o'clock in the day he was discovered fast asleep by a mourner who had inadvertently mistaken the outhouse for the lavatory. Murto slept with his mouth wide open and the deep snores came rumbling upwards like thunder from the caverns of his throat. The publican's son was alerted but the joint attempts of both men were not sufficient to wake him. Finally a horse and rail was sent for. It took the combined efforts of seven men to load him into the rail. When this was done his body was covered with tarpaulin and he was taken home. The owner of the horse and rail went to the rear of Murto's house, heeled his car and unloaded his cargo, without ceremony, outside the back door. He then kicked the door hard and long and took off as fast as he could in case the Pom might think he had been Murto's drinking companion. How she got him into the house was a mystery. Some say she used an old window shutter as a lever and bit by bit managed to ease him inside. Then she covered him with a quilt and a blanket and left him until he was obliged to go on duty that night. He woke hours later with a flaming head but reported for duty nevertheless. He touched several of his colleagues for money but got none. No one had money in those days except a few shopkeepers and professional people such as doctors and lawyers and the like. Anyway he never paid back what he borrowed. He bided his time until midnight.

Then he started to raid the pubs. From every one he exacted his toll. He would first knock gently at the public house door. He knew the secret knock of every one. When the publican would open up and peer out expecting to see a familiar face Murto would whisper: 'Guards on public house duty.'

'Would you drink a pint?' the publican would ask.

'Would I drink a pair of 'em,' from Murto. He employed this tack on all the pubs which were engaged in after-hours trade until his head was cured and his belly full of free porter. If any publican refused him a drink he summonsed him on the spot. He had the longest reach I ever saw in a human being if there was anything to be grabbed that cost nothing. When he was in digs he had a boarding house reach to outclass all boarding house reaches. If another diner took his eyes off his plate for a split-second Murto's huge paw would descend on the plate and sweep whatever was on it. When the astonished victim looked around to see who had taken his supper Murto's face would be the picture of innocence. He had no time for colleagues who were under six feet in height.

'Small guards is no good for nothing except small women,' he would say. It was said of him that he drank thirty pints of porter give or take a few pints every day for thirty years which was no mean achievement when you consider that he did not pay for a single pint. He would call for a drink all right when in company but somebody else always paid for it. It's a sad fact about many unfortunate people in this country but they will insist upon buying drinks for guards even if it means going without food for themselves and their families. Murto and his equals always took advantage of these people. On the other hand it was and is an acute source of embarrassment to most guards who like to buy their own drink and be beholden to nobody. Poor Murto. He could never get enough of strong drink. He passed from this hard world at the tender age of sixty-one, only one year before he was due to retire. He was on temporary duty at a village carnival where he was not known to the proprietors of the public houses. At midnight, acting on orders from the local sergeant, Murto and a few other guards started to clear the pubs. The sergeant meant business so there was no way Murto could come around free drink. The last pub they raided was owned by a widow who had never seen Murto before in her life. Murto was well aware of this and as he was leaving the premises he took hold of his forehead and staggered all over the place moaning painfully.

'Oh my poor man,' said the widow, 'what ails you?' Murto made no answer but he pointed dramatically at his chest. The widow at once went inside the counter where she seized a bottle of brandy and a glass. She poured a full tumbler and held it to Murto's mouth. He was now seated on a chair with his hand inside his tunic. He swallowed in dribs and drabs until he had the measure inside of him. The widow in her innocence filled the glass again. This time Murto took the glass in his own hands.

'Do whatever you have to do,' he told the widow. 'I'll sit here awhile till the pain goes.'

The widow, it transpired, had to go to the outskirts of the village to collect her two daughters who were attending a dance in the marquee which had been specially erected for the duration of the carnival.

'Go away cratur,' said Murto magnanimously. 'I'll hould the fort till you get back.'

'Help yourself to what drink you want,' said the widow. 'I won't be long.'

'I might try another small sup so,' he called out weakly. When he was alone he polished off the contents of the brandy bottle and liking the taste of it went inside the counter where he found a second bottle. What happened in the meanwhile was that the widow, as soon as she stuck her head inside the entrance to the marquee, was asked to dance. Knowing the house was in safe hands she waited till the ball was over. When she returned there was no sign of Murto or of two full bottles of brandy which was the widow's entire stock of that wonderful amber liquid.

It was Seán O'Conlon of the Special Branch who pieced together what happened afterwards. It would seem that Murto consumed the brandy in question in less than forty-five minutes. On his way back to the barracks he found himself weakening so he entered a meadow where he sat for a spell with his back to a cock of hay. After a while he fell asleep full stretch on his stomach. Around three o'clock in the morning he swallowed his tongue and was suffocated. God be good to him. He wasn't the worst of them. We shall not look upon his likes again, not in the uniform of a civic guard at any rate. Remind me sometime to tell you about the two women who proposed to myself and Mick Drea.

My love to Gert and the child

Your fond uncle

Leo

Super's Office
District Headquarters GS

Dear Leo

Good man yourself. I am most happy with your report. Monasterbawn has never given me any headaches thanks to you. From the point of view of peace and quiet it could be looked upon as the showpiece of the district. I note from your latest dispatch that you intend coming out next year. I am fully aware of the fact that you are entitled to retire any time you like but I would ask you, as a personal favour, to reconsider. This district needs men of your calibre. Think about it. I spent the first ten years of my career in a village no bigger than Monasterbawn. I had a sergeant who was always at his wit's end trying to restrain me. I knew it all, of course, in those days. But for that sergeant I wouldn't have lasted three months in the force. He was a father and mother to me. At first I couldn't understand why he ignored most of my reports or why he would pooh-pooh what I regarded as vital information. As time passed I began to appreciate his wisdom. The first boob I made was to arrest a man I found climbing over the back wall of a garden which surrounded a handsome detached house on the outskirts of the village. I lugged him straight to the barracks despite all his protestations. I demanded a statement from him but he demanded to see the sergeant. What an awkward, uncooperative scoundrel he was. The sergeant appeared in his pyjamas.

'Go home Jim,' he told my prisoner.

'Thanks Pat,' said he and out of the door with him. I ranted and fumed after that and for weeks there was a coolness between us. How dare he dismiss my valiant efforts with a few words, without even consulting me. A month later I caught the same man climbing over the same garden wall. I arrested him a second time and took him to the barracks. Again the sergeant appeared and again he told my captive to go home. After that we didn't speak for three months except in the line of business. What a fool I was. Every week without fail I would see the same man climbing over the same wall. It took me years to discover that he was a local farmer, the henpecked husband of a sexless and careless wife. He was a decent sort of man despite his aberations. The woman he was visiting was a buxom, sexy-looking lady in her forties who lived with her married sister and whose small back room overlooked the wall which her lover so often climbed. Everybody knew what was going on except the man's wife and myself. After that I wasn't half as brash or officious. I learned that nightfall, as far as a civic guard was concerned, was but the overture to another sorry tale on the human situation, another chapter in the mighty tome of human lunacy. I often despaired of the human race after a month of nights. Even in that tiny village the hours of darkness were filled with shuffling, silent shapes which were identifiable after a while as prominent or common or worthless members of the community. Night-time is for lovers, lawbreakers and cats. Sometimes on misty, chilly winter nights I would pass a pair of lovers intent on their kissing and cuddling in a shady place off the beaten track. I'm ashamed to say curiosity often got the better of me and I would draw aside as soon as they parted from each other in order to see who they were. I was once shocked to the core for the woman was the respectable mother of a family. I ceased to be shocked thereafter and I would take it in my stride, the rare time I would see a married woman of impeccable character, dressed in raincoat and headscarf, furtively scurrying homewards from the arms of another man. I learned too that there were reasons for this kind of carry-on, not good reasons but reasons all the same, often almost amounting to justification. It might be spite for an uncaring spouse or revenge on an unfaithful partner or it could be that some foolish woman had fallen for the looks and lingo of a Casanova. Often it would be love, pure and unadorned. I was the only witness to the isolated and uncommon. Happily for those whose paths crossed mine in the dark of the night I was a witness who would never testify. A layman with whom I was once drinking insisted, during the course of our conversation, that civic guards were dour, uncommunicative fellows who seemed reluctant to join in normal conversation. An exaggeration, of course, but not without a grain of truth. I tried to explain to him that a man who knows so much about the people of his community has to be cautious when communicating with others lest he slip up and bring somebody into disrepute. This he refused to accept saying that guards should let their hair down the same as everybody else. Personally speaking my experience is that it pays to be careful and conservative when conversing with members of the general public. Personal opinions Leo are a luxury which you and I just cannot afford.

I'll wind up now but not before I compliment you on the fine job you're doing in Monasterbawn. I wish you would not look upon the difference in our ranks as an excuse for not calling to see me when you're in town. There's always a bed here for you. Give my regards to the Widow Hansel and keep up the splendid work.

As ever

Joe Fahy

Toormane Hill
Monasterbawn

Guard Molair

Raid the Widow's and do us all a favour by catching yourself. Do something about the young drunkards who shout and yell on their way home at night. Scum is what you are and a low bastard to boot. Be careful don't you give the Widow a child, and try to have the grace of God about you.

Signed
A TT

Garda Barracks
Monasterbawn

Dear Ned

Many thanks for yours of yesterday. I see by the papers that O'Connell Street is dominated at night by young thugs. Too much is expected of the guards. How can a handful subdue a horde when the public looks on and for the most part enjoys it. You can't have law and order without consent from the public. Without their back-up the uniform is only a target for thugs. God forbid me but I loathe gangs whether they be religious, political or sporting. You'll find when you sort them out that there isn't a good man in the bunch. Your decent man won't run with gangs no matter what their purpose. Good men don't form gangs. Only the scum of the earth do that.

You ask about Flash Maldook. Well what they say is true. He was the greatest ladies man since Casanova and having a guard's uniform was no disadvantage to him. The women loved him, married, single or otherwise. He had a pencil moustache, dark brown eyes and curly black hair on top of a head that was without a brain of any kind. He was a handsome scoundrel however. Make no mistake about that. When he flashed those white teeth of his and shook his head so that his curls danced on the rim of his forehead few women could resist him. It was a woman who got him into the guards. In those days you didn't need much education. She was the Reverend Mother of the local convent in the town where Flash resided. The poor woman went on her knees to the local sergeant to get him out of town. Damage had been already done to two of her pupils and the party responsible was our friend Flash Maldook. The sergeant groomed him for the guards and eventually he got him in. As I said already the uniform crowned him. Even if he had wanted to he couldn't keep the females away. As fond as the women were of Flash he was even fonder of them. He lasted a year. He was forced to flee to Canada after it was discovered that a score of pregnant women had named him as the sole cause of their predicaments. He was a legend in his own time. They say that women swooned when he entered a dance hall and the whispers would spread like wildfire: 'Maldook is here. Maldook is here.' Some say he was shot dead by a jealous husband in Montreal while more say he joined an order of monks and devoted his life to God as an atonement for his sins. You won't knock an old dog off his track and what I say is that Flash Maldook is still fornicating with females whether in Alaska or Nebraska, whether white, black, mottled or brown.

One thing is sure. He sired them on the tops of mountains and the depths of valleys, up against hall doors and halfdoors, against hawthorn hedges, turf-ricks and oatstacks, in rain or shine, on dry ground and puddle, in the backs of motor cars and in the fronts of motor cars, upstairs and downstairs, in haysheds and turfsheds, byres and barns, in nooks and crannies and all over the place till he transported himself through necessity across the wide Atlantic. I'll close now. I see my friend Jerry Fogg, the postman, at the window. I wonder what brings him at this late hour. There's trouble. It's written clearly on his face. It's bad trouble. Jerry wouldn't look like that unless there was death in the background. I'll conclude.

Your fond uncle,

Leo

PS I was right. All hell has broken loose here. A husband and wife on their way home to their abode a mile from Monasterbawn were knocked down and killed by a car which did not stop. A few moments ago Mocky Trembles of Jackass Lane stumbled across the bodies. I'll close. Say a prayer for us.

Uncle Leo

Garda Barracks
Monasterbawn

Dear Superintendent Fahy
Here is the report as requested. At twelve minutes past twelve on the morning of 11 April it was brought to my attention by local postman Jerry Fogg that a serious accident had taken place in the roadway known as Jackass Lane which is the only northern approach to the village of Monasterbawn. I proceeded immediately to the spot and there beheld two bodies, both lying approximately on the middle of the roadway and exactly thirty-one feet apart. They were the bodies of a man and a woman known to me as John and Sheila Glenn, husband and wife and the parents of six young children whose ages range from four months to ten years. Upon examination I perceived that they were both dead or as like to dead as I could make out. Priest and doctor had already been sent for. There were forty-feet brake marks at the right side of the roadway and a foot long torchlight which had apparently been in use by the deceased was still switched on when I discovered it on the grass margin near where Mrs Glenn lay. I instructed the postman Fogg to notify the district headquarters by the barracks phone while I remained on the scene of the accident to take comprehensive measurements by tape.

At twelve twenty-nine Doctor Bawney, the local MO and coroner, arrived on the scene. After a brief inspection he ordered the bodies to be removed to his surgery where, after a thorough examination he pronounced John and Sheila Glenn dead. An ambulance removed the bodies to the mortuary of Ballincarra district hospital, it being the nearest such place to the scene of the accident. Attached find two copies of the coroner's report.

Signed

Officer in Charge

Monasterbawn GS

Leo Molair

Personal

Dear Joe

For the love and honour of God will you do all in your power to prevent what looks all set to be a massive inflow of garda personnel. I know this area like the back of my hand and I can tell you straight that the bigger the number of strange faces the less likelihood of receiving any worthwhile information. Strange accents are no asset either and the superintendent, the two inspectors and the four detectives might as well not be here at all. All they will succeed in doing by their continued presence is to frighten the wits out of the local population and even make these good people wary of myself since they will have no choice but to identify me with these intruders. I know they are well trained and highly proficient in every respect but with all due respect what you require here are district men only led by yourself or you could bring in men like Jim Brick of Derrymullane and other outlying stations, men who know the people and the countryside and who are known and trusted by the people. With the brass out of the way the tip-offs will come. The locals will be making their own seemingly innocent enquiries here and there and a picture will emerge in time. The normal pattern of life has been disturbed and from the looks of things there will be more turbulence. A consensus of local opinion would tell you that no useful purpose will be served by the presence of so many strangers. They honestly feel that they're being made a show of. Consequently they close up. Any fair-minded person would agree that we should have been given first chance what with our knowledge of the area and the goodwill we have built up over the years. Fine then if we failed. Bring in the city men and give them their chance. I'll tell you a true story which will better illustrate what I am trying to prove. When I first came to this place more than thirty years ago I was looked upon as a stranger. It took several years before the people began to accept me as one of their own and even then there was the invisible barrier that always exists between the civic guard and the public but I knew all I wanted to know as soon as they came to accept me.

However, on my first day, while patrolling the village I was taught a valuable lesson. It was a fine summer's afternoon and there was nobody to be seen in the main street save an old, bearded man with a blackthorn stick. He sat on the wooden seat near the village pump. I bade him the time of day and stood idly for a few moments admiring the mountains of Mullachareirk in the hazy background. One stood out above the others and I was curious as to its name. I pointed in its general direction and asked the old man if he would tell me. He looked first at the peak and then he looked at me:

'I am here,' said he, 'man and boy for seventy-five years and I never noticed that mountain till now.'

I got the message and knew it would take time and patience if I were to win the confidence of these people. Do what you can Joe. We will never know who killed John and Sheila Glenn unless the investigation is in our hands. This is purely personal.

As ever

Leo

Main Street
Monasterbawn

Dear Guard Molair

It is with extreme regret I take up my pen to write to you. I have just come from the church where I have spent the past hour in prayer and meditation and beseeching the Mother of God to intercede for me and to guide my conscience in the right direction. It is my bounden duty to write this letter and inform you that the hit-and-run monster was in Fie's public house on the night the Glenns were slaughtered. He was in conversation most of the night with Margie Fie, the mistress of the den. It could be bad whiskey he got that blinded him when he went behind the wheel. Don't spare her. Act now.

Devoted wife and mother of a large family

Main Street
Monasterbawn

Dear Guard Molair

It is high time that someone in authority clamped down on the after-hours drinking that goes on at Crutt's shebeen which is the right name for it, may God forgive me. Everyone is saying that more drunken drivers leave it after hours than you would find coming from the city of Cork after a Munster final. Everybody says it must be in Crutt's the man responsible for this hit and run got the drink. Where there is smoke there is fire. Everybody says it and everybody can't be wrong and to see the Crutt one marching up the main aisle of the chapel like she was God's anointed. It would turn you against religion. Indeed it would and wouldn't you be inclined to ask yourself what is the good in being honest when the likes of her can scorn the laws of God and man and walk around brazen like she was as pure as the driven snow. Hell is a light punishment for the proprietors of Crutt's public house.

Signed

Indignant housewife

Toormane Hill
Monasterbawn

Guard Molair

The chickens have come home to roost. You have reaped the harvest of the shut eye and the turned back. On your shoulders fair and square must be placed the blame for the deaths of poor Mr and Mrs Glenn. May the faces of their innocent children haunt you to your deathbed although you won't see any deathbed for it is you has the prime head for an axe and fine soft neck for a rope, you that condoned after-hours drinking and ignored the warnings I sent you. It's you who should stand trial but you won't you wretch. May your conscience, if you have one, pester you till your days run out and you go to face your God. Think about what you have done, your crime against those orphaned babes.

Signed

A TT

Garda Barracks
Monasterbawn

My dear Ned

No doubt you have by now read the whole sorry business in the papers. They did a fair enough job, allowing for all the groundless speculation and interviewing of local fools. They must dress things up too I suppose. I enclose a copy of my report plus a personal note to my chief Joe Fahy. You will also find a copy of the coroner's report. They may interest you. I had no written answer to the letter I wrote Joe Fahy. No blame to him for this. He came to see me, however, and we had a few drinks at the Widow's. There was nothing he could do. Mind you he agreed with most of my submission but he is himself subject to his own chief. He told me there is a prescribed machinery specially geared towards the crime in question and ready to move instantly into operation for the very good reason that scents grow cold and time covers most things. I asked him if there was any hope of just having the two local squad cars, their crews and all the men of our district alone just for a week but he ruled it out saying he had a moral obligation to accept all the help he could get and that he was under strict orders to follow routine and proven methods. My dear Ned I do not boast when I say I could do a better job than these outsiders, no blame to them, if I were given the manpower and transport and permitted to deploy it in my own way. But I'm only the man on the spot who knows the people and the area better than any man in the entire force. They haven't asked for my advice once, just questioned me over and over like all the others involved in the case. They are stomping with big boots where tiptoe walking in soft shoes is absolutely necessary. They are closing doors instead of opening them.

The super also told me that the nationwide publicity was an advantage. The photograph of the six children in particular which appeared in two Sunday newspapers should bring home to those who might know something the fact that the perpetrator of the dastardly act must not be allowed to go free. The photos should prick consciences. They should but will they? Somewhere in the Monasterbawn district I'm sure, a mother or a father or a sister or brother or a whole family knows that one of its members is responsible for the taking of two lives yet nothing will induce them to talk. If young folk were responsible the parents know and vice versa. You're up against native craft and cunning here. Ordinary police methods won't work. I'll keep you posted about events. Quite frankly I'm pessimistic. In an area like Monasterbawn when solutions don't surface at once they have a habit of never surfacing. Love to all.

Your fond uncle
Leo

The Mountain Road
Monasterbawn

Dear Guard Molair
You can pretend you was never in receipt of this. I would not care to be known as a man as writes to guards. I would like to see you. Slip up this way after dark and I'll have something for you, something that will do you good although I owes you bugger-all after the persecution you gave me. Come on your lonesome and tell no one.

Thade Buckley

PS That bull that gave you the run did the job himself crossing a gate. He got held up by a noose of thorny wire and hadn't the patience to wait. Don't come if there's a moon. I don't want the country seeing you.

Thade Buckley again.

PS I always lets on I'm illiterate so no one is going to believe you anyway if you say 'twas me wrote this letter. It pays me better to be illiterate.

TB

PS Don't come in a car whatever you do. Better you didn't come in uniform. Better you came in a hat and coat and I can say 'twas some chap enquiring after the services of my stud greyhound, Flashing Dango.

    Yours faithfully

    TB

Garda Barracks
Monasterbawn

Dear Joe

This is confidential. I was right all along. The brass have really put their feet in it. Yesterday I received a garbled message from a Mr Thade Buckley of the Mountain Road. He farms his mountain acres about five miles from the village. I deduced from the message that he knew something about the hit and run. I waited till well after dark and cycled to my rendezvous. There was no light in Thade Buckley's but this did not surprise me as I knew he wanted our meeting to be as secret as possible. The moment I dismounted he emerged from behind a hayrick and thrust a bottle into my hand.

'That's for yourself,' he said. 'Something to tickle the balls of your toes.'

It was a bottle of poteen, the last thing in the world I wanted.

'Is this why you told me to come up here?' I asked him.

''Tis a good drop,' he said, 'a special drop, the last of a good brew. When I got it you were the first man I thought of.'

I nearly went berserk at this. It gave me all I could do not to strike him. I took him by the throat and brought him to his knees.

'I'll beat you to pulp,' I told him, 'if you don't tell me the real reason why you invited me.'

'I don't know what you're talking about,' he whined. 'I swear it.'

'Come on, come on,' I said bringing him to his feet and chucking him about till he was dizzy. He still maintained, however, that his reason for inviting me was the poteen and the poteen alone. I tried different methods. I released him and offered him a cigarette.

'Tell me about the hit and run,' I asked him offhandedly.

'Hit and run,' he laughed at this. 'Cripes 'n mighty man,' said he, 'I gave the morning long on that one with them detectives and that superintendent with the moustache. The morning long I gave and they quizzing me left and right, together and single.'

I knew that any further interrogation would be a waste of time, that the barriers were up. He had intended telling me something, knowing I wouldn't disclose my source. He knew he could trust me on that score. He knew from experience that I was a man who could be relied upon but the visit that morning from the detectives and the super had silenced him effectively and eternally. Nothing on God's earth would now induce him to part with his secret. I have my own suspicions but no proof at all. I'll report everything.

As ever

Leo

Fallon Street GS
Dublin 13

Dear Leo

My old friend. It's high time I wrote to you. I often have a good laugh when I remember the old days. Last Sunday I earned twenty-five pounds overtime. What a change. I often worked a long, hard and dirty month for the same amount not all that long ago. Your nephew is a fine lad, a bit over-conscientious on occasion but settling in nicely and will, no doubt, be a credit to the force in a short while now. I have a keen interest in him. By the way I'm a grandfather. My oldest daughter has a boy and a girl and my son has a son and heir with four months. I'm as bald now as a billiard ball, me that had a head of hair that blinded the women of Mayo, all but one and she, I'm told, died in England a short while ago.

That's a dirty business that hit and run you have. Without a tip-off you have little chance. At least that has always been my experience. The parents, of course, are the really guilty ones. They know damn well when something's wrong, particularly the mothers. Sometimes both parents know but mostly it's the mother and she hides it from the father unless the damage to the car is too obvious. Almost every hit and run would be solved overnight if parents made a brief examination of the son's car the morning after when a hit and run has taken place locally. Most of them prefer to close their eyes. This is also particularly true of wives whose husbands spend most nights in the pubs and clubs. Theirs is a difficult choice but they do the easy thing, cover their eyes when they don't want to know, cover their mouths when they do know. In the short term it must seem to pay but in the long term the awful secret, too late now to be revealed, eats away at the mind like a vicious cancer. I wish you luck in your investigations. Drop me a line when the whole thing is over.

Your old sidekick

Mick Drea

PS We have lost the city streets to hooligans. The calibre of our men is as good as ever but physically we cannot hold a candle to the giants who dominated the city when I was a rookie. They would be suspended or dismissed altogether if they employed such tactics today. The spotlight nowadays is on the actions of the guards, never the hooligans. A low profile is what we are supposed to present. We must never retaliate. What many forget is that an effective police force cannot expect to be over-popular.

How many times lately have I wanted to smash my knuckles into the leering faces of cowardly scuts and blackguards, hell-bent on provoking me, you might say trained to the ounce in the art of provocation.

I bridle as any red-blooded man will bridle when I am taunted and teased, spat upon and cursed, called a pig and an animal and a free-state bastard whatever that means. I am challenged by drunkards and braggarts. I am called yellow, lily-livered, cowardly etc. I bridle but always I keep my temper and so we stay a step ahead of the lawbreaker.

Every job has its problems I have no doubt. Still ours is often unbearable. There are areas here where the inhabitants would cheerfully kick you to death for no reason at all. The uniform is enough. There is nothing from the general public by way of support. I often wish there were posses or vigilantes. Then the public might have some idea of what we have to contend with. But you have enough on your plate without my side of it. Drop a line sometime.

Mick

Garda Barracks
Monasterbawn

Dear Mick

Your letter brought back memories of old times. The past came drifting back to me again and I found myself walking along the narrow roads of Mayo like as if 'twas yesterday. Do you remember all the girls without lights on their cycles we used to stop at night after the dances? Fair play to us we never gave one a summons. You were the fierce man Drea for the cautioning so you were. Do you remember all the good-looking ones we escorted home for their own good moryah? Do you remember the lassie with the red hair that stole my cap? I called to her house a few days later by the way to find out how many hens, cows, ducks, pigs et cetera they had. The father gave me the numbers in good heart and we sat down to the tea.

'Will you also put it down in your returns,' said he, 'that I have four marriageable daughters and every one of them with a head redder than the next.'

We had a royal evening and my cap was returned to me before I left. Hard to believe but not one of those lovely girls was alive when I called that way again during a holiday four years later. All had been carried off by consumption.

I'm happy here Mick or at least I was happy until this hit and run. There isn't a day but we have a visit from some detective. They watch the comings and goings of the villagers and the pubs are losing trade steadily for no man wishes to have his movements recorded no matter how innocent or law-abiding he may be. The village was depressed enough after the accident but this constant harrassment is as much as it can take. They even have nicknames on the visitors now. One is called 'Catsfoot' because no one ever hears him approach. There is another and they call him 'The Pale Moonlight'. His first question is always: 'Who were you with last night?' There is another sinister-looking chap, an inspector, who has a habit of scratching his posterior. 'Itchybum' they call him. Then there's 'The Big Wind' who breaks wind all the time and finally there is a giant of a fellow who walks like a lady. 'Tiptoe through the Tulips' they call him.

They see to it that the pubs close on the dot. With characteristic loyalty the regulars of Crutt's and Fie's are gradually drifting away to other pubs in the nearby villages. I had the usual anonymous letters from Crutt's and Fie's, both without a word of truth but they had to be handed over. The visitors took them seriously and acted accordingly. They questioned every man, woman and child who was seen entering or leaving either pub. It would take a brave man to go into one of them now. This whole business has me in the dumps. The respect I've earned over thirty years is being eroded. If only we could solve it things would soon return to normal.

I think I know who's responsible for this business myself. I'm keeping my own counsel just yet. There's little to go on. Mocky Trembles of Jackass Lane says he heard a loud thump around the time the accident would have taken place. Then he says he heard a car start and leave the scene for the direction of the Mountain Road. He was beating the wife when I called to see him. I intervened and gave him a good kick where it won't show.

'You'll kill her one of these days,' I warned him.

'There's no fear of that,' said Mocky, 'don't I know to the stroke what she can take.' Goggles Finn says he heard a car pass at the time but he never turned to look. He was too busy watching Aggie Boucher as she togged off for bed. Aggie herself saw the car pass but could give no clue otherwise. Aggie had a fellow up one time for carnal knowledge. She was dating a middle-aged mechanic and in her own words in court he often started her engine. The mechanic had a son who was a total failure with women so what did he do but give the son his own coat, hat and spectacles and sent him off one dark and stormy night to meet Aggie at their favourite trysting-place which was a hayshed convenient to Monasterbawn. The mechanic was a man of few words who always got down to business as soon as he arrived on the scene. Aggie did most of the talking asking how was this and how was that and never waiting for an answer only always pressing on to the next question or commenting at length on the state of the country in general and the state of Monasterbawn in particular. She took the mechanic's actions for granted, making no comment during the preparatory stages of the encounter, during the act itself or afterwards. There are apparently many women who behave like this in these circumstances and Aggie Boucher was one of them.

The son had been carefully briefed by the father and he carried out his instructions to the letter. It was a big moment for him since there was no other way he could possibly come to close quarters with a woman. For a while all went well. The preliminary stages were negotiated successfully and the heart rose in the son of the mechanic after this first hurdle was cleared. Gently then he laid her on the broad of her back on the hay. With a becoming sigh just like the father he got directly down to business. It was a task to his liking and he lay into it with a will, with too much of a will alas for suddenly Aggie Boucher pulled out from under him and started to screech like a stuck pig. She reported the incident to the barracks and identified the son of the mechanic. It should never have gone to court but it did. The son denied the charge and the father backed him up by insisting that he was Aggie's lover on the night in question. Aggie stuck to her guns. She was asked by the judge how she could be sure it was the son in the darkness of the shed.

'I knew at once,' said she, 'for there is no one has the fine even stroke of the father.' The judge who himself was a middle-aged man held in her favour.

To get back to the hit and run Aggie saw the car but no more could she tell and it is highly unlikely that she would tell if she saw more. Thade Buckley obviously saw the car too but he has been frightened off and there is nothing to be done with him. About a mile from Thade's there is a farm owned by Malachy

Rattin. He has a wife, three sons and four daughters. They have an ancient Austin and a tractor but neither was involved in the accident. I'm sure about this. I thoroughly checked both vehicles unknown to them while they were drinking in Monasterbawn. The Rattin girls are sonsy types who spread their favours widely although I am told that the oldest girl has a steady man. If he has a car he could have driven her home on the night of the hit and run. I was up there yesterday on my own. They offered me tea which I accepted. I told them I was looking for information and then went on to explain that if there was a passenger in the car which was involved that person would most certainly escape scot-free if he or she came forward and made a statement to the guards. I thought I detected a twitch on the face of the girl who had served the tea but oul' Rattin intervened immediately.

'Yesterday,' said he, '"The Big Wind" and "Tiptoe Through the Tulips" were here. "Tiptoe" drank out of that very cup in your hand. We told them all we knew which was damn-all. We answered every question they put to us. It would be a great ease to us now if we was left alone and not have the neighbours raising all sorts of talk over guards coming two days in a row.'

I apologised for any embarrassment I might be causing and expressed a desire to speak to the girl alone. The father was inclined to object but when I asked if she had anything to hide he agreed. I led the girl out into the roadway out of earshot of the father or any other who might be listening.

'You're the eldest girl,' I said to her. She nodded demurely. 'And you're doing a strong line I hear.' Again the demure nod. Too demure to be true.

'Tell me,' said I, 'what part of the world does your young man hail from?'

'Tooreenada,' she answered.

'That would be the best part of twenty miles from here?' I said.

"'Tis no secret where it is,' said she as demure as ever, 'isn't it carried on the signposts.'

I was dealing with a tough chicken, well drilled by the Da and well used all her life to dealing with curious strangers. It wasn't my first time calling to the Rattin household. I could put forty minor crimes at their door but I could never prove one. They were always on the one word every one of them, produced and rehearsed by the Da with never an extra line or part of a line no matter how often you questioned them.

'Tell me Miss Rattin,' said I, 'what is your young man's name?'

'His name,' said she, 'is McMorrow, Joseph McMorrow. They calls him Sikey.'

'And was Sikey at the dance,' I enquired, 'the night of the hit and run?'

'He comes every Sunday night,' she answered demurely 'but sure didn't I tell all this to "Big Wind" and "Tiptoe" and before that to "Catsfoot" and "Itchybum".'

'Sure if you told it to them you can have no objection in telling it to me.'

'My Da is your sound man,' said she.

'How come?' I asked.

'He says that there's no good to be got o' guards.'

'Now Miss Rattin,' said I, 'was your young man driving a car the night of the hit and run?'

'No.'

'And how did he come to the dance?'

'With his brother.' She started to tap her foot impatiently. She drew a cigarette butt and a box of matches from the sleeve of her cardigan and soon she was puffing away in full content. Something told me that she knew more than she was disclosing. She was nervous and worried and she did not altogether conceal .

this successfully. I tried another tack.

'Had Sikey ever a car?' I asked.

'He had but he sold it three months ago.'

'Does he ever hire out a self-drive?'

'No he don't.'

'Does he ever borrow a car?'

'I don't know.'

'Since he sold his own car did he ever come driving another car?'

'Once only,' said she, 'and that was two months ago.'

'And where did he get that car?'

'He borrowed it from a cousin I think but he was covered for wasn't he stopped the same night by the White Mice and let go at once.'

I thanked her and let her go. I noticed a peakishness about her and there was a decided swing to her walk. I was sure she was pregnant and had been for some time. If Sikey was the father it would be in the girl's best interests to keep her mouth shut. When I got back to the Barracks I compared notes with the inspector. He agreed when I suggested Sikey should be questioned. He promised to do the job himself. Said it was the best lead to date.

If you are ever in this neck of the woods be sure to call. I always keep a good drop. No man will be more welcome. We must continue to keep in touch now that we have started to correspond again. I intend to come out next year. Have you decided one way or the other yet?

All the best for now.

Sincerely

Leo

Derrymullane GS

Dear Leo

I haven't time to drop over since the fellow here took queer. He was always bad but for the past few weeks he hasn't appeared much only talking to himself. I can hear him in the day room. There's no more talk now of your hit and run. A nine day wonder that, add a few weeks. I was doing a bit of arithmetic lately and I discovered that there have been seven unsolved hit and run cases in this district in the past five years as against one solved and he gave himself up after a day. Family affairs, every one of them. I can hear your man at it upstairs. He had an uncle for a bishop. That's how he became a sergeant. That's as far as he got however. The real trouble with him is that he thinks he's a super. That's why he won't speak to me. He feels he'd be letting down his rank. Whenever I want him to sign something or confirm something I have to pretend I'm a super too. I go up and knock at the door and put on an English accent.

'Who's out?' he calls.

''Tis me,' I tell him. 'Superintendant McDoogle.'

'Come in. Come in,' he says. After that we get down to business and the affairs of the station are easily sorted out. Superintendent Fahy knows the score. His advice is to leave well alone unless the man becomes dangerous. Three times I knocked on the door yesterday and got no answer. Finally I had to pretend I was the commissioner. All was well after that. The other night he ordered me to sandbag the doors and windows saying he had word of an IRA attack. He mightn't be too far wrong the way things are going. Sooner or later the post offices of our own district will come under attack. It's happening elsewhere. Why shouldn't it happen here? Whisht. Here he comes. He had just ordered me to suspend every civic guard in the station for disrespect to the superintendent. He keeps forgetting there's only the two of us here. It can't go on. Almost every day now he has visitors to his upstairs room. Sometimes he tells me who they are and why they came. Other times he cannot say a word for security reasons. On Thursday he had a call from Princess Grace of Monaco. Apparently she wanted him to take charge of the police force there. Later that day there was a deputation from Saudi Arabia. He introduced me to these. One of them was a very nice man by the name of Haji Puree. The others were a dour lot. That night a superintendent from Scotland Yard called to pay his respects. He was on a fishing holiday. He told him if we ever decided to leave the guards the Yard will be delighted to have us. Our man already works for them and for the FBI and Interpol in a consultative capacity. This morning there was a lot of noise upstairs, an attempt on his life by some Chinese agitators. He managed to beat them off.

What am I going to do? I can't give up on him. Last Sunday I spent the whole day on checkpoint duty. When I came back that night he told me that he had made an important arrest. Apparently there had been a papal spy in the area for some weeks. For some reason known only to the Pope she had been watching the comings and goings at the barracks in Derrymullane. At first I thought he was up to his usual capers but then I heard a dull thump from the area where the cell is located.

'Be careful,' he cautioned.

'I will. I will,' I promised. 'I'll just have a look.'

'There's no point,' he said angrily, 'she hasn't a word of English.'

'I'll take a look anyway,' I told him.

'It's against regulations,' he warned and moved to stop me.

'Did she say anything?' I asked.

'The usual,' he replied.

'What was that?' I asked.

'She pleaded diplomatic immunity.'

Meanwhile there were several thumps and some other unidentifiable, muffled sounds from the direction of the cell. He had by now unloosened his tunic and drawn his baton.

'I have a duty,' he said proudly, 'and no power on earth can dissuade me from carrying out that same.'

'What's that noise upstairs?' I said.

'What noise?' he asked suspiciously.

'Italian voices,' I said.

He was upstairs like a flash and there was pandemonium above. I'm telling you the furniture paid for it. I hastened to the cell while he was out of the way and there bound and gagged was Mrs Hussey the char. She was in a shocked state but fair play to her the first question she asked was to find out if himself was all right. She must have known with a while but kept her own counsel. There are more of them that would have us noted. I sent her home. She assured me that no one would hear a word from her. The commotion upstairs had ended and he was coming down the stairs with several dangerous-looking Italians in tow. One had a scar and another a limp. They were a terrible assortment of cut-throats. We managed to lock them up. He said nothing about Mrs Hussey. At the back of his mind somewhere he knew he had done wrong. He was right now however. He had the real villains under lock and key.

We took their names but every man Jack of them pleaded diplomatic immunity and swore like troopers at us. Christ I'm beginning to be as bad as him. It can't be too long now before he cracks. I'll let you know. He'll have to be moved quietly. Have you really made up your mind about coming out? I couldn't afford it just yet. The kids are too young awhile.

As always

Jim Brick

Garda Barracks
Monasterbawn

Dear Ned

I hope yourself, herself and the ladeen are fine. The story here could be worse I daresay. We are disappointed naturally over the hit and run. All our visitors have gone and so alas have the children of the dead pair. They've gone to a good place, run by sisters. Before he left the inspector told me about his interview with the prime suspect, a chap we'll call Sikey. Mick Drea will have filled you in on the story so far. I told him all in my last letter. This fellow Sikey is from a place called Tooreenada about twenty miles away. He is doing a strong line with a young one called Rattin from the Mountain Road. The inspector who was christened 'Itchybum' by the locals is a tenacious enough fellow, highly intelligent but with a downright bad manner which has antagonised everybody. There is no doubt in his mind, or in mine, that Sikey was the driver of the car which killed John and Sheila Glenn. He was in town that night. He did drive the Rattin girl home. He was seen by at least two locals who will never come forward. The car was one of twenty crocks owned by a cousin of his with a run-down garage. It had been in a crash but so had every other car in the cousin's lot. Sikey's brothers, three of them, his cousin and all the Rattin girls will swear that Sikey had no car of his own on the night of the hit and run. Sikey is to marry the Rattin girl at the end of this month. A friend of the Widow Hansel's told her that there would be a baby less than a month afterwards. Those who know that Sikey killed the Glenns can salve their consciences by telling themselves that the young mother and child would be the real victims if their evidence was the cause of convicting him. All the Rattins know, all Sikey's people and at least two others know but the Gardai know nothing. It's sickening. There may be more who know but you may be sure they'll never talk.

There are certain elements in every community who have always obstructed or conspired against the guards, who have closed ranks and stood firm when one or more of them was accused or suspected of something. It is a feather in their caps when we fail to right a wrong or punish a transgression and by God they show it in their faces when we accost them in the streets after a victory. There is the provocative, knowing smile that every one of us knows so well.

This is the eighth serious hit and run in this district in five years. There have been five deaths and four maimings and there is nothing to show that it won't get worse. The mothers know and the wives know and sometimes the fathers and other members of the family know. There are cases where the neighbours know. In all there must be a hundred people who could help us solve these killings and maimings but not one single, solitary voice has emerged so far from this community of so-called law-abiding people. They all know but us. That's the way it's always been and unless the make-up of mankind changes that's the way it always will be. If that's the sort of law they want that's the sort of law they deserve.

Thade Buckley's stud greyhound Flashing Dango was also killed the other night by a driver who did not stop. I thought this might soften him but so far he has remained silent. That was the mourning after the death of the dog. They have been drowning their sorrows in Crutt's and Fie's for the past three nights but always leaving on the dot of closing time and never unsteady on their feet or showing the least sign of drink. When they see me patrolling they whisper among themselves and there is the faintest trace of derisive laughter. I march on and keep my feelings to myself. The wheel turns slowly but turn it does and some day it will stop at the right number or at least I hope it will. Take good care of yourself up there and good care of herself and the kid as well. Now that I plan to retire you'll probably see a good deal of me from time to time but that's a fair ways off yet and the future is in God's good hands. I had better sign off. I'm up to my eyes between passports, school attendances, dog licenses and noxious weeds and on top of that a report that Mocky Trembles has the wife murdered. This must be the hundredth time. There's a complaint from a mother that her seventeen year old son has been served with cider at Fie's and is currently out of his mind. Jamesy Cracken, all seventy-four years of him, has just now attempted to rape the daily help. Monica Flynn has reported the Bugger Moran. That particular naughty boy has been exposing himself again. Goggles Finn has been peeping in the wrong windows. If only he would confine himself to Aggie Boucher's all would be well. Last night he spent an hour trying to watch the postmistress undressing herself. Will the long shameful, pitiful parade never end or is there any way in the world's face to divert it. I think I'll call on Jerry Fogg and take a saunter in the general direction of the Widow's, have a game of cards maybe with a few of the boys and down a few pints. God knows I have them well earned this day. Write soon.

Your fond uncle
Leo

Fallon Street GS
Dublin 13

Dear Uncle Leo
Enjoyed your letter. You never know but a break may come in that hit and run case when you least expect it. It can be terribly frustrating when the public won't come forward. They foolishly

believe that it's the function of the gardai and the guards alone to solve crimes but a police force is only as strong as the moral fibre of the public it represents and what the public really wants is not to be bothered in any way or embarrassed by the publicity the courts can bring or drawn into things against their will. The public would like to see us winning the war against crime. I have no doubt about that. However, they would like to keep their eyes shut while we are engaged in the struggle.

The reason I am writing so soon is that I am off to the Border for a term of duty. Herself and the kid are off to the mother-in-law until I come back. It's my second term so I know what to expect. You'll be hearing from me.

Your fond nephew
Ned

Monasterbawn GS

Dear Mick

You remember our friend Jim Brick? Well he's been stationed next door in Derrymullane for years now with a sergeant who thinks he's a superintendent. God alone knows what he has suffered in silence for the good name of the force. At last his suffering has come to an end. On Wednesday night last I received a phone call from Jim saying that his man had become violent and was barricaded in a room upstairs. It would be two hours before a squad car became available because of a bank robbery in the village of Tooreenada. I had no choice but to contact Jack Fie the publican, who is a tight-lipped fellow and has a car. Fie's wife is a sharp-tongued dangerous gossip but the man himself is a decent sort who never has a bad word to say about anyone. Although henpecked to the limits of his endurance he is an agreeable and obliging man. When I asked him to drive me to Derrymullane he agreed at once and we set out in a blinding rainstorm for that place. When we arrived there was no change in the situation. Jim met me at the door. I introduced Fie and the three of us made our way indoors. We decided our best bet would be to transport him to headquarters where the Garda doctor would be available. At all costs Jim wanted no commotion. His sole aim was to get the poor man out of Derrymullane without attracting attention. With this in view we sent Jack Fie upstairs with the following instructions. He was to knock upon the door and inform the sergeant that he was to come at once to meet the Minister for Justice who was waiting for him in Mallow and that a staff car was available to transport him thence.

Jim and I waited at the foot of the stairs. Jim had a pair of handcuffs at the ready. Upstairs we heard the door open and heard Jack Fie's voice.

'This way, sir,' he said and indicated the way downstairs. They came slowly, the sergeant first, Jack Fie second. They exchanged remarks about the weather. At the foot of the stairs the sergeant stopped. Jim and I saluted and prayed silently that there would be no trouble. Suddenly the sergeant turned and struck Jack Fie a solid blow on the jaw. Fie fell in a heap at the foot of the stairs. I tackled the sergeant down low by his ankles while Jim endeavoured to get the handcuffs on. The man had superhuman strength. All we could do was to hold on to him until he weakened or we did. Suddenly he went limp and started to weep. Then he spoke rationally.

'It's all right Jim,' he said, 'there's no need for the bracelet.'

Then as sane as ever I saw a man he got up and went straight to the car. He sat in the back without a further word.

The most recent reports indicate that he has a good chance of returning to normalcy although he will never return to the force.

The basic reason for his condition, according to those who knew him, was the fact that he had been bypassed for promotion several times while colleagues of his with less experience and ability were pulled up over his head. As the years went by he began to stagnate in Derrymullane with no outlet for his talents. A normal man might make the most of it or just go to seed as many good men did but not our friend. A new sergeant arrived yesterday in Derrymullane, a spick and span merchant, something of a martinet. The barracks of Derrymullane won't be long knocking the taspy out of him. Better still a couple of chip shop rows and a few weeks on checkpoint duty when the wind is from the north with sleet in it and you'd be ashamed to let a dog out of doors. I'll close for now hoping to hear from you at your convenience.

Take good care
Your old pal
Leo

Monasterbawn GS

Dear Joe

At the moment things look black but I have great hopes that someone somewhere will talk when the dust settles. I have just received another letter from Thade Buckley but I haven't opened it yet. If there was a blue riband for the ripest rogue in Monasterbawn Thade would win hands down. He had his share of misfortune too. His oldest boy was killed about ten years ago in a fall from his motorbike. Inevitable since he never wore a helmet. Today whenever I see a young man without a helmet on a fast machine I feel like cursing the parents who saw him leave home without suitable headgear.

The first time I prosecuted Thade was for the larceny of a pair of shoes. It was old Dan Turndown's wake. He was laid out in his best for all to see in his son's house on Toormane Hill. All night the neighbours called to pay their respects. They praised the corpse, accepted a drink and sat for a while in the kitchen.

It was well into the morning of another day when Thade arrived. He went straight to the wake-room to say a prayer for the soul of Dan Turndown. When he returned to the kitchen he declined the offer of a drink on the grounds that he had a cow calving.

A little after daybreak the woman of the house rose from her bed. The first thing she did was to visit the wake-room with a view to tidying up. It was she who noticed the torn wellingtons on the feet of the corpse. It was a month later, at a wren dance in Toormane, that I caught Thade Buckley dancing an eight-hand reel in Dan Turndown's new shoes.

Still I had better read the letter. I'll be in touch.

As ever

Leo

The Mountain Road
Monasterbawn

Dear Guard Molair

Sunday night will be quiet here with all gone to pubs and dances saving myself and my missus who has too much sense for that sort of thing no more. Nine o'clock would be fine time to meet under the lone eye of Ballygownalawn Bridge where no one will see or hear saving what few fish there is in the hole down below. This time I'll have something that will warm the cockles of your heart and no codding. No poteen this time but a thing you would dearly love to know.

There is wretches loose in this countryside that should be dangling from the gallows and their seed and breed should be strung up with them and their corpses left outside the gate of churches so as honest people know what they have done. Is it people I ask you that would harm innocent creatures? Is it monsters that would take the life of an innocent dog that brought credit and renown to Monasterbawn and the nation? Be here Sunday night at nine and tell no one. It is no good for you to go to supers or the likes with this as I am illiterate and can get several to swear to that effect. Remember Ballygownalawn Bridge at nine o'clock on your lonesome.

Signed

Thade Buckley

PS The bull you prosecuted me for I took to Derrymullane Mart. He was not a full bull since he got himself perverted by the thorny wire I told you about. He is what they call a Dildo. He could perform all right but no good would come of it. The man I sold him to has no way of knowing this but all is fair in love and war as we learned in school long ago.

TB

PS In the name of God let you not wear a uniform in case someone might see me going up and you going down. If you should come across anyone on the road that knows you let on you're looking for bald tyres. In this country there is a fierce crop of these as you know yourself and if you were to summons them all you would bankrupt the parish of Monasterbawn

TB

PS What I have to tell you will put your mind at ease for once and for all concerning a certain item that has caused a deal of commotion in these parts lately.

When Leo Molair came down from the mountain he was elated as Moses was elated after God had entrusted him with the Commandments. Although the information which Thade Buckley had imparted to him was not nearly so important as God's revelation to Moses it was, nevertheless, priceless in its own context. Infuriated by the untimely demise of his dearly beloved greyhound, Flashing Dango, Thade had unflinchingly put the finger on the man responsible for the deaths of John and Sheila Glenn. It was, as Leo and 'Itchybum' had surmised, Sikey from Tooreenada. Thade himself had not seen the actual incident but his youngest daughter had. She had immediately informed Thade who responded by threatening to break her neck if ever she mentioned a word to anybody. She had also seen another witness, Goggles Finn, who promptly ran off as soon as the victims were smashed to the ground.

Later when Leo confronted him with this he admitted everything and identified Sikey of Tooreenada as the driver of the car. Sikey's companion at the time was the Rattin girl who carried his child. After the crash he left the car, made a brief inspection of the bodies and drove off.

Leo was commended by his superintendent Joe Fahy who assured him that the evidence against Sikey was so overwhelming that there was no way he could escape prison.

So life went on. Time passed and came the last summer of Leo Molair's life as custodian of the peace in Monasterbawn. He looked forward to his retirement and engaged a builder from Derrymullane to erect a bungalow on the plot he had long before purchased for such a purpose. He was on his way to Derrymullane to meet this man when the unexpected caught up with him.

Some said later that since he was out of uniform it was none of his business but most held that being the man he was no other course was open to him. At precisely ten o'clock he left Monasterbawn barracks and mounted his bicycle. At one minute past ten he cycled *past Monasterbawn post office. He got no further. Seated in a car parked directly outside the building was a young man who was known to him as a subversive. He had once seen him during an anti-government demonstration in the city. As Leo was about to pass by the man tried to cover off his profile with his hands. It was too late. Leo had recognised him. At once he linked the man's presence with the fact that it was family allowance day and that a substantial amount of cash would be in the post office. Leo dismounted and, as he did, a number of things happened.*

Main Street
Monasterbawn

Dear Ned

It's high time I dropped you a line. At the funeral I couldn't help but notice your resemblance to himself. You asked me to send you a personal account of what happened. At a minute past ten on that awful morning a man entered Monasterbawn post office waving a gun and demanding that all the money on the premises be turned over to him. I was in the office at the time with Mrs Dully the Postmistress. She handed over the money which amounted to six hundred and ten pounds. The man ran into the street still waving a gun just as your Uncle Leo was entering the post office. He seized the robber by both hands and disarmed him. I was standing just inside the window at the time but my feet were stuck to the floor. I was paralysed by shock. The robber's accomplice who happened to be sitting in a car parked outside lowered the window and pointed a gun at your uncle. He fired two shots. The first struck Leo in the chest but did not seem to take immediate effect. The second struck him in the forehead. He fell dead at once. The two men drove off. Nobody knows who they were or where they came from. All we know is that they murdered the finest gentleman ever to come into our midst and left a void that will remain through my time and yours and beyond. There's no more I can say except that I'll tend to his grave as if he was my own father till I'm taken away myself for, in truth, that is what he was, a father to me and mine and to every man, woman and child in his care.

Yours faithfully

Jerry Fogg

LETTERS OF AN IRISH PUBLICAN

MARTIN MACMEER *the publican, mine host of Journey's End, a popular tavern in the village Knockanee in the county of Kerry, initiates a series of letters to a friend in the city. Betimes he will epistolise to others. Harassed by the changing tempers and idiosyncrasies of his customers he bids to defeat frustration by noting their antics, mannerisms, virtues, faults and general behaviour. Underneath his counter, on a good-quality jotter supplied free by Guinness's Brewery, he would appear to be doodling the time away. In reality he is logging the arrival and departure of customers and faithfully recording their words and actions.*

We should perhaps take a brief look into the background of Martin MacMeer. In most respects he is an ordinary publican committed to the serving of drinks hard and soft and committed too to the onerous task of having to listen to the problems, real and imagined, of all those who enter his premises. He is a bachelor by choice.

'I have no notion,' he was once heard to say, 'of becoming a martyr.'

A good figure of a man with a kind face he is now balding a little although women find him attractive. He is not easily ruffled but can be as short-tempered as the next when confronted with an awkward customer. When we find him in Journey's End he is past forty. He was not always a publican. In his eighteenth year he entered a seminary but on discovering that he was not cut out for the priesthood abandoned the idea altogether after two fruitless years and was fortunate to find a position with a newspaper.

Here he received some formal training as a reporter. As a result he was not long in acquiring the jaundiced eye of those who adhere to that occupation.

When Martin reached the manly age of twenty-five his widowed father tapped his last barrel and was called away to that place where all ales are clear and all spirits indisputably proof. Some weeks after his father's death he was summoned to town where the family solicitor promised to acquaint him with the contents of his father's will. Martin sat twiddling his thumbs in the waiting room wondering what lay in store for him. A maternal uncle who died prematurely some years previously had made a rather remarkable will which Martin remembered with some trepidation.

The name of the deceased uncle was Tom Long and the will was as follows: 'I Tom Long, being of sound mind, drank every penny I had before I died.'

There was no need for Martin to worry as he subsequently discovered. His father's entire possessions which consisted of a few thousand pounds and the inn known as Journey's End passed into his hands and so he became the proprietor of a public house. It is here we find him twenty years later putting pen to paper. He writes to a former colleague and friend from his newspaper days, one Daniel Stack, now a senior reporter with the same paper and as astute a judge of the human situation as one would be likely to find.

Journey's End
Knockanee
County Kerry

Dear Dan

The last time we met was in Ballybunion when we were both so drunk we should have been declared a danger to shipping. That was last summer two years ago. You suggested at the time that I should write a book about an Irish publican. I doubt if I could ever come up with a book but from time to time I will forward, not for publication, a running commentary on the prevailing situation. Enough said for now. My love to Briege and the kids.

Your old sidekick
Martin MacMeer

Editorial Department
The Irish Leader

Dear Martin

Good to hear from you. Delighted you have decided to do a spot of writing. Why not change the names of the characters and the location and earn yourself a few pounds in the process. Whatever you decide I shall be looking forward to an inside look at public house life in rural Ireland.

In haste
Dan

Wellington Heights
Dublin

Dear Martin

I am the stout female solicitor who spent so many nights in your lovely pub during the summer. I am the one who used to play the piano and drink the green Chartreuse. I can do other things too but we will not go into those now. What I want is this:

Could you find for me an old house, derelict or in reasonable repair that I might convert into a summer home near the sea at Knockanee. A place with a view would be ideal. If you can oblige I would appreciate if you would let me know and I will purchase provided the price is not too exorbitant.

I have fallen in love with Knockanee and the characters who live there all the year round. My eventual aim is retirement but that will be a long time yet. I must say I always found you most courteous, too bloody courteous as I recall when I called to say goodbye to you. Anyway do what you can for me.

Your sincere friend

Grace Lantry

Journey's End
Knockanee
County Kerry

Dear Dan

From where I sit I can see the rude Atlantic covered with white horses from point to point and off to its furthest horizons. On my right is Loop Head, drooping and lonely and on my left Kerry Head bull-necked and powerful. Between is a great plain of pure sea, churned and choppy now but in a few months time it will gently caress the browning, full-breasted bodies of young lovelies from distant cities. I must confess that I look forward to that time although I like this month of March the best of all. I like it for its promise and because it is neither summer nor winter. I love it for its freshness and if you want to know the sea for her true self March is the time to study her face and to fare where she holds court.

I see now that a brace of cormorants have entered the scene. They fly south in search of food, breasting the spitting seas of March. Gulls, of course, are mewing everywhere and there is a sting in the wind, a sting of salt, healing as a chest of medicaments and fresh as a kiss from a laughing girl. I know now that I could be happy nowhere else and and I am glad I made that fateful decision to resign from the *Leader*.

Here comes the first customer of the day, a hard case by name of Madge Dewley, the relict of a drunken schoolmaster and resident in a place known as Seaview Heights but known locally as Tipplers' Terrace. The inhabitants of this particular area would drink whiskey out of a sore ear with the difference that they will not be caught at it publicly. They are secret drinkers or so they think. Their neighbours could tell you to the drop what they have consumed.

Madge approaches the counter now bearing a brown message bag which contains three empty pint bottles. She smiles. I don't trust that smile. However, I will say this much for Madge Dewley. She is the soul of consistency. She never said a good word for anyone in her life, friend or foe, man or beast.

'Tis one right hoor of a day, Martin,' she says.

'Tis all that,' I reply. She opens the message bag and withdraws the empty bottles which she places upright on the counter.

'Give us up three pints of stout,' she says. I do her bidding. While I draw the high stout and allow it to rest she explains her case as she always does. She knows I do not believe her but she lies as convincingly as ever.

'I'm making a couple of porter cakes,' she informs me for the thousandth time, 'one for myself and one for my sister Kate in Cork that married the postman.'

I keep drawing until the bottles are filled.

'How's Mrs Malone?' I ask for devilment, knowing they do not get on.

'The poor creature,' says Madge, 'she don't stop farting from one end of the day to the other. You'd swear you was next door to a machine-gun post.'

I cork the bottles and wrap them thickly with newspapers lest they break in transit. Madge produces another empty from her coat pocket.

'You can throw a half pint of whiskey in that,' says she, 'I'll be making a trifle tomorrow.'

I do as I am told and she pays me my dues.

'If you like,' I suggest, 'I'll send them up at lunchtime by one of the young Malones. They'll be passing from school.'

'No thank you,' Madge announces politely, 'breed, seed and generation of that crew drank drop down but they'll drink none of mine.'

Madge bids me the time of day and exits. I watch her small defiant figure as it braves the stormy weather. She pulls her hat tightly over her head and changes her booze bag from one hand to the other. Her supply will last for two days. She can't afford any more. She is not poorly off. She has a modest pension and she lets most of her home to holiday-makers during the summer and autumn. I like her. I admire her. The only thing that will ever get the better of Madge Dewley is that which gets the better of every man and woman sooner or later. She pauses for a moment and rests the bag on the ground before ascending the stony path to Tippler's Terrace. Eva St George, the landscape artist, in spite of the wind and the cold, descends with her trappings. Madge refuses to give way and Eva is forced on to the roadway. No salutation passes between them. Eva will walk as far as the point and in the lee of the ruined castle commence a new painting. Nobody ever buys her paintings and her house from attic to basement is a jumble of canvases. Asked once for her opinion of Eva's work, Madge Dewley replied thus: 'I wouldn't allow her whitewash my lav, not if she was to pay me.'

Eva sees me through the window. She waves and I wave back. On her face is a look of radiance which says I will capture the tossing white waves today and the tumbling clouds and the glinting black rocks. If only she could paint. I'll close for the nonce. I'll be in touch. Love to Briege and the kids.

Martin

Journey's End
Knockanee
County Kerry

Dear Grace

Re yours of Saturday last. I think I have discovered a place that might suit. It's perched high above the Point with a fine prospect of sea and coastline. It is dilapidated but not beyond repair. The owner is a man by name of Peadar Lyne. I suggested to him that he have it valued by an auctioneer and then to put a price on it. This way there would be no suggestion of chicanery and there can be no soul-searching later on. I think it might be bought for three thousand. It stands on a quarter acre. A bit of gardening would do you no harm.

The reasons I was so courteous when you called to say goodbye last summer are as follows: It was three o'clock in the morning when you called and Father Pat Hauley the parish priest and his brother Father Ned, home from California, had you well-covered through the lounge window. I had them over for a few drinks since Father Ned was departing the following day for the States. Number two you were in bathing togs and that would be fine but for the fact that the upper piece was draped round your neck. Number three I never in all my born days saw anyone as drunk as you were then.

Hence the courteous reception. Try it again sometime and you may find me less hamstrung. I may be only a publican but I am not indifferent to the better things in life. It is too true that we, the publicans of Ireland, are the most lied about, the most abused, the most reviled of all God's creatures. Through the years we have been the sole target of fire and brimstone preachers and other itinerant, lusty-lunged missionaries belatedly loosed from their lonely cells and brimming with religious taspy.

We have been cursed by orphans and widows, damned by the wives and children of habitual drunkards and we have been consigned to eternal and exquisite agony by the mothers of this green and lovely land. Fair play to us it has all rolled off our backs like rainwater off a duck. The weaker amongst us have given in under the strain and the terrible injustice of it all. All is quiet now but let there be a disaster or an accident, a drowning or any damned calamity whatsoever and they'll pounce with a vengeance on the evergreen scapegoat i.e. your overworked Irish publican.

I don't know why I'm telling you all this. Why don't you drop down and see the cottage if you have a mind. There are no seas as capricious as the seas of March and no breezes as fresh or fair.

Yours sincerely
Martin MacMeer

Sandhill View
The Old Mill Road
Knockanee

Dear Mr MacMeer

I am aware that my husband John sometimes drinks in your pub. I am asking you in the name of God to serve him no more drink. He put us all out on the street the other night and when I tried to steal back into the house with the kids he struck me with his fist in the face and knocked me. This happens all the time when he has drink taken. Neither I nor my five children have ever enough to eat. The last time I bought shoes and clothes was at a jumble sale. I have stopped going to Mass. I am ashamed of my clothes and I am nearly always marked about the face. I can't leave him on account of the children. There is no misery greater than ours. Think of that, Mister MacMeer, the next time he asks for drink. I am also writing to the five other publicans in Knockanee. There is nothing personal.

Sincerely

Mary Hauley

Journey's End
Knockanee
County Kerry

Dear Dan

I have been blinded by a vision. I have been shattered from head to heel by the loveliest, sweetest creature that ever trod the sands of Knockanee. She was there under my eyes all the time but it took divine intervention for me to behold her as she really is, an angel pure and gracious, a fragile breath of utter loveliness. Alas she is only eighteen and is spending her final year at the Convent here in Knockanee. Her name is Antoinette Lingley. She is the daughter of a local housing contractor. I swear to you, Daniel, never was a fool of forty so woefully smitten. This is my vision splendid. She is dark-haired, sloe-eyed and willowy. Her skin is creamy and clear and she walks like an Olympic gymnast. She knows I exist because whenever I salute her she smiles and winks. You'd swear she knew my trouble. The mother, Lily, unfortunately, is one of the greatest straps ever to dangle her legs over a golf club stool, a brazen, stuck-up tit-tosser with a reputation for having popped in and out of bed with any available buck more times than she can actually remember. The father Jim Lingley is a decent skin, a man you'd have to like. He knows the score too but he loves Lily as he did the day he said, 'I do.'

There is no figurine of brass as hard as Lily. She has one abiding fear and that is your friend and mine Madge Dewley.

It is fear of Madge's tongue rather than anything else. Lily was in the bar here one morning last summer having a gin and tonic with Surgeon Casby from Cork. Casby wears white trousers, blue blazers, yellow socks and fawn suedes. He talks through his nose and finds it impossible to speak without first lifting his eyebrows to look down at a person. In short he is the epitome of snobbery and the kind that Lily has always desperately courted.

On the occasion Lily used her best Wimbledon accent and whenever old Casby squeezed her thigh she reacted by squeezing his. Halfway through the second gin and tonic Madge walks in with her message bag. Making no attempt to conceal her business she addresses me in a loud voice.

'Martin, you son of a bitch, I'm in one hell of a hurry. Give me out three pints of porter. I am baking two porter cakes, one for myself and one for my sister that married the postman in Cork.' So saying she planks the three empty pint bottles on the counter. At the time Lily is telling Surgeon Casby about her childhood in the village of Kilseer. Suddenly Madge starts to sing raucously to herself. The surgeon and Lily look on nervously. Madge's song is about Kilseer. She addresses herself to Lily:

Montana for cowpokes
Newcastle for coal
Chicago for gangsters
But Kilseer for your hole.

Poor Lily is mortified. Chuckling to herself Madge orders a half pint of whiskey for the mythical trifle. How such a mother as Lily could produce a daughter such as Antoinette is beyond me. I dare say natural goodness, like natural genius, will out at any

LETTERS OF AN IRISH PUBLICAN

cost. I will close for the present. I'll write again in a few days. Love to Briege and the kids.

As ever
Martin

Wellington Heights
Dublin

Dear Martin

You're a darling entirely. I'll try to pop down the weekend after next to have a look at Peadar Lyne's place. I enjoyed your letter but was somewhat disappointed when you closed with that dreadful piece of bull, yours sincerely. With bated breath I consumed your closing lines about the capricious seas of March et cetera. I was certain you were setting me up for a dirty weekend but then you went and spoiled it all with your yours sincerely.

Anyway thanks for going to so much trouble. Do you think you could find me a place to stay overnight or are all the guesthouses closed for the off-season? I know the hotel is but you are well in the know and I'm sure you'll have no bother at all fixing me up.

Yours sincerely
Grace Lantry

PS I am a much soberer girl in the springtime.
GL

Journey's End
Knockanee

Dear Mrs Hauley

I have just received your letter. You have no idea how upset its contents have made me. I will, of course, do as you request and refuse your husband drink when he calls again. I sincerely hope the other publicans will do the same. Indeed I am pretty certain they will. We are not a bad bunch even if we are painted otherwise. My dear Mrs Hauley, I would dearly love to help you. I could loan you some money. You need not worry about repayment for the present. If there is anything in the world I can do please do not hesitate to call upon me.

Yours most sincerely

Martin MacMeer

Editorial Department
The Irish Leader

Dear Martin

Is anything the matter? Just as I was beginning to enjoy those letters you suddenly stop. I was getting a tooth for your characters especially Madge Dewley. Your obsession with Antoinette Lingley is a natural phenomenon befitting your age. I have no doubt it will pass. Intransmutable as it may seem now there will come a time when you will smile at your present condition.

I hope nothing is amiss because seriously I am interested in finding out more about the good folk of Knockanee. Briege will be going to hospital shortly. Another natural phenomenon, the result of an error in judgement after the Journalists' Ball. I look forward to hearing from you within the week.

As ever

Dan

Sandhill View
The Old Mail Road
Knockanee

Dear Mr MacMeer

Please do not communicate further with me. If my husband knew I had written to you he would nearly kill me. He is too cunning to kill me outright. He would suffer for that. Please for the sake of myself and my children, forget us.

Mary Hauley

Journey's End
Knockanee

Dear Dan

Sorry for the delay between letters. The truth is that I have had a fairly hectic time in the interim. Easy for you to be dispassionate and philosophical about Antoinette Lingley. You haven't even seen her. She is the cause of many a backward look from dotard downwards to juvenile delinquent. One of the worst incidents to occur in the bar since I took over happened last Friday night. I have been assaulted and intimidated by gangs of youth on rampages and I have survived onslaughts from the most vicious thugs during the Whit and August weekends but Friday night's incident leaves these in the shade. Some time ago I received a letter from a most unfortunate woman. She asked simply to stop serving her husband with intoxicating drink. She had good reason to make such a request, believe me.

On Friday night at eight o'clock the bar was empty. I sat looking out the window thinking futilely of Antoinette and surveying the salty Atlantic all aglimmer just then, swathed in gentle moonlight and reflecting the glitter of a million stars. Ah my dear Dan, there is no sea like the Atlantic. She is a thing of a thousand moods. Turbulence, tranquillity, peace, passion, savagery, serenity. They are all there. There is no epic that would do her justice. She is too great, too vast, too exotic. She is the empress of seas.

While I sat there meditating I heard the door open and then the deep voices of two males. Looking around I saw that one was the husband of the woman who had written to me, one John Hauley. He was accompanied by the chief thug of the district, a horrible individual by the name of Joesheen Jameson. The latter is a familiar figure in the country's leading jails. His crimes chiefly consist of assult, theft and attempted rape to mention but a few.

Earlier in the week I had refused Hauley for drink but on that occasion he was alone and easy to handle. In fact he was as docile as could be and took my refusal quite well. Obviously it rankled him in the meanwhile because normally, bad as he is, he would not be seen in the company of a man like Jameson.

Instinctively I guessed that serious trouble was in the offing. I am without a phone and I never employ staff across the winter and springtime months. My regular customers, Peadar Lyne, Eve St George and the others would not be arriving for an hour or so. I had no way of contacting the barrcks and even if I had I wouldn't want to involve Mick Henderson the sergeant. He is due to retire next year. All right if one of the two young guards was on duty but I happened to know that one was on holiday and the other strongly courting a girl in Tralee. No chance of catching him at home during his off duty period.

There was a lot of menace in Hauley's approach. He produced his pay packet and withdrew a pound. His opening reminded me of a poker player the strength of whose hand it is impossible to determine.

'I am calling,' said he in a deadly earnest fashion, 'for two halves of Scotch.' I looked at Joesheen who stood in the background. He wouldn't know Scotch from urine.

'Sorry,' I said, 'I cannot serve you.'

'I want to know why,' Hauley leaned across the counter and so did Joesheen Jameson.

'His money is as good as anyone else's,' Jameson put in.

'I want no arguments now, boys,' I said calmly, 'and I want no trouble. If 'tis drink you really want there are several other pubs in the village where you'll get all you want.'

I figured if they left and were refused in the other pubs they might get into their heads that the whole village was against them. I could see, however, that they were already carrying a lot of drink, that I had been Judased by a fellow publican. It is the like of this particular Judas who gives us all a bad name.

'If you don't leave,' I lied, 'I'll send for the Civic Guards.'

Suddenly the pair unleashed a flood of expletives fouler than anything I had ever heard in my life. It was plain to see that Hauley's vanity had been severely pricked by my refusal earlier in the week. It must have festered. Word of such things spreads and trivial incidents assume new proportions. He works with Jim Lingley the contractor and naturally there was nasty banter on the site. I know what site chat can be like. Grown men can be exceedingly vicious.

Unexpectedly Hauley seized hold of a heavy ashtray and flung it at the shelf of bottles behind the counter. The ashtray smashed to pieces and two bottles of gin fell to the floor as a result of the impact. These also were smashed. Joesheen seized me by the tie and attempted to haul me out over the counter. I resisted easily. Hauley seized a small table and flung it at the shelves. Two more bottles, this time of whiskey, fell to the floor and were smashed. Hauley was berserk by now. The language still poured forth foul and filthy. He came across the counter. I decided it was time to evacuate. I vaulted across the counter and walked straight into a left hand swung wildly by Jameson. He caught me napping so much so that I almost fell. That settled it as far as I was concerned. He started to draw back his right hand to deliver the *coup de grâce*. My God he was cumbersome. I stepped inside him and smashed a good right into his mouth. I felt his teeth crunch. I stepped in closer as he reeled backwards and let him have a really good one in the same place. He sat on his arse without further ado.

Hauley, who was a witness to all this, had now lost all of his bravado. His face was pale. He knew I meant business. He ran round me with surprising speed and got through the door almost taking the damned thing with him. I contacted with my left shoe and felt it crack between the cheeks of his evil posterior. He ran down the street holding on to his gems, shouting in agony.

I lifted Jameson to his feet. It gave him all he could do to stand. I helped him outside and gave him a push in the general direction of his home. So much for that part of it. It is elementary for a fit man to handle half-drunks. Worse was to follow. I stood in the doorway and watched Jameson stagger his way homewards. He wouldn't forget his visit to Journey's End for many a day.

Meanwhile Hauley skulked in the shadows. I could see that he was still holding on to those which we all hold most dear. After a while, his condition improved and he entered the licensed premises of the widow McGuire's. I knew Kathy McGuire's form. She ran a good house. He didn't stay long. It was obvious that she had refused his request for drink.

The next place he tried was the Stella Maris, a licensed premises next door to the widow's. He spent barely a minute there. It was gratifying to see that the other publicans of

Knockanee were being faithful to Mary Hauley's instructions. This sort of treatment would soon send him home a chastened man and since he only acts up when intoxicated there was every reason to hope that his wife and children might have a respite from his tantrums.

His next port of call was the Hy-Brasil View owned by Dixie Megley. A minute passed and then two. Five more came and went, yet he did not reappear. Dixie Medley then was the Judas. I locked up shop and went down the street. I entered Megley's and there I beheld John Hauley drinking a pint of beer. As soon as he saw me he skedaddled.

'What's the idea?' Dixie asked innocently from behind the counter.

'Don't you know?' I said.

'Know what?' he asked with the same innocence.

'Come off it, Dixie,' I advised him, 'you received a letter the same as the rest of us.'

'Look here, MacMeer,' he said coldly, 'I don't tell you how to run your business so don't tell me how to run mine. I have a family to rear and I serve who I like. If Hauley didn't get his drink here he'd get it elsewhere.'

'That's a lie,' I shouted. That was when I made my mistake.

'Don't raise your voice a second time in my premises,' he cautioned. 'If you do I'll send for the Guards.'

He had me there. There was much I wanted to say to him. I had a parting shot.

'If your livelihood makes you sink so low,' I said, 'you should abandon it.'

So saying I made my exit. I was depressed and down and out and I was in need of a stiff drink. I decided that I would not reopen my premises that night. As I was about to enter the widow McGuire's I was hailed by a soft, cultivated voice and at once I recognised the portly form of John O'Donnell, Guinness's representative for the area.

'My dear Martin,' said John, 'how good to see you out of doors. Shall we indulge in a quick one?'

I have always found John to be the most agreeable of companions. We entered the widow McGuire's together where we joined forces with the remains of a wedding party. A hearty sing-song followed and no more can I tell you if you were to give me the keys of the Kingdom of Heaven. My love to Briege and the kids. Her confinement can't be too far away now.

As ever

Martin

It should be revealed here that our friend Martin MacMeer is not above indulging in the occasional bout of sustained boozing. Four times a year and sometimes five he embarks upon what the good folk of Knockanee call a shaughrawn. Loosely translated and in drinking parlance this would mean a skite or batter. These shaughrawns usually end when the subject is physically exhausted and totally dehydrated by the ravages of continued drinking.

Martin MacMeer is no exception. After three or four days he may be seen sitting peaceably albeit drowsily in the lounge of a hotel in the town.

Having arrived at this near-comatose condition he waits silently for one of his friends to collect him. As a rule this act of mercy is undertaken by John O'Donnell of Guinness's or by Eva St George or by Peadar Lyne. The last-mentioned it is who does it most often. Lyne is the owner of a pick-up truck. On the bottom of this he places an old mattress and thereon he dumps the exhausted body of his friend Martin. No word passes between them. In a day or so Journey's End is again open to the public and Martin MacMeer, mine host, would appear to be his old self.

Let me stress that he is no alcoholic. After such prolonged bouts of intense boozing he can return without difficulty to normal drinking habits, i.e. three and sometimes four pints of stout before retiring each night. The fact that he makes the occasional break is merely the Celtic extension of his character. This nomadic streak is a legacy from his Celtic forbears who once trudged across Europe and Asia in search of grazing and diversion.

The same legacy is inherited by all true Irishmen. But in some it is so dormant as to be everlastingly still. Slowly recovering he writes an imaginary letter to his beloved. He does not put pen to paper but speaks his heart to the listening sea.

Journey's End
Knockanee

My dearest Antoinette

You cannot know that for weeks past I have craved your company. It is I, Martin MacMeer, poet and publican, who called out to you from the depths of his anguished and sorely smitten heart. My love for you is a physical ache that hurts me day and night. In the darkness I see your young face shining like the Day Star. I imagine your dark hair falls and spreads and tumbles and tosses before my eyes.

Oh how I wish it were winter when the hail drives noisily across the rooftops hammering at door and window and the bitter wind churns the seas to white foam. Oh to have you in my bed (wedded of course) under the starchy white sheets, to shelter you from the cold and the dark. Oh my lovely Antoinette, my spirit aches for your nearness. Gentle and pure as is my love the lust of my manhood cries out for your tender body. The well of my love is deeper than the deepest ocean. The strength of my love is stronger and fiercer than the wildest tempest. Oh how would I love you, my dream, my angel, my sweet rose petal.

Do not think me an old fool of forty. There is more to me than that. There is the desire to cozen you through the nights and days of winter and spring and to help you bloom across the summer and autumn.

What can I say to spell out my deep and lasting love for you? What new mixture of words can I spread before you, dear, enchanting schoolgirl? I see your moist red lips all day long. I feel your sweet breath upon my shoulder and oh those sloe-dark eyes that weaken my every resolve and enmesh me totally so that I am a witless captive fit for nothing but to grovel at your feet.

Take pity on a fool of forty who through no fault of his own has been struck by the lightning bolt of your heavenly beauty. Do not spurn me without thought. I am wounded enough as it is.

Your slave
Martin MacMeer

Editorial Department
The Irish Leader

Dear Martin

Your letters have become so erratic of late that I am concerned for you. I hope all is well. Is it the girl Antoinette? If it is please remember, my dear fellow, that she is but a transient fad of the forties. For God's sake keep in touch.

As ever
Dan

Editorial Department
The Irish Leader

Dear Martin

You might as well know now that I intend haunting you until such time as your letters complete the picture of life in Knockanee as seen through the eyes of a publican. Quite frankly I intend to use the letters as a base for a work of fiction so for God's sake get on with it. I can use the money. Briege came up trumps and produced a pair of twins, one of either sex. She sends her regards. Please write soon.

As ever
Dan

Journey's End
Knockanee

Dear Dan

Please forgive me for the delay in the letters. Use the bloody things for whatever purpose you like and the best of luck to you. Under separate cover you will find a pair of suits for the new arrivals. I hope Briege thinks they're suitable. They were selected by a friend of mine, a lady from the big city, a solicitor by name of Grace Lantry who has been overwhelmed by the simple charms of this place and is determined to settle down here.

To this end she has just planked down three thousand pounds for an old house, the property of my friend Peadar Lyne who no longer has any use for it since he came to live in the village itself. She spent last weekend here. I could not find suitable accommodation for her because it was off-season so she coolly announced that she would have no objection to staying here at Journey's End. I couldn't very well throw her out. Her visit, which I shall never forget to the day I die, coincided with Old Jimmy Cossboy's wake. Grace arrived at eight o'clock in the evening just as I was loading up Peadar Lyne's pick-up with the wake order, the biggest wake order I ever received incidentally. Since I was locking up to attend the wake I invited her along. She drank twice as much as anyone there and was a tremendous hit with the old lechers and the likes of those that were never within an ass's roar of a liberal-minded woman. I discovered that she had no religion of any kind. During the recital of the litany she chimed in with her own piece. There we were after the rosary, all kneeling on the floor, as sanctimonious a circle of arch-hypocrites as ever supplemented the obsequies of an unwanted old man.

'Holy Mary,' said the woman of the house.

'Pray for us,' we all answered dutifully. So it went on.

'Tower of Ivory,' said the supplicant.

'Pray for us,' we all answered.

'Bangers and mash,' said Grace Lantry.

'Pray for us,' answered the entire assembly. Need I say more about the effect she created? We arrived home drunk as sticks about half-past five in the morning. Peadar dumped us at the door. If you don't mind, she wanted to sleep with me. I pointed out that it was hardly the time and place and if you don't mind she says that she can't sleep alone. I asked her if this meant she was habitually promiscuous, and she neatly countered by explaining that she had a cat for company in her flat. I couldn't resist her. The woman is a veritable cannibal for sex. I won't be the better of her for a month. Nourishment I want at my time of life, not punishment. While I was tending bar she knocked around most of the time with Peadar Lyne but she failed to register there. Peadar always claims that he was the only white man ever to screw a mermaid.

Says he, 'After jockin' a mermaid you'd never again have mind for ordinary women.'

When I reprimanded Grace for butting in during the Litany she told me that she thought it would only be right and proper to liven up the proceedings. Old Pettyfly, the well-known barrister, has lived in retirement here for some years now. I introduced him to Grace and they had a great confab.

A few days later he waylaid me and I walking along the strand, trying to recover from the excesses of Grace and strong drink.

'That was a nice handful you introduced to me lately,' said he.

'Are all of your profession like that?' I asked jocosely.

'Not quite,' he said, but then he grew serious. 'I'll tell you one thing,' he confided.

'Yes,' I said eagerly.

'The law never stood back from it,' he said proudly.

You should have seen Grace at the Mass for Jimmy Cossboy. She did the opposite of what everybody else was doing. When all stood for the Gospel she sat down and when all sat down she stood up. It was plain to be seen that she was as foreign to the inside of a church as an unbroken colt to the starting gate.

She's gone back now but she will be calling regularly. She's too much for me. I'll have to think of something. I'll sign off now. Tomorrow is the annual Knockanee cattle fair. I'll be in touch.

As ever

Martin

Wellington Heights
Dublin

My dear Martin

I can't tell you how much I enjoyed last weekend. What a surprisingly shy and, of course, refreshingly chaste individual you are. I've never met anybody quite like you. Do all publicans know as much about human nature? I daresay they must being at the front line, so to speak, from morning till night.

I've been telling my friends about Peadar Lyne's exploits with the mermaid. Is there any truth in it? I think he was having me on. How does he manage when there are no mermaids? There is a divorcee who lives in the flat next to mine and she assures me that she would give the number one mermaid a run for her money any time.

There is so much more I want to say to you but it is very very wrong and very foolish to trust oneself to paper as many of my unfortunate clients know to their cost. I shan't do anything with the house this year but I expect to be coming into quite a sizeable sum next year from a paternal investment many years ago. I'll get down to business then. Meanwhile don't do anything I wouldn't do.

xxxx
Grace

Journey's End
Knockanee

Dear Dan

The Knockanee annual cattle fair has just ended and presently permeating the entire scene, indoor and out, is the smell of fresh dung. Before I describe the day's happenings I want to put you a simple question. When a lady appends a lot of kiss crosses to the end of a letter is she being serious? Is there a special significance? Is it commonplace? Let me know as I am a man who values freedom more than most.

It was a great cattle fair with excellent prices. As usual they came in from the hinterlands with caps and ashplants and long coats, honest men who would give you a lick of an ashplant as soon as they'd look at you. True Celts every one. There were only two fights in Journey's End and these were mild enough compared with other years. The other pubs had their fair share of rows but by and large the violence would seem to be going from cattle fairs. Most of the farmers, big and small, have cars of their own now. They, and especially their children, tend to be a little more sophisticated. Still they retain many of their old features, some deplorably bad, others upliftingly good.

I'll say one thing for your aged countryman in this part of the world, He knows what frills are but he's not a man for them. What a change they are from a lot of the upstart new rich of today with their requests for Scotch on the Rocks, Bloody Marys, Asses' Elbows and what have you.

The first two customers to come in here this morning were middling-sized farmers from Cunnacanewer.

'Martin, my lovely boy,' said one of them, Mick Hayes by name, 'throw us out two small ones.'

What a classically simple request, most endearing to a publican's ears. Two small ones! They didn't ask for Scotch or Irish or Canadian, just two small ones. They couldn't care less as long as it was honest whiskey and if it wasn't honest they would not be long in telling you. It also shows that they trust the judgement of the publican to deliver a whiskey that should suit their particular tastes. In effect what they are saying is this: 'give us two halves of whiskey, Martin, a good honest whiskey that would suit the likes of us.' No illusions of grandeur here, no stupid pretensions. They are followed by others who call for the same. Each man will have four, maybe five halves of whiskey, no more. No force on earth will induce these men to have another whiskey. They regard the whiskey as a base for porter and a sound method of heating a cold interior.

After the whiskey it is your half-pint of stout. They will drink that all day long, taking a short break now and then to inspect the cattle or to close a deal. They will make a long break in the middle of the day to visit Dolly Cotter's pieshop. There one can have a hot mutton pie immersed in rich, goodly soup. These mutton pies served thus are also regarded as a great base for porter. In addition to mutton pies they can have cold meat and tea or a plate of good boiling beef at Heffron's eating house. No embellishments needed here. An eating house is a place where you eat and should be so called.

The day wears on and deals are made. Subsequently countless libations are poured and there is a rough all-round air of good fellowship. Of course the crowd is suitably interspersed with blackguards. These are loud and uncouth men who have disgusted their wives and children down the years. The only place they will be listened to is in a public house and believe me, Dan, it's no picnic for a publican to have to endure their curses and other crudities for the length of the day.

Sometimes I can't take any more so I come from behind the counter and throw them out. They are never any use when faced with somebody their own size. I watch them too in mounting disgust when they try to insist on buying whiskey and brandy for men who don't want it. I never serve in cases like this. Fitter for these wretches to hand the money over to their wives. No fear. The dirty braggarts will drink, drink, drink till they can hold no more and then stumble home like cattle to abuse and manhandle their innocent families.

It is the Judases amongst us again who betray all humanity when they serve drink to sated monsters like these. Any decent publican will always stand up to these defilers of home and family.

Then there is the townland thug who tends to bully smaller men who have kept out of his way successfully until they meet at the pub counter. I have seen quiet, decent men humbled by these cowardly scoundrels.

I will not tolerate the presence of these men under my roof. I will serve drink to no man who will not show respect to me, to my house and to my customers. When a man comes into my pub he comes into a sanctuary and he is entitled to drink in peace.

I have seen bands of smelly young thugs from the bigger towns and cities trying to take over peaceful pubs in this little resort during the summer weekends. They show no respect at all for age or sex. They want things their own way. Well they just can't have things their own way. They will behave and obey my rules or they won't be permitted to stay here.

A good pub is entitled to the same respect as a good home. I intend to see, no matter what the outcome, that it receives that respect.

As I say, Dan, the fair is over and there is now only the smell of droppings and the odd tuneless sing-song. Most of these farmers and labourers will go home happy, knowing a welcome from wife and children awaits them. Should anything happen them there would be tears and anguish in their wake. The grief would be indescribable.

What of the drunkard who abuses the sanctity of his home? There would be no tears, nothing but a blessed, secret relief if he walked in his door no more.

I'm tired after the day. When I am occasionally very busy like this Madge Dewley gives me a hand in the kitchen, making sandwiches and the meals for myself and the part-time barman. She's getting old but she insists on coming.

I enjoy the cattle fair atmosphere. It is still a big event in the calendar of the Knockanee countryfolk. I fear, however, that it is passing from the scene and in your time and mine, Dan, the cattle will no longer be stood outside the doors of houses in the public street. Progress will put an end to it all, the way it put an end to an honest day's work and outdoor piddling.

I'll close for the present. Do not forget to answer the question concerning the kiss crosses. It may not seem important to you but to me it could be a matter of life and death.

Hold everything. She's after coming into my house. She approaches my humble counter with a heavenly smile on her radiant young face. Her eyebrows droop over her dark eyes. She blushes modestly. I swear that the blood has left my face and that time stands still. Oh God how I would love to hold that pale, lovely face in my hands.

'A bottle of gin please, Martin. It's for my mother. She'll fix with you herself. Oh and I nearly forgot. A half dozen bottles of tonic water.' You have guessed who it is. Antoinette of course. I fumble for the gin and the smaller bottles of tonic. I allow a bottle to fall from my hand. I nearly fall over myself trying to recover it. Oh what a hapless fool of forty am I. I find a box and wrap the bottles over and over with pages from old newspapers. I stall for time with futile questions about the weather. I ask her how her studies are going and other polite, needless queries. All the things I had planned to say are stuck in my throat. With a celestial smile she is gone. The place is like a shrine but barely vacated by a beatific vision.

Oh you pitiful fool who should and could have spoken your

mind. What matter if she burst out laughing. The thing would be forever said and on second and third thoughts she would maybe come to reconsider you.

My claim would be staked and even if I never struck gold at least she would know how I felt about her. How many are there in the world who suffer the way I do?

I'll abandon this epistle for the moment. You'll hear from me soon.

As ever
Martin

Peadar Lyne writes to Grace Lantry in answer to a letter she has sent him. It is the first letter Peadar has ever received from a body revolving in such an outward sphere. It is confidential. In it she declares her love for Martin of Journey's End and requests Peadar to put in a good word for her whenever he can without, at the same time, letting Martin know her intent. She explains that a direct approach might frighten him away. She also questions him about the mermaid.

Sleepy Valley
Knockanee
County Kerry

Dear Grace
So you want to be his grace before and after meals and always with the greatest attention and devotion no full stops or commas or like hold-ups that get in my way dodge the fences and keep going to the post I'll hop a ball now and then but offers no hope hes dyed in the wool bachelor with notions of young wans like all that age last kick if you know what I mean still no harm keep trying ah the mermaid seen likely droppings wan morning comin from seven Mass says I mermaids for sure and after trailin awhile

seen her sittin combin her hair on a rock near Knockanee Point just ablow the castle whistled her and she turned she was on the point of divin toughen says I the days long mounted no bother in the world the finest ever straddled kept shakin her tail the whole time wanted me to go in the water and do it there good job I was bate Id be in with her to my watery grave like many a sailor She gets nasty when I wont jump in flakes my oul man with a belt of the tail to this day scales on it sure as my mother in the grave. I never seen her after searched up and down from the Point to Donnelly Rock but no trace. One flake of a mermaid and no woman ever satisfies from the only white man ever hammered a job on a mermaid.

Peadar Lyne

PS Try Coaxiorum with Martin.

Editorial Department
The Irish Leader

Dear Martin

Many thanks for your long letter concerning the Knockanee cattle fair. It is important to record events like these if, as you say, they are in danger of disappearing from the scene. All goes well here. Briege and the new arrivals are fine. She says the lady solicitor has good taste. We both appreciate your thoughtfulness in purchasing the gifts.

You ask about the significance of kiss crosses. I would not take them too seriously. For years I harmlessly corresponded with a number of girls and we must have expended thousands of such crosses between us. On the other hand if she is not given to lightweight statements you would want to watch your step. One minute you are as free as the air and the next thing you know you're in hot water. It is a very tricky business any way you look at it. Women will use any and all lures in the matter of hooking the fish that suits their taste. All I would advise you at the moment is tread warily. Please keep writing me letters.

As ever
Dan

Demented from thinking about Antoinette Lingley the livelong day and indeed during most of his waking hours, Martin decides to confide his true feelings to his good friend Mother Martha, Headmistress of the Compassionate Convent School where Antoinette is a student. Over the years Martin has supplied the convent with bottled stout and brandy purely as tonics for the elders of the Compassionate community. The delivery of these items was always a most discreet mission and undertaken only by Martin himself. Even though the monthly order might be for a mere few glasses of brandy and a bare dozen of stout the number of eyebrows that might be raised by revelation of such deliveries would surely pass belief. Unfortunately, Mother Martha is in retreat when Martin calls. As a result he puts pen to paper.

Journey's End
Knockanee

My dear Friend

I have no one to turn to but your good self who I trust and respect more than any woman I know. My plight is that I have fallen in love with one of your senior students, Antoinette Lingley. The feelings I store for her are pure in the extreme. Else I would not dare write to you. You can help me. Would it be possible for me to speak to her in your presence? She is too young to be without a chaperone and we both know, alas, what her mother is like. Because of my age it is likely that her father may mistrust my motives. So it is to you I turn, dear friend. Can you see your way towards helping me?

Yours in J. C.

Martin MacMeer

Journey's End
Knockanee

Dear Grace

Many thanks for your letter. I doubt if there is any truth to Peader Lyne's claim in connection with his mastery of the Knockanee Point Mermaid. On the other hand Eva St George claims to have seen a mermaid one evening in June some years ago. The old people in Cunnacanewer maintain that June is the month when mermaids appear to humans. It was twilight when Eva saw her mermaid. The light was poor and she could easily have been mistaken. In the first place she is an artist and you must know, as a solicitor, the sort of hallucinatory testimony one can expect from such people.

In the second place early June is the time for the start of the peal salmon run. They move in their thousands from outside the estuary up to the spawning beds of the Feale and Shannon rivers. Needless to mention they are hotly pursued by hordes of hungry seals. I have no doubt that what Eva saw was a basking seal endeavouring to digest a suffocating feed of fresh salmon. If one is to believe in the existence of mermaids we might as well start believing in leprechauns as well.

Cynics around here argue that Peadar Lyne probably raped a seal on that memorable Sunday morning. They say he was so drunk at the time that he could not tell the difference. It is well known that he was not returning from seven o'clock Mass as he claims but from a shebeen party in Cunnacanewer.

Some nasty-minded neighbour of his wrote an anonymous letter to Sergeant Mick Henderson demanding that Peadar be arrested and charged with self-confessed buggery.

So much for the mermaid. I am indeed glad you enjoyed your weekend. It was a nice break for you. Unfortunately, I will not be able to host you any more. The summer season is now almost upon us and I'll want the rooms for the two girls I normally employ across the summer and autumn.

You'll have no problem, however, as most of the guesthouses will be open in five or six weeks' time and the hotel is due to unlock its doors on the first day of May. Then there is the caravan park if you had friends with you. You could always stay in the house you bought. It wouldn't be too bad in the summer if the place was properly aired.

You'll have no difficulty at all. I expect a very busy season so that I will have very little leisure time. In fact you could say that I will have no time at all.

Every good wish

Your humble

Martin

Compassionate Convent
Knockanee

Dear Martin

Where else would you turn in your time of trial and temptation but to your friends. I have read your letter carefully and burned it lest it fall into unsympathetic hands. We have a few pairs of those here, odd as it may seem. I am enclosing a prayer to Saint Jude. In future whenever you think of Antoinette I want you to recite the prayer. In addition I want you to do the Stations of the Cross. Time and faith will heal your wound.

Yours in J. C.

Mother Martha

Wellington Heights
Dublin

Dear Martin

I fear I detect a certain note of coolness in your letter. There was no need to tell me about the reopening of the hotel and guesthouses. I already know when they open. Remember I stayed in Knockanee last summer. You need not worry. I would not dream of imposing on you during your busy season. Have I said or done anything unwittingly to offend you? You must know I would not hurt you for the world.

The tone of your letter worries me. Am I no longer welcome at Journey's End even as a customer? Please do not worry over me. I'm so depressed I could cry.

Love

Grace

Journey's End
Knockanee

Dear Mother Martha

Thanks for the Saint Jude prayer. I appreciate your advice about the Stations of the Cross too but I beg of you to intercede for me with Antoinette. You know my intent is honourable. All I ask is permission to speak to her in your own presence. What can be wrong with that? Will you please reply by return?

Yours in J. C.

Martin

Journey's End
Knockanee

Dear Dan

I'm in a right kettle of fish. Grace Lantry has her sights raised and is beginning to employ her womanly wiles. I fear a stern resistance is going to be necessary here and even at that, the outcome could be doubtful. The other side of the picture is that I still crave Antoinette Lingley. She means all the world to me. What am I to do? Love to Briege and the kids.

As ever
Martin

Compassionate Convent
Knockane

Dear Martin

I do sympathise with you. I really do. I had better begin at the beginning. If it were any other senior girl I would intercede for you with her parents' approval but in the case of Antoinette I cannot and will not. Let me explain.

Our founder as you may know was Jean Marie Colette McMangerton. On land willed to her by a great-aunt she built our first humble retreat and with the kind permission of the then bishop started her community of fourteen sisters. That was in 1848 when the need for an advanced form of education, not belittling the hedge schools, was sorely needed. The same year saw the death of poor Dan O'Connell who won Catholic emancipation for his people and was rewarded ever after by the most vile and slanderous character assassination. No Catholic would ever do the things of which he stands accused.

To get on with it. For the past few years there has been a steady decline in our numbers and so far this year there has been no application for entry into our novitiate. This may be purely a passing phase in our long and holy history but it could well be the death knell of the Compassionate Sisters.

There is still hope for us however. Antoinette Lingley is as angelic a child as ever drew breath and we have great hopes that she will join our order after she does her Leaving Certificate at the end of next term. She never wears minis or make-up but is as diligent a girl as ever sat in a classroom. She deserves a better mother than the one she's got. I have no wish to be uncharitable. The message I have for you is this, my dear Martin. Antoinette will not be the bride of any mortal man. She will be the bride of Christ as a Compassionate Sister. She has said nothing about it yet and maybe she does not know it yet but I know. I am certain that any day now she will announce her decision to become one of us. It could be the turning point for the Compassionates. If a girl as pretty as Antoinette decides to become one of our company other girls may follow her example. I am sure she is an instrument of God.

I am so sorry, dear Martin. What about this girl from Dublin who stayed with you recently? We hear everything here, everything. God bless and keep you.

Yours in J. C.

Mother Martha

Journey's End

Knockanee

Dear Dan

The reverend mother of the Compassionates in the local convent informs me that Antoinette is to become a nun. I cannot believe that a girl with eyes as mischievous as she will content herself shut away from the bright lights for the remainder of her life. I still long for her no matter what the reverend mother says. I will wait and play my cards as they are dealt to me but holding my best trump for a final onslaught.

If you ever want to hear all the gossip and family scandals of a town or village keep away from the barracks of the Civic Guards. They have to search for news but whatever the reason people with spicy stories and family scandals make straight for the local convent. I would recommend the local convent to any investigator carrying out an examination of the town's inhabitants. The nuns know everything.

Here is the order in which I would place the best sources of information:

first, the convent.
second, the barber's
third, the public houses

The convents are omniscient. The barber's shop is fairly reliable and the pubs are fifty per cent accurate. There are other sources such as gossip shops and the various societies that constitute a town's activities, creameries or any place where people foregather in sufficient numbers. Believe it or not Mother Martha of the Compassionates knew that Grace Lantry stayed at Journey's End over the weekend I told you about. That's all she knows but like all women she has a bloody useful imagination with a finished intuition for drawing the worst possible conclusions. Yesterday I was delivering a bottle of brandy and a few dozen of stout. They give it to the old ones to help them sleep or to buck up the heart in the cold mornings.

'Were you at the barbecue, Martin?' Martha asked.

'What barbecue?' I returned although I was responsible for supplying quite a large share of the booze and unfortunately, turned down an invitation to attend.

'Of course you weren't at it,' said Martha. 'I'd have heard if you were.'

Now I'm curious as the next man and I must confess I had heard certain rumours. Eva St George had mentioned it and Mick Henderson enquired if I had been at it. Madge Dewley in typical fashion announced that Sodom and Gomorrah were only trotting after it.

'I hear we have a nudist colony at last,' she said the other morning when she arrived for a half-gallon of porter to make two porter cakes, one for herself and one for the sister that married the postman. That postman must have a right surfeit of porter cakes by now.

According to Madge the most dreadful fornication took place. Eva St Geoge's account was less colourful. I knew the Mother Martha would have the true story. As it is the whole village and the entire county is literally buzzing with the news. Here is what actually happened. You have heard, no doubt, of Lochlune, the lovely wooded lake about three miles north of Knockanee. It's not really a lake, of course, and yet it's not quite a lagoon. It's composed of salt water and its levels depend on the tides.

Lochlune is a very beautiful place, more so at night when the moon shines on the waters and the winds rustle the leaves of the wild ash and laurel. It is a haven for courting couples who walk the lake shore in the long summer evenings. I often fancied myself walking hand in hand with Antoinette as the red sun sank slowly beneath the western horizon.

One thing is certain and that is Lochlune will never be the same again after the barbecue. Lily Lingley, the mother of

Antoinette, imagines herself to be the C-in-C of the snob mob
in this zone but it was Millie Dewey, the solicitor's wife, who
thought up the idea of the barbecue. A few weeks ago she
returned from a holiday with her sister Delia in Southern
California. The place she chose was lovely Lochlune of my
romantic fantasies. Millie Dewey threw the idea around and a
committee was formed. Some of its members were Lily Langley
and Eva St George who, because she is regarded as an artist, is
always invited to whatever is happening. They decided upon the
night of Saturday last to hold the first ever barbecue in the
district of Knockanee.

They had Dinny Pats, the local halfwit, out all day collecting
driftwood for a great fire and generally preparing a site for the
revels. The guests were carefully chosen, all the upper crust with
the noble exception of that frigid few who are a bit too upper. I
will deal no further with the preparatory details. The upshot of the
whole business was that the entire affair was an utter disaster.

Knockanee was delighted as was all Cunnacanewer and the
other townlands of this ancient barony. Most delighted of all
were those who were not invited but who felt they should have
been. At ten o'clock just as the party was sitting down to eat
the rain came down in torrents. It came driving in from the west
in great grey veils that made visibility extremely poor. The party
was pretty drunk at this stage, all being nicely tanked up before
attacking the grub. There was a wild scramble for shelter during
which Lily Lingley was accidentally tripped. She fell headlong
into Lochlune at its deepest point and narrowly missed being
drowned. There was nobody sober enough to rescue her. She
managed to clamber out. Dooney the dentist hit his head off a
branch of a tree and had to receive eight stitches.

Millie Dewey, I feel sure, is sorry she didn't stay in Southern
California. She had the hardest luck of all. She slipped on a slimy

rock and fractured her hip after an unholy row with her husband. The car in which she was being driven to hospital skidded and crashed into a telephone pole. She broke her wrist and received two black eyes. I know and Mother Martha knows and all his friends know that Tom Dewey would never strike Millie but he is being blamed for both black eyes and no one believes the story about the crash despite the fact that the car is almost a write-off. People believe only what they want to believe. A group of seven people, including Dan Slatter the postmaster, rushed for the doubtful cover of a nearby sandhill when the storm broke. They could not have hit upon a less suitable place for lying on the sand in the lee of the dune was Dan's daughter Imelda and an obscure labouring boy who lived locally. They were not saying their prayers and they were not building sandcastles. A bloody fight followed in which several became accidentally involved because of the dark and the teeming rain. Other groups joined in.

Fists flew and kicks were drawn. Nobody was sure what was happening. Most imagined they were being attacked by a group of outsiders. Consequently the safest course was to hit first and ask questions afterwards. Finally it wore itself out and the exhausted remnants of a once proud party straggled homewards.

They certainly gave the people round here something to talk about. The Lochlune barbecue will go down in history like the night of the big wind. All the casualties have not yet been counted and there are wild rumours of running duels between jealous husbands and over-zealous Casanovas. I'm certain there isn't a word of truth in this.

You may wonder how convents know so much. It is because sooner or later they are told everything. They are the repositories for the top secrets of the community. Over a drink one night in the lounge old Father Hauley, the parish priest, confided to me as follows, 'If I want to know something I go to the Compassionates. If they don't know I shorten my sails and end my quest for knowledge.'

On another occasion Mother Martha confided thus: 'They come to us for blooms and shrub branches for their altars and mantelpieces. We give freely. I suppose they feel they owe us something and endeavour to repay us with interesting titbits. It is an easy matter to sieve the grains of truth when one is an experienced assessor. We often hear as many as twelve versions of the same tale. Our experience helps us to deduce the true story from the whole collection.'

So you see, my dear Dan, the Spanish Inquisition never really ended. Still the Compassionates are harmless enough and their charges are as dear to them as life itself. The Lochlune Barbecue may have been a disaster for those involved but for the rest of us it was a heaven-sent diversion.

Lochlune deserves better of us mortals. You remember Callanan's romantic lake poem:

Tis down by the lake where the wild trees fringe its sides
The love of my heart, my fair one of heaven resides.
I think as at eve she wanders its mazes along
The birds go to sleep to the sweet, wild twist of her song.

Poor Callanan. He knew what love was too.

Peadar Lyne is right plank in the middle of one of his notorious week-long boozes. The curate here is a tiny, inoffensive man by the name of O'Dee. He takes a walk round the village at night and interferes with nobody. As I say he is diminutive in size and always walks warily.

Last night Peadar emerged from the Widow's at the same time that Father O'Dee was taking his midnight constitutional.

Peadar was well and truly on the jigs after his third consecutive day on straight rum. His vision may have been badly blurred. Whatever it was he seized Father O'Dee by the throat and rammed him up against the Widow's front window. He was then heard to say: 'Give me your gold you rotten hoor you.' Passers-by intervened but found it impossible to subdue Peadar who insisted he had captured a leprechaun. I now have a tough one to write to Grace Lantry so I'll close for the present. Love to all.

As ever
Martin

Journey's End
Knockanee

Dear Grace

I assure you that you have offended me in no way. I would be a churl indeed if I did not assure you of the warmest of welcomes as always when you come for your summer holidays. How you could think otherwise I cannot fathom. Be assured Grace of a seat at my counter for as long as I am the proprietor of these premises known as Journey's End.

The weather is greatly improved here. The local news is of a barbecue that was held at Lochlune. Reports are exaggerated beyond words and there are ungodly tales of rape, adultery and worse. These reports are hotly denied by the participants but nothing can now save them from the truly abominable tales that are in full circulation. Talk of this barbecue has spread to nearby towns and God alone knows how it will end.

I am sorry you were depressed when you wrote last. That is life, isn't it, up one day, down the next. I know what it's like. The things that get me down most are funerals. No matter how awkward it is one is expected to attend and it doesn't matter whether one was once acquainted with the deceased or not. They take a lot of my time and in the wintertime when they are most abundant it means I have to close the bar to attend. What difference does it make anyway? I'm sick at the sight of gaping crowds round a hole in the ground. Yesterday I made a vow. I shall forthwith cease to attend funerals of all kinds. The next funeral to be attended by me will be my own. All the publicans for miles around are conspicuous at every funeral. I suspect they attend for business purposes. I watch them walking solemn-faced to the next of kin. Then comes a long shake-hands and a longer, sadder shake of the head to wring the full tragedy out of the occasion. I am sick of pretending to be sad, of shaking hands with people I hardly know. Yesterday I attended my last funeral. I don't care who dies now. They'll be buried without me. Anyway there are so many publicans with nothing better to do that I shall hardly be missed.

From where I sit at this present time I can see Eva returning from her day's painting. She waves and I wave back. Here comes Peadar, red-eyed, wrinkled and shivering from stem to stern, like an ancient hooker that has lost every tack of its sail and is at the mercy of mountainous waves.

'In the name of all that's good and holy,' he cries out, 'make me a hot whiskey as fast as you can.'

Madge Dewley arrives for a second cargo of booze. Today is pension day and she can indulge herself.

'Make it two hot ones,' Peadar instructs me with a badly broken voice.

'Stick it you know where,' says Madge, 'I want none of your drink.'

I will close now and see to their wants. Be assured that all is well between us. I regard you as a very dear friend and I would hate if anything were to damage that friendship.

Sincerely, as ever

Martin

Wellington Heights
Dublin

Dear Martin

I'm so glad all is well between us. You had me worried for a while. I thought it was all up. I am delighted to hear you say otherwise. It is so important to me that you have the same regard for me. Believe it or not I have already heard reports of the Knockanee barbecue. It's common knowledge here that a married man was stabbed to death but that it's being kept hush-hush. A colleague has also confided that two women stripped naked after drinking too much and danced like dervishes round the barbecue fire. One is still in hospital after the beating her husband gave her. Has the body of the poor woman who was drowned been recovered yet?

Other people I've met over the past few days tell me of countless horrifying incidents straight from the lips of commercial travellers who have come direct from Knockanee. One never knows does one? I would have thought that women of that age should have more sense. Yet I can understand what firelight and liquor might do to a middle-aged woman especially if she had been confined to her kitchen for a long period beforehand. Before I close, dear Martin, let me tell you once again what immense joy your letter has brought me. To put it mildly I would say that you have made my day. It is so worthwhile to have an understanding with someone like yourself. 'Bye for now.

xxxxxxxxxx

Grace

LETTERS OF AN IRISH PUBLICAN

Journey's End

Knockanee

Dear Dan

It is as difficult to escape the clutches of Grace Lantry as it is for a salmon to shake off a hungry lamprey. I may have to plead the old religious issue if she gets any closer. That's one great advantage in being a Catholic when the opposing party is of another persuasion. Can you think of any other way I might shake her off? I would go as far as to plead insanity if needs be. As I said so often I treasure freedom above all else.

This is an astonishingly tenacious creature. She deliberately picks false meanings from simple straightforward statements. I am no match for her. That is why I call upon you to come to my aid. Think of something. Love to Briege and the kids.

As ever

Martin

PS What do you say to telling her I am already married with a wife across the Irish Sea in Camden Town or some other likely place?

M

Editorial Department

The Irish Leader

Dear Martin

I have discussed your case with Briege and we are agreed that you should not lie to the girl. She deserves better, such as a simple thing called the truth. Just tell her you are determined

[143]

to stay a bachelor, that you value her friendship but that a permanent legal union would not suit you. Once will do to tell her. Write soon.

Dan

Compassionate Convent
Knockanee

Dear Martin

I think it is but fair to tell you that Antoinette has left school and will not be coming back. Thereby hangs a long and harrowing tale but it is not for me to tell. It will be many a day before I get over the shock of what has happened. May God give me the strength to carry on. My faith has received a severe jolting. Maybe what happened was ordained by the almighty God to test me.

It will do you no good, Martin, to come looking for further information. I am entering a self-imposed retreat in an effort to recover my composure.

Too many parents have fallen down on the job and have left it up to us. We do what we can but we never can replace parents. Many of them are now content to look the other way. They have surrendered to rebellious offspring and go around pretending that all is well. They are the worst criminals of all, those parents who will not see.

There is now no cowardice worse than the cowardice of parents who will not face up to facts, who refuse to recognise that rearing children to be useful members of society is a full-time, complicated, sensitive vocation without parallel in the whole range of serious callings.

Failing a child is a transgression of truly great magnitude, so great that I know of no punishment to fit such a crime.

I will close. It is just that I felt you ought to know.
　Yours in J. C.
　Mother Martha

Journey's End
Knockanee

Dear Dan

Antoinette Lingley, the object of my love, is a fallen angel. She has been a fallen angel for some time. She was found out one day last week during the French class at the convent. Mother Martha teaches French and when she instructed the class to produce their Maupassant textbooks Antoinette Lingley who sits in the front seat right under Martha's nose was first to whip out her book. Alas and alack she also whipped out something else. It was in a package and what was inside was made of rubber.

'And pray what is this?' Martha asked as she recovered the package from the floor. She gently opened the package and produced the rubber object. Her face showed puzzlement. A girl in the back seat giggled but otherwise there was a ghastly silence.

'Well?' Mother Martha asked, growing somewhat annoyed.

'It's a balloon,' Antoinette Lingley announced.

'So it is,' said Mother Martha and she waved a mild finger of admonishment at her favourite. 'You are far too grown-up,' she chided, 'to be playing with balloons.' So saying she put the balloon in her pocket.

'Let us proceed with the first short story,' she said with a shake of the head and she was rewarded with a beautiful smile from Antoinette. Some days passed and Mother Martha fell to thinking. Antoinette Lingley must have problems in the home if she resorted to balloons for playthings. Instinctively Martha blamed Lily Lingley. A great feeling of pity for Antoinette stirred inside her. She was determined to shelter the girl at all costs. A week passed and Doctor Sugan called to the convent to examine one of the older sisters. When the examination was complete he made his usual report to Mother Martha. Seizing her opportunity she mentioned Antoinette's interest in balloons. Sugan was on the point of dismissing the whole business as a girlish prank when suddenly a sly look crept over his face.

'What sort of balloon was it?' he asked.

'Just an ordinary balloon in a package,' Martha replied.

'You're sure it was in a package,' Sugan's worst suspicions were now almost confirmed.

'I have it right here,' Martha told him. She produced the package and handed it to the doctor. Sugan sighed as doctors are wont to do when confronted with the hard facts of life.

'My dear Mother Martha,' said he sorrowfully, 'this is no balloon.'

'What is it then?' asked Martha.

'Pray be seated,' said Sugan.

That, my dear Dan, was how the *exposé* started. It is now clear that Antoinette and the Lingley housemaid known locally as Kitty Bang-Bang entertained hundreds of young men from all over the country, from everywhere, in fact, except Knockanee. Antoinette ticked bottles of gin in every pub within a radius of ten miles and assured each publican that her mother would pay. Who would ever believe that a creature so beautiful would tell a lie?

My own balloon of innocent love is well and truly burst, Dan. Scandalwise it has almost equalled the Lochlune Barbecue.

Last evening Madge Dewley arrived for her cake and trifle ingredients. The customers present, including Peadar Lyne, were discussing the Lingley case.

'Kicky mare, kicky foal,' said Madge.

'Black cat, black kitten,' said Peadar.

No one said another word. I'll write soon. Love to Briege and the kids.

As ever
Martin

Wellington Heights
Dublin

Dear Martin

I have to go abroad for a period on behalf of my company. I cannot say for sure when I will be back but I doubt if I will see Ireland this summer. There are a number of legacy problems to be sorted out and these will take time. What I am asking is this. Will you write to me when I am in the States? I will let you know where I will be staying. I doubt if I could endure the loneliness there if I did not hear from you regularly. I heard the story of the Lingley girl. I remember her. She used to lie near me on the beach at Knockanee. I always sized her up as a game piece, only awaiting her chance. Some of her posing would do credit to a professional. I can imagine her bamboozling a man with those dark eyes and that angelic smile. I'll be in touch as soon as I land in New York.

xxxxxxxxxx
Grace

Journey's End
Knockanee

Dear Dan

The summer season is only a few weeks away and already the ladders and the paint pots are everywhere. It's almost impossible to get a tradesman. The lovely Antoinette has left Knockanee and is, by all accounts, working as a receptionist with a doctor cousin of her mother's in Dublin. It is alleged that this doctor runs a very tight ship, Rosary every night and Mass every morning not to mention pilgrimages to here, there and everywhere. Add to this a lights out stricture at ten-thirty and you will agree that Antoinette is in for different times. I still cannot get over it. Ah well. Life must go on.

As I write this I am also watching my uncle Matthew, my late mother's brother, as he engages in conversation with some of his neighbours from the hill country of Cunnacanewer. Matthew is a priceless old gent with a fabulous repertoire of yarns relating to his friends and neighbours. Did I ever tell you that this is a Cunnacanewer house? By this is meant that the folk of Cunnacanewer would not dream of drinking elsewhere when they visit Knockanee on business or for football matches or cattle fairs. The reason is, of course, that one of their women, my mother, was once established here as mistress of the house. In the case of the Widow McGuire's it is a house frequented chiefly by those from the northern end of Knockanee. The widow herself is one of the Dwans from the Point so that no man from the Point or nearabouts will leave his business in other than the Widow's. Dixie Megley hails originally from Knockriddle and consequently his is a Knockriddle house.

Of the lot I would rate the Cunnacanewer crowd the cheeriest and the decentest. They can be shifty too and extremely clannish. At football games they have been known to attempt all sorts of wickedness including cheerfully endeavouring to kick a few referees as well as players on the opposing team and partisans. Not too long ago they tried in vain to castrate a chap from a nearby town. The reason was that the fellow raped a young Cunnacanewer girl working there. You will not be surprised to hear that, ever since, there is tremendous respect for Cunnacanewer girls wherever they go.

Otherwise the menfolk are a well-meaning lot with a great well of songs and folk tales. Nowadays it is common for women to patronise pubs but when I was a young fellow it was out of the question. Not so with Cunnacanewer women or indeed those from the other country townlands. They always drank with their men, mostly halves of hot port or whiskey. Their shawlies or poorer women who were not as well off as the farmers' wives would drink mulled porter the round of a Friday which is market day in Knockanee as well as being pension day. It is the busiest day of the week outside the high season time. They are well behaved in the pub and apart from spitting on the floor, spilling an occasional drink or puking without warning are model customers. Now and then they argue and on rare occasions they fight.

In their clannishness lies their strength. They love the pub. It is where they arrange to meet. If the women go shopping their parcels are delivered to Journey's End where they collect them later. They just would not think of entering another pub. I am one of their own so to speak and thus am worthy of their support.

Towards evening they will sing and maybe dance a few reels if an itinerant musician happens to chance by. This is the ultimate pleasure. Their type is fading fast. The shawls are disappearing one by one. The strong boots and the wellingtons are on the way out too as are the grey flannel, collarless shirts. My uncle Matt informed me this morning that an old woman who lives near him went on her knees to pray when she saw a Cunnacanewer turf-cutter going to the bog wearing low shoes and a collar and tie. There was a time, not so long ago, when such a garb of a weekday denoted only one thing. It meant that the wearer was on his way to court to answer a charge. The old woman rose from her knees when the man with the low shoes had passed and declared that the end of the world must surely be at hand when such flagrant profligacy was allowed to pass without punishment.

Grace Lantry is going to America. Thanks be to the Almighty God say I. She will be gone for the summer season and in a letter she told me that she would die with loneliness if I didn't write to her regularly. Talk about birdlime being sticky. How does a man release himself from the grasp of a determined woman? She misinterprets every line I write, always edging her way towards committing me to a marital direction. Love to Briege and the kids.

As ever
Martin

Journey's End
Knockanee

Dear Grace
So you are off to America. Isn't it fine for you. I may not be able to write as often as I would like. In fact if the season is going to be as busy as I think I may not be able to write at all. When the day ends I find myself fit for nothing but the bed. We will all be looking forward to seeing you when you come home.

As ever
Martin

Editorial Department
The Irish Leader

Dear Martin
More please about your uncle Matthew and the colourful folk of Cunnacanewer. There must be thousands of tales to be taken

down. A word of advice about Grace Lantry or indeed about any female who is unattached. If you must write a letter make certain you show it to a solicitor before you send it. I know far too many victims of thoughtless letter writing who would today be glad now to eat the paper on which they committed themselves for life. An ordinary man is no match for a scheming woman. Have the law on your side from this day forth whenever you put a pen to paper.

Briege is pregnant again after all our caution and care. We will definitely have to take positive steps after this. Don't forget to let me know more about Cunnacanewer. She sends her love.

As ever
Dan

Wellington Heights
Dublin

My dear Martin
Thanks for your wonderful letter. I realise, of course, that you will not have time to write to me across the summer. Never mind. I'll write every day to you. It is heartening to read that you look forward to seeing me again. I look forward to seeing you too and will head straight for Knockanee when I return.

When you go to bed exhausted during the summer make sure you go alone and think of me over in New York dreaming of you and the day when we shall be united again. I will be flying out early tomorrow morning and will write the moment I land. I must visit the pubs in New York and bring home all the latest techniques. I may be able to give you a hand behind the bar on occasion.

Do not worry about me while I am flying. I shall return safely and it will seem like no time at all.

xxxxxxxxxx

xxxxxxxxxx

Grace

Journey's End

Knockanee

Dear Dan

I have decided to ignore all future communications from Miss Grace Lantry. The next thing you know she'll have a halter slipped on me and I'll be another marriage martyr. Every word I have ever written to her she has miscontrued. She'll hear no more from me. Love to Briege and the kids. That's great news entirely about the new arrival or is it? About the people of Cunnacanewer. They were here again yesterday for the semi-final of the Kerry Junior League. An umpire was knocked unconscious after deciding to abandon the game. Some onlookers were also hurt. By and large it was a quiet enough game when you consider that Cunnacanewer were matched against their arch-enemies Kilcogley.

Madge Dewley arrived after the game with her message bag. There was nothing but noise and confusion when she entered. When she approached the counter there was dead silence. She ordered four pints of stout for the porter cakes and a half pint of whiskey for the trifle. Not a word of any kind until she had left the premises. Astonishing you may think. Not so really. Madge already has had some runs-in with the Cunnacanewer crowd and they have a healthy respect for her as a result. I remember the last time the Cunnacanewer crowd were here she entered as usual and ordered the ingredients for the cake and trifle. As she was leaving a young chap spoke up.

'I hope you enjoy your bit of trifle, missus,' said he. Madge looked at him witheringly for what seemed like an hour. Then she spoke.

'That your rear exit might close up and fester,' said she. 'That it might break out under your arm and that you might have to take off your shirt to relieve yourself.'

Even by Cunnacanewer standards this was an outstanding curse. Hence the silence when she entered. The moment she left there was bedlam again. A row started between some Cunnacanewer boys and supporters of the visiting team. They entered Journey's End without thinking. In such cases I never interfere. It wouldn't do any good anyway. They wear themselves out in minutes and they are always contrite afterwards. They make it up with their foes and new friendships are established. That is the way with country people.

There is a backwoods retreat in Cunnacanewer called Cooleen. About a dozen or so families farm there and my uncle Matthew tells me that the married men emit loud, long shouts of exultation at the peak of their copulations. Since copulation usually takes place at night these shouts can often be heard all over Cunnacanewer.

A curate who once ministered there went around to the heads of the families in Cooleen and asked them to show some restraint as these audacious, nocturnal outbursts were the talk of the entire parish. He was told bluntly that their fathers and forefathers before them had shouted in triumph and exultation during such occasions and they would continue in the old way until time came to an end or their seed failed.

An unusual development to the situation is best manifested in the following addendum by my uncle Matthew. Picture a peaceful night without trace of wind along the slopes of Cunnacanewer. The lights are out in every homestead and no man walks abroad.

Suddenly the peace is shattered by a mighty roar from the direction of Cooleen. Many are awakened instantly all over the hill and those who are not turn restlessly in their shaken slumbers.

At the base of the hill a man turns to his wife and speaks as follows: 'That's Mickeen Derry above in Cooleen. I'd know the voice anywhere. He's after a good cut tonight.'

This, according to my uncle Matthew, is commonplace and the minute a climax is heralded by a roar the identity of the man involved is known to all who are listening.

There was serious trouble once when the roar of a man living in a house in the south of Cooleen came instead from a house in the north of Cooleen.

'Ho-ho,' said all who heard, 'there's adultery rampant in Cooleen tonight.'

Truth to tell however there are only two recorded instances of misplaced roars in Cooleen over the last three generations. Poteen was the cause of one and the other was an old buck of ninety who was only pretending. Only a fool would give himself away by roaring if he was misconducting himself.

Sometimes there are roars in the middle of the day but this is only where you have newly-weds. My uncle Matt maintains that as long as these roars are heard the future of Cooleen is assured.

I will close for the moment as I want to get a few early nights' sleep while I can. Love to Briege and the kids.

As ever

Martin

PS Expect very little from me for the next few months, say until after the fifteenth of August, when things return to normal. The two girls who work with me for the summer arrive tomorrow. The season will begin in earnest then.

M

Journey's End
Knockanee

Dear Grace

Many thanks for your letter. Twenty-one pages takes a long time to read. That is why I am a month late in answering. The season here is at its peak. I am glad you are settled down nicely and falling into place. A retired American has come to live in Knockanee. He bought Christopher's great house beyond the Point. He must be aged eighty if he's a day. His name is Ernie Saschbuck. After making a pass at the Widow McGuire to which she did not respond he asked if there was a lunderin' house in the place. The widow told him she did not understand.

'You got a knockin' shop in this neck of the woods?' he asked. Still the widow did not understand.

'You know where I can find me a plain ornery cat-house?' Ernie tried another tack. Still the widow did not understand.

'Ma'am,' said Ernie, 'it sure does you credit you don't know what I'm talking about.' Since then he has settled in nicely. The parish priest Father Ned Hauley told me that he called to Ernie to remind him that his Station was coming up.

'What Station, man?' Ernie said. 'I'm here a month and I ain't even heard a train whistle.'

Still and for all when Father Ned explained that it was a Station Mass Ernie could not have been more cooperative.

I'll sign off now. That's all I have to say. I'm too busy to write more.

Your humble servant
Martin MacMeer

Editorial Department,
Irish Leader

Dear Martin

You can't be that busy. For pity's sake drop me a line. I'm only just getting to grips with public house life at this stage. I'm just getting to know the characters. When did Madge Dewley's husband die? Did she have a family? The Widow McGuire? What age is she? I know I'm asking a bit much but I'm dead curious as I am trying to formulate a pattern for a book.

Briege is all right, a little peaked sometimes but that's to be expected when you consider her condition.

Write soon.

As ever

Dan

Journey's End
Knockanee

Dear Dan

We are in the middle of an early August heatwave. Things are quiet till evening. Every rational holidaymaker is stretched below on the beach or bathing beyond at the Point. It is a lovely day with the faintest suggestion of breeze from the west and a blue sky without a speck of cloud. It's a day for all ages, to suit all tastes. Before I proceed further let me tell you that I am badly marked about the head and face after the August weekend. A number of youths came in here and tried to oust the other customers, in short tried to take over. I went outside the counter and asked them to leave. When I opened the door to usher them out one hit me from behind with an ashtray. Several of his accomplices joined in and I was beaten senseless. The same gang wrecked the Widow McGuire's and caused a serious disturbance at the Stella Maris. We all refused to serve them, all except Dixie Megley. If he had refused they would never again come to Knockanee. Later that night he had to run to the barracks for Civic Guards. I wonder what sort of homes these inhuman little wretches come out of or do they behave in those homes the way they do outside.

Today's parents are the main cause of teenage violence. They should have tamed these animals before unleashing them on an innocent public. What they do is turn their backs and wash their hands.

The Judas publican who serves under-age youngsters with intoxicating drink must take his share of the blame too. These kids just cannot cope with strong drink. I've seen teenage girls endeavouring to practise the world's oldest trade after drinks in certain public houses.

Worse than this, of course, is the publican who serves the early morning prowler. Let me explain. As soon as it's light a hunger for drink consumes certain unfortunate gentlemen. They will scour the pubs of a town or village before their breakfasts looking for a pub that's open. As always there is one Judas. These unfortunates who need the drink are not evil people. They need help and they need it from publicans as much as they need it from everybody else. I have seen them with grey, wrinkled unshaven faces prowling the streets and alleys. Most pubs will say no but we have that small, abominable handful who will do anything to make a sale. It is criminal to serve men like these who have no solid food in their stomachs. I once asked another publican why he did it.

'Because the man was sick and needed a cure,' he said.

'But what of his wife and family?' I entreated. 'What about his job?'

He did not answer. He could not. To answer your questions. Freddie Dewley, Madge's late husband, said his last goodbye to these climes in the winter of nineteen-sixty. He died from drink. It is as simple as that. There was no family. There had been a boy who was knocked down and killed by a car at the age of four. Neither Madge nor Freddie were heavy drinkers before that. In fact Madge never frequented pubs and Freddie's limit was a few pints of stout at weekends. It was the loss of the little boy who was, by every account, a bright, intelligent, lovable little fellow that led them to drink.

I haven't seen Madge with a few days. She lets her house for the summer and lives in a little annexe till the visitors have gone.

The Widow McGuire is a fine woman of about fifty who looks forty and she has an imposing bosom, lovely red hair without a grey rib. How she keeps it red is her business. She runs a good pub where a man can drink in peace and be sure of what he's getting. There's always some dicey drink going the rounds. Any port which shelters foreign trawlers also shelters a share of dubious brandy which is distributed cutely from time to time to certain publicans.

The Widow McGuire was married to the late Martin McGuire, a decent skin. He was drowned one pleasant July evening while collecting lobsters from his pots off the Point. Like most fishermen he could not swim a stroke. Some say he probably received a bite from a conger eel trapped in a lobster pot and that he recoiled so violently he must have fallen backwards into the water. The Widow has two sons. Tom the older is studying medicine at Cork University and Wally the younger is still at secondary school.

Your friend and mine, Peadar Lyne, is boozing away quietly and knocking off lonely middle-aged female visitors by the new time. No wonder he never married. We had a good season generally apart from the trouble at the weekends. Teenage drinking is going to be a national problem in a few years. On the sexual side Knockanee is no worse than any other seaside resort. Stories may circulate but there is little change in the relationships between your average boy and girl. There will always be loose women but I think these are the exceptions that prove the rule that the vast majority of our girls are decent in the extreme.

From time to time scandal breaks like a giant wave, unexpected and refreshing. The latest worthwhile stories concern Lily Lingley who is enraptured by a young wavy-haired band vocalist of twenty-one and Surgeon Casby who is never seen lately without a young blonde who can't be out of her teens yet. These are but the poppies in the wheatfield however, the bad pennies that keep turning up, the nettles amongst the potato stalks.

The trek from the beach is starting as the gentle Atlantic breeze grows cooler and the first chill puffs of the winds of evening alight on the near bare brown bodies of bathers and beach addicts. Times have not really changed as far as the relationship between men and women is concerned. Men and women will always lust after each other given the proper climate. However, all these things pass and life goes on regardless.

As ever
Martin

No new address yet

Its me Peadar one from Cunnacanewer thick red legs you must have seen her fair enough oul figure cook at the Stella Maris Im after rising a flag there she announced last night theres more marksmen in town says I oh no says she Im not that kind that I'd be a target like you'd see in a carnival for every pellet gun around. Cant be sure would say she was round the course before a few times and wound up in winners enclosure I told her bolt a bottle of gin and have a hot bath not that kind but as little says she cant go home and tell father and mother and worse still brothers working at Killclough Quarry look like gorillas tear you apart Id swear just for the gas of it one solution at present hit for Kilburn and go to ground until storm blows over maybe she might lose you know Cunnacanewer crowd as well as me so what better for me to do. Tooraloo Ill see you before Christmas tell stout woman widow Missus Goody from Belfast staying at hotel will not be able to meet her tonight previous appointment.

Your oul segocia,

Peadar.

Will send address let me know lie of land.

Peadar.

Apartment 5B
Sesame Arms Hotel
Woodison Park
New York

Dear Martin

Don't worry. This will be short and to the point. I will be home very soon. You are not my 'humble servant' as you said in your letter although I am flattered that you so prostrate yourself.

One of the embassy crowd here, a secretary aged about forty with a bright diplomatic future, took me to dinner one night last week and again this week. I would not go out with him the third time although his intentions are honourable.

He has me persecuted for the last few days. Finally I had to tell him the sober truth, that there was somebody else. I want to be fair to you and true to you. I will not be seeing him again.

For the present take care. I will be home on the 3rd of October which is only six weeks away. I'll come down the first weekend.

Now you have to admit that was not very long.

Goodbye love

xxxxxxxxxx

xxxxxxxxxx

Grace

Journey's End
Knockanee

Dear Dan

The big news is that Peadar Lyne is married. She is Fidelma Belton from Cunnacanewer. Everybody says he is lucky to have married such a fine girl. I was his best man at a simple ceremony. The knot was tied by Father Ned Hauley. In sprinting parlance you might say that Peadar went off before the shot and was punished by being brought back to the starting line where he will now remain until he or Fidelma gives up the ghost and from the look of Fidelma she won't be giving up the ghost for a long time.

Peadar returned rather unexpectedly from England where he had been for a few days. He returned with two of Fidelma's brothers who invited him home to marry their sister.

So much for that. I am being driven into an almost indefensible position by Grace Lantry. She now presumes she has an understanding with me. I never met such a woman. What am I to do? I have stopped writing to her but I don't believe that will do any good either. She will be coming home in less than six weeks and it is her avowed intention to come down here the minute she returns. I cannot flee from here. I have to stand my ground. I have a business to run. I wish I could do a skip to Malu like any other cornered wretch. Love to Briege.

As ever

Martin

Editorial Department
Irish Leader

Dear Martin

You have my sympathy. One statement in your letter amuses me. You say you never 'met such a woman'. There are thousands of Grace Lantrys ever hovering over likely prospects using every wile, every base dodge to turn what was an innocent friendship into a liaison of permanent misery. On at least three different occasions I was almost walked into it by the likes of Grace Lantry. I had to face tears, threats of suicide and God knows what. Each time, after a most harrowing period of constant soul-destroying assault, I was lucky to escape. Finally I met a woman I wanted to marry.

My advice is stand fast. Hold on to your territories and strengthen your redoubts and redans. Entrench yourself in the stressed concrete of the negative answer and be ever vigilant. A moment off guard could spell your downfall. Relax your vigilance for a second and the jig is up. Finally, never underestimate your enemy. If you do you will pay the price.

You mention teenage drinking in the context of national problems. Can nothing be done?

Love from all here

Dan

Journey's End
Knockanee

Dear Dan

You asked about teenage drinking. You always have had the problem since the crushing of the first grape but in those early times it was done within the commune or family so that it rarely grew out of hand. When I was a teenager there were scares and woeful predictions. There was plenty teenage drinking. I drank myself. I was lucky because drink agreed with me and I knew when to stop. I cannot say the same for many of my companions.

What parents and teachers fail to grasp in these days of affluence and drink-availability is that, in order to succeed at any given pursuit, there must be training beforehand. If the teenage drinker is to be a successful drinker he must be coached. By successful drinker I mean a boy or girl who is not violent, abusive or irresponsible in drink; a boy or girl who drinks in moderation at certain prescribed times such as weddings, local festivals and family celebrations. That is the primary function of alcoholic drink, i.e. to complement happy occasions and to add more cheer to parties and functions. Drink has other uses but I will not go into these now.

To drive a motor car a young man must be taught first how to drive, drilled in road regulations and made to acquire considerable experience in car handling before submitting to a rigid test. To otherwise inflict him upon his fellows would be murderous.

Should not the same code apply to intoxicating drink? Alcohol is as potentially dangerous a weapon as a motor car. Yet the tragedy is that youngsters often embark on a night's drinking with no previous experience of carrying drink. The result of course is nearly always disaster. Still it goes on despite the fact that alcoholic beverages unwisely consumed can set boys and girls on the high road to moral and physical collapse.

It is my experience as a publican that where you have a father drinking with his son there is rarely any danger of that boy's future in respect of alcoholism. This is supervised drinking, carefully, skilfully guided instruction in the art of social drinking. If the father takes the interest or the mother in the case of the daughter there is little danger of later over-indulgence when the boys and girls go out in the world. I can only speak from my own experience. Only the parents can point out the pitfalls, show by example that strong drink can be used to enjoy oneself and not to ultimately destroy self and others.

Another danger which I have noticed is the evil influence of thugs and bullies who advocate drunkenness as a virtue, i.e. judging a fellow by the amount of drink he can carry. This, of course, is an atrocious yardstick. I will stick to what I believe about parents guiding their offspring through the dangerous tides and shallows of alcoholism to the safe shore of general sobriety. Let the parent be the pilot and his family will be safe from the ravages of stupefaction, poverty and ill-health. In short they will instinctively know the way to a safe anchorage when caught amid the heavy seas of drunken sessions. Conversely it is similar to dropping a ball of paper into the depths of the ocean. For a while it will bob gaily and wilfully all over the surface but slowly the salt sea will penetrate to its core and there is nothing but a bloated mass which must disintegrate inevitably.

So to parents I would say this. To spare your young the agony of alcoholism, be by their sides when they most need you.

Love to Briege and the kids.

As ever

Martin

Kilteary Lodge Hotel
Kilteary
West Cork

On the honeymoon weather you could say perfect grub good but
could do with more meat cut too thin paddling to-day picked
a few periwinkles ashamed to ask hotel boil them its all before
me now isnt it couldnt be nicer to tell the truth the way she tries
but would rather pick my own apple than have it picked for me
still youd have to like her shes for a fellow on his side if you
know what i mean and on the loving side a week bed id make
no battle with her sent cards to Madge Eva the widow and all
the gang check up on my property see you Monday bar a fall.

Your oul segocia

Peadar and Fidelma

Journey's End
Knockanee

Dear Dan

I have a tragic tale to tell. On Sunday last Madge Dewley
appeared as usual with her bottles for the cake and trifle
ingredients. She looked wan and miserable as if she had endured
a severe illness. When I taxed her with this she cut loose and
called me a baldy ram. She pulls no punches. I advised her
against taking so much as she did not seem at all well. I offered
her brandy but she argued that she was entitled to respect at her
age. I was immediately sorry and I filled her bottles. That night
there was a fire in the little annexe where she lived across the
summer and autumn. She was badly burned and died before
anyone could get to her. The only worthwhile possession she
had, apart from the decrepit furniture was a locket and chain

which she wore around her neck. When I opened the locket there was a picture of her husband and the little boy they lost in the accident.

I will say no more except that I pray the three are together again.

As ever

Martin

Editorial Department
Irish Leader

Dear Martin

An idea has occurred to me apropos your position with the possessive Miss Lantry. Here is what I suggest. I will write her an anonymous letter in which I will reveal that I am a devout Catholic mother who has known you all your life. I would inform her that you are a known sheep and hen-rapist and petty thief with deep-seated homicidal tendencies. That shouldn't be long in putting a damper on her ardour.

Another approach would be to write and say that I am the mother of your half-grown, half-starved, badly-wronged child. If the position becomes desperate you will have to take desperate steps. Let me know what you think.

Now will you let me have an account of the burial of Madge Dewley? Who attended? What was the general reaction?

Briege was never better. She wants to know when you are coming to see us.

As ever

Dan

Journey's End
Knockanee

Dear Dan

The funeral of Madge Dewley was one of the biggest in living memory. Cunnacanewer turned out in force as did the whole population of Knockanee. It transpired that she had no sister married to a postman in Cork. In fact she had no sister at all nor does there seem to be a trace of a living relative. The little annexe in which she died was filled with old newspapers which caught fire while she was drunk. In fact she used these as bedclothes. It was a terribly threadbare place, reeking with poverty. The house itself was not too bad. There were beds and chairs and a table but beyond that little else of value. This is true of the houses of most heavy drinkers. The little ornaments of brass, glass, copper and china that are the outward symbols of moderate wealth elsewhere are nowhere to be seen. No treasures are hoarded in the long travail through life. There is little evidence of the trappings of independence. In most cases nothing at all remains. The moneys that would normally be used to buy bric-a-brac of one kind or another go to buy drink for one purpose or another. In the case of Madge the purpose was to shut out the memory of the husband and child she loved. She drank to forget. Others drink, believe it or not, in an effort to remember lost, loved ones or occasions of love and joy. There are those who drink out of pure selfishness. More, unluckily for them, are possessed of enormous and insatiable appetites for intoxicating liquor. Some drink because of disillusionment whether it be marital or sexual or common everyday failure. In the side effects of this drinking is where the awful tragedy is most apparent in the wives who have to forego normal style for want of pocket money and who say nothing because of pride or shame, in the children who die the death every day from embarrassment of every conceivable kind, in the everlasting miserable, grinding poverty of every drunkard's dependant, in the hopeless, shameful, degrading, dehumanising day-to-day struggle to make ends meet and in the non-stop shouldering of the back-breaking burdens.

In the middle of all this is the publican. Not all publicans see or know what is happening behind the scenes in the world of compulsive drinking. Some are insensitive. Others like myself who know and feel and sense the trouble do what we can but in cold analysis our positions are somewhat desperate. Yet publicans are there and are legally entitled to stay there. It is a tough job that might be bearable in spite of the long hours and the danger of assaults and the abuse if only we could be sure that we were not doing wrong from time to time. We cannot be blamed for alcoholism but there is much we can do, much we can prevent.

The only true salvation for the alcoholic is that incomparable body of great souls known as the AA. There are many who do not want to hear of it but therein lies the only salvation for otherwise incurable drinkers.

Madge is gone. She might say, if she were alive, that the drop of drink made life bearable for her. She might have turned to her God like other women and there found partial solace or at least enough to survive. She chose her own road. We buried her 'dacent' as they say. She deserved to be buried thus for she never lost her dignity.

This, in the last analysis, is the nub of the question, this basic matter of human dignity. Without it there can be no such thing as a worthwhile existence. There is nothing to equal the honour and the elevation of mind and character that is to be found in the dignity of man and woman. This massive virtue is corroded by excessive drinking. Gone is all the illustrious heritage of true humanity, the gravity, the nobility, the exaltation, the justifiable pride in one's own strength of character. The great stag that is human dignity is humbled and dragged down by the hounds of self-indulgence.

When dignity goes there is nothing left. Be sure that drunkenness and dignity cannot stay together in the same body. It's as simple as that.

About Grace Lantry. I doubt if she would be duped by a letter of the kind you mention, nor would she, in my opinion, be the least bit affected by the revelations you propose. I'll keep in touch concerning her.

Love to Briege and the kids.

As ever

Martin

Greenfields Hotel

Highfield Parade

Cork

Dear Martin

I have left Knockanee temporarily. My reason for so doing is that I want to think. You know Ernie Saschbuck who drinks at the Widow McGuire's? Of course you do. He wants to marry me. He is over seventy and I am only forty. Do you think we would have any chance together? I am not worried about his ability to perform the customary duties. I expect him to try his heart out and we all know the world loves a trier. The question I want you to answer if you can is this. I don't know how to put it. We've always been such good friends you and I. Well this is it.

I would not dream of marrying him if you disapproved. I would do anything you ask. I think you know that. That is why

I am writing to you. If you would rather I should not marry him I will return home at once and tell him we will never share the same bed together. I will not, however, return to Knockanee until I hear from you.

Your dear lifelong friend

Eva St George

PS Not a word to anyone. You know what they would say. I can see the word abortion fluttering on their lips as they grimace at one another when news of my absence spreads.

Eva

Journey's End
Knockanee

Dear Dan

Women. Women. Women. What predators they are. We have vilified innocent sharks and stalking tigers who seek only to have a decent meal but we have glorified women, the most incessant and possessive predators of all. We have put prices on the heads of foxes and squirrels but we allow women to rove about freely, seeking whatever prey they may presently fancy.

Seriously Dan. I have a letter from Eva St George which should be framed. At sixty-two years of age she professes to be forty and is worried lest people might imagine her to be pregnant. I wrote to her a while ago in answer to a letter which she sent me from Greenhills Hotel in Cork. Eva St George pregnant! A regiment of the French Foreign Legion exiled for a year backed up by the crews of two aircraft carriers at sea for another year wouldn't put her by way of child.

She asked me if she should marry Ernie Saschbuck who is eighty and growing mankier by the day. I answered by return and told her she should wed him at once. The sooner the better as far as I'm concerned. I feel I have struck another blow for my personal freedom. I'll write shortly. Love to Briege and the kids.

As ever

Martin

Old Point House
Beach Road
Knockanee

Dear Martin

Jim and I will be married twenty-one years on Saturday. We are having a few friends in for a bite of supper and a drink or two. We would love to have you along in view of our old friendship. Let me know within the next few days. Jim bids me to tell you that he will be most disappointed if you don't show up.

Sincerely,

Lily Lingley

Journey's End
Knockanee

Dear Dan

Peadar is well settled now in Knockanee and seems mightily pleased with himself. As I write there is a storm rising and the sea is a mass of swirly grey foam. Far out I can discern a tanker as she battles her way towards Limerick. Seagulls drift inland before the gale and the torn clouds tumble recklessly overhead. It's nice to be seated snugly indoors on a day like this. In comes a tiny man by the name of Bluney, Jerry Bluney. Already I have several other customers and all look up eagerly to see how I will react to Bluney who, incidentally, is nicknamed the Holy Terror.

He is the most inoffensive and mildest little man imaginable, the most likeable and lovable little person who ever drew breath, a deeply religious little gentleman who haunts the chapel, a smiling, harmless soul until he gets two pints of porter inside him.

Then he is a little demon, a vicious, treacherous blackguard who will shout his way home challenging all comers and waking people from their well-earned repose. It's a mystery to me that he hasn't been killed years ago. I take perverse pleasure in refusing him for a pint. I adopt the same angelic smile that he wears himself and in a sugary voice I tell him that I will not serve him. With a polite nod he withdraws. Later tonight he will stand outside my door on his way home with a few pints of porters inside him.

'Come out, you cowardly baldy bastard,' he will shout at the top of his voice. 'Come out, till I tear your heart out. Come out, you spoiled priest, you cut-jack till I throttle you.'

That's just a sample. A cut-jack, by the way, is a stallion ass or in electrical terms an ass whose light bulb has been taken from its socket, or, if you like, a donkey with a diminished under-carriage.

In Knockanee also there is another tiny gentleman whose name is Roderick or Roddy O'Dill. Roderick is known locally as the White Hope. Ever since Jack Johnson defeated Tommy Burns and became the first black man to win the heavyweight championship of the world white sports fans have clamoured for a White Hope, that is to say a white heavyweight who would wrest the title from the negroes. It is my contention that no white man would ever have held the title if black boxers had been given equal opportunity but I think all sportsmen know this.

Later when Louis dominated the scene there was further clamour. About this time Roddy O'Dill was brought into court by his wife to defend a charge of assault and battery. Arriving home drunk one night he demanded that the frying pan be taken out and that sausages, puddings, kidney, etc., be fried for him. When his wife pointed out that he had neglected to provide her with the wherewithal to purchase any sort of provisions he assumed a fighting stance and struck her a blow on the mouth. She fell to the ground.

In court his defence was that he mistook her for Joe Louis because he had more than his share of drink taken.

'Another white hope' said the justice and the name stuck. Wherever he went thereafter he was called the White Hope, derisively, of course, because no man loves a wife beater. Many an honest man often drew a belt at his beloved but that was that. They never made a habit of it. So did many an honest woman flatten her partner with a blow from a suitable kitchen utensil but that was the end of it and there was a making-up of great proportions.

For years the White Hope staggered home on weekend nights boasting to all and sundry as follows: 'I am the White Hope. I have beaten my wife two hundred and fifty-seven times and tonight I will beat her for the two hundred and fifty-eighth.'

So saying the drunken little wretch would stagger home and if she was there before him he would insult her or assault her according to his mood. In his fighting career he had over three hundred victories and only one defeat. His defeat came about this way. His family, apart from his unfortunate wife, consisted of one son and two daughters.

One night he came home drunk and aggressive. He demanded meat but there was none to be had. He first started to berate her and then he started to pummel her. He forgot one thing. During all the years of beatings his son had been slowly growing into a man. When he heard his mother's cries he became frightened as always but then slowly and inevitably a great fury took hold of him. He came downstairs and told his mother to go upstairs. She did as she was bade. The son then inflicted the following injuries upon his father: two black eyes, a broken nose, a fractured jaw and three fractured ribs. He went upstairs and kissed his mother and sisters before leaving home. He was never seen again in Knockanee. After that the White Hope never laid a glove on his wife nor did he ever take an intoxicating drink.

If the district justice had been less facetious and more just on that far-off court-day and handed him a month in jail the son might never have been called upon to do what he had to do.

I have an invitation to a twenty-first wedding anniversary at Lingleys'. I'll let you know all about it in due course. Love to Briege and the kids.

As ever

Martin

Wellington Heights
Dublin

My dear Martin

I have just arrived back in Dublin. I will be down on the weekend after next. I look forward more than I can say to seeing you. All I ask, seriously, is that you don't throw me out. I have some most interesting local news which I shall not put down on paper. You don't have to worry about my motives. I have no intention of railroading you. I just want to spend a quiet weekend with my favourite people. I have a lovely wedding present for Peadar and his bride. I have another for Ernie and Eva. Eva did well for a girl of sixty. I'll say no more for now, dear Martin.

xxxxxxxxxx
xxxxxxxxxx
xxxxxxxxxx
xxxxxxxxxx
Your dear friend
Grace

Journey's End
Knockanee

Dear Dan

You-know-who is back but, apart from a hundred or so kiss-crosses, seems to have lost the initiative. Amen say I. She hasn't alighted here yet but is due shortly. There was intense activity by the Civic Guards here on Sunday night. Following a spate of poison pen letters, probably written by an envious publican, all the pubs were raided. The letters, of course, could have been written by a housewife who is getting no money to run the house but my guess is that it was a publican whose business has fallen off. We have such a publican here. Journey's End was mentioned in one of the letters. I was accused of serving drink to under-age customers at all hours of the morning.

The Widow McGuire was the first to be raided. The time was ten-thirty which is a half hour after the legal closing time. When Mick Henderson was granted access by the Widow's son he was astonished at what he saw. Kneeling all over the bar were hatless men of all ages. The Widow was reciting the Rosary and the assembly was diligently answering.

'Guards on public house duty,' Mick announced. Then he addressed himself to the Widow.

'How can you account,' said he, 'for the presence of these men on your premises?' No answer from the Widow. Together with the Guard who accompanied him Mick knelt down and answered the Rosary like all the rest. When it was finished Mick repeated his question: 'How can you account for these men on your premises?'

'We were saying the Rosary,' said the Widow.

'In honour of what?' asked Mick.

'For the Pope's intentions,' said the Widow. Since there was no sign of intoxicating drink to be seen and since Mick didn't really want to prosecute the Widow he cautioned her and warned her that there were to be no more after-hours Rosaries. He then cleared the house. I was next on his list. There were Peadar, Ernie Saschbuck, my Uncle Matt and three of his Cunnacanewer cronies. First came the knock at the door. Then came the announcement 'Guards on public house duty.' The three Cunnacanewer men, as if they had been rehearsing for years, silently swept all drinks from the table and disappeared upstairs. Immediately I opened the door. Mick entered followed by Guard Batty Cronin.

'How can you account,' asked Mick, 'for the presence of these men on your premises?'

'They are all authorised persons,' I answered. 'Peadar works here part-time as you know and this man is my uncle and resident here.'

I must confess that I was stuck as far as Ernie Saschbuck was concerned. Mick, however, came to my aid.

'And this man,' said he, 'is an American citizen.'

Batty and he then bade us goodnight and went off about their business. The Stella Maris was packed and there was a roaring sing-song which could be heard on the street. From everyone's point of view this was considered fair game so names were taken and the licensee charged. The last pub to be raided that night was Micky Holohan's at the other end of Tipplers' Terrace. He had heard on the grapevine that Guards were raiding but like many another foolish publican never dreamed that he would be visited himself. When the knock came Micky moved all his customers into his aged mother's bedroom and lighted two candles on a table next to the bed. Next he placed a crucifix in the old woman's hands and tucked a missal under her chin.

'Play dead,' Micky told her. The old woman was as frail as a starving bird. She looked the part. The customers stood round respectfully with their drinks in their hands. A look of mourning appeared on each face. Micky went downstairs where he admitted the sergeant and guard.

'Anyone on the premises?' asked Mick Henderson.

'Just a few friends,' said Micky. 'My poor mother passed on a short while back and there's no one in the wake-room bar mourners.'

'You have my deepest sympathy,' said Mick, 'You will take no exception I'm sure if Guard Cronin says a prayer over her. I'm a bad warrant to climb stairs lately.'

'He'll be most welcome,' said Micky gratefully. Head bent in sorrow he led the way upstairs and found a place, far from the bed, where the Guard could kneel in comfort. In the weak candlelight the old lady looked like a corpse. Batty Cronin was convinced. Clutching his cap in his hand he left the room. In the street afterwards as he and the sergeant wended their majestic way towards the Barracks the older man spoke confidentially. 'You know something, Batty,' said Mick Henderson. 'it wouldn't surprise me one bit if that old lady were to rise from the dead shortly.'

Micky Holohan's mother, as prophesied by the sergeant, did rise from the dead and Micky to give him his due was down to the barracks first thing in the morning to reveal the joyful news.

'It must have been a coma she was in then,' said Mick Henderson.

'The very thing,' said Mickey Holohan, who wouldn't know a coma from a running nose. ''Twas a coma for sure.'

'Anything is better than a full-stop, Micky,' chimed in Batty Cronin who had been listening in the dayroom.

I have a visitor. There is something about him. He did not walk in. He sidled in silently. He looks the very epitome of humility, a shabby excuse for what he should be or might have been or what he once was. You gather at once that he is kind and gentle. You know immediately that he would never make a fuss. His pale cheeks are indrawn. Somewhere along the line, in his quest for liquor, he lost his false teeth and, I would suspect, his spectacles for there is a red trace across the upper of his nose. He could do with a shave and a new raincoat. I daresay he could do with a whole new body. He is most respectful, the relict of old decencies, as they say in Cunnacanewer.

'A small Irish and a bottle of stout.' He places the money meticulously on the counter. I serve him and he swallows. He literally melts with relief before my eyes. Now I'm sure that he is an alcoholic. I call Peadar to ring a number in Listowel. Help will be along shortly.

I had better sign off and take charge of this man. Love to Briege and the kids.

As ever
Martin

Compassionate Convent
Knockanee

Dear Martin

I so enjoyed the Lingley party the other night. It was so old-fashioned it took me back to parties I attended as a child in the great house of an Ascendancy neighbour. Everything was done in style and dignity and songs like 'The Last Rose of Summer' and 'Greensleeves' were accorded pride of place. I liked your rendition of the Foster songs particularly 'My Old Kentucky Home'. What an accomplished pianist Surgeon Casby is. Martin, it's a long time since we had a chat. Come and see me on Saturday morning.

I am out of touch with events for the past few weeks, ever since the retreat. The town could be burned down and I wouldn't know about it.

Please bring a bottle of brandy, a dozen stout, a bottle of your best sherry and a dozen of assorted minerals. Also I would like if you tendered your full account as from Christmas last. We must owe you a small fortune. Take care of yourself.

Yours in J. C.
Mother Martha

PS Deliver the goods and the bill at the rear entrance. Then come to the front. The hall door will be open. Walk straight through to the sitting room.

MM

Journey's End
Knockanee

Dear Dan

Christmas is coming. Therefore, you will find a lull in the letter-writing as business usually improves across the season. Grace Lantry has come and gone. She is due back again for Christmas. She stays with Peadar and the wife as a paying guest. This time she did not push herself. She was content to remain in the background. Would you say that she is a reformed, new Grace Lantry or the old Grace with a new bag of tricks? I think that she has calmed down a lot as a result of her American visit. I am prepared to accept her on that basis. I shall, of course, not shed a whit of my usual vigilance.

The party at Jim and Lily Lingleys was an outstanding success. It was attended by what the Lingleys believed to be the more refined elements in the village. If you don't mind I sang a selection of Foster's songs from 'De Camptown Races' through 'Old Virginia' to 'My Old Kentucky Home' where I closed the door. Needless to mention I was nicely tanked up. I'll say one thing for Lily, she has a liberal hand with a bottle. Among the guests were Mother Martha, Father Hauley, Father Dee the curate, Doctor Sugan. Ernie and Eva Saschbuck, Surgeon and Mrs Casby who drove from Cork for the occasion, Mick Henderson and his wife, the Widow McGuire, Peadar Lyne and his wife as a concession to me and quite a few others whose names do not come to mind immediately. There was a buffet-style supper with every conceivable delicacy. I recall lobster, crab and escallop. There was salmon and sea trout. I saw turkey, tongue, beef, ham, mutton and a variety of salads. Some stuffed themselves. I am certain that they must have suffered afterwards. I swear I never saw such glaring examples of gluttony, mostly by the better off, believe it or not. Buffets always terrify me for the rampant near-cannibalism that goes on, the unmitigated greed and the ungoverned gorging. I had a satisfying meal and plenty of drink afterwards but some who should know better.had to be carted home. If you wanted to get rid of these elements permanently the thing is to offer them a succession of invitations to buffets. As long as the victuals and liquor are free they will always overdo it. It would be a mere matter of time before they eventually succumbed to gluttony.

We were all photographed together for the local paper and the photographer went around afterwards asking for our names. I'm certain we will be painstakingly dissected by the locals as soon as the paper comes out on Friday. That is the price of fame even if it is fame for a day only. It must be great to be a halfwit or a recluse or to be habitually in the background or to be a dodger. No responsibility and one is answerable to nobody. One's advice is never sought. One is never asked to stand at a church gate or sit upon a platform. Yet one can be part of it all and enjoy the occasional discomfiture or destruction of those who take part or take sides. I suppose the truth is that most people are like this. The others are merely the entertainers. I will sign off now and write as soon as I have anything of importance. Love to Briege and the kids.

As ever

Martin

Wellington Heights
Dublin

Dear Martin

I expect to be down next weekend. I want you to promise me
something. Under no circumstances enter any bonds or agree-
ments, engagements or bargains until I see you. If you do your
life will be a shambles before you know it. I am not at liberty
to convey the explosive news which I have recently heard. Let
me give you a final warning. Make no promises of any kind to
anybody until we meet face to face. You can do as you please
then.

xxxxxx
Your dear and faithful friend
Grace
xxxxxx

Journey's End
Knockanee

Dear Dan

Antoinette Lingley is home. She is a chastened, cowed rather sad
Antoinette. Yet in a way she is more beautiful. I think she may have
been blamed in the wrong. I am not saying that she is an angel.
What I would suggest is that she was easily led, being an innocent
and credulous girl with no experience of the world. The other day
I went to visit Mother Martha at the convent and we had a long
chat about the village and about the goings-on. She filled me in
on any number of matters of which I was ignorant. She produced
a bottle of brandy and poured a few stiff doses for me. She never
touches a drop herself. She told me her father had been a confirmed
drunkard. While we were chatting who should arrive but Lily

Lingley who informed us that Antoinette was home and would, most likely, be staying home and helping her father in the office.

Mother Martha insisted we both stay for lunch. She pressed a convenient wall button and in a matter of seconds a shining-faced nun appeared. Martha informed her that the visitors' dining room was to be made ready. After another brandy we repaired to the dining room where we were served with an excellent leek soup. There followed a main course of truly succulent roast beef, pot-roast potatoes and a variety of fresh vegetables. This was followed by a rich trifle, flavoured to a nicety with good quality sherry. Then came the coffee and then the chat.

When Antoinette left Knockanee in disgrace she went to a relation who employed her as a receptionist. You know all this. I recall telling you in an earlier letter. What you do not know is the following. Before her disgrace Antoinette was studying for all she was worth. The Leaving Certificate examination was her target. Weakened by non-stop studies and further bemused by parents who took it for granted that she was inviolate and therefore invulnerable, Antoinette was easy meat for the housemaid Kitty Bang-Bang.

Let me dwell for a while on the Bang-Bangs. They are indigenous to a place called Toorytooreen, a townland at the other side of Cunnacanewer hill. Their real names are Mulleys. Kitty Bang-Bang would be a daughter to Nellie Bang-Bang and Nellie Bang-Bang a daughter to Molly Bang-Bang who was first invested with the title. How old Molly whose real name was Shayton deserved to be so called nobody knows. One may safely deduce that it is not a nickname you could expect to see conferred on a member of the Children of Mary. No more will I say in this respect. Anyway Toorytooreen is noted for pishogues, black magic et cetera.

Before Kitty Bang-Bang came to work for the Lingley's Antoinette was a wide-eyed innocent. Before Kitty left Antoinette was a hardened woman of the world. Lily Lingley assured us that her daughter was first hypnotised and then doped by Kitty Bang-Bang. It seems logical anyway you look at it. How else can you account for the incredible transformation of innocence to evil. As a seasoned reporter you will have to agree that Antoinette's downfall was not entirely due to herself. There had to be an outside force. These things do not just happen out of the blue.

Anyway to proceed with the story it transpired that Jim and Lily Lingley went one weekend to Killarney to a builders' conference. They spent three days away from home all told and upon their return Lily noticed that Antoinette looked a little drawn and appeared to be listless. She was not in the least worried at this stage as these periods of listlessness are common to all girls. She thought it was perfectly natural for Antoinette to look pale and wan at regular intervals. Across the spring Jim and Lily spent a number of weekends in Dublin and Cork. They spent a week in London. Lily assured us that they would never have gone on these trips if they thought anything was amiss at home. It was during these absences that the orgies took place. Did I tell you that a number of obscene photographs were found in Antoinette's room afterwards. I have not seen these nor do I want to but Lily told us that if one was to judge from the expression of abandon and wantonness on Antoinette's face there could be no remaining doubt but that she was under the influence of some very potent drug whether shop-bought or home-brewed. My uncle Matt will tell you that there was a love potion, commonly called Coaxiorum, in wide use in Toorytooreen up to the late nineteen forties before the great guns of Europe

LETTERS OF AN IRISH PUBLICAN

blew a millon myths and fables into total obscurity.

However, to press on I do not suggest for a minute that Coaxiorum was used. The point I would like to bring out is that some form of potion, drug or charm was used on Antoinette. Mother Martha, after hearing Lily's account of the business, declared that she was convinced that Antoinette was the victim of a fiendish intrigue between Kitty Bang-Bang and certain unscrupulous perverts who were prepared to stop at nothing to have their way with Antoinette. Martha then gave us a resumé of Antoinette's career from the day she entered the convent to the afternoon of the balloon. The girl had been a model of perfection up to that fateful day.

I myself have no doubt about her innocence. I was too hasty to condemn her. The only excuse I can offer is that everybody else was doing it at the time and I was working on the obnoxious premise that if everybody says so it has to be.

Winter is here in real earnest, my friend. The seas have been murderous these past few days with foaming, mountainous breakers thundering ruthlessly on rock and beach. Love to Briege and the kids.

As ever
Martin

Sleepy Valley
Knockanee

Dear Grace

Hop on your bike fast the jig is up they have your man rightly banjoed the reverend mother and Lily Lie Low and the balloon merchant with the face like Marie Goretti such a gang reverend mother innocent enough dont know her oats thats all say now the young wan doped by Kitty Bang-Bang all lies Bang-Bangs every bloody one of em decent oul skins would lie down all right but whats that this day and age and wholl gainsay not you or me for sure nor devil a man with red blood and sound tackling. Lingley outfit need no dope nor nothing else mother and daughter game to the tail bred for the caper nothin come out of a box faster Martin goes around moonin and broodin like he'd be suffocatin they have the sign put on him for sure better he be borned a rabbit he now surrounded on all sides no escape better you buzz down fast dont wait for starters orders or flag to go up or the man in black will have the knot tied oh yes seen the mother and Mrs Casby headin for Journey's End last night fierce hurry throwin' the hot sups in all directions ho-ho say I dont delay talk about sellin a jennet pretendin tis a pony nothing the equal of Lily Lie Low you might lift a leg but you wont pull it ho-ho say I catch asleep a weasel very down to earth these days all put on for Martin all moryah stand easy I was a private myself if you twig all the blame now on Kitty Bang-Bang poor cratur her grandmother got the nickname first poor Molly God be good to her fowlers up that way scourin Toorytooreen for pheasants one fowler chats up Molly nice slip of a girl then time pass poor Molly showin the signs Molly no English in those days all Irish in Cunnacanewer and Toorytooreen father and mother quiz her hard who covered her first bang bang said Molly meanin twas the fowler thats the true story harmless poor people part the goods for a bag of toffees no more bother no sense as I say God help us all rich and poor no one the match for the Lingley daughter the hardest case I ever came across and I met a few in my time hard as the black rocks smooth as Lochlune tricky like the sea herself you have the law you might have a chance youll want all you have Eva placed in good position daubin away up the road a bit can see all comins and goins reports all that goes on we cant hold out much longer all rockets gone battery low last sos going down for third time dont notify Martin poor man bewitched another martyr for old Ireland another victim for the long hairs.

Your friend

Peadar Lyne

Journey's End
Knockanee

Dear Dan

All hell has broken loose. The storm has come when I least expected it and I am tossed like a cork right smack in the middle of the maelstrom harried by raving maenads not knowing where to turn. I am writing this in the loneliness of my bedroom. The door is locked for safety's sake. I don't want to be caught again in the terrible crossfire of female accusations.

Grace Lantry arrived last night. She came in the middle of the engagement party. Did I tell you I was engaged to the fair Antoinette for a few hours? Grace soon put an end to that. There we were, all good friends, a jolly good company as the song says, when she arrives without a word of warning. Present were Antoinette and her mother and father together with their friends the Casbys and all the others who were at the anniversary party at Lingleys. I was seated outside the counter in the thick of the rejoicing. Eva and Peadar were behind the counter and we were all having a wonderful time. Grace said or did nothing for a while. She accepted the green Chartreuse which Peadar handed her and she seemed to relax. She sat near Surgeon Casby who promptly took his hand from Lily Lingley's knee and transferred it to Grace's. She lifted the hand and inflicted a sharp bite on it. Everybody else thought she had kissed it but I knew from Casby's face that he had been bitten. This should have forewarned me the way a ringed moon warns a sailor but I was sated with liquor and looking lustfully at the shapely young thing who was to be my bride. Time passed. A number of songs were sung. I myself contributed. A cold plate was handed to everyone. Lily, Mrs Casby and Mrs Lyne had prepared these earlier. There were numerous toasts. It was at the end of her toast that Grace made her onslaught. She literally took the Lingleys apart. She did it carefully and systematically. Her training had prepared her well.

Here is the cold truth backed by hard facts. Antoinette did not go to a relative in Dublin to act as his receptionist. She stole three hundred pounds from her father and went to London where she had an abortion. After a week's rest she went after a job. She had little difficulty in finding one as a photographer's model. The photographer had less difficulty in convincing Antoinette that her finer points deserved a wider audience. Grace produced some of the erotica in which Antoinette had been involved with some well-developed young gentlemen.

This was bad enough until Grace revealed that the younger Lingley, in a matter of months, became the most sought-after and expensive call-girl in London.

Why then you may well ask, my dear Dan, did she chose to abandon a calling for which she was ideally suited and which she thoroughly enjoyed. The answer is twofold. Firstly she broke the rules. She spoke about her clients. Apparently this is something you can never do in this particular profession.

Secondly she acquired an unfortunate ailment common to the trade. Of this I will say no more. You are a man of the world. You will draw the correct conclusion. The aim was to foist her over on me. You would think that having been once bitten I would be twice shy. Alas no. I am a mere mortal, a thing of flesh and bone and temperament. I was snared a second time. But for Grace I would have been snared for eternity. If I had been married when she arrived she would not have told me. There but for the grace of God, my dear Dan, I would have gone. I will arise in a short while now and go to the Widow McGuire's where I will consume one large brandy. I will then walk towards the shore until I arrive at the abode of Jer Taxi. His correct name, of course, is not Jer Taxi but that is how he is called. I shall commission Jer Taxi to drive me to the town of Listowel. From there I propose to embark upon a long shaughrawn. It will be some time before you hear from me. I have the feeling anyhow that I am writing the closing chapter. It is a critical time for me. I feel that Fate is closing in on me. I'll say no more for the nonce.

Love to Briege and the kids.

As ever

Martin

So it was that Martin MacMeer embarked upon his last and most memorable shaughrawn or, as he liked to call it himself, his purification pilgrimage. He was absent from Journey's End for a period of seventeen days which brought us up to a fortnight from Christmas. This final shaughrawn was something of a local record. In the town he bade farewell to Jer Taxi and proceeded to the lounge of an hotel where he was warmly received by his old friend Anna Stacey. At nine o'clock he left the hotel. We must rely on hearsay if we are to trace his movements after this. He was seen in a variety of places during the following seventeen days. If it was not he who was seen it was surely someone who bore a remarkable resemblance to him. In a letter from Glasgow he was the chief news. This letter was written to a Mrs Josie Maldowney of Tippler's Terrace by her sister Hannah who is married in Glasgow. She maintained that she saw him staggering past the Citizen's Theatre as she and her husband were leaving after a show. She called after him but he lurched off into the darkness taking enormous strides. He was positively identified by several Cunna-canewer and Knockanee exiles who saw him in places like Soho, Streatham, Cricklewood and The Strand. His eyes were glazed and he did not stop when called upon to do so. One witness wrote to say that there was a whiff of stale drink off him that would knock a horse down.

He was seen in Kilkee by moonlight and in the town of Nenagh in Tipperary a spirits salesman identified him leaving a hotel.

When he returned home to Journey's End, a worn and exhausted man, Grace Lantry was waiting for him. Aided by delicate broths and slight but highly palatable snacks she won him back to health. They married on the fifth day of January as soon as the Christmas season had all but expired. They now live happily in Knockanee and if we are to believe Peadar Lyne there will be napkins soon on the rusted clothesline which extends across the back yard of Journey's End.

Letters of a Country Postman

The Postman writes to his friend Hamish MacShamus

The Ivy Cottage
Lisnacoo
Ballyfee

Dear Hamish

Steam is your powerful weapon. You can use it to heat homes and hospitals. With steam you can manufacture all kinds of metal. Bless my soul but you can drive a train with it or cook your supper with it and that's not all for if you have a sufficiency of curiosity and cunning you can read the minds of your neighbours with steam. You can discover their innermost thoughts and secret yearnings and the progress of their offspring and kinsfolk in distant places. You could write the history of a parish with steam and I ought to know for my immediate superior, my postmistress Katie Kersey, once mastered the use of steam as no other before or since, for the sole purpose of furthering her knowledge of the fortunes and misfortunes of those who dwelt within the bounds of her postal district. The only instrument she used was a small aluminium kettle with a spout as slender and shapely as the youngest wand of a willow. From this spout, as the water in the kettle began to boil, there emanated a powerful jet of whistling steam strong enough to rise a blister on the most calloused palm or subtle enough to sever the flap from the most hermetically sealed envelope.

You may say here with some justification that anybody with a kettle to hand could steam open an evelope. Agreed. However, it is not the manner of opening that matters for please to remember my dear Hamish that the letter must be closed again and in such a fashion that its ultimate recipient will have no idea that it was tampered with.

Katie Kersey worked in absolute privacy. First she locked the door of her kitchen and from the depths of her apron extracted a small pincers. Then she rummaged through the mailbag until she located the letter she wanted. Using the pincers she took a tender hold and placed the prized epistle in the path of the escaping steam. Once while thus engaged she was seen through the kitchen window by an old woman who wished to make a phone call. Katie had neglected to draw the curtains. Later when she admitted the old woman she explained her actions: 'Toasting a taste of bread I does be there by the fire,' she said.

As soon as the steam had softened the gum the flap curled outward and upward so that the letter within could be extracted without difficulty. For this purpose Katie used the pincers. What followed then amounted to a ritual. With infinite care as if they were breakable objects Katie would place the letter and the envelope near each other on the spotless surface of the kitchen table.

In the dresser the showpiece of a motley kitchenware collection was an ornate casserole adjudged by local experts to be a hundred years old and now far too fragile and cracked to suit the purpose for which it was originally intended. Lifting the cover Katie would gently withdraw a pair of immaculate white gloves, a Christmas present from a niece who is a member of a religious order. Delicately Katie would pull on the gloves, smoothing them over her podgy hands like a surgeon readying himself for an important operation. Next came her spectacles, wire-rimmed with powerful lenses. These she polished with a fragment of convenient chamois. Time after time she puffed her moist breath upon the lenses, polishing them immediately after each puff until at last the requisite glossiness had been achieved. Then with a mighty sigh of contentment she would plop into her favourite chair to savour the contents of the dispatch.

Sometimes she would content herself with one epistle. On other occasions she had an insatiable appetite and would read several at one sitting. Her knowledge of the postal district was all-embracing yet she never once revealed either by word or deed that she knew anything more than the simplest inhabitant of the place.

While Katie read she sobbed and sighed, moaned in distress, laughed in exultation, frowned, smiled and scowled as she digested titbit after titbit, woe after woe, triumph after triumph, disaster after disaster. The moment a letter was finished it was resealed with the aid of the kettle and if necessary a smear or two of judiciously applied gum. These acts alone, however, were not enough. There were many in Lisnacoo who were not above examining letters under magnifying glasses to see if they had been tampered with. When the letter was closed Katie would place it at the corner of the table. Then with the aid of a chair she would sit on it with one of her ample buttocks. The whole fourteen stone of her was tilted on to this solitary buttock. It was a precarious balance but when the buttock was removed the letter was flat as a pancake and impregnably sealed to boot. Even the closest inspection failed to reveal any sign of interference.

Many is the sly smile that appeared on Katie's face and she sitting in the church on Sunday mornings. The saintlier and more sanctimonious the communicants the more knowing the smile. Often half aloud she would say to herself in a true spirit of justification as certain pious people returned with bent heads from the altar: 'Only God and myself knows the kind they really are.' Fair dues to her she kept her mind to herself except alone when her niece the nun arrived for a few days holiday. Then all was revealed as the saying goes and as to whether it went any farther your guess is as good as mine although in all fairness regarding nuns there are those who fervently believe that the only word you'll get from one is the word of God. For the present all the best. See you in the summer D.V. Fond regards to the missus and family.

As ever
Mocky Fondoo

Sarsfield Mews
Upper Shoe Street
Cork

Dear Mocky

I hope you remember me. I am the curly-haired young fellow who used to follow you on your rounds through the village of Lisnacoo and the postal district of Ballyfee. You were always very kind to me when my parents and I were on holidays down there. You remember I always told you I would one day become a postman. At last that day has dawned and after many an up and down I am off on my first round next Monday morning. It's a country district about three miles from the city. Of course I have a van which is more than you ever had. What I would really appreciate are a few basic tips about the snags which are likely to beset me. I am most anxious to be a success at my job the way you always were. You must be forty years at the game now so anything you might have to convey to me would be of help. Every good wish to you and yours.

Sincerely
Frank O'Looney

Wangle Avenue
Off Sidberry Row
Glasgow

Dear Mocky

This is to tell you I shan't be spending the holidays in Lisnacoo this summer. The wife wants to go to Malta. I'll miss the fishing and the bit of poaching. What I'll miss most is your company over the beer in the 'Lisnacoo Elms'. Not to worry. We'll be back next year. You know it often occurred to me to ask you about the women in your life. Uniforms, they say, attract all types and I'm sure a postman is no exception. Write and tell me all the news when you get a chance.

Your sincere friend

Hamish MacShamus

Sradbally Lower
Ballyfee

Dear Mocky Fondoo

How is it I gets no letter at all and them lightin hures of Caffertys down the road gets several in the week and a big bundle at Christmas. Even the Feens that had all belong to them in an out of jail for robbery and buggery gets their share including parcels. What in God's name are you doing with my letters? I'll swear there is thousands of dollars gone astray or robbed from aunts of mine in America. One Christmas card I got entirely and that was a nice one from Cronin the butcher in Lisnacoo threatening me with law over three rack chops I swear I paid the thief for. Bring on my letters at once do you hear and the money that's inside in them or you'll hear about it.

Nance Nolan

PS I see Katie Kersey at the chapel and she having a new coat. You own wife is never short of style neither.

The Ivy Cottage
Lisnacoo
Ballyfee

Dear Hamish

I agree that uniforms have a fatal fascination for certain women but a postman's more so than any you care to name. I'll grant you ours is a secure, pensionable position, respected by the public as few others are but there's a lot more to it than that. From the ages of fifteen to seventy in my range of experience I have seen sane, sensible women lose their heads over this humble uniform of mine. It's a sort of disease that blinds them to everyone else and they spend their time, after the germ invades, waylaying and inveigling innocent and not-so-innocent postmen.

From the day I delivered my first epistle I found myself in deep water with the opposite sex. When I wore civvies women tended to ignore me but when I went out into the world a fully-fledged, fully-uniformed postman I found myself in a new and deadly game. Of course, I was single then and not a bad-looking chap even if I do say so myself. I thought I knew it all but alas I was no match for some of the conniving dames along my route.

The first odd bird I encountered was a buxom, black-eyed bundle of mischief in her thirties. She had three children who bore no resemblance whatsoever to each other which is no great surprise seeing as how she wasn't married. One morning I made the fatal mistake of offering her a cigarette. She accepted it as if it were a proposal of marriage. I had a terrible job keeping her at bay after that.

There was another, a sonsy widow, fair, fat and fifty-five who would complain of having a severe pain in her belly every time I called to deliver her social insurance. First she asked me if I knew of any cure for it but after a while when we got to know each other better she wanted me to feel it to see if there were any dangerous lumps on it.

The worst I met was a fiery, red-haired Dexter at the southernmost end of Ballyfee postal district. She was the only daughter of departed parents and facing up to her fiftieth year like 'twould be her twentieth with a gait on her like a waterhen and a screech to match. In my first week she took a daft and unyielding fancy to me until I took to thrusting her letters under the door after that.

What did she do one day but send herself a registered letter which it was my solemn duty to deliver. I remember it was a fine day in June with a lovely blue sky that boded well for hay, the kind of day that a postman on his bicycle loves best of all. Against my will I dismounted as soon as I reached the entrance to her house. I knocked at the door but there was no response. I knocked a second time, louder and longer than the first but still there was no reply of any kind, not even the bark of a dog or the miaow of a cat. I lifted the latch and peered into the kitchen but there was no sign of life. There was a fire in the Stanley and on it the kettle sang gently but no trace whatsoever of the damsel herself. I called out her name which was Gracie, Gracie Goddy she was nicknamed although her true title was Grace Godleigh. There was no answer. I opened the back door which led out into the haggard. Again I called out her name and threw in a few prolonged halloos for good measure. I came back into the kitchen clutching the letter in my hand. That's one of the cardinal rules of the post. A registered letter must be signed for. At the time a cat's paw would have suited me fine but there wasn't even a cat. No witnesses, animal, human or otherwise.

It was then I noticed the bedroom door ajar. I was nonplussed. I had no choice but to knock. Knock I did but there was no answer. I stood back a respectable way and peered in. If it gave me all I could do to fend off Gracie Goddy in the wide spaces of her kitchen it was odds on I'd have no chance at all in her bedroom. There she was with a large comb in her hand and she propped up on the bed like a mermaid on a headland with her red hair thrown down over her shoulders, loose and shiny and her two breasts as bare as a brace of outsize pumpkins.

I knocked once more at the bedroom door. To do any more would be in excess of my duty.

'Come in lovie,' said Gracie in a sort of a sing-song.

'I can't,' I said, ''tis against regulations.'

She muttered an unprintable word about regulations. It wasn't for my hearing of course.

'Rules was made to be broken,' she called out.

'I have my job to think of,' said I.

'All right,' she said resignedly after a while, 'I'll come down so.'

Down she came. I turned away and looked out the window. There was a blackbird picking worms in the haggard so I concentrated on his antics. I don't know what I'd have done only for him.

'Sign there,' I said pointing my thumb backwards over my shoulder to the registration slip which I had placed on the table. I waited then for a decent space and threw the letter over my shoulder. I had to turn, however, to collect the receipt. I had one glimpse of her as I snatched the slip. All I recall is a huge pink and white mass, a shuddering, heaving, breathing mass, a mighty moaning, groaning mass. I bolted through the front door forgetting my pencil. I remember too hearing a great volcanic sigh coming from somewhere in the depths of Gracie Goddy.

She got married about two years after to a small, bald-headed man who drove a wagon for Duffy's Circus. It is interesting to note that he wore a green uniform and peaked cap. They went to Australia after she sold her place.

Even after I married there were several who refused to throw in the towel. There is no doubt but that the uniform was at the back of it all. Better looking men than I such as vets, inseminators, insurance agents, seed salesmen and warblefly inspectors seemed to enjoy immunity. You could be a film star and escape without notice but pull on a postman's uniform and you were a target for every sex-starved damsel in the district. If I availed myself of half the chances I was offered I'd be growing daisies for no man born of woman could possibly possess the energy to satisfy these famished females.

Our local dispensary doctor is a man of the world by the name of Mongie. I asked him one night and we taking our pints in the 'Lisnacoo Elms' if he could explain this obsession with uniforms. He said it was probably a traditional thing, that over the years postmen seemed always to be set upon by dogs and women. I don't see how I can disagree with him. The man before me, Willie Liddy was a notorious Lothario and the man before that was a bit of a playboy too. My immediate predecessor for all his conquests was crossed in love when he set about choosing a permanent partner. She was a farmer's daughter with her eyes set on land. She married land and left our man in the lurch. He went out of his mind for a while and suffered suspension as a result. He was found sitting one morning on Kilcoo Bridge with a powerful odour of whiskey all round him. His bag of letters was open on his lap. Every so often he would fling one on to the roadway and say: 'She loves me'. For every one he threw on the roadway he threw another into the river and cried: 'She loves me not'. In no time at all his bag was empty and he fell off to sleep by the bridge. Luckily the letters in the river floated long enough to be picked up by net fishermen in the estuary while the ones on the roadway were rescued by passers-by who quickly sobered up poor Willie and sent him off on his rounds.

Ah dear I could go on all day about the uniform but alas I must now present myself to my postmistress, the one and only Katie Kersey or Katie the Steamer as the locals call her. From her I will collect the post, sort it with the only other postman in the district, my colleague Micky Monsell, then mount my bicycle and hit for the countryside of Ballyfee. Micky does the village of Lisnacoo and that part of Ballyfee which lies to the north of it while my territory consists of all the land to the south and west, a considerable area of approximately twenty square miles and roughly two hundred households.

I hope you enjoy the holiday in Malta. God knows we'll miss you this summer which incidentally will be my last one in the employ of the department of post and telegraphs. I'll be sixty-five in September and due to retire after fifty years in the service of the same employer.

For the time being I'll sign off. Regards to all.

As ever

Mocky Fondoo

The Ivy Cottage
Lisnacoo
Ballyfee

Dear Frank

Many thanks for yours of the fourteenth inst. Of course I remember you and I always knew you would be a postman one day. There are some men born to be postmen and I have no doubt but that you are one of those. It's hard to know where to begin if I am to advise you. There is no teacher like experience as you will find out but still a few pointers from an old stager might do no harm. You will find almost everything you need in the official rules and regulations but there's always more to a game than you'll find in the books. There are the things that cannot be written down. I will try to pinpoint trouble spots for you:

Number 1: Be discreet when you deliver a registered envelope. Let none look upon it except the person whose name it bears.

Number 2: When you deliver ordinary letters, if indeed any letter can be called ordinary, hand it to its legal owner face downwards if there are other persons present. This way neither the handwriting of the sender or the postmark can be seen.

Number 3: Never take tea in the same house two days in a row.

Number 4: Never let any particular house adopt you.

Number 5: Never appear drunk in uniform although at Christmas it's all right to be merry. People expect it of us.

Number 6: Always make sure you do not wear a uniform when becoming romantically involved with a woman.

Number 7: Keep one eye open for signs of want. There is much we can do.

Number 8: Remember there is no door so familiar that it can't do with a knock.

Number 9: Beware most of all of idle women. They'll play with you the way a cat plays with a mouse and often with consequences as dire.

Number 10: Never forget that in your sole custody are the innermost thoughts of the hundreds of souls entrusted to your care. In the most fragile and perishable of paper containers you transport tidings of priceless value for those to whom they are addressed. Remember that when a man entrusts his most private thoughts to paper he lays his reputation and character on the line. You sir carry his good name in your hands. This is the most valuable possession a man has. A man may reveal his sins in confession but he is capable of revealing all in his letters. In the last analysis he is dependent for discretion on you and you alone. Often you will convey expressions of the love that blossoms pure in the hearts of men and women. No trust could be more sacred. Transport these and all your other commissions with tenderness and care. I would forfeit my life rather than submit one of my letters to anyone but its rightful owner.

Number 11: Treat department inspectors as you would men from outer space, with caution, reserve and respect.

Number 12 and Last: Never forget that you are paid to deliver letters, not gossip.

I wish you luck and success in your career and I hope that what I have conveyed to you may be of some use to you. If you ever find yourself in a jam you'll know where to find me.

As ever

Mocky Fondoo

Sradbally Lower
Ballyfee

Dear Mocky Fondoo

I see you delivering at Feens yesterday. There was a bundle in your hand you hure and you goin' in. Who would be writin' to them Caffertys that had five out of their six daughters knocked up by travellers and soldiers and not a note of any sort for me as never did a thing out of the way to no one. There is fierce cuffuffling goin' on somewhere to say a woman of my standing does have to play second fiddle to disgenerates. All my letters are in a big heap somewhere hidden by villains in the post office or burned by those that begrudges me what is mine. The next person I'm goin' to see is the minister for post and telegraphs and we'll see how many will have jobs when I'm done.

Nance Nolan

Sradbally Upper
Ballyfee

Dear Mocky

I hate to bother you but I have no course left open to me other than writing to you. I know how persecuted you must be from people who think their letters are being mislaid and hold you to blame. I haven't heard from Jack in a fortnight which is unlike him. He was nearly always on the dot up till now and I can't understand why I haven't heard from him. It's not that I'm short of money. I have some spared out of what he sends me. Still it won't last much longer. Also I'm worried in case something has happened to him. I wrote to Miss Kersey the postmistress asking her if maybe the registered letter had gone astray. She answered by return and told me that there was no likelihood of such a thing and if there was that my husband would have the receipt and could make a claim.

Unfortunately this tells me nothing and so I am appealing to you. Would you enquire in the proper place for me or look around in the sorting office to see if the letter was mislaid. I'm worried sick Jack might have lost his job or maybe he has had an accident. It's no fun with three young children. Do what you can for me Mocky and I'll be forever thankful to you.

Sincerely yours
Kitty Norris

The Ivy Cottage
Lisnacoo
Ballyfee

Dear Hamish

The fishing season opened yesterday and I landed a nice nine pound cock fish with a two and a half inch blue and silver in fairly high water. Others did not fare as luckily and catches are well down on other years considering the quality of the water. I am all alone at the moment. The missus has gone to America to spend a holiday with my two daughters who are married in New Jersey. She'll spend a second period with my two sons in the Bronx. Altogether she'll be gone three months. Although it's only a few days since she boarded the plane at Shannon I already miss her more than words can tell. All the crowd here send their regards. You'll be missed in the taproom especially for the chorus of 'Loch Lomond'.

The only news of importance is that the postmistress's niece, Sister Gabrielle, is spending a few days holiday with her beloved auntie. At night the pair sit in the kitchen and Katie reveals all that there is to be known about the fortunes of the people of the postal district of Ballyfee. To the casual listener it sounds as if a litany is being recited with the nun offering short responses every so often. What she is really doing is egging Katie on when she hesitates before the juicier parts of her revelations. She does not steam the letters open any more except on very rare occasions. Very seldom indeed do I come across a bum-flattened epistle these days. Every second house in the district has a telephone and all she has to do is listen. Sometimes, in an effort to catch her out, the party at the other end of the line might ask: 'Are you there Katie?'

Her answer to this is: 'You wouldn't be on the line you fool if I was elsewhere.'

She misses nothing although she was nearly poisoned lately when she copied a cure for flatulence on to her pad. She keeps the pad handy when she is reciting for Sister Gabrielle. She looks to it for cues whenever she falters in the middle of a tale. The cure for flatulence consisted of a large dose of Cascara Sagrada mixed with boiled rhubarb. The whole thing was a set up by a pharmacist's assistant working in Cork who happens to be doing an on-and-off line with a local flier. Otherwise she's a lovely girl in every way. It just so happens that some women are born cold, others warm and a rare few hot, a very necessary and sobering few for the survival of the sanity of that awful conglomerate known as the human race. Anyway our man was one night talking to the flier whose name I won't mention, not because I'm a gentleman or anything but because in my heyday I had a great appreciation for this type of young lady. While he was talking Katie was listening. Our man was at his most persuasive when our friend the flier expressed reluctance about spending a weekend in Cork. Our man reminded her of past joys and was becoming most elaborate in this respect when Katie cut him off without warning. She has her limits.

Our friend was thus forced to make the long journey to Lisnacoo. His timing was wrong so he returned to Cork unappeased. While in Lisnacoo the flier informed him of Katie Kersey's doings and let it fall into the bargain that Katie was a chronic burper sounding off like a bullfrog as I can personally verify from one end of the day to the other. During the course of the flier's next phone conversation with the pharmacist's assistant she asked him if he knew of a cure for flatulence intimating that her grandmother was a martyr to this noisy malady. The pharmacist's mate then related the cure which he said was prescribed for Rose Kennedy by a Harley Street specialist.

Subsequently in the course of the morning between the hours of nine-thirty and twelve Katie Kersey paid a record number of nineteen visits to the toilet and did not quite make it on two.

They sit now at night herself and the saintly Sister Gabrielle while Katie recounts the broken engagements, the cross-Channel abortions, the infidelities, the lusts and longings, the ups and downs of the Ballyfee subscribers and others further afield.

You may ask why people don't report her. The answer, of course, is that they might be saddled with worse and anyway what harm is she doing. There are meaner ways of getting one's kicks and but for the nun and I daresay a few of her cronies in the convent no one knows a damned thing. Another reason is that only part of what she hears is true and the young bucks of the parish have a habit of inventing unlikely tales for her titillation and their own amusement in the long winter nights. One day the parish priest's housekeeper might be pregnant, a woman of sixty-three, another it might be the reverend mother of some convent. True or false Katie would absorb all and relate all to the nun.

Katie is also probably the last of her kind. Her likes were as common as bogwater and I starting out but now for better or for worse they are gone from the scene. Reasons? Today people prefer to live their own lives. In Katie's heyday in rural Ireland for the want of fulfilment and involvement they were forced to live other people's lives. It was that or go nuts. Only once ever did I see her lose her control. There's a fishing village about seven miles from here with a crowd of resident trawlermen who would do anything for diversion when the weather is unfit for fishing. One night they coaxed a Spanish colleague into making a phone call to Katie announcing that he was the new Papal Nuncio, Doctor Elbrigandi. Katie burped in surprise into the mouthpiece to be informed in broken English by Doctor Elbrigandi that she was being excommunicated for farting. Involuntarily she spluttered back with injured innocence that she was a burper not a farter but by this time the Spaniard had hung up on her.

I'll close now as I have to tie a few minnows for Sunday's fishing. I have never lost so many. The river gets dirtier and snaggier every season and I often wonder how the salmon come upriver at all. You'll be for Malta one of those days. Send a card if you think of it and while you're at it will you engage in an act of charity and send one to Miss Nance Nolan, Sradbally Lower, Ballyfee. Don't sign your own name. Just sign it 'The Knight of Malta'.

As ever

Your oul' segocia

Mocky Fondoo

Sarsfield Mews
Upper Shoe Street
Cork

Dear Mocky

A thousand thanks for your letter and for the twelve good rules as Shakespeare said when referring to the game of Goose. Your advice should be pinned up in every post office in the country. What you wrote came to mind only last Thursday. I was delivering a seed catalogue to a farmer when his daughter chimed in and asked me to stay for a drop of tea. She asked me if I liked griddle bread and I said I adored it which is the honest to God truth. Every day since there is a cup of tea and a few slices of freshly made griddle bread waiting for me around lunchtime. Lately she has taken to adding a nicely boiled fresh egg. I can handle her, however. Make no mistake about it. By the way lest I forget. You said nothing about dogs in your list. Already I've received two bites and was lucky to escape without several more. Every good wish to you and yours.

Sincerely

Frank O'Looney

Sradbally Lower

Ballyfee

Dear Micky Fondoo

Bad cess to yourself and Katie the Steamer for the robbin' thieves that the pair of ye are. That's a great postboy is Micky Monsell that does the other route. There's no fear he passes a door. An I payin' Cronin the butcher yesterday for rack chops and buyin' a bit of boilin' that decent postboy lifted his cap and bade me the time of day. But I'm easy now about yourself or Katie for who should write to me only the Knight of Malta himself. You dassent interfere with royal post like that. Maybe now you'll give the rest and spare me the bother of writin' to the minister. No wonder Katie does be smilin' and talkin' to herself and she sittin' on her rump in the chapel with her leather coat and who paid for your one's trip to America?

Nance Nolan

The Ivy Cottage
Lisnacoo
Ballyfee

Dear Kitty

I am indeed sorry to report that there is no sign of a letter from Jack, registered or otherwise in this post office. The first light day's post I get in the coming week I'll call to Sradbally but maybe you'll have news before that. I hope the matter will be straightened out by then. If not I shouldn't worry. The postal system is not foolproof and a genuine mistake may have been made.

Your friend
Mocky

The Ivy Cottage
Lisnacoo
Ballyfee

Dear Frank

You're not a month on the job yet and already you have broken one of my most important instructions. Don't ever forget that I am fifty years at this caper. You say you can handle this farmer's daughter who has the griddle bread and boiled eggs waiting for you every day. That griddle bread and those boiled eggs must be paid for and if you're not careful my cocksure friend you'll find yourself picking up the tab. What amuses me is your belief you can handle her. You will find to your cost if you're not careful that it's a lot easier to handle nitroglycerine. Can't you see she's spinning a web made of eggs and griddle bread, a web from which there is no escape once you tangle with the weakest strand? I know the pattern like the back of my hand. Next thing now you'll be getting trifle or roasted apples or semolina pudding on top of the eggs and griddle bread or maybe you have a preference for something special like apple tart and cream or mandarin oranges. Have no worries. She'll find out what it is and that will be another strand around your throat. Can't you realise you're walking a tightrope? Give yourself a chance, before you settle down, to wear the arse off one pair of pants at least. Remember what I said in my letter. Never take tea under the same roof two days in a row. Yet here you are taking tea and more besides in spite of all my warnings.

So you've been bitten by dogs. Will you tell me which postman has not? Every one of us must adopt his own strategy for dealing with this menace. No two dogs are alike but every dog, behind the facade of viciousness, is a coward. My predecessor, Willie Liddy, was badly bitten by a mongrel cow-dog on his first day out. Willie was anything but a patient man. After the bite he ignored the dog and went looking for its master. When he found him he left the impression of a size eleven boot on the fellow's behind.

'If that dog bites me again,' Willie warned him, 'you're a dead man.'

The dog never bit him again.

In this business it is wrong to blame the dog. The master or mistress must always be held to blame. My colleague Micky Monsel who delivers in the northern half of the district is nicknamed Dogmeat for the simple reason that dogs will not leave him alone. Wandering curs recognise him when he's off duty and single him out for attack. In uniform he has no peace at all. For some years now he wears wellingtons to protect his calves and ankles from the fangs of his tormentors. Certain postmen are unfortunate in this respect. Some aspect of their appearance, attitude or manner seems to bring out the worst in otherwise well-behaved dogs. Even suave, elderly, well-bred dogs with pedigrees are transformed into snarling savages the moment Dogmeat Monsell lifts the latch on the gate where they stand with innocent faces looking as if the last thought in their heads was the biting of a postman. Approval and welcome are written all over them. They are the types of dog one instinctively pats on the head, dogs with honest, good-natured faces, faces that inspire trust and confidence. Yet the moment Dogmeat turns his back a terrible transformation takes place. Dogmeat has a theory that people use postmen as guinea pigs in order to turn harmless curs into watchdogs.

With me it's different. I like dogs and get on fairly well with all types. Occasionally I meet an exception but I have a prearranged strategy for dealing with these. I look them in the eye until they skulk off with hangdog looks. There are rare occasions when this does not work and when one meets a really nasty mongrel the owner must be confronted and told that until such time as the dog behaves deliveries must be suspended. With some dogs I have struck up lasting friendships and these follow me on my route until the domain of another dog is reached. Here I am handed over to the dog in charge who in turn will escort me to the bailiwick of the next dog. Often I have been attacked for no reason by pairs of dogs and on occasion by packs of three or four. The exercise here is to isolate the ringleader and concentrate all your energies on him.

However, no matter what precautions a postman may take there is no guarantee of immunity. Alas all the suspicion and mistrust is on one side. It is in the nature of a dog to express hostility towards callers but especially towards postmen so it has to be the uniform.

'But,' you may say, 'has not a Civic Guard a uniform?'

He has but he also has a baton and whatever a dog may do it is not likely he will attack a man who has a weapon. More important, owners see to it that their dogs are on their best behaviour whenever a Civic Guard calls around so we may conclude that the owner is every bit as cunning as the dog. I am firmly of the belief that there should be some sort of compatibility or competence test before a person is allowed to take charge of a dog because I have often found that there is more animal in the man than there is in the dog. Often too a sensitive dog can read his master's face and upon seeing worry or fear inscribed thereon, because of the impending visit of a postman, may foolishly presume that the postman is an enemy. Those who receive letters every day take letters for granted but a man who never receives a letter has good reason to fear one when it is delivered unexpectedly. Of course there is a chance in a million that he may have inherited money. More likely, however, it is a bill or some other request for money from friends or relations. Just as in newspapers and other forms of the communications media there is more bad news than good news in letters. Therefore, to the one-letter-a-year man the postman has to be the bearer of bad tidings. He may avoid the Civic Guard or the process server by the simple expedient of skipping out the back door and spending his day in the wilds until danger has passed. He cannot do this with the postman because there is always the outside chance that the letter may contain good tidings or because of the million to one chance that it may contain news of a legacy. While hope keeps springing in the human breast there is always the possibility that news of a legacy may spring from the postman's bag.

That's all for now except to issue a final warning. Better men than you were collared by tea and griddle bread.

As ever

Mocky Fondoo

PS It wasn't Shakespeare who referred to the twelve good rules and the royal game of Goose. It was Oliver Goldsmith, the same man who referred to every fool in the countryside from swain to parson but made sure to say nothing about the postman. We have accounts of cripples, schoolmasters, spendthrifts, geese and watchdogs but no mention of you know who.

M. F.

Templebawn
Ballyfee

Dear Mister Fondoo

I hesitates ere I writes to you as my matter is most private. I was expecting a small parcel with special goods in it which has not come. As it was medicine would you treat it with care and not open it don't all the good go out of it.

Your sincere friend

Catriona Cooney (Mrs)

Sradbally Upper
Ballyfee

Dear Mocky

I cannot thank you enough for calling and for your kind offer. I have written to my mother for help. She's fairly well off. I'm certain that Jack is in hospital somewhere suffering from loss of memory.

I have written to the parish priest of his district and to a few other people I know. It's a bit too soon to notify the police. There were other times when a few weeks went by without hearing from him and once a month passed without my getting a copper. It was the time he hurt his leg. The letter you brought the last day was unsigned. It was from someone in the neighbourhood who seems to know an awful lot about me and about Jack. It was a dirty letter. Thanks again for all your help. I hope we hear from Jack soon as I'm getting really worried.

Yours sincerely

Kitty Norris

The Ivy Cottage

Lisnacoo

Ballyfee

Dear Hamish

I don't know where to begin. The news has been piling up. The latest is that the last of the Burley sisters has married into another big farm west of Lisnacoo to a bachelor wild by the name of Jack Silky who is up to the top of his two hairy ears in debt. The Burley lady had the money, however, and the mystery here is where she came by it and indeed where did her sisters come by it for the four of them are married into the biggest farms in these parts. Many is the registered letter I delivered to their mother across the years but what could be inside I asked myself except a few pounds at most. The Burleys you see were illiterate and spent most of their growing years avoiding the classroom. Where then did they make the thousands when all that any of them spent in London was two years?

For me the mystery was solved the other night in the 'Lisnacoo Elms' when the last of the Burleys stood me a drink the night before the wedding, slipped me a fiver too and thanked me for the faithful way I had delivered her earnings to the mother. She was half drunk and as the night wore on she grew drunker still.

'You did well in England,' I said cautiously.

'Better than I'd ever do here,' she said.

'Were you in service?' I asked.

'You might say I was,' she replied with a smirk.

I smirked as well but I kept my mouth shut.

'The Burleys mightn't be able to work the brain so good,' said she proud as you please, 'but they makes up for it by working the other thing.'

I got the message but I feigned ignorance. She sighed at my innocence.

'What I often gave away here,' said she, 'for a fist of gooseberries or a fag I gets a score of notes for over there.'

On the tragic side there's a lovely woman living in Sradbally Upper. Her name is Kitty Norris and it would seem that her husband has deserted her. I think the truth may be dawning on her at last. She has also been receiving anonymous letters from a gentleman in the area. I think I may know who he is. He fakes the writing but it isn't easy to pull the wool over the eyes of a postman.

Jack Norris was always a bit of a playboy. He gave up a good job here to go to England where he said the pickings were better. How any man could leave a woman like Kitty Norris is beyond me. I fear he has taken up residence with another woman which, alas, is not an uncommon practice with those who leave their wives behind when they go abroad. The trouble is that there was no need for Jack to go. He seems now to have deserted poor Kitty and from here on she will be dependent on her mother for the bite and sup or any other charity which might come her way. What a fall this is for a proud and lovely girl. I remember when she first came to Sradbally Upper as a young bride. She brightened the kitchen with her blushes and the countryside with the sound of her voice. What madness possesses grown men to forsake such beauty?

Last week I was reported to the postmistress by a Mrs Catriona Cooney of Templebawn. The postmistress has no real authority over me if I wanted to go by the book. The head postmaster is my real boss. Katie, in turn, reported me to the postmaster. What happened was this. A small box addressed to Mrs Cooney was damaged in transit and had to be returned to the district office for reparcelling. The district postmaster is a man by the name of Mallvey. He is an ex-army man, fond of strong drink and strong language but as genuine a scout as you could meet. Many's the postman he's saved from suspension. When I entered his office he was looking out the window, standing with his hands on his hips. There was an overseer by the name of Dick Cavill seated at a table on which was a small cardboard parcel which had almost disintegrated because of bad parcelling and rough handling.

'What do you make of that Mocky?' Mallvey said without turning his head.

'Don't know sir,' I told him.

'Pick up the shagging thing,' he said, 'and examine it. Tell me what you see.'

I lifted the parcel. I groped inside and withdrew some of the contents.

'Now what do you make of it?' Mallvey said turning around.

'French letters,' I said.

'Exactly,' said Mallvey. 'Bloody well disgraceful using the Post for such purposes. Now Mocky I must ask you a question. Did you open this parcel?'

'No sir. I've never seen it before now. Katie never showed it to me.'

'That's good enough for me,' said Mallvey. 'Do your duty Dick,' he addressed the overseer.

'Very good sir,' said Cavill. 'What method shall I use to dispose of them sir?'

'Consign them to flames,' the postmaster's voice was full of mock indignation, 'and see that every last one is burned to a frazzle.'

'Yes sir,' said Dick obediently.

'They'll be mounting them bareback in Templebawn till the next consignment comes,' the postmaster quipped.

I followed Dicky Cavill downstairs to the basement where there was a furnace. On his way he transferred the contents of the package to his own person.

'Witness this,' he said to me as he flung the empty package into the flames. 'Witness the destruction of these instruments of depravity, these sheaths of iniquity. The lechers of Templebawn will be without sport tonight. I swear to that on the eighty-two balls of Ali Baba and the Forty Thieves. Come on, we'll have a drink somewhere before I drive you home.'

I remember well the time when we had a list of banned newspapers and magazines pinned up in all offices. There was the *News of the World, Truelife Detective, The Naked Truth* and several others. The clerks in the district office and their wives and relations had great reading in those days, those of them that were interested in pictures of naked men and women and true tales of bigamy, rape, murder, sadism, bestiality, buggery, infidelity and other uncommon doings too numerous to mention.

The publications I mention would nearly always be concealed inside religious magazines or British newspapers which were deemed acceptable by the censors. When they were well wrapped and hidden so that no sign of them was revealed they would find their way to the people to whom they were addressed. When they were not it was the duty of the postal clerks and sorters who handled them to take them from their wrappings and destroy them. The sorters and clerks were not fools so they took the magazines home or gave them to friends who were in dire need of diversion in the long nights of winter. Sometimes they burned them but only when they were read by all who had wanted to read them. The Irish censors must have been the most naive and backward men of any age in the Island of Saints and Scholars. It was a poor post office that hadn't a comprehensive library of banned magazines in those benighted days.

I'll sign off now. I must write to the wife and fill her in on all the goings-on of Lisnacoo and greater Ballyfee no matter how trivial. She doesn't write at all herself. She had a mild stroke some years ago as you know. For the present then Hamish all the very best.

As ever

Your oul' segocia

Mocky Fondoo

Sarsfield Mews
Upper Shoe Street
Cork

Dear Mocky

You were right about the drawing power of the uniform. I'm fighting them off as best I can. No need to worry about the damsel who provides the boiled eggs and the griddle bread. Her name is Rosanna McDoogle. One of the clerks in the head office here was marking my card the other night but he made no mention of Rosanna so she's no tracker. Only last Thursday she had my favourite feed waiting for me when I struck the house at dinnertime. I could eat spare-ribs and cabbage from morning till night. I must have let it drop, in passing, that I liked them for the plate was piled high with ribs of the finest quality. There is no danger of my getting involved in a serious way. This is a decent sort who just wants to be friends.

Friday last she asked me to bring out a parcel of bikinis on appro from the city. I won't have a chance till Saturday afternoon. She has promised she'll let me select the most suitable one on Monday when I call. She plans to go abroad for a fortnight in July. We have a great chat when I call. There never seems to be anybody around although she has brothers and sisters and both parents living. She is the oldest of the family. She says she's only twenty-eight but I suspect she's a bit older.

I'll remember what you wrote about cross dogs. The man who retired from this route just before I was appointed always carried a small ashplant. He struck first and asked questions afterwards. Dogs left him alone. I don't want to go around trailing an ashplant so I'll try your methods.

Have no worries about my marrying Rosanna McDoogle or anybody else for ten years at least. I'll wear the arse off twenty pairs of pants before I join the ranks of the martyrs.

Sincerely

Frank O'Looney

PS Was there a postman by the name of Bugler McNulty? I mean did he really exist and was he the character people make him out to be?

Frank

Sradbally Lower
Ballyfee

Dear Mocky Fondoo
No letter. No parcel. No card. I wrote to the Knight of Malta and I got no answer. I wrote to know would he have any old suits for my brother Dan or shoes and know would his wife have any summer dresses that she had no use for but divil the word. The Knight's clothes would suit Dan. Our Dan is the dead stamp of Prince Philip. Don't do away with this parcel like you did the others.

Nance Nolan

Wangle Avenue
Off Sidberry Row
Glasgow

Dear Mocky
Just back from Malta, nice and brown. So is the wife. In no way can it be compared with Lisnacoo and Ballyfee with the mountains all around and the green, green fields and the waterfalls not to mention the people. Now that the wife's whim is fulfilled it's Lisnacoo for me for evermore. I sent your friend a Maltese calendar and a sheaf of brochures. Should keep her quiet for a while. Sorry to hear about that nice woman in Sradbally Upper. I remember her. Old lechers like myself don't easily forget a face and a figure like that. You'll find a gift under separate cover. It's only a wooden cross but it's artistic and it's peculiar to the island where it was made. Tonight I intend to write to the 'Lisnacoo Elms' booking my spot for next year. I'm

tired so I'll close for the moment. I look forward to hearing from you.

Your sincere friend
Hamish MacShamus

The Ivy Cottage
Lisnacoo
Ballyfee

Dear Frank

I grow more amused at your assessment of Rosanna McDoogle. Will you take my word for it that an eligible bachelor can be anything with an eligible spinster except good friends. Such a relationship between a man and a woman may last for a short while but, because of the nature of the bashte, as the saying goes, must exceed the bounds of friendship in a matter of time. Keep that in mind when you're measuring Rosanna for bikinis. Believe me Frank if you had no job and no uniform you'd be as much in demand by the Rosanna McDoogles of this country as a Christmas tree in the middle of January. Try to stand back and have an objective look at your exact position. You're lunching at McDoogle's regularly at considerable expense to oul' McDoogle you may be sure. You are selecting bathing costumes for Rosanna. Does it not strike you as sinister or odd to say the least that there is no member of the McDoogle family present while you are on the premises stuffing your gut with spare-ribs and cabbage? Does it not strike you as odd that they receive a letter or letters every day of the week? What important role in the community does oul' McDoogle play to say that he's barricaded with letters every day of his life?

In normal circumstances a small farmer like McDoogle might receive a letter once a week. I can see McDoogle clearly in my mind's eye. There he is, saddled with a wife and large family with the eldest daughter Rosanna showing every sign of becoming a permanent fixture. This is a state of affairs which can be intolerable in a small house where it is no fun making ends meet. Oul' McDoogle is driven almost to the point of distraction. The wife turns to novenas. Suddenly the prayers are answered and salvation in the shape of a rookie postman appears out of the blue. Spick and span with his postal van and his new uniform he is too precious a catch to be sought after with ordinary bait. Here's a man with a fine pensionable position, a civil servant and a respected figure to crown all. We want a big net with small meshes for this fish.

However it's not yet too late. Pull out now before your paunch is pulled to the ground by spare-ribs. Don't hesitate for another moment. You are in grave danger. At least give yourself a chance to put your first Christmas on the job behind you as a single man. You're too young for marriage. Great God you're not yet twenty-one years of age and already you're on the point of being hooked for life.

You ask about the Bugler McNulty. Yes he existed, Patrick Augustine Stanislaus McNulty, pride of the auxiliaries and the terror of overseers, with more suspensions to his credit than any ten postmen anywhere. You could, I suppose, call him a lover of the outdoors if only for the good reason that he slept more often out of doors than in, rarely ever being sober enough to find his own way home. He mislaid, lost and damaged hundreds of parcels and letters. Yet he was never sacked, the chief reason being that he was rarely reported by his victims. He was unbelievably popular. Despite having a mountainous and circuitous route he started his first day without a bicycle. On his first assignment he headed straight for the local creamery where outlying farmers came with their milk every morning. Here he would distribute most of the letters to their proper owners and to neighbours of the owners who would deliver them, if they remembered, as they returned home from the creamery. Most of the letters were delivered one way or another in due course but, unfortunately, a small number fell into the wrong hands and here is where the Bugler's troubles started. Here is what happened.

Not all the farmers would go directly home from the creamery. A few would spend most of the day in the nearest public house playing rings or darts or maybe debating the progress of national and international affairs. Outside horses, ponies and asses were tethered to telephone poles, church railings or to each other. Some owners thoughtfully provided their animals with bundles of hay but most of the unfortunate creatures just stood there resignedly and patiently until their masters could drink no more or until their monies were exhausted.

All this time important letters for neighbours lay forgotten in their pockets. Upon reaching home, well and truly befuddled by drink, a member of the household would see to the untackling of the horse or pony while the lord and master sat down to his dinner. After dinner he would generally be overcome by drowsiness so he would either park himself by the fire or take a turn in the bed. Not all wives would rummage through his pockets while he slept but there were a few who would, a few who hungered for news and companionship, who lived in semi-isolation, in desolation and despair, whose loveless marriages were poor fodder for the hunger and loneliness. For these there was nothing to whack the reading of a neighbour's letter to lift one out of the blues. It was easily located and read. Lacking the subtle craftsmanship of Katie Kersey the women in question were left with no option but to destroy the letters once they were read.

Inevitably complaints came in and an investigation followed. The upshot of the ruction was that the Bugler was suspended for a fortnight and cautioned that if he ever again broke the rules he would be dismissed. He promised the postmaster that he would never visit the creamery again. He was true to his word. From that time forward he let it be known that those who wanted letters for themselves, their friends or their neighbours might obtain same by visiting a certain public house where he would be in residence from morning till night. Not only did this arrangement simplify the Bugler's task but it also resulted in his being stood round after round of free drinks from grateful clients, particularly those in receipt of registered letters or those who did not want their spouses to know that they were receiving letters.

It could not last and following complaints the Bugler was called before his postmaster. He was asked to defend his actions.

'You told me to stay away from the creamery and I did,' the Bugler said.

'But I didn't tell you go to the pub,' the postmaster pointed out.

'You didn't,' the Bugler replied, 'but you didn't tell me stay away from it either.'

'Damn you,' the postmaster shouted. 'You know the rules. You took an oath.'

'I know. I know,' the Bugler said placatingly, 'but I'm not able for the long journey into the hills.'

'You have a bicycle,' the postmaster reminded him.

'It's punctured,' the Bugler told him.

'You have an allowance of one and sixpence a week to maintain that bicycle,' the postmaster persisted.

'You wouldn't maintain a pair o' drawers on one and six a week,' the Bugler replied.

'Every other postman with a rural route uses his bike without complaint so why shouldn't you?'

'It makes me dizzy when I mount up,' the Bugler responded.

'Then you'd better be on the lookout for a job that won't make you dizzy,' the postmaster said. The Bugler made no reply to this. He sat there, wordless, with his head in his hands. From time to time he would look beseechingly at the postmaster who was a soft-hearted man behind the facade of authority. A large tear left the Bugler's eye and proceeded slowly down his face towards the side of his mouth where he demolished it with his tongue. He looked for all the world like an old hound slobbering for mercy before its master. The postmaster turned his head away. The Bugler was reinstated after a fortnight and for a while his work was exemplary. Then one day he mislaid his bag. When he reported for work the following morning he could give no account of it. He was suspended for a month at the end of which time he recovered the bag from under a bed in the house of a widow where he often spent more time than was necessary. Not a letter had she touched. All were eventually delivered and as the Bugler put it when he was once again confronted by his postmaster: 'A late letter is better than no letter at all.' For the present I'll bid you adieu and hope you come to your senses soon in respect of Miss Rosanna McDoogle.

As ever

Your oul' segocia

Mocky Fondoo

Sradbally Upper
Ballyfee

Dear Mocky

Sorry to trouble you with my burdens. I will hand this letter to the first passer-by in the hope that it reaches you before you set out on your rounds tomorrow morning. I hate asking you but I have nobody else to ask. My mother is in hospital after an operation and won't be out and about for another week at least. Would you bring the following items with you if you can fit them on the carrier; a half pound of tea, a quarter stone of sugar, a half stone of flour or three large pan loaves, two boxes of matches, a half pound of margarine and a pound or so of lean bacon. I never thought I would see the day that I'd have to beg from a friend.

I'll pay you back in a week or so when I hear from my mother.

Yours sincerely

Kitty Norris

The Ivy Cottage

Lisnacoo

Ballyfee

Dear Hamish

Steam, we are told, is the first man-made source of power and is there anything, I ask you, as incomparably efficient as the steam turbine. The first tiny turbine was invented about nineteen hundred years ago by Hero of Alexandria but I strongly suspect that steam was used as a source of power before that. We are told that as far back as two and a half thousand years before Christ the Egyptians were making good quality paper from a reed called Papyrus. Now, if they were making paper you may be sure they were writing letters and if they were writing letters they were using envelopes or, if not, some glutinous or sticky substance was being used to seal their private communications and secret dispatches. If this was the case, and there is no historical evidence to suggest otherwise, we can take it for granted, human nature being what it is, that steam was in wide use in Egypt and thereabouts so that curious people might acquaint themselves with the correspondence of their friends, neighbours and relations.

You may wonder why I open on this note. The reason my dear Hamish is that there is a return to steam as a source of power in the kitchen of Katie Kersey, the postmistress of Lisnacoo. The evidence is overwhelming. We are in the middle of a telephone strike so that all news from that source has dried up. Also when the laundry van called here a few evenings back I noticed among Katie's aprons and bibs one pair of gloves, immaculately white. The kitchen door is locked for long periods and the curtains are drawn. Finally, to set the seal in favour of my suspicions, a number of letters addressed to prominent people are bottom-flattened to such a degree that you could say with absolute certainty they were autographed by the large left buttock of Katie Kersey. Like Michelangelo or Picasso her work is unmistakable.

The trouble is that while Katie's style is instantly recognisable the standard has dropped far below those fine classical examples of her pre-telephone period. Her finished work has now become sloppy and careless. One still encounters the occasional epistle where the master buttock of the artist can be seen but these are isolated cases and, by and large, those letters which are not partly open are often only partly closed. Age has caught up with her and unless her work improves or the strike ends quickly more than her age will be catching up with her.

I don't want to see this happen so I may take steps myself if the worst comes to the worst. I happen to know that the nun is due next weekend and it could be that in her anxiety to tank up with a full complement of news Katie is rushing her work with the result that there is carelessness. At the moment there is a run of watery gum on the market or so I tell those who look with jaundiced eyes on their letters. They all know Katie's form and many have devised simple code systems to safeguard important communications. Cracking codes is child's play to a woman with Katie's cunning and experience. The harder the code the more fun she knocks out of it.

Six more weeks and I'll be a free man. It's about time after fifty years. Still my friends on the route tell me out of the goodness of their hearts no doubt, that I don't look a day over fifty. It's nice to hear it even if there's no truth in it. I understand the lads in the district office and my colleagues are to make me a presentation followed by a booze-up and buffet at the 'Lisnacoo Elms'. Dogmeat Monsell is in charge of the affair and every man, woman and child in his route knows all about it.

That's all for now my dear Hamish. Best regards to the wife. Write soon.

Mocky Fondoo

Sarsfield Mews
Upper Shoe Street
Cork

Dear Mocky,
Still single and will be for many a long year to come. You're a born pessimist that's what you are. We picked out a lovely red bikini. You could fit the lot into a small envelope. It was a tricky job but we managed in the finish. We tried several before finding the right one. What a figure this girl has. Maybe she's a bit big around the hips but what of it. I've never come across the likes of her in all my born days. 'Tis a case of no holds barred in dead earnest. Rosanna McDoogle is the fastest piece of goods since the first ray of light penetrated the darkness of the universe. I

have it all and it's costing nothing, spare-ribs, griddle bread, the works. You were right Mocky. You said she'd come up with what I like best of all and she has. Thanks for all your help and advice.

Sincerely

Frank O'Looney

PS Why was the Bugler McNulty so called? You made no reference to a bugle in your letter.

Frank

The Ivy Cottage

Lisnacoo

Ballyfee

Dear Brigid

The house isn't the same without you. Indeed life isn't the same without you. I long for the hour when you'll be back in our bed again. 'Tis a black spot, is this place since you went. The only other creature, apart from myself, who comes and goes is the cat. Other than him there is nothing and at every hand's turn there is some little thing to keep reminding me of you. I heard from Hamish MacShamus. He's back from his holiday in Malta and seems to have enjoyed himself although Lisnacoo is still his favourite haunt and he hopes to be with us next year.

There isn't a whole heap of news. Fishing is poor and we constantly ask ourselves have we seen the last of the Atlantic salmon. The river is no place for such handsome and elegant visitors in these dirty times.

The stalks of the new spuds are showing well and should be in their prime against the time you come home. I sat a half hundred of cabbage and 'tis coming strong too.

'Tis only now that you're gone I realise the full truth of the old saying that a woman's work is never done because, God knows, there is always something to do around a house and when you think you have the last job done you find the next job facing you. The post is easy work by comparison.

I have the turf cut and, please God, the pair of us will enjoy the heat and the sparkle of it across the winter. The hens are laying as good as ever, the cow milking well and the cat has a shine on him for I have him spoiled entirely.

It won't be long now and I'll be taking off this uniform forever. The post was a trade I loved from the first day I slung the mailbag across my shoulders but there comes a time to end a thing and to tell you the truth I find myself yielding a little lately so 'twill be an ease when I retire. With the help of God we'll knock many a good day out of it yet.

On the black side of it poor Gracie Goddy's husband is dead but word has it she'll marry the second man at once if she can lay hold of him.

The last of the six Cafferty girls is knocked up. The blame is with a lorry driver, they say, who used deliver carrots and onions in Lisnacoo. Others hold the guilty man to be a wisp of a fellow who plays a tin whistle with a travelling folk group. He's that small you'd wash him in a saucepan but accounts have it he's the sire of a score or more since he took to the road. Appearances are the last thing a body should go by in the judgment of a man. Look at this mote that would hardly bait a mousetrap yet by all accounts he can put the come-hither on all and sundry and leave his mark besides.

Kitty Norris's husband seems to have deserted her. That's the talk anyway.

There is trouble looming for Katie Kersey unless the telephone strike ends quickly. She is opening letters at random now but worst of all she sometimes omits to return all the pages to the envelope. Later when she finds a lost page under the table or blown by a draught of wind to the top of the dresser she forgets where it came from. Other times she reads a rake of letters at a sitting but she returns them to the wrong envelopes so that Maggie Cafferty might be in receipt of Katie Feen's letter or vice versa. Susie Dill, the Flier, might receive our parish priest's, Father Kimmerley's letter or worst of all, God between us and all harm, poor Father Kimmerley might find himself reading a red hot love letter from that pharmacist's assistant below in Cork city. 'Tis a cruel mix-up.

The complaints have started to pour into the district office. If Katie only paid more attention to the replacement of the letters and the resealing of the envelopes all would be well. People would have their suspicions but there is damn all you can do with a suspicion only be addling yourself from day to day and maybe grievously wronging innocent people.

There is little more I can think of offhand except to give my love to the children and to my grandchildren. There is no need for you to answer this or to bother with any sort of a letter or card until you're ready to come home. I'll have all things ready and will be at Shannon to greet you. Dogmeat Monsell will drive me down. That will be the happy day for me. For the present now take good care of yourself and if there is anything you want let me know and you won't be wanting it long.

Love as always
Your devoted husband
Mocky

Guess Where
Ballyfee

Poor Mocky
While the cat's away the mice will dance. What did Kitty Norris

give you in return for the messages you took her? It must be a great thrill for a fellow of your age with hardly enough ribs to cover the small of his poll. They say women get a great kick out of baldy men. The best thrill of all they say is to rub the head of a baldy man. You can feel his brains underneath and tell what he might be thinking. Ha – ha! You should have more sense Cocky Mocky at your age. Don't you know sex is bad for the hearts of the aged. What a pity if you should expire before you retire.

Guess Who?

Sradbally Lower
Ballyfee

Dear Mocky Fondoo
It must have broke your heart to hand in the parcel from the Knight of Malta last week. There was lovely books in it that my brother Dan is reading these days but no sign of the summer dresses or the suits I asked him for in my letter. I hope they don't go astray like all the other parcels that was sent to me or fall into wrong hands. If the cap fits yourself and Katie can wear it.

Nance Nolan

The Ivy Cottage
Lisnacoo
Ballyfee

Dear Frank
The Bugler McNulty as I told you was born Patrick Augustine Stanislaus McNulty. His parents died when he was a gorsoon of ten. With the remainder of his brothers and sisters he was sent to an orphanage. He escaped and worked for a farmer until he was fourteen. Then he joined the army. When he left the

army he was appointed an auxiliary postman. He was christened the Bugler not long after his second suspension. As was to be expected he behaved in a model fashion for a short period after this suspension. In his extensive route there were several major crossroads created for the most part by lesser, uncharted byways which crossed a major road at intervals. These uncharted byways might ramble into the hills for miles until they had serviced the last of the houses in the hinterland.

The Bugler let it be known after a while to those concerned that he had no notion of cycling or trudging to these out of the way dwellings so he bought a policeman's whistle in a second-hand shop in Cork. At each crossroads he would blow this whistle to let the inhabitants of the far-off cots know that the postman had arrived. But, you may ask, was there not the likelihood that the whistle would bring the inhabitants of every cot within whistle-range to the crossroads rather than just those for whom the Bugler had letters?

Quite so. In the avoidance of his duties I must hand it to the Bugler for the man was never less than brilliant. Let us suppose that there were seven houses in that area of roadway or byway stretching from the crossroads to the last house and let us suppose that he had letters for the first, third and sixth houses.

He would blow on the whistle, one long blast for number one house. Then he would pause for several seconds before blowing three blasts for number three house. Then would come another pause before letting go six blasts to notify house number six.

Alas this system worked only on fine days when the whistle blasts carried without difficulty to the ends of the roadways. However should there be a breeze the end houses could not pick up the sound. Should there be a gale not even the first house could pick up the sound. There was no option open then to the Bugler except to deposit all the letters in house number one until such time as they were called for by the inhabitants of numbers two to seven. This was all right where the owner of number one house would not steam open a letter or two to satisfy her curiosity.

Again it was a situation that could not last and the Bugler was once more suspended. Still there was no doubt that through trial and error his methods were becoming more sophisticated. After the whistle he invested in a bugle. He bought it off a man who used to play the last post over the graves of members of the old IRA. This unfortunate man had his jaw broken in a row over politics so the bugle was of no more use to him. On his first day out after his summer holidays the Bugler McNulty sounded his bugle at the first crossroads. Two hares broke from the nearby hedge and birds of all shapes and sizes burst from the bushes at either side of the road. The sound of the bugle, however, carried quite clearly to the end house despite the fact that there was a fresh wind blowing down the path of its notes. Only when a gale force wind blew was the sound of the bugle inaudible. Gales were infrequent enough and at last the Bugler McNulty was happy. His system was almost foolproof.

It lasted for several months or precisely until the week before Christmas when the Bugler, who was well and truly sotted after liberal doses of whiskey, stout and poteen began to mix his notes. In addition there was no interval between them. The drinking lasted for a week and caused no end of trouble to the hill people. Inevitably there was a complaint and Dick Cavill was sent out from the district office. He found the Bugler in an advanced state of drunkenness under a holly bush and he endeavouring with all his might to blow his horn. Naturally he was suspended but the district office was always proud of him and at union meetings throughout the country clerks and others would boast of his exploits to anyone prepared to listen. He only used the bugle in emergencies after that. So now you know why he was called the Bugler McNulty.

How is your girlfriend Rosanna? I have the distinct feeling that the time of the spare-ribs and griddle cake is coming to an end. Don't ask me how I know. I have a sixth sense about these things.

I have issued enough warnings so that the pitfalls should be quite clear to you. However I will say this. It is never too late to escape the clutches of any woman but to do this the sternest kind of resolve is needed. Put in for a transfer now before it is too late.

As ever

Mocky Fondoo

The Ivy Cottage
Lisnacoo
Ballyfee

Dear Hamish,

To be a successful postman you need the patience of Job, the sagacity of Solomon and the perception of Plato. In addition you must be prepared to hear all, see all and say nothing. It is not easy to become a postman. You must have a knowledge of Irish. Only last week an auxiliary with twenty years experience who wanted to become a full-time, pensionable postman was turned down because he could not name a single book written in Irish. Apparently he would have been appointed if he had known the name of such as *Twenty Years a-Growing* or *Jimín Mhaire Thaidg*.

Cavill the overseer was conducting the interview with a scholarly looking fellow from the head office.

'Have you any foreign language?' Cavill asked in the vain

hope that he might still manage to salvage the job for the applicant.

'I have a smattering of massage parlour Swedish sir,' our man replied.

'By the six buttocks of the three musketeers,' said Cavill slapping his thigh, 'but that's a good answer, an imaginative answer.' The man from Dublin, however, was not impressed. Apparently regulations were regulations and a knowledge of Irish was necessary.

'Say something to us in the native tongue,' Cavill begged in a last despairing effort.

'*Lá brea,*' said our friend. This is Gaelic for a 'fine day' Hamish.

'I declare to God,' said Cavill, 'but he's made an accurate observation. It is a fine day.'

'*Lá brea,*' our friend repeated himself.

'By the twelve tits of the Vestal Virgins but that's fair comment,' Cavill said. The man from Dublin shook his head indicating that the interview was over.

I myself became a postman the hard way. I passed the civil service examination at the age of fourteen after a long session of special coaching by my teachers. I spent four years as a telegram boy before I was allowed to lay hands on my first letter. I learned all the tricks for survival but I never had to use any. I was good at my job and I liked my job.

In my telegram days the Bugler McNulty was ticked off regularly for late deliveries or for arriving back at the office hours behind time. His argument was that he had too many calls when in point of fact he had too few. Always on his return he reeked with the smell of intoxicating drink. One morning he found an overseer waiting for him. This was a taciturn martinet of a fellow. The overseer was astonished at the end of the day to find that the Bugler had been telling the truth. But how had he managed to dupe this expert?

Over the preceding months he had been collecting windows – i.e. bills which had been posted by local merchants to debtors along his route. The Bugler dare not do this with normal mail but nobody wants a bill so he was quite safe. On the morning in question the overseer sprung himself upon the Bugler out of the blue. From the moment he received his bag the overseer fastened himself to the Bugler's side. The collected bills were hidden behind some wainscotting in the sorting office. The problem was how to get at them without being spotted by the overseer. As they were leaving the office the Bugler turned to one of the clerks at the counter and in a very refined accent addressed him:

'Like a good chap,' said the Bugler, 'would you mind fetching my lunch from the sorting office?'

There was a general titter at this both from the customers and the clerks. Wasn't it well known that the Bugler's sole means of sustenance was porter. The clerk, however, sensed that the Bugler was in trouble.

'Where is it?' he asked while the overseer fumed at the doorway.

'In the wall pantry,' the Bugler informed him. Then in a whisper he revealed that it was behind the wainscotting. The clerk disappeared and returned at once with the parcel. It was covered with cobwebs but the Bugler fobbed it inside his bag before the overseer could catch a glimpse of it. Outside the door the Bugler mounted his bicycle and the overseer mounted his. When they left the village the Bugler dismounted and informed the overseer that he was going behind a ditch to answer a call of nature. In a matter of minutes the bills were mixed with the normal mail. It was late that night when the pair returned.

In less than a month I'll be delivering my last letter. I don't know what I'll do apart from the fishing. The wife has sent word that she's staying in America until Christmas. The children need her. 'Tis lonely enough as it is. There is nothing else that is noteworthy. I'll close for the present. Regards to the wife.

As ever

Mocky Fondoo

PS The phone strike is still on and the longer it lasts the more precarious Katie Kersey's position becomes. The nun seldom comes now although it is widely known, in spite of their holiness, that some nuns have an insatiable appetite for news and chocolate.

Sarsfield Mews
Upper Shoe Street
Cork

Dear Mocky

How do you fight them off? There's a widow now does have a glass of hot whiskey ready for me if there's the slightest chill in the mornings. She sweetens it with sugar and flavours it with a slice of lemon and some cloves. Rosanna was never better. We had a midnight swim recently in a stream about a mile or so from her home. What a night we had racing through the rushes and pelting water on top of one another. She's the sweetest sod that was ever put into the world and there's no obligation of any kind after a night with her. What about those anonymous letters? Did they stop or did you find out the sender? Let me know all at your convenience. I have more women than I can cope with. I never believed it possible. My wildest dreams have come true and it's all due to the uniform.

Sincerely

Frank O' Looney

Sradbally Upper
Ballyfee

Dear Mocky

Please don't think I'm taking advantage of you. This is positively the last time I'll bother you. Could you bring the usual items with you and I'll fix up with you at the end of the month.
   Kitty

The Ivy Cottage
Lisnacoo
Ballyfee

Dear Frank

As the tree falls so shall it lie or if you want it another way those who live by the sword shall perish by the sword or maybe you think you're blessed with a special immunity. No man with his possessions intact who behaves as you do can escape his destiny. No doubt, however, you'll keep making hay while the sun shines. At least you'll have the memory when the storm clouds appear.

About the writer of the anonymous letters I have a happy tale to tell. We nailed him, Dogmeat Monsell and myself but we spent many a miserable night before we succeeded. No doubt you'll unknowingly deliver many an anonymous letter. You can take it from me that you'll never deliver a greater evil to the innocent persons who are at the receiving end. The chief cause underlying the writing of these dreadful epistles is jealousy. There is no other reason. The writers are consumed with it so that it becomes an illness from which there is no reprieve. Dogmeat and I suspected the same man. His name: Jonsy Josey McDill from Sradbally Lower. He lives with his mother and sells pool coupons, Sweep Tickets, et cetera for a living. What made me suspect him in the first place was a chance remark dropped by a woman of my acquaintance whose husband is in England. She is a Mrs Norris, Kitty to be more precise. Jonsy Josey chanced his arm with her several times and in the end became so amorous that she was forced to bar him from the house. I had nothing else to go on. Dogmeat Monsell on the other hand had his own way of discovering the scoundrel. When I first told him that Kitty Norris and I had been receiving anonymous letters in the taproom of the 'Lisnacoo Elms' as we were enjoying a few pints together one night he concluded immediately that Jonsy Josey McDill was the man. When I asked him for proof he said he needed none.

'He looks like a writer of anonymous letters,' said Dogmeat. 'Under that calm exterior lurks a slimy merchant. Have no doubt. He's the man.'

Dogmeat wasn't surprised when I told him of the incidents with Kitty. Suspicions, however, were of little use unless we could catch him red-handed. There was always the distinct possibility that we could be completely wrong. We had no clues at the beginning but then they began to appear and a pattern that was to solve all our problems began to emerge. The first anonymous letter which Kitty Norris received was posted the night before. On this night occurred a very severe rainstorm. The second letter received by Kitty was posted the night before as well. On that night there was a fierce gale blowing and you wouldn't put a dog out of doors. The letter I received was posted the night before and was still damp when I located it in the post office that morning. It had been raining heavily the night before. Here at last was a pointer. Whoever the writer was he or she only posted a letter upon a particularly bad night and with good reason. You won't find many people abroad on wet and stormy nights. The chances of meeting anybody are slender in the extreme. An ideal time, therefore, for dirty work.

Each wet or stormy night afterwards Dogmeat would park his van outside the post office front door. The front faced on to the roadway and the back, which was provided with a door, as close as possible to the letter box. With a dozen of stout between us and a dart of poteen now and then we would sit in the rear of the van. Any person coming or going the road would see that the vehicle was empty at first appearances. There was no way of knowing that we sat behind the front seats swigging away at our porter bottles and conversing in whispers. At the least sound from the roadway we dried up altogether and held our breaths. Then on the fourth night which happened to be squally, wet and unfit for travel we heard the sound of muffled footsteps on the roadway. As they came closer we lay flat on our backs in case our visitor should decide to peep in through the windscreen. Several times we heard the light footfalls circling the van. Then they stopped and the vital moment was at hand. My heart thumped in my breast like a drum and my breathing became so strained that I feared it must give me away. Then we heard a rustling movement as if a cape or raincoat were being loosened or tightened. Of one accord we burst through the backdoors of the van. There stood Jonsy Josey McDill with a letter in his hand.

Upon seeing us he let out a terrible screech the likes of which would remind you of nothing but the death squeal of a stuck pig. Before we could lay hands on him he took to his heels with Dogmeat and myself in hot pursuit. As he fled along the roadway he tore pieces from the letter and flung them into the air. We nailed him on the outskirts of the village just as he was about to take off across country. But for a despairing dive by Dogmeat the scoundrel might have escaped our clutches. We confiscated the remains of the letter and collected the pieces as we retraced our footsteps. In the kitchen of my own cottage we sat him near the fire and pieced the letter together. It was addressed to Kitty Norris and it contained page after page of the most heinous obscenities. He cringed and whined and trembled by the fire but neither Dogmeat nor myself could find it in our hearts to feel pity for him. He begged for mercy and explained that no door would be opened to him if word of what he had done spread throughout the countryside. He was particularly vulnerable, he explained, because of the type of work in which he was engaged. As he sat there whimpering, Dogmeat and I held a whispered council and after a while came to what we considered to be the most sensible solution. Jonsy Josey was to pay one hundred pounds forthwith to Kitty Norris. He was never again to write another anonymous letter and he was to pay a daily fifteen minutes visit to the parish church asking God's forgiveness. This was to be the price of silence until we decided to review his case again in the not-too-distant future. For good measure we assisted him to the bounds of the village with several well-aimed kicks in the arse. He handed me the money the following day and in turn I handed it over to Kitty. It was a godsend to her. The husband sends her nothing whatsoever.

I myself am of the belief that people who write anonymous letters are in need of psychiatric treatment and also perhaps they need more understanding and compassion than we are prepared to give them. However there can be no disputing the fact that it is the most foul resort to which a man can turn in order to vent his spleen on his fellow human beings. I'll say no more for now except to warn you that unless you avoid the McDoogle traphouse you will get your fingers burnt.

As ever

Your oul' segocia

Mocky Fondoo

PS Another likely way out of your predicament is to involve yourself with as many women as you can at this present time. There is safety in numbers.

   Mocky

Templebawn
Ballyfee

Dear Mister Fondoo
I hesitates ere I writes to you. There was a parcel posted to me lately by my sister Nancy in London. When I went to enquire to the head office they told me the parcel's contents was exposed and that they were destroyed according to the law. Now Mister Fondoo what would they want with confiscating fingerstalls? Fingerstalls is what is known as medical objects. There is another parcel coming soon, better wrapped with the same commodities inside and I implore of you to see that they gets delivered. My poor husband has very sore fingers as might get festered easy if not wrapped with care.

   Your sincere friend
   Catriona Cooney (Mrs)

Wangle Avenue
Off Sidberry Row
Glasgow

Dear Mocky
I have a few days leave coming up and I am at a loss to know what to do with it. The missus wants to go to London to do a spot of shopping. Then there's my brother Angus in Kilmarnock I haven't seen for years. If I go to London I'll buy you something suitable to mark your retirement. I'm sorry for Kitty Norris and

I have an idea what it must be like for her but don't you think my old friend that the answer to her problems lies in her own hands. Far be it from me to offer a man of your background and experience unwanted advice. However I feel that in view of our long friendship I have earned that right. Here in Glasgow there are thousands of Kitty Norrises. They seem to manage quite well after a while. There are state aids and other agencies to help them as I'm sure there must be in your country and I think Kitty would be well advised to get in touch without delay with one of these. The least that would happen is that there would be an easing of her financial worries. There are generous allowances for deserted wives. What I'm trying to say Mocky is that you and I, in spite of our ages, are maybe fools at heart and more susceptible than most to the plight of a lovely woman like Kitty. I am not suggesting for a moment that you are enamoured of her or have been smitten with one of those latter-day obsessions so common to fellows of our age. What I'm saying is that you might be overconcerned and as a result might become more involved than is wise. I speak from experience. Just bear in mind that there is a limit to what you can do for her, that you are restricted by other commitments. Oh dammit all Mocky my real worry is that you might make a fool of yourself. I hope I haven't said too much. A few years ago I became overprotective towards a girl in the office after her father died. I should have known better. I made a fool of myself. It's so bloody easy to make a fool of oneself when there's a young woman involved.

Write soon and let me know the details of your retirement and all the other odds and ends of news concerning Lisnacoo and Ballyfee. I'm tired out at the moment so I'll conclude.

Yours sincere friend

Hamish MacShamus

Sradbally Lower
Ballyfee

Dear Mocky Fondoo
My letter to that lovely decent man, the Knight of Malta has
been returned to me marked address unknown. They don't
know much that don't know where Malta is.
　　Nance Nolan

The Ivy Cottage
Lisnacoo
Ballyfee

Dear Bridget
I hope you're having a great time. The weather is fine here and from
everywhere these days comes the sound of mowing machines as the
meadows begin to fall in the hills and valleys. I would have written
sooner but I have been up till all hours of late and the sleep is playing
hell with me. There is the devil to pay here. The office was visited
today by the postmaster, two overseers and the local Civic Guard
who has been holding a sort of watching brief. I was questioned
closely myself until Mr Mallvey stepped in and announced that I
was above suspicion. Katey refused to answer any of the questions
put to her and pretended she knew nothing about anything. The
real cause of all the rumpus was the mixing up of two envelopes,
almost impossible to distinguish from each other because of a
similarity in size and bulk. What happened is this:
　　One of the letters was addressed to Father Kimmerley the
parish priest while the other was intended for Catriona Cooney
of Templebawn. Father Kimmerley's letter contained samples of
cardboard and plastic Saint Patrick's Day badges manufactured
by cash-strapped nuns. His Lordship the Bishop had misgivings
about the quality of the badges and because Kimmerley has a

reputation in artistic matters the bishop wanted his opinion before making any decision concerning them. The letter which was addressed to Catriona Cooney contained five plastic packets of contraceptives. By some mysterious means, well known to all who know Katie Kersey, the Saint Patrick's Day badges wound up in Catriona Cooney's envelope while the contraceptives ended in Father Kimmerley's. With the contraceptives was a short note from his Lordship:

'Let me know,' it said, 'what you think of these. If you approve I'll give the nuns a free hand in their manufacture.' With the badges was an equally short note from Catriona's sister:

'One day,' it read, 'I hope these will be for sale publicly in Ireland.'

I don't know what the eventual outcome of this wretched mix-up will be. Katie seems to be wearing up well although there is a tenseness barely visible for all her outward calm. She has no one to fall back on. The nun has made no appearance since the trouble started. No blame to her. She dare not involve herself in any sort of scandal. Katie has never been very communicative. She has always resolutely depended on herself and herself alone. Of course they really are wasting their time asking questions. The combined forces of the Gestapo and the NKVD wouldn't knock a single tittle out of Katie Kersey. I must say, however, that this is the most serious business yet.

There is no more to report except that I miss you every day and night and long more than anything else in the world to have you back home again. Not to worry too much about the children. Things will sort themselves out. Everything works itself out in due course. Give them my love and let me assure you and them that all of you are constantly in my prayers.

Your loving husband

Mocky

Templebawn
Ballyfee

Dear Mocky

I hesitates ere I writes to you. All's well as ends well as the lady said what thought she was expecting and was not. Father Kimmerley landed here. I'd have run in hide if I seen him in time. The man is a saint and 'tis well I knows his views on certain matters but he spoke out whatever. Says he what's yours is yours and what's mine is mine Catriona. We made our exchange and he bade me God bless. All's well as ends well.

Yours sincere friend
Catriona Cooney

Cahircoddle Heights
Cahircoddle Upper
Cork

Mr and Mrs Percy McDoogle
request the pleasure of the company of
Mocky and Bridget
on the occasion of the marriage of their daughter
Rosanna
to
Mr Frank O'Looney
in Saint Mary's Church, Cahircoddle
on
Friday, July 31st
at 2 o'clock
and afterwards at the reception in
The Silver Birch Hotel
Cork

RSVP

The Ivy Cottage
Lisnacoo
Ballyfee

Dear Hamish

I appreciate the sentiments expressed in your letter and take no exception whatsoever. You always had an uncanny knack of hitting the nail upon the head. Kitty Norris has gone. There's a FOR SALE on one of the windows of the house and rumour has it that she left in an attempt to rejoin Jack in England. She must have located him because I understand that the house was in their joint names. I remember the day it first dawned on her that he was two-timing. It was I who delivered the letter just a few months ago. It was written by a school friend of Kitty's to whom she had written requesting information about Jack. The friend was blunt. Jack was shacked up with a divorcee who also happened to run a boarding house. He has stopped sending money. His wife and children might have starved but for me. That's another matter altogether, however, and I don't expect any kudos for that.

I remember that letter well. I knew by the handwriting it was from a woman and the postmark told me that it was dispatched from the same postal district from which used arrive Jack's registered letters. Kitty asked me to wait while she read it. This is common enough along the route. The letter might require an immediate answer and only a churlish postman would not respond. When she finished she laid the letter on the table. Tears appeared in her eyes. It was a bitter blow. Certainly she had given Jack no cause to be unfaithful. She had, in fact, been a model wife and no one but a restless and discontented wretch would consider leaving her. She laid a hand on the table and fought to keep back the tears. I'm sure she must have asked herself why her beauty and fidelity had been so heedlessly spurned by the only man to whom she had ever given herself. A woman will never fully recover from a blow like this. The tragedy of her situation was reflected in her face. The next thing was that I found her in my arms. For a long time she sobbed out her sorrow. There was no way I could alleviate her misery except to wait until the last tear had fallen.

I held her in my arms for as long as she wanted to be held and released her the moment she wished to be released. I'll never forget the warmth of her tears on my face or the soft tender touch of her dark hair as it whispered unholy thoughts to my overworked heart. Foolish old man you will say but a man can be old and not be blind to beauty in distress. Age may do a lot of things but it does not make a man insensitive. All it can do is make him old. Now that she's gone I know how old I really am. I had come to look forward to bringing her groceries from Lisnacoo and if there were times when she hadn't the money her wants made no great inroads into my reserves.

I cannot say that what I felt for her was completely lacking in carnality but I think I can say that my own loneliness because of Bridget's absence and her undeniable beauty were factors that made my visits to her the most exciting prospects of these lonesome days.

As you said in your letter the answer to her problem was in her own hands all the time. The simple and natural solution was to follow her mate. After all she had taken him on for better or for worse and then there were the children. Not all women would go after him. I'm glad she didn't tell me beforehand that she intended leaving. It was characteristic of her to leave with the minimum of fuss. To be honest Hamish I'll miss her, not the way I miss my wife but the way I'd miss a memorable landmark such as a favourite stretch of water or the brow of a hill lighted by the red rays of a declining sun. There's more to it of course than just that. I have no doubt you understand. There is an ache for which there is no immediate cure. Enough of this foolishness. These are luxuries beyond a man of my years and on top of that the show must go on. For the present then I'll sign off. Regards to the missus. I hope you enjoy your few days off.

As ever
Your oul' segocia
Mocky Fondoo

Sarsfield Mews
Upper Shoe Street
Cork

Dear Mocky

Don't say it. Don't say I told you so. By this time you will have received the invitation from Percy and Mrs McDoogle. The uniform has turned out to be the rope that finally hung me although that's harsh because Rosanna is a fine girl and will make a splendid wife. You were right when you said I wouldn't wear out my first pair of pants before joining the ranks of the martyrs. It must be an all-time record for a postman, three months on the job and already engaged to be married.

Now I have a very special request. Could you see your way towards being my best man? There is nobody I'd rather have. You would want to let me know by return as the moment of truth is at hand. The reason for the early date is that Rosanna will be due about six months after and the McDoogles don't want to give the neighbours anything to say. I've only known her three months which may not seem like a long time but by the hokey I saw more action in that space of time than most men see in a lifetime. The baby will be a premature one to the tune of three months so suspicion is bound to be aroused. However, as you so often said yourself people only addle themselves with suspicion. I wish you luck and joy on the occasion of your retirement. You were a man I always looked up to when I was a gorsoon down there and I could see from the way the people looked at you and spoke to you that you were highly regarded in your district. You were a bit proud maybe and you often refused a good dinner when you shouldn't have but, by God, none of those people would ever dream of putting a hard word on you.

Don't delay in answering this. I can get plenty to stand up for me around here but you're the man I want whatever is in you. Rosanna sends her love and we both look forward to having you at our wedding.

Sincerely

Frank O'Looney

PS That widow I told you about who makes the hot whiskey for me keeps lodgers now and then. I'll book you in there for the night as soon as you let me know you're coming.

Frank.

The Ivy Cottage
Lisnacoo
Ballyfee

Dear Frank,

Congratulations on your engagement. Let me assure you that you have broken no records. Dogmeat Monsell delivered his first letter to a young widow by the name of Katie-Go-Down of a Tuesday morning in May close on thirty years ago and on the following Saturday the pair were spotted in the city of Limerick where they went to purchase an engagement ring. That amounts to five days. They were married the following Saturday which amounts to twelve days. Now that's a record for you. Her real name was Kate McKenna but she was nicknamed Go-Down after her father Micky-Go-Down who used the expression 'go down damn you' to chastise his dogs or to disagree with humans. They live happily Dogmeat and Katie and as soon as I retire in a week's time it is almost certain that Dogmeat's son Martin will step into my shoes. He's qualified for the job.

I'll gladly be your best man although I believe you should have asked some friend of yours nearer your own age. Still I'm honoured and flattered. Katie Kersey was carried away yesterday on the nun's instructions. Katie hasn't been herself for some time. Three days ago she was suspended from her position as postmistress after the biggest mix-up in the history of the post office. In the end nobody was receiving the right letters but believe it or not there is talk of submitting a petition to the minister to have her reinstated.

The night before she was taken away she attempted to say mass in the phone booth which stands outside the post office. She read the Gospel from the telephone directory starting at random with the word Jordanian and ending quite solemnly but quite accidentally with the phrase *Jubilate Deo* from the famous canticle of the same name. She looked like a high priestess in her long nightgown. It transpired later from what could be made of her sermon that she was praying for forgiveness for the souls of Lisnacoo and Ballyfee. In the middle of the ceremony Father Kimmerley arrived and led her indoors quietly. Doctor Mongie was summoned and she was put under sedation. I understand she's quite happy in her place of confinement. She spends the day reading invisible letters and seems to knock great enjoyment out of it. You might say she's chewing the cud. Dick Cavill has taken over the running of the post office until somebody new is appointed.

'By the twenty breast nipples of Niall and the Nine Hostages,' said he, 'but this is the greatest mess since Moses came down from the mountain.'

There's little else of interest. In view of the fact that the wife is in the States I presume it will be all right if I bring Dogmeat Monsell along to the wedding. He has a car and in addition he might be a better candidate for your widow's favours. See you soon then.

As ever
Your oul' segocia
Mocky Fondoo

The Ivy Cottage
Lisnacoo

My dear Bridget
Well it has happened at last although I can still feel the strap of the bag across my shoulders. The Bugler McNulty once told me that it never really goes away. As I write this the hammers of hell are pounding in my head. When I handed in my bag for the last time last evening Dick Cavill suggested we make for the 'Lisnacoo Elms' for a farewell drink and to discuss arrangements for the presentation and dinner which is to be held on my behalf later in the year in some hotel in town. We went into the back lounge where a huge bright bouquet of summer blooms greeted us from the open hearth. Dick called for two whiskies and while we sat there reminiscing I felt a great loneliness inside me. The tears came to my eyes. I think Dick understood for he placed a hand upon my shoulder and said in a low voice: 'Fifty years is a long time. By the eight kidneys of the Four Horsemen of

the Apocalypse,' said he, 'but it's a long time old son.'

Then one by one all the gang started to drift in until soon every postman in the district was present. The postmaster came and so did the clerks and soon the beer flowed. At the height of our sing-song the door opened and who should appear in his tweeds and old grey beard but Hamish MacShamus. Very soon he was as drunk as the rest of us and we lifted the roof with the chorus of 'Loch Lomond'. I do not remember going home to the cottage. All I remember is being awakened an hour ago by Hamish who handed me a mug of tea and informed me that the water in the river was dropping fast and it would be fit for fishing in less than two hours. It's a strange feeling that's on me since I woke. I doubt if I'll ever really get used to it. There's a guilt in me that shouldn't be there and it's as if the people I served for so long were beckoning me to get on with the job. Even if I wanted I can't do that now.

There were many other well-wishers who sent cards and letters and the letters weren't without their tokens of appreciation. There was also a parcel which contained one of the loveliest fishing spools I ever saw. The sender was anonymous, somebody in England. It could be one of a thousand. I won't tell you how much I miss you but it will be a long summer and a longer autumn without you. For a while then my love I'll bid you adieu.

Your loving husband

Mocky

LETTERS TO THE BRAIN

INTRODUCTION

Because I am the central point of the body it is fitting that I should be the one to write this introduction.

To some I may appear to be no more than a very ordinary depression in the middle of the abdomen but this is the whole point. The abdomen is the recognised centre of the anatomy and I am the centre of the abdomen. Therefore, I am the very core, the kernel, the centre of the centre. Let no one dispute my entitlement to authorship of the foreword.

In the matter of selecting the contributors for this long-overdue series of invocations I willingly leave myself open to criticism.

Let me say at once that this is purely a personal choice. I am certain that if the liver, the kidneys, the bladder or even the eyebrows, none of which are included here, were to nominate the contributors the selection would bear little resemblance to mine. This is to be expected; no two aspects of the body's organs are alike in either taste or temperament so that the last thing that should be expected of us is unanimity.

Nevertheless I have striven to be impartial and unprejudiced in so far as it is possible for any appurtenance of the human body to be. The reader will be familiar with other anthologies, treasuries and compendiums and will, no doubt, concur when I submit that any selection no matter how honestly or how painstakingly chosen is but a reflection of the anthologist's own personal philosophies, attitudes and convictions. This is not to proffer an apology for this selection; rather it is a justification.

Some of my fastidious readers will ask why the rear aperture? To this I say, why not? If this seems to be too simplistic an answer let me add that I personally find the area in question to be one of the less edifying regions of the body which I have the honour to represent as navel-in-residence but I did not allow my personal squeamishness to militate against such a selection. I gave this particular choice a great deal of thought before I eventually decided in its favour.

The rear aperture, I told myself, is not my kettle of fish but the rear aperture, more than any other area of the body, has something to say and whether I like or dislike the tone, content or flavour of its pronouncements the rear aperture has a right to be heard if only for the reason that what it has to say must perforce be vastly different from anything else we are likely to hear in the many splendid contributions which I have solicited over so long a period. I often, in fact, despaired of ever bringing my daunting task to a finish.

Others will ask, why not the breast nipples? They are perfectly entitled to ask and I will endeavour to answer to the best of my ability. The breast nipples are near neighbours of mine and it must seem somewhat churlish to the gentle reader that I deliberately overlooked them when I was in the process of dispatching invitations to the selected organs and others.

Indeed the breast nipples are unobtrusive and yet sensitive. Together, in fact, we form an isosceles triangle and you cannot get much closer than that.

Other organs and aspects have offered themselves as contributors from the moment it became known that I had this undertaking in mind. Politely but firmly I declined every offer except those I had already chosen without reference to any authority save my own.

One of the great difficulties in compiling a work of this kind is having to reject a contribution which has been commissioned in good faith. Thanks to all the powers that be there was only one instance of this. I must confess that when I first invited the eyelashes to submit a contribution of roughly 1,500 words I had some misgivings. I had already accepted an important address from the hairs of the head and *began to think that perhaps my readers might be put off by a surfeit of hairs. Add to this the fact that I was shamelessly importuned by the hairs which grow between myself and the nether quarters to consider a rambling exposé which they maintain would truly titillate the reader. Naturally I declined the offer. The contribution from the eyelashes exceeded in length all the other contributions put together although this was not the sole reason why the opus was returned to its author. In short it was downright boring and reeking with distasteful vanity. From its contents one would be forced to conclude that but for the input of the eyelashes there would be a total breakdown of the body's other components. I returned the bulky manuscript and suggested to its author that it should be published as a separate volume.*

There are, I most willingly concede, many other worthy claimants for inclusion. There is the blood, the very stream of life, the saliva which plays a most important role and the lungs whose contribution cannot be measured. On the liquid side once more there is the urine, the perspiration, the tears et cetera, all worthy of inclusion but perhaps at this juncture I should emphatically stress that this is not a medical journal; rather it is a somewhat whimsical and often jaundiced series of onslaughts on the brain.

Another difficulty arose as I drew up the list of proposed contributors and this was, for me personally, the most serious dilemma of all. Should I, the navel, make a contribution or to put it another way was I, the navel, deserving of making a contribution. I might have consulted with others but in the last analysis I felt that the decision should be mine and mine alone. After a great deal of thought I decided against. In the first place my location has placed me next door to the epicentre of certain activities which would be more appropriate to the pages of a Sunday tabloid than the foreword of a book which may well appear in reputable bookshops and public libraries.

I live in the hope that some of the organs or aspects which I have chosen for my selection will one day compile anthologies of their own and honour me beyond words by inviting me to contribute to theirs. I realise that I may have unwittingly omitted some who deserve to be included but I have diligently and ruthlessly scoured the anatomy and its invisible extensions lest I perpetrate an injustice against a deserving case.

Many may wonder why I could not find room for the backbone. The answer is that symbolically the backbone is fairly represented in the following pages. Another thing about bones is that they are associated with skeletons rather than living persons and Tom Scam, who is the personification of my brain, is a living person whose bones are still concealed by his all too mortal flesh. Finally, were I to include the backbone, there would be an avalanche of claims from other bones. In short, there are just too many bones.

Others will wonder why no muscle has been considered and this despite the fact that there are thirty score muscles in the body. My answer is, which muscle do you pick? Rather than offend the hard-working, industrious five hundred and ninety nine, I decided to choose no muscle at all.

The eyebrows I deliberately omitted because all eyebrows are cynics. It isn't that I dislike cynics but the eyebrows are the least articulate. All they can do is arch themselves.

Some may say that in writing this introduction I have deliberately masterminded a navel contribution. This is not so because I have not addressed myself to the brain as have the other contributors. What I have tried to do is to bring about a better understanding of the body's constituents and in addressing one brain I hope that the contributors will, as a consequence, succeed in addressing all brains and improve the general coordination without which the body must fail to function properly.

I think the book has succeeded in achieving what it set out to do in the first place which was to alert the brain of one man to the fast-developing crisis in his body. I hereby extend my heartiest thanks to *the contributors and wish them continuing success in their various undertakings.*

The Navel

THE STOMACH WRITES

Dear Brain

I am your best friend. Never once have I broken faith. I came into the world a normal healthy, hard-working maw and have survived until now without the slightest sign of ulcerous infiltration.

I have, for your pleasure and relief, calefacted 10,000 farts, no two of which have ever been exactly alike in volume or tone. I regard this as my greatest achievement. I have sent out into the world a selection varying from the sublime to the ridiculous, from the twittering to the grating, from the hushed to the explosive. Often strident and harsh they have shocked and stunned the sensitive listener. Other times they assumed pitches lyrical and haunting which no musical instrument could emulate.

These sounds are sometimes mistakenly taken for revelations or confessions of the posterus whereas, in point of fact, they are, as the street artist frequently proclaims, all my own work. It is I who creates. The posterus merely releases.

From my strife and turmoil come unmistakable expressions of joy and discontent, of anguish and elation. How wise was he who stated that there can be no great art without suffering and, certainly, you have made me suffer my share. Would that you had eaten like a normal man. I might have enjoyed a normal life but no! You always over-indulged. You could not and would not settle for your normal share. In the end I was obliged to come to the conclusion that true felicity is to be found only in starvation.

From that fateful moment when you first licked your young lips after being introduced to O'Shonnessy's sparkling cider I was to be flooded and overtaxed beyond my utmost capacity. There were times when, quite honestly, I thought I must surely burst.

Often you were forced into opening a second front. You were obliged to call the gullet into play during long periods of eructation.

How well I remember once after trying for hours to digest a massive intake of boiled turnips and gammon I gave up the unequal struggle and allowed nature to take its course. I recall it was at a residents' association meeting, a heated one if ever there was one, having to do with the manner of resistance which might be adopted to prevent the cutting of some dangerous and decaying trees in the vicinity.

Everybody had spoken but you. You sat stupidly in your chair unable to whisper much less to vociferate. Is anything more eagerly awaited, I ask you, than the utterance of a man who has kept his mouth shut whilst around him others are pontificating. There was silence as the chairman asked if you would like to make a contribution. It was the gammon and turnips, however, which did your speaking for you. They erupted into one of the loudest and most vulgar belches I was ever forced to initiate. The effect was the same as if there had been an unexpected clap of thunder. One anxious lady fled in terror from the chamber. The other females remained glued to their chairs fearfully awaiting a second eructation. The chairman, not fully aware of what had caused the explosion, made the sign of the cross and in a strangulated but solemn whisper entreated the immediate succour of the Three Divine Persons whilst others appealed to the Blessed Virgin not to desert them in their hour of tribulation.

When the initial shock had been absorbed you did the only

decent thing possible under the circumstances. You rose, excused yourself and made your apologies to the chairman before exiting with a hand over your mouth lest a second explosion rock the building to its very foundations. You were never asked to speak thereafter.

Had you not come from healthy stock you would be feeding worms this long while. Fortunately for you, you were always possessed of a stomach which was capable, as your mother once boasted, of digesting an anvil.

On another occasion, after you had returned home with your wife from a dinner dance, one of your neighbours claimed he was unexpectedly awakened from deep sleep. He had left the dance earlier like the sensible man of moderation that he was and was sleeping the sleep of the just when his slumber was disrupted. Granted the same fellow tends to exaggerate but he positively swears that during dinner he saw you eating sufficient mashed potatoes and onions to keep a small army on the march for several days. According to the neighbour you left the kitchen where your wife was preparing some tea and took yourself to an outhouse. Here you were heard to belch so outrageously that the corrugated iron roof of the outhouse was lifted several inches into the air in a veritable haboob of dust before settling once more on its supports. It was then that I was paid a belated but much-prized compliment:

'That man,' said the neighbour, 'has a stomach like a boa constrictor.'

Alas and alack I am at this time so grievously overworked that I would not be surprised if a duodenal ulcer was forming in the uproar of my digestion. It is truly a miracle that I have survived so long without succumbing to a cancerous tumour or to one of the other evil visitations to which all stomachs are subject.

If one of your more comprehensive belches could be fully analysed by a computer my story would be heard at last and you might come to your senses. If some sort of machine could be devised into which you might belch several times in the round of a day, and if a spoken interpretation could be forthcoming, I would a tale unfold that would bring tears from a hardboiled egg.

Please to remember during your more complacent moments that I have been rumbling a long time now. Soon, all too soon, the lava will come spurting from your mouth and I shall be emptied forever. Yet, for all my rumbling and grumbling, my puling and my puking, my external naval area is the most presentable part of the entire anatomy. Even females who are averse to nude masculinity will reluctantly concede that the male belly is less obnoxious and more bearable than the buttocks, for instance, or the back or the chest or the callops, or indeed what have you! Let us, however, leave my outside to those who would have truck with it and let us return to the interior from which much is to be learned if one is prepared to listen. Listen to me my son and I will keep you healthy. The burp and the belch and all the revelations of the posterior, lisping or loud, must be given ear. These are my true sentiments and they contain much that will lengthen your days. I am the soul of patience. You have been stuffing me with impossible burdens of food and drink for the best part of a lifetime. By all the powers that be I should be out of commission long ago. I should have been supplemented, of course, by a second stomach or, at the very least, should have been rested for long periods. I never was, and this raises the question: how long more can I continue as I am? This is entirely up to you and, fortunately, it is not yet too late. Moderation will do both of us the world of good but moderation was never for you. You regarded moderation as a mortal enemy. You are a man who demolished two mature lobsters and a bottle of potstill whiskey for his forty-ninth birthday. In my youth I would have regarded such a monumental intake before bedtime as a mere repast, a challenge to my digestive juices, but nowadays I am put to the pin of my collar to cope with paté and toast.

I remember once aboard a train as you returned with a party of other drunkards from a rugby game the barman announced that all the bottled stout had been consumed. You resorted, as did your friends, to whiskey. Seated across the aisle was a mild-mannered book-immersed gorsoon whose mother dozed fitfully close by. As the whiskey mingled with a dozen or more bottles of stout and, of course, the prime fillet steak, the French fries, the onions and the mushrooms and the gases remaining from the morning's gin and tonics, there began a series of mild burps which gradually blossomed into boisterous belches.

I recall how I rumbled gently as the raw whiskey made you hold your breath before searing its way downwards into my crammed interior. There came from me, unsolicited by you, first a snarl followed by a whine, and then a succession of minor, almost inaudible rumbles. It was my way of intimating to you that enough was enough, that I needed to be rested. You persisted, however, and as though to keep me in my place threw back a glass of undiluted whiskey as if it were a spoonful of lukewarm soup. It was then that I held forth as I never held forth before. First came an inharmonious, low-key cacophony which increased in volume until all the passengers in the seats contiguous to yours lifted their heads in fear, most notably the gorsoon who sat across the way. Not knowing where the sound came from his face registered considerable alarm. When I attained a crescendo of baying and howling the alarm was quickly replaced by fear and then abject terror. He leaped from his seat and sought refuge in his mother's arms. She, poor creature, disturbed from her unquiet dreams, bestowed upon him the absolute comfort of her arms as he called out to all within earshot that there were lions and tigers in the carriage.

You were obliged to beat a hasty retreat to the toilet where my rumblings eventually subsided. When you returned some time later your neighbours, drunken companions apart, had taken themselves well out of earshot and occupied some vacant seats at the far end of the carriage. It was not the first time you were responsible for an evacuation of this nature.

There was the occasion of the excursion and I think you will agree that this is the one incident of all the incidents in your life that you would most like to forget. At the time you were a mere eighteen and it was with considerable reluctance that you accompanied your mother who expressed a desire to spend a summer's day beside the sea. She prepared a lunch of chicken and salad which subsequently proved to be highly palatable as well as being extremely beneficial and easily digested. As soon as the lunch was consumed some elderly friends of your mother's happened along the beach. You excused yourself and informed her that you would like to have a swim and take in the amusements of the resort before returning to take her to the station. As a result it was not you but the contents of yours truly which were obliged to swim. These contents included the delectable salad so lovingly prepared by your mother, a large bag of periwinkles, a double portion of fish and chips before you started drinking and a second smaller portion when you felt peckish after you had drunk your fill.

At the time you were still a long way from graduation to beer and stout but you were a comparatively old hand as a dabbler in O'Shonnessy's sparkling cider, a beverage which you had been flooring successfully if excessively since your fifteenth birthday.

Now in your eighteenth year you were to indulge to an unprecedented degree in what the manufacturers euphemistically labelled 'the produce of the home orchard, pressed out of mature and luscious fruit'.

On the return journey you deposited your mother near the window in the front seat of the carriage directly behind the engine which was as far removed as possible from the carriage you had terrorised on the outgoing journey. You need not have bothered for the good reason that your victims had observed you as you entered the station and shrewdly waited for you to deposit yourself before availing of a carriage at the other end of the train.

Experience, like history, is a net from which it is difficult to extricate oneself but those homebound travellers should have learned from my rumblings and grumblings on the outward journey and should have extricated themselves at once from where they found themselves and awaited the arrival of the next transport.

All went well during the first few miles but then your brimming bladder began to expostulate and you relieved yourself in the toilet. It was here that you made the *faux pas* which was responsible for the disaster that followed. You had, in the tavern, out of sheer bravado, purchased a baby bottle of Jamaica rum which you concealed in your trouser pocket to relieve, as you told yourself with a smirk, the rigours of the return journey.

How wise was he who said that you cannot put an old head on young shoulders. Unscrewing the cap you swallowed the entire contents of the baby rum. Such was the impact of this fresh intake that you found yourself panting for air.

But for a succession of breaths, long and deep, I would never have been able to retain that powerful Caribbean potion. Shaking your head and swallowing hard you drew yourself erect into a semblance of sobriety. The toilet, it transpired, was situated at the very end of that very last carriage and who should be seated in the seat outside but the same gorsoon you had routed on the rugby train. He made at once for his mother's lap, the naked fear rampant in his eyes. In the seats close by sat several other passengers, all alarmed, forewarned by the quaking boy and his anguished mother. Now, fully alerted to your presence, they sat rigidly upright in their seats.

For a moment you stood apologetically surveying them. You noted the pretty white frocks of the two genteel sisters in their early twenties and were hurt when they frowned upon seeing you. There was an elderly parson and his wife, a frail creature dressed in a leopardskin swagger of indeterminate age and a red bonnet weighted down by an assortment of multicoloured wax fruits. Finally there was a trio of nuns, hooded and veiled with beads in their hands as they silently recited the evening prayers.

As you stood uncertainly, unable to make up your mind whether you would be capable or not of maintaining your balance, you were suddenly suffocated by a feeling of nausea. Then came the upheaval prompted by the earlier and injudicious intake of the Jamaican rum. A torrent of cider issued in wanton abandon from your open mouth. In it was the undigested flotsam of periwinkles, chips, fish, chicken, salad and every other particle in my beleaguered depths. It would be the vastest and most drenching vomit you would ever make and I say this knowing you to be a veteran of a thousand upheavals. What an ecumenical puke it was! It equally drenched the Roman Catholic nuns and the Church of Ireland parson as well as his horrified wife. The end of the stream which contained the majority of the undigested French fries and all of the barely chewed fish was distributed evenly over the mother and son and the pretty white dresses of the mortified sisters.

Still spewing the remains of the record-breaking retch you lurched forward without as much as a word of apology leaving in your wake a vomit-covered and utterly shattered company of innocents who between them, the clergyman apart, had never consumed as much as a solitary pale sherry in their entire lives. They sat now reeking in unfamiliar filth, too stunned to utter the slightest protest. The clergyman was the only person to pass comment. Imagine my surprise to hear a man of the cloth suggest that it was I, the stomach, which was to blame for the entire catastrophe. Said he in a voice shaking with disdain:

'The scoundrel can't stomach his liquor!'

To associate me with the appalling misbehaviour of my proprietor was an injustice of the greatest magnitude and to think that it came from the mouth of a uniformed Christian. It was you, the Brain, who was totally responsible and it was you, you craven coward, who slyly departed the scene when the damage was done.

The fact that I have survived intact to this day is ample testimony to my mettle. I am, however, prepared to forget the past. There is little profit in remembering ancient wrongs although I can never quite erase the sight of those genteel people endeavouring to clean themselves as you sneaked drunkenly to the leading carriage.

The tragedy was compounded by the fact that they had believed themselves to be safe. I believe that Robbie Burns created the most truthful and profound stanza of all time when he leaned on his plough to address himself to the mouse who habitation he had unwittingly destroyed:

The best laid schemes of mice and men
Gang aft a-gley
And leave us nought but grief and pain
For promised joy.

How blissfully they sat before you were called to the toilet, and then in a trice how shattered! I could recall for you other indiscretions but the excursion puke as I would like to call it is sufficient for our purpose. It is now high time you came to your senses.

Look then to my upkeep and maintenance and spare me henceforth from the indigestible and the unpalatable. I will reward you well for it is true to say that when I fail you everything else will fail you as a matter of course. Remember this when next you tax me. I cannot go on forever; time to wind me down, to give me the rest I so richly deserve or I will growl you out of your appetite and groan you into an early grave.

Sincerely

Your Stomach

The Posterior Writes

Dear Brain

What a shapely and ornamental article I was in my heyday! How rotund and fulsome, how firm yet buoyant, how curvaceous yet slender! Oh how eminently pattable was I, how kneadable, how caressable! How trim! I was as shapely a backside as ever adorned the end of a trunk, as ever overlooked a thigh or collop, as ever saucily sported itself before the eye of misfortune!

How I scorn the term buttocks; they remind me of so much dead meat.

They have labelled me bum, bottom, backside, arse, croup, rump and coccyx but what care I! I am what I am, a simple posterior designed to enforce the rut, to break the fall, to suffer the kick, to steady the scrum, to sit on the fence, to press the case, to soften the shock, to bear the brunt.

I have been threatened with more kicks and, perversely, invited more kisses than any other part of the anatomy. Alas, I have received too many of the former and none of the latter. I doubt if it will ever be resolved whether posteriors were just made to be kicked or whether the brain draws the kicks upon us. It's like trying to decide which was there first, the hen or the egg, the whore or the pimp. I have watched silently as our own feet, left and right, aimed themselves after a retreating posterior whose owner had been aggressive or insulting. Similarly I have seen you kick a bending figure on the rear end for no reason at all. I heard you justify your actions afterwards by suggesting that as surely as stones were made to be flung so were arses made to be kicked; your very own words my dear lord and master.

Unlike Gaul I am only divided into two parts. Yet there exists no partition for we are really one. Can you imagine a posterior with only one cheek? Could anything be more ridiculous? I remember the first kick which ever jolted me into the harsh realities of coexistence. You were but a ten-year-old whilst the man who kicked me was eighty. Much as I resented that kick it was, I felt, richly deserved. You had callously taken the life of one of his three ducks, the remnants of a once populous clutch which he had vainly hoped would provide him with eggs for his daily needs. The stone which you flung would not normally arrive within an ass's roar of the target but on this tragic occasion the duck was smitten on the very top of its head. Death was instantaneous. You were caught in the act and the old man implanted a kick which you were to feel for several weeks afterwards. That was the first of many. Kicks, however, I could accept but not permanent disfiguration which was to be my lot when you reneged on your fees in a seedy massage parlour. Before you had time to draw on your trousers the madame, quick as a flash, inscribed the sign of the cross with a razor blade on my left cheek where the mark remains to this day as a caution to masseuses everywhere that they were not to be duped by your innocent face but were to demand their fees in advance.

Some months later as your mother handed you a towel in the bathroom she could not help but notice the transverse lacerations which dominated my left cheek. Shocked beyond words she demanded an explanation. Hastily wrapping the towel around me, thereby concealing the crude disfiguration, you explained without batting an eyelid that it was part of an initiation ceremony. Inveterate liar that you were you convinced the poor woman that you were now, as a result of the sacred inscription, a member fully-fledged of a society devoted to the propagation of the Catholic faith, a society which expressly forbade its members to wear their hearts on their sleeves but rather wished them to pursue their vocations secretly and discreetly. You brought tears to the poor woman's eyes when you explained that the reward for such unselfish devotion would come not in this life but in the next. She never doubted you and you salved your conscience by convincing yourself that you wished to spare her the seamier side of your more mundane activities.

As the years rolled by and your paunch began to protrude so did I begin to obtrude in the opposite direction until the specially tailored slacks and trousers which fitted your once lithe figure so admirably had to be disposed of for good to be substituted by the baggy britches which are anathema to females. Drink was the chief reason for my expansion. You might have held the obesity at bay had you moderated your intake and indulged in jogging or even walking, although my innate honesty compels me to recount an isolated occasion when you ran several hundred yards without stopping until your goal was attained.

You had dined well, as I remember, but then there was never an occasion when you did not dine well. On the evening in question, while the stomach laboured incessantly to digest the beef, the pudding, the potatoes, the assorted vegetables, the gravy, the sweet and the cheese, you fell into a deep slumber in front of the sitting room fire. Around you sat your loving family, your well-preserved, pseudo-aristocratic wife and charming daughters. Your snoring soon dominated all the other sounds of the room. After a while the snores grew fitful and uneven. Your wife, believing you to be the victim of a nightmare, called into your ear that there was no need for alarm. When you spluttered into wakefulness she repeated the assurance.

'No need for alarm!' you echoed in consternation as you noted the hands of the mantelpiece clock. The time was twenty minutes to eleven which was the precise and blessed hour the taverns closed their doors for the night. You leaped from the armchair like a scalded cat and without donning hat or overcoat dashed out of doors and ran through the streets like a man demented until you reached the nearest pub.

If I were ever asked to nominate that part of your body which was subjected to the most exercise I would, without hesitation, declare wholeheartedly for your right elbow although that same elbow has added, you might say, to my dimensions more than anything. I recall a particular night when the circumference was extended by a full inch, most of which accrued to me. You drank several pints of beer, retired to a hotel where you ordered a mixed grill which contained all the orthodox constituents from chop to liver, but which in this instance was enriched by several medallions of black and white pudding. You salivated and snorted like a starving hyena. The proprietor of the hotel was so taken by your appreciation that he added several further medallions of the puddings in question. Alas, because of their saline contents you consumed another half gallon of beer.

I just cannot forgive you for repeatedly indulging yourself in such a gluttonous fashion. You have made me ungainly and obese. Bad as this is the worst of all is that nobody cherishes me. You have never uttered a single word in praise of me or a word in my defence. There are no poems or songs about me or my equals. The only praise I ever received was when I accidentally came in the way of a kick at goal during a football game. Somebody shouted from the sideline, 'Good arse!' Beyond that nobody ever singled me out for approbation. I have no dignity. It's been eroded over the years by your failure to keep me in shape. I once had innate dignity and when innate dignity is eroded there is no substitute. Acquired dignity is less sensitive.

I am often mildly irked by the veneration which is accorded to my female counterpart - it seems to be an object of immeasurable esteem as well as being a powerful source of titillation and infatuation. Men are frequently quite carried away by moderately attractive female posteriors and just as you slobber over your food so do the lecher and the philanderer slobber over the curvaceous sit-me-down of the graceful female. In fact I recall on occasion after you had emerged one morning from a newsagent's in the metropolis, you were so attracted by the pair of bouncing female buttocks in front of you that you followed their proprietress blindly for over a mile until she disappeared through a doorway. Granted the female posterior is smooth as silk, eminently hand-cuppable and more capable of exciting the male onlooker than any other aspect of the female make-up. There is simply nothing to compete with it. Woe is poor me by comparison. Many a worshipful devotee will tell you that of all the world's vistas the female fundament is the most surpassing whereas even the most chaste will not deny that, in all its unclad glory, it is the most intoxicating of prospects. But enough! I digress too much.

I have, for too long, succumbed to base matters. How can one be analogical when one descends to the very bottom! Despite my lowly position, however, I must not despair. I cannot draw myself up nor can I alter my situation. Yet I am strangely content. I do what is required of me and I believe I do it well. Little is seen of me and maybe that is just as well. All exposure has ever done for me has been to bring ridicule down upon me. I can still hear the derisive whoops from the day the seam of your trousers burst when you stopped to tie your shoelace as you searched for a Christmas turkey in the market place. You slunk home with your inadequate hands vainly trying to cover the exposed area which was the title bestowed upon me by your kind-hearted mother. I am, I must painfully conclude, an object of derision. I do not deserve to be, hairy though my lineaments may be and coarse my features, with a central situation which does little to enhance my overall appearance. If I were permitted to choose my epitaph it would read as follows:

Faithful down below he performed his duty.
No posterior deserved more to be raised aloft.

If I could leave my impression, my mark as it were, upon this paper I would be proud to do so, so that maybe one day a discerning soul might read my lines as the clairvoyant reads the palm and tell the world of the vilification to which I have been subjected and declare the true warmth, the true loveliness that I exude. If posteriors have a dream then mine would be to hold myself up to a mirror and ask:

Mirror, mirror on the wall,
Who is the fairest of us all?

To which the mirror would instantly reply:

Thou art, oh arse!

Remember, dear brain, that dreams sometimes come true. All you have to do is address yourself to moderation and unremitting exercise and I might be transformed into a posterior trim and shapely, which might be exhibited in public as a shining example of my kind.

Sincerely

Your Posterior

THE LIPS WRITE

Dear Brain

There was a milkman, a curly-haired, chubby-faced fellow who might, to the casual onlooker, have seemed twenty when he must really have been sixty at least. He was that kind of person. Age, it would seem, made little impression upon him. Your father had known him for years, or so he used to say, which means the man might have been eighty. His fountain of youth was his whistling. First thing in the morning, after the cocks had crowed and the last of the rooks had flown, his exhilarating serenading could be heard as he cycled upon his round.

What a happy man he must have been! He never whistled a drab melody. He excelled at the stirring march and he would empty his heart to nurture the sweet chords of love which he warbled, free of charge, morning after morning for all and sundry.

Dour veterans of the marital confrontation relented and turned in their beds to celebrate sweet sessions of amorous rapture and all because of this incidental input. The morning was transformed into a backdrop for his princely rendition. He contributed more to the rescue of foundering marriages than any human intermediary could ever hope to, and not unwittingly, I might add.

It often seemed to us lips that he was transported here from some heavenly sphere for no other purpose than the upraising of downcast hearts. How I secretly yearned that you, one day, would purse us into an instrument which would fritter away depressions and upraise the human spirit to its loftiest pinnacles!

Surely the pipings of that dear departed milkman had their roots in his immortal soul and yet it was the orifice of the contracting lips that modulated and measured the bewitching torrent of empyreal sonority which charmed and delighted all those fortunate enough to be within earshot. We, too, might have attained to such fluency had you but persevered after your early failures. There wasn't a child in the street who did not try to emulate that milk-carrying maestro.

We remember once of an icy morning how he fell from his rickety bicycle, spilling the contents of both his pails and breaking two front teeth into the bargain. Poor fellow, his lips were brutally lacerated. The tears formed in his eyes as the white streams of freshly-drawn milk coursed irredeemably towards the nearest channel, but how quickly he transformed misfortune into triumph.

Supporting himself on his right knee and placing his left hand over his breast he pursed his shattered lips, oblivious to the agonising pain. Then, extending his right hand to his invisible public, he gave the performance of his life. That redition of 'At the Balalaika' was the performance for which he would always be remembered. Not even the combined efforts of Nelson Eddy and Ilona Massey in their illustrious heydays succeeded in wringing such total ecstasy from this immortal lovesong. Long before he finished, the underemployed lips of that once dreary street were never so utilised in pursuit of loving fulfilment, and to think that it was a simple pair of mutilated lips which created the mouthpiece through which this masterpiece was delivered. For the listening lovers in the silent houses it was a never-to-be-forgotten experience. Some had never even dreamed of aspiring to such unprecedented ecstasies. Remember, their moment came only after years of waiting. If the world and its people could only wait long enough everybody would, eventually, be kissed by someone, be loved by someone.

However, we lips were not designed for whistling alone. On a more realistic level we accurately direct the airflow that cools the steaming soup, the scalding tea, the gum-blistering stew. Alternatively, we warm the freezing fingers with the comforting breath, but it is at kissing that we excel.

Kissing can be a precarious business, as many a rueful participant will verify. We were designed to kiss and we are capable of producing a true multiformity of kisses. Our kisses may be blown and wafted from our pouting embouchure by the eyes or by the hands, but the imposition of lip upon lip conceals more hazards than thin ice on a bottomless lake.

Lips love to kiss but we also kiss to love and this must never be forgotten by those who would recklessly disburse kisses at every hand's turn. 'A kiss on the brow for the dead we loved,' your late and pious father used to say. 'A kiss on the cheek for a friend but a kiss on the lips,' quoth he, 'is the most imponderable of all propositions and should never be undertaken lightly, especially by those who foolishly presume they are fully aware of the dangers involved.'

In its own time and in its own place and in conditions blessed by love the kiss will melt the icicles of frigidity and replace the pinched cheek with the amorous suffusion. Of all the earth's moistures there is none so delicate as that of the lips nor can the subtlest velvet match their smoothness of texture. When poised to kiss there are no dewier petals on land or sea.

We, your very own lips, are ambassadors from the court of true love and deserve the respect and deference which are the dues of all accredited envoys. Sully us not by debasement or defilement and do not ever shape us for the spit of ridicule, foulest of all human ejaculations; neither pout us for the contemptuous grin but be aloof and restrained so that we may buttress your dignity and beautify your wrinkling face.

Be not an imitator of posterior windbreaking but whistle cheerfully in the dark for the benefit of those who may be affrighted. We have served you well and will continue to serve but we are a sensitive pair and would remain pursed rather than be party to grins and grimaces which may hurt another.

You have, alas, imposed us on the lips of females we would rather have shunned and disgraced us by not imposing the gentlest and sweetest of kisses upon the fair face and virgin lips of the lovely Lily Lieloly. Still and for all we are prepared to light for you the golden lamp of love, preserving its mellow glow through all your days and nights and trimming it to last your fretful pace till the final Amen is murmured!

In your lifetime, dear brain, you have kissed far and wide. Be thankful for your share and pity the lips starved of kisses. How goes it in the ancient ballad:

'Tis I my love sits on your grave,
And will not let you sleep
For I crave one kiss of your cold, cold lips
And that is all I seek.

Yes indeed; that is all he sought, poor fellow, and you who are blessed with a living wife and who knows not the pain of loss may kiss when you choose and yet would kiss elsewhere and put your lips for auction to the first bidder. You remind me of the improvident mule who vacates a barely nibbled pasture for the promise of sweeter clover behind the next hill, but then, in matters hymeneal, you could never see the wood for the trees. Would you had piped sweetly but once in your lifetime rather than the chirpings cheap and lewd wasted upon the passing lass. Unmusical and unromantic crow, you never turned a solitary female head whereas the true whistler serenading from his soul wooed the delicate ear and won the most precious heart. We, your lips, are God-given and whether we pout, whistle or kiss, we remain yours to do with as you will, but we would beseech you to employ us in order to issue the sweet whisper rather than formulate the braggart shout which shatters the female ear and dispatches discord like a raging fever through your house and every house.

The sweet whisper is the very distillation of love's gentle presence and we would have you know that we have responsibility for the processing and distribution of all whispers, sweet and secret, long and short; therefore, engage us unreservedly in this respect and you will be as well rewarded as we will be fulfilled. Where shouting, threats and posturings fail, a whisper carefully wrought and intimately delivered by the lips will always succeed. When our modifying sensitivity is bypassed by the shout and the scream respect is shattered and civility dies.

Look to your lips, dear brain, and the harmony that is absent from your life shall be implanted. We shall infuse in you the fire that shines through the spirit of love and when we part there shall be revealed for the first time the smiles of which you were always capable but never uncovered to a world in dire need of a produce so refined. We should, perhaps, now draw to a close. We look forward to better times and to remaining firmly closed in the face of unjust criticism and broadsides of a malicious nature.

Sincerely

Your Lips

THE KNEES WRITE

Dear Brain

Our fondest memory is supporting the lovely Lily Lieloly when she sat on your lap in the rear seat of a motor car as you journeyed home from a dance one blissful summer's night many years ago. We were proud to give service to one so splendid and innocent. Although the journey took over an hour we never flinched and, if needs be, would have happily borne her till the pleasurable commission made us numb.

Later you were to use us for the transportation of creatures infinitely less savoury and immeasurably more seductive but our fealty was and ever will be to Lily Lieloly. Had we but wings we would one day bear her safely to the very portals of heaven. For her part, unlike so many others, she never made us feel knobbly or unsolicited. We regarded ourselves, in fact, to have been devised for the sole purpose of ministering to her in matters of transport. Enough of Lily, however.

We recall with dismay the countless times we wobbled as you trundled homewards in your cups. We became scarred and battered beyond recognition when you would stagger, then stumble and finally fall, sometimes on your posterior, other times on your hands but more often than not on us poor knees.

We knees are ungainly enough without adding to our aesthetic inelegance. Whatever it is about knees and despite their undeniable usefulness to men and women, nobody seems to love them. We have never heard it said of a man that he has lovely knees and rarely indeed would you hear it said of a woman. Women in fact, from what we manage to gather whilst listening to their conversations, very often loathe their own knees, particularly if they are unusually knobbly, crinkly or over-convoluted. It does not matter that we play the role we were ordained to play and that without us there would be no footloose movements of any consequence. Out of commission we spell total stagnation and, even when we suffer minimal damage, travel by shanks's mare is restricted.

Once we felt you fall clumsily on us when you were swearing love to a rather podgy-faced woman at a distant orgy. You very nearly permanently damaged us, so heavy was this infatuated collapse, this prurience-inducing gratulation, this dastardly declaration of lunatic libidinosity. More offensive still was the raucous and unladylike laughter of your pickled pick-up as she contorted herself drunkenly in appreciation of your loutish tomfoolery. We were sore for several days following that particular exhibition.

We recall with delight how you were overcome on the occasion by your own alcoholic fumes and were unable to perform.

We would now like to refer you to a function for which we were, we firmly believe, designed by God. This is for the sublime purpose of paying Him the homage that is His eternal due, although you would argue in drink that if you were invited into the world and given the choice of acceptance or refusal you would have declined the invitation and stayed where you were, wherever that was.

You were always a great man for flying in the face of God, forgetting, you poor benighted mortal, that you may one day have to crawl on your hands and us in supplication before His throne, and that day may not be as far away as you think. Now to that function for which we were specially designed; i.e. making you kneel in prayer. Alas it is the one function for which we were never even partially utilised and it is the one function in which we would have been pleased to involve ourselves. It was Saint Paul who said: 'At the name of Jesus every knee should bend.'

Paul was, of course, referring to the followers of Christ and must surely have meant every Christian knee, two of which have been possessed by you since the day you were born. However, neither of us can recall anything remotely approaching the faintest semblance of a genuflection since your sinless and virtuous mother was borne away to the plains of heaven by the nine choirs of angels. Neither did you kneel to pray at the anniversaries of your parents' death.

Although these were not deliberate sins of omission we, nevertheless, find your negligence to be bordering on the unforgiveable.

How is it that your late father could always manage to find time for prayer, always make it a point to bend us on the floor or the pavement or in the fields which he loved to traverse in obeisance to his heavenly benefactor! How often we foolishly wished we were his knees instead of yours but those were transient aspirations for, through thick and thin, we are still determined to support you and though somewhat rickety and wobbly we will persevere with the struggle to support your ever-extending paunch and inexorably fattening buttocks and thighs.

We lovingly recall your father as he would gently lower himself into a kneeling position to thank the appropriate saint for some favour received. Even when he would recover the pipe or the spectacles which had been mislaid for but a few moments he would cross himself and kneel in thanksgiving.

The only occasion in recent times that we remember you kneeling in real earnest was when the right knee of one of your enemies guilefully connected with that prized and sensitive area commonly referred to as your private parts!

At once you fell to your knees clutching the affected spot, uttering hideous screams and gasping for breath until you were stretchered away to the nearest infirmary by some of your cronies. Even they would not deny that you had at last come into your entitlement for you, in your day, were never slow to inflict the same punishment on those who had incurred your wrath! How true the old adage: 'Those who live by the sword shall die by the sword.'

You didn't die then but you knelt as you never knelt before and, alas, have not knelt since nor have you the slightest notion of kneeling. We beg you to do so before a day dawns when infirmity will preclude any possibility of your kneeling and that will be the time you will want to kneel most so that your supplications for salvation will be properly delivered. Tennyson, to whom your father was devoted particularly towards the end of his days, asks:

> For what are men better than sheep or goats
> That nourish a blind life within the brain,
> If, knowing God, they lift not hands of prayer
> Both for themselves and those who call them friend?
> For so the whole round earth is every way
> Bound by gold chains about the feet of God.

You would do well to utilise us more while we are willing and able to accommodate any prayerful postures you may hopefully adopt before it is too late.

We have been most wrongfully deprived of our right to participate in divine worship. Millions and millions of knees fulfil their proper roles every Sabbath while we languish and pine for our heritage.

I don't know for sure how medical texts might describe us but more than likely we would be delineated as being joints of the ginglymus type in the middle part of the human leg. We are the articulation between the femur, tibia and the patella. This is what they have to say about us in medical journals but this is a somewhat clinical analysis. There is much more to us that has not been revealed by the followers of Hippocrates.

In all wars from the lowly skirmish to the decisive battle the knees have played vital roles. Without us every rifleman who ever aimed his weapon would be at a disadvantage. Remember the position favoured in extended-order infantry drill in which the soldier kneels on the right knee, rests the left forearm across the left thigh and grasps his rifle in the position of order arms with the right hand above the lower hand. It is we who are at the very nub of this manoeuvre. Upon our mobility depends the very life of every soldier in charge or retreat.

It is we who enable the thirsty traveller to kneel by the roadside spring and it is we who stiffen to attention when the anthem of our country is sounding and yet we cannot recall a poem or song in praise of knees, but then it is also true that the horse which earns the oats rarely receives them. We care not because we know that virtue is its own reward and we are content while we are able to serve.

We had hoped – oh! impossible dream – that one day you would be summoned into a presidential presence and honoured for services to your fellow man. We saw ourselves bending so that you might kneel upon the tasselled mat. For us this truly would have been a moment to cherish. Only a knee can kneel and kneeling is the *sine qua non* of knighthood. Then would come the laying on of the royal sword followed by the royal command, Arise Sir Knight!

Sir Thomas Scam. It sounds right and proper but alas your activities over a lifetime were more suited to the jailyard than the palace. In fact there are many who would suggest that you should be permanently incarcerated, roundly whipped every day and made to lie on beds of nails at night. We must be thankful that nobody ever suggested you should be made to kneel upon broken glass.

We now feel obliged to conclude, and still we entertain the hope that you will see fit to make more use of us at wayside shrines and ancient oratories, before the sacred tabernacle and representations of the crucifixion, in cemeteries and places of holy pilgrimage, in mosques, synagogues, pagodas and temples of every denomination, in grand cathedral and humble chantry. Avail of us we beseech you so that you might give thanks to your creator for the life He has breathed upon you and for the longevity He has thus far granted you. Weigh upon us in every holy place and make it known to the giver of life that for every breath you are grateful to Him and mindful of His unparalleled munificence, for life is the father and the mother of all gifts and cannot be estimated in human terms. Press upon us then without delay so that we may contribute to your belated atonement and ultimately share in your salvation.

Sincerely

Your Knees

The Tongue Writes

Dear Brain

It was I who was obliged to deliver the utterance which contained the first lie you ever told. It was a deliberate falsehood devised to ingratiate yourself into your mother's good books after she had chastised you following a fit of petulance.

You had been sent to your room like many a small boy before you. It was a job I detested and as you know by now I can be a very sensitive fellow indeed with the power to react when an injustice is perpetrated against me. As you lay in your room endeavouring to count the myriad patterns of wild oats on the wallpaper you hit upon a plan which very nearly proved to be the death of your mother. You staggered from the bedroom clutching your breast, announcing in tones of agony from the top of the stairs that you were going to die. You blundered unsteadily downwards towards the hallway to where your mother had hastened from the garden where she had been engaged in the pruning of rose bushes. She was at first petrified upon hearing your screams and then spurred into action like all mothers by concern for your safety.

Upon beholding you she instantly fainted but luckily for all concerned her collapse coincided with the visit of an itinerant chimney sweep who ministered successfully to both of you, to your mother by gently slapping her face and to you by stoutly implanting the toe of his wellington fairly and squarely upon your pampered posterior.

How often has it been said that a kick in the right place often put a man on the right road! Certainly it was true of that occasion for you never employed such a dangerous form of deceit on your poor mother again.

You were, however, to dupe her and others in a complexity of ways for the remainder of your life. How frequently have we heard it said of scandalmongers that their tongues should be cut out. I am just another organ and, therefore, for everything I say you must be held responsible. You dictate to me and I articulate. I fulfil my other roles as a matter of course. I concern myself with assisting the teeth and throat in the vital acts of chewing and swallowing. My mucous membrane attaches itself to food, sloshing it through gum-induced saliva, retaining and refining it for the titillation of my tastebuds and at the end of these pleasurable proceedings dispatching it gratefully past the tonsils, my roots and down the deep throat to the receptive stomach.

I am filled with the most sensitive nerve fibres which issue rebukes and warnings to the entire nervous system as well as the mouth. From my fold to my papillae to my apex I am involved in essential activities for the betterment of the body as a whole and while I do not wish to sound boastful I believe it could be argued that I am an organ who bears great responsibilities as a contributor to the well-being of any given human.

I could go on about my physical philanthropy but these functions I have cited are as nothing in comparison to the awesome power which sends millions of words tripping off my apex day after day. Most of these I will concede are meaningless and although packaged in phrases and sentences it can be safely said that were they never uttered there would be no loss whatsoever to the world. There are countless men and women who have utilised me on a round-the-clock basis and who have never issued a word of common sense. There are millions who use me for nothing better than criticising and maligning friends, neighbours and institutions. There are, mercifully, a gracious and godly few who never employ me for the voicing of evil commentary about others and but for these kind-hearted souls the world would be a more damnable place than it already is. Their example stands out like sweet birdsong in a shadowy grove. As for those who employ me for the distribution of the truth they slash through hypocrisy and cant the way a comet sears through the heavens at night, and yet they do not wound or maim nor do they use the truth for their own advancement. Indeed they wound themselves more by adhering to it, cut themselves adrift from the safe anchorage of convention and expose themselves without raft or lifebelt to the hostile seas of suspicion.

I remember a female teacher, one of the few who refused to be taken in by your pretended illnesses. When you blamed another boy for your own piddle-stains on the freshly whitewashed gable of the schoolhouse she requested you to stick out your tongue so that the world might see the black mark on its surface, proof if any was needed that you were already at that tender age an unrepentant liar.

You obdurately refused to exhibit me in public. Now I am an organ which never entertains aspirations towards vanity and thrusting me forth in public, medical examination excepted, is not my idea of fun because I am not in the least pretty or personable. The better organs never are.

However, on that occasion I fervently wished that you would for we tongues have properties with which we suffuse ourselves and were you to make a spectacle of me on that occasion I would have been as black as the bottom sod in a raised peat bank.

Organs are not capable of acting independently of the brain but they are capable of reacting, often with embarrassing consequences.

There are many men who believe that it is both proper and natural to tell lies to women and indeed they believe that those who tell the truth to wives, especially, are leaving the side down, as it were. Fortunately most women do not believe daylight from the opposite sex who would use them for their own ends. I once heard your own wife admonishing your daughter for believing what she had been told by a neighbourhood rapscallion. Said your long-suffering spouse on that memorable occasion:

'My dear, you are not to believe a word of it and from now until the day you die you are not to believe a single word you are told by a man, especially a married man.'

Would that more females had adopted your wife's sensible philosophy. It is impossible to estimate the amount of anguish they would have been spared and more difficult still to measure the volume of tears that would be left unshed. Of the two known sexes man is the bigger liar. Ask any tongue for confirmation and I will be borne out. In fact the more daring of the males will invent the most outrageous lies to save themselves, to justify an injustice, to convince themselves that wrong is right and to seduce and subsequently ravish innocent females.

I know what I'm talking about. All too often have I uttered your distortions against my will. Right down through history man has shown himself to be the master of the big lie. It succeeds, though not for all time, when all else fails. It is easy enough to convince a gullible public; the difficulty arises when a once honest man is forced to convince himself.

Nazism, apartheid, religious bigotry, Klu-Kluxery and tainted patriotism flourish in a climate where men begin to believe their own lies. Soon those very lies become institutional maxims and truth shivers in the shadows like a pariah.

Worst of all, however, is when I am deliberately silenced by you. Silence has contributed more to misrule and tyranny than all the lies that have ever been told. If tongues had articulated what the brain knew to be the truth there would be no place for the tyrant or the dictator.

Sometimes courage momentarily wins the day and the brain ordains that the tongue should speak out, but just as the tongue is about to articulate the courageous condemnation the words are halted at the tongue's tip where they languish and fade.

When the foul deed is executed how often have we heard the sideliner say that it was on the tip of his tongue to shout stop but he thought that surely somebody else would say it for him Give me the lie anytime before a wilful silence, a silence that watches coldly and callously while evil smothers good. Yes, bad as the lie is give it to me before silence.

What a quidnunc you have been. You would be the first to accuse women of having a monopoly on gossip but women are, for the most part, harmless tattlers although there are some who have permanently ruined the innocent as well as the guilty. Women are mere relayers of more outrageous fibs manufactured by man. Even your sainted mother was not above carrying a tale of dubious origins and little substance.

How many innocent holidaying girls are alleged to be absent because of illicit pregnancies and had their characters ruined and their marriage prospects decimated. Did not you yourself add to these defamations without batting an eyelid, more so if the girls in question were of outstanding character. You shamed me then and indeed I would have preferred on such occasions if somebody had cut me off and tossed me to the dogs. You tried to salve your conscience by suggesting that you were only parroting the disclosures of other small-minded men.

How I loathed your silence when your friends were being slandered, but is that not the story of most men's lives? I would have swelled with pride had you invested me with the diction to defend them.

I have no longer any doubt but that men are the harsher and more venomous gossips. Women gossip mostly for the sake of ingratiation but men do it because it's a crime to use a sword but no crime to pierce a heart with the malicious innuendo. Men manufacture. Women distribute.

How I remember the facility with which you broke so many hearts. Oh the gorgeous phrases so sonorous and so mellifluous that flowed from my core as you wooed the greener girls of the countryside! Even I was transported on the run-up to your first conquest, but I quickly grew disillusioned as you trotted out the same base blandishments to female after female.

You scored a bull's-eye once in every ten throws of the amorous dart. This was good shooting by any standard but how you lied and cheated, always using me to convey the oft-repeated piffle which women seem to lap up like starving cats at a milk basin. They are easily flattered, poor creatures, and they never tire of hearing their praises sung. One day, inevitably, they become hardened after perfidious onslaughts by the likes of you.

When you would hear that a girl's heart was breaking after you tired of her you would quote the sages and say time heals all. I wonder, however, how many of these sages were jilted or betrayed by those they loved. When you fell in love with Lily Lieloly you experienced purity and sanctity and beauty but these were not enough for you. You wanted more but Lily denied you.

I remember how you brutally defined true love ever after.

'True love,' said you with a smirk, 'is when a chap wants a girl to hold his hand instead of his population stick.'

Glib isn't the word for you. I would sooner you had mouthed the mimesis of a fart. There is much more that I could add but there are other organs anxiously awaiting their turn. Before I conclude I would ask you to use me sparingly when your dander is up. Use me most to forgive and forget and when evil assails you use me not at all.

Sincerely

Your Tongue

THE HAIRS OF THE HEAD WRITE

Dear Neighbour

As we write a white hair falls to the page. It should remind you that you are now in the autumn of your life and that at last you might consider comporting yourself accordingly so as not to embarrass us further.

We who were once black and curly grow thinner and more fragile by the hour. Yet we still manage to compliment each other and how we wish that humans as a whole could do likewise. Here, living together in total harmony, one will notice blacks, browns and yellows, whites and off-whites with occasional strands of uncommon silver.

At this stage of your life, as seen by others, we present a picture of overall greyness and this is as it should be having regard for your years, wasted and otherwise. It is about this greyness that we propose to address you. We might dwell upon other aspects of our relationship with you such as the time you shaved your cranium to the very bone after beholding Yul Brynner in *The King and I* or we might mention the time you dyed us all red or the time you opted for that infernal white splash, but since these were fads we feel that to dwell upon them would be to defeat our real purpose which has to do with the present time and not the past.

Of late we are growing grey for the second time and would like to remain grey this time. The first time was roughly five years ago. We well recall how your long-suffering wife, the once luscious Penelope Fitzfeckid, and your daughters looked on with mounting alarm as the fine white streaks encroached upon the ebony thatch to which they had been accustomed for so long. They imagined, poor feckless creatures, just as Keats's bees imagined that warm days would never cease, that we would never change colour or lose so many of our brotherhood to the passage of time. For our part we were perfectly satisfied. Nature was taking its course. The inevitable was happening. Worse if you were growing bald. Now that would have been calamity! We fear nothing more than approaching baldness. For us baldness means the end of everything.

Back, however, to those females of yours. Of course, you would never give ear when they reminded you that you were consuming too much alcohol or behaving like a lecher or spending too much time with your cronies or not spending enough time at home. Your vanity, the most prickable part of your make-up was pricked once more. When they subtly suggested to you that the grey might be kept at bay you readily acquiesced and were induced to part with a substantial sum to initiate the first action against what was right and natural.

They purchased for you at a reputable pharmacist's a bottle of Greyfix, a mixture which was guaranteed to retain the natural colour of the hair and this by merely using a small quantity of the miraculous composition whenever a grey hair hove into view. Even the cranium itself with whom we are constantly in touch had no objection to our growing grey. Only you, the brain, would disapprove.

You should know by now that a man with a dash of grey in his hair need never grow a moustache or a beard to prove his masculinity. The grey shows that he has been there and back. The white filaments stand out like stripes on a sergeant major or campaign ribbons on a veteran. This is why most grey-haired young men marry early and successfully and this is why women are so attracted to otherwise ordinary-looking men who have nothing going for them save a touch of grey in the hair.

You should be on your bended knees in thanksgiving that you have greyed with such distinction. Were we hairs but brains we would cherish every last grey rib atop the cranium. Whatever else it may be about the colour grey one thing is absolutely certain: it has an extraordinary effect on females of all ages. We, the hairs, believe that it gives the impression of accomplishment. Certainly the man with a discreet tinge of grey has a head start over his rivals. He doesn't even have to ogle the lady of his fancy. His grey hairs do all the work for him. We also believe that women have infinite trust in grey-haired men. There is a fatherliness about them; they radiate concern. They may be no more than common rogues like yourself but women, more than men, are firm believers in the old legal decree that a grey-haired man is innocent until proven guilty.

Even if all the hair is not grey it would be sufficient if the hirsute area above the auricles were ever so slightly tinged.

When you anointed us with Greyfix it worked admirably as far as you were concerned. We were as black as ever we had been and your cronies wondered at the redoubtable napper which defied the years and refused to play host to a single grey hair.

You were a man apart for a while but in the end people grew suspicious. Add to this the fact that a tiny but ominous bald patch made its appearance on your poll. At first this was easily concealed by the deceitful deployment of some of the longer hairs in the patch's vicinity but as time wore on and the bald patch expanded its holding we remaining hairs became painfully aware that it would only be a matter of time before it made an outright bid for monopoly of your entire crown. If anything you became even more panic-stricken than we were and wisely you decided to withhold further applications of the much-vaunted Greyfix. It was the wisest move you ever made and ever after when we would hear people say that poor old Tommy Scam hadn't a brain in his head we would bristle as we never bristled before.

While our numbers did not increase there were no further losses and you vowed to allow nature full rein, sustaining and maintaining your remaining hairs. We have served you well and we have survived the excesses which have done for so many of our immediate colleagues and for greying hairs on every pate all over the world. We feel like parodying old Polonius as he addressed his son Laertes in *Hamlet*:

Those hairs thou hast and their adoption tried
grapple them to thy poll with hoops of steel.

I am certain that if Laertes had been allowed to grow older and greyer those would have been the precise words used by his father. The Elizabethans were great warrants to coin the colourful phrase. The father of this day and age would be more likely to say, 'Keep your hair on, son.'

If you had persevered with the application of the murderous Greyfix we have no doubt whatsoever but that your head would now be as bald as the proverbial billiard ball.

It is, we believe, a fine thing to grow bald naturally because all bald men are possessed of shapely, presentable heads which look dignified as well as romantic. However, brains like yourself who forfeit precious ribs through vanity are possessed of mediocre craniums which need considerable camouflage when our artful coverage is withdrawn. What a sorry sight you would be without us. A duck out of water would be infinitely more prepossessing.

We would now like to issue the following statement as an assurance to those who are apprehensive about growing grey and we would expect you to instruct your writing hand that the statement be written in characters clear and submitted to the world through whatever means you may think most effective.

Grey hairs are the harbingers of tolerance and maturity. They complement the lines that come with age and remember too that from a sartorial viewpoint grey goes with everything. For a black head a man needs sprightly feet whereas for a grey head a sensible pace is all that is required. No great feats are expected from the men whose heads we adorn whereas a man with bright colours might be expected to perform feats as colourful as his hair. The old Gaelic poets must take their share of the blame for derogatory attitudes towards grey hairs. When they wrote of men with black hair they compared it to the raven's wing and when they spoke of men with red hair they said it was burnished like the sun. When they spoke of men with fair or blonde hair they said it glistened like gold but when they spoke of men with grey hair they said of them that they were as grey as badgers or as grey as goats.

They should have said as grey as mottled silver or as grey as an evening sky or grey as doves at daybreak or grey as a stand of winter beeches or grey as the Burren of the County Clare or grey as the snowy owl or grey as the Northern Diver. There are a thousand beautiful shades of grey. There is the gentle grey of sea mist, there is the silvery grey of slates under a full moon and there is oyster grey in the bed of the sea. It's great to be grey when you come to think of it.

For one of the finer tributes paid to us grey hairs we must look once more to Shakespeare. In the first act of *Julius Caesar* when the conspirators are selecting their henchmen, the requisite characteristics of the various nominees are taken into account. Somebody suggests Cinna the poet and the motion is carried.

'Let us have him,' says his nominator, 'for his grey hairs.'

No more than his grey hairs, mark you. We would also like to make it clear that we male hairs do not expect females to retain their greyness just because we insist upon doing so. For us, however, the retention of our natural grey is the paramount consideration. Even the theatre today has the good sense to realise that black and white are no longer the dominant shades of drama. Greys are now preferable to sheer blacks and whites because unlike these primary colours grey has many shades, each more subtle than the next.

Of all colours we may also presume that grey is the most conciliatory by virtue of the fact that it never obtrudes or dazzles. It has, we believe, a calming quality and we have noted inflammatory situations where the timely arrival of a grey-haired man had the effect of imposing peace and tranquillity upon the warring factions. We who are grey have spoken and, happily, we find ourselves in this time and place presentable, abundant and hopeful that we will never again be subjected to chemical pollution.

Sincerely

Your Grey Hairs

THE MEMORY WRITES

Dear Brain

I recall a votive mass commissioned by your loving mother for the fulfilment of her private intentions. Your father had gone to his grave but six months earlier and if there are choirs of angels in the regions beyond they were surely gathered in their entirety to sing that sainted soul into heaven.

For his likes, heaven if there is one, with its indescribable effulgence and pain-free felicity, was most certainly devised as a just need for his humanitarian activities during his all too short stay in this crucible we call the world.

You were in your late teens and, like all mothers, yours still cherished delusory hopes that you might yet entertain a vocation for the priesthood. The votive candles shimmered in their polished candelabra and no sound save the rustle of the sacred vestments obtruded into that solemn place other than yours and your mother's gentle breathing.

How is it that occasions like these which are designed to impose pious sentiments on the participants very often induce responses which are far from spiritual, responses alas which are the direct opposite of those intended. I am only your memory and cannot choose what you wish to recall. I am a good memory and I store much that is eminently quotable and well worth visual replay, but you prefer to summon up the less savoury aspects of your tainted past.

Instead of praying for your father's soul you permitted your mind to wander to a visit of Connelly's Circus when it had played a matinée in your childhood, and what was it you thought of? The elephants, the lions, the horses and ponies, the juggler, the monkeys? No indeed, oh most lascivious of wretches! Even in the sacred place where you and your mother came to worship you might have been partially forgiven if you had remembered Loco the red-nosed, potbellied clown who had every child under the canvas in stitches.

Earlier that morning I had high hopes for you. Quite unexpectedly and delightfully you recalled glimpses of the snowy summits of the South Kerry mountains in all their pearly whiteness as they strove to survive the warming winds of a bright May morning. There is a godly gleam from mountain snow when the sun assails it. I would have forgiven you if this recollection had persisted throughout the celebration of the holy mass for there is a deep spirituality secreted in the beauties of nature, a spirituality so glorious that God is forever manifesting Himself and his artistry through its magnificent intricacies.

No such lofty pursuits for you, however, who preferred to resurrect the only scene in that particular circus which provoked criticism from the local parish priest, who described it as obscene. That was when Mona Bonelli, the Italian contortionist, wearing only the skimpiest of briefs and the barest of bras danced on to the centre ring under the spotlight's glare. Her dazzling smile captivated all present but you more than any. Immediately she lifted the hoop through which she would thrust her seemingly boneless body you started to drool and slobber like a starving hound on beholding a string of pork sausages. Granted the girl was sensual and sinuous, even voluptuous when she felt so disposed, but there was a hardness and a craftiness about her which you refused to recognise.

All that concerned you was the way she displayed her shapely body as she twisted and screwed her muscular limbs. There were, I will concede, no angles to her, no warps nor wrinkles nor blemish that could be perceived by the naked eye. With curves she was bountifully endowed and aided by the make-up, the perpetual smile, the shimmering sequins on her scant apparel and the bright spotlights she did succeed in unsettling the less discerning and non-artistic males among the audience.

Long before her performance drew to a close you were completely carried away, and to think that you would preserve this far-off exhibition for the sacred occasion devoted to your father's memory.

I have forgotten the number of times you have recalled Mona Bonelli and countless other scantily clad and unclad visions to induce nocturnal slumber when by the simple expedient of saying your night-time prayers your conscience would just as easily have entrusted you to the waiting arms of Morpheus.

You could not know, of course, poor, weak-willed organ, that the glamorous Mona Bonelli was in reality none other than plain Biddy Muldoon from the county of Waterford and that she was not the nineteen-year-old titian-haired beauty that she was supposed to be. Rather was she a forty-year-old, mousey-haired, drop-out housewife who had allowed herself some years before to be seduced and latterly taken in tow by the moustachioed ringmaster of Connelly's Circus. Her deserted husband had ever after made it a point to remember the ringmaster in his prayers, day and night, 'For,' said he to a freshly acquired helpmate, 'he has taken the scourge of my life upon himself and heaven will surely be his lot, for he will suffer his hell in this world.'

Later that evening, the same Mona Bonelli or Biddy Muldoon was seated in the local hotel where your father had invited you to partake of an orangeade whilst he sampled the excellent potstill whiskey for which the hostelry was renowned. Mona Bonelli, the luscious, titian-haired teenager from the land of the Tiber and the Po was now showing every single one of her forty years and deprived of the glamorous aids of her contortionist's trade she looked a very ordinary creature indeed. You failed to recognise her and even when she vainly tried to ogle your late, lamented father by crossing and uncrossing her still shapely legs you still could not call to mind the body that had transported you such a short while before.

I can never comprehend why you still persist in remembering the more tawdry experiences of your past especially since I carry a large stock of beautiful visions which you would have no trouble to remember if only you made the effort. Among other things I have an excellent range of truly beautiful faces including those of your ageing mother and your long-suffering spouse and, of course, the innocent faces of your children. I lovingly preserve those of your maiden aunts and benevolent uncles and, dare I mention her name, the lovely Lily Lieloly. No memory could be blamed for cherishing that angelic face.

I have an exciting repertoire of sporting occasions from the lowliest of donkey derbies to the heart-stopping drama of the Aintree Grand National, from your own humble contributions on the playing fields to the dizzy heights of the great Olympics. No television set will ever serve you as well as I do and yet you all too often employ me to recall the basest of your activities.

I have a priceless accumulation of sunsets, no two of which are alike and were you to excavate my recesses you would find such an array of wonders treasured over a lifetime that your heart would be permanently uplifted. There are my vaults of cloud formations, cataracts, dawns, twilights, sunbeams and, of course, my seascapes ever ready to reveal themselves.

Remember the blizzards, the cloudburst and the fuming, raging anger of the oceans. Remember the rolling reverberations of the great thunderstorms, the crackling, the booming and the lingering echoes as the turmoil spent itself in the all-absorbing bosom of the sky. Remember the surging, sweeping floods, their inestimable passion concealed in the sibilant deceptive surges.

Oh those rampant, riotous waters, dirging and delving and loamy! I can bring to mind the sounds and the pictures in an instant. Just say the word and I will recall for you the first kiss, the first embrace, the first love of those halcyon days when your heart was unsullied and pure. I have so much that is elevating, so much that will bring you closer to the ideal of self-purification, the only ideal which will truly prepare you for the transition from a known state to an unknown. Prompt me, poise me, nudge me to work for our good. Resist the evil pressures that would have me prostitute my talents so that your unworthy whims might be gratified. Let me resurrect for you the glories and the good deeds, so few in your lifetime to date. Upon recalling these you may go forth and emulate, thus inspiring me to renounce the inglorious and the ignominious.

I will conclude now but before I do I would like to recall for you the most heroic incident which might be credited to you. You were but seven then and you were in the company of an even younger girl who happened to be your playmate of the time. As the two of you passed Drumgooley's farmyard gate, having wandered from a rustic picnic organised by your mother, who should come fussing and flapping from the fowl-run but Drumgooley's gander, a fearsome creature with a nerve-shattering cackle whenever he felt his flock was in danger.

Bravely you ordered your young charge to run for her life while you manfully stood your ground and diverted this bloodthirsty barnyard braggart until she had run clear of danger. Allowing for your age and size this was a monumental feat of bravery, of selflessness, of knight-errantry. It was, however, never to be equalled in the long years that followed but in recalling it I may perhaps remind you that there was a brief but glorious while when chivalry was your long suit.

Finally I would ask you to use me for the betterment of your immortal soul while conceding that I must also be spiced a little now and then if I am to be entertaining as well as exalting.

Sincerely

Your Memory

THE FISTS WRITE

Dear Brain

You have never used us on the face of a woman and for this we partially forgive you. You have never used us on the face of a child and for this we are also ready to partially forgive you. You have never used us on the face, head or body of a man who was down and for this too we partially forgive you. Alas, I cannot forgive you everything, though I wish I could.

I remember the night you smashed to pieces every breakable object in the apartment of your partner in your last *affaire d'amour*. So terrified was that unfortunate creature that she threw herself at your feet and begged you to leave but no! You persisted in pursuing your orgy of destruction which was later to cost you dearly in financial terms for you were obliged to foot the bill *in toto* for every shred of damage you caused.

Oh poor, foolish, vain fellow! Know you not that affairs are the most short-lived of all relationships. Even a fist knows that. An affair comes like a jet aircraft from the east, dominates the heavens overhead for a few brief moments and then disappears / into the western skies and is never seen or heard from again.

An affair is like an air-filled toy balloon which takes off in all directions at once when its wind is released. It rasps, snorts, squeaks and screeches with a passion and ferocity unbridled, and then flops on the floor a tattered parody of its former self. An affair is a mere sneeze which gathers slowly and disperses quickly. You should have known this and accepted your rejection when your correspondent announced that she had her fill of you and fancied another.

You raised us instantly, your loyal and long-suffering fists, and spent your fury on the inanimate. Battered, bloodied and bruised you thrust us inside your coat and staggered to your home where you didn't even have the common courtesy to lave us with ordinary tapwater or dab us with iodine. We suffered for days on end because of your carelessness.

We will be the first to admit that we are only part-time organs. Sometimes we come and go like lightning, other times like flash floods but alas there are times when you retain our services far above and beyond the call of duty and these are the times when we dislike you most.

It is easy to justify the clenching of a fish as a weapon of defence or as an instrument which might be used to strike a football or a punchbag or indeed for involvement in a fair bout of fisticuffs where the protagonists are willing and able to take each other on.

However, there is a time to unclench, to release, to forgive and forget and to carry on with the business of living and this is where you frequently failed us, for you would not instruct your heart to relent.

So it was that we were unwillingly retained when we might have been peacefully broken up into our many components. Being part-time organs provides us with many compensations so long as you, the proprietor, use us as part-time employees.

When your anger goes we go. In fact we need never exist if you were not so quick to react, if you were not so easily incited, so readily influenced for all the wrong reasons.

We fists are often petrified and activated for reasons of which we rarely approve and if you were to ask the average fist why it is so clenched and why its knuckles show so white, that fist would shake its figurative head in sorrow and frustration and then hang it in shame. We know because we are fists and a fist is not an instrument of affection or love. It does not lie down with peace and harmony. It is hard and hurtful and the longer it remains in this state the less good it bodes for those whom it may encounter. It has little discernment while it remains closed and often all and sundry can fall foul of it with disastrous consequences for its victims and proprietor.

Please remember that ninety-nine times out of a hundred there is no need of us even though you may think otherwise. You, the brain, are solely responsible for our inhumanity, our obstinacy, our inflexibility and only you, the brain, can soften and subdue us.

There are happy days, weeks, even months when we are non-existent. Our various parts fill other useful roles while we are dormant. Then, unfortunately, as a result of a chance remark, an allegedly unkind cut, a ridiculous, meaningless slight, we are mobilised once more and alerted for destruction even though it is a mobilisation that all too often backfires, leaving you with a bloody nose and broken fingers.

We will now, before concluding, pose you a few questions, Have you ever seen a clenched fist in the company of a laugh? Have you ever seen a fist being clenched while its owner rendered a lovesong? Have you ever seen a man with clenched fists embracing a woman? Have you ever heard of a man who made love with clenched fists or a man who stroked a girl's hair with his fists? Of course not for the good reason that a fist only does injury whereas the actions to which I have referred call for softness and tenderness.

The only really good thing about us is that when your anger subsides we are dissolved. Now that the years are creeping up on you I think it is high time you retired us altogether. Dismiss us for once and for all and show the world that you have come to terms with yourself and the people about you. Grey hairs and clenched fists seem to us the most unseemly of companions. Wrinkles and clenched fists look even more ridiculous. Retire us at once, in God's name, before you make a complete fool of yourself!

    Sincerely

    Your fists

THE PENIS WRITES

Dear Master

I write to you as the most reviled of all your organs, objurgated and calumniated since the inception of copulation and constantly blamed for misdeeds which I freely admit to perpetrating – but always on your instructions. Anything I have ever done has been instigated by you.

There I would be pendant and somnolent and occasionally out of commission when suddenly you would shout 'tenshun!' and I would be obliged to spring instantly into action.

I was ever ready because eternal vigilance was my motto since I first became aware of your extraordinary and ungovernable proclivity towards the opposite sex.

Now that you have moved on into the years one would expect a katabolism or some slight contraction in the carnal drive. If anything, alas! you would seem to be more inclined than ever before towards sexual debauchery and would motivate me around the clock if you could bring yourself to stay awake that long.

God grant a silver bed in Heaven to your sainted, paternal grandmother; it was she who said that the body should be seven days dead before the penis would fully subside and even then she contended there were isolated cases where this much-maligned organ was seen to be still the outstanding feature in resurrected cadavers which had been interred months before. If this is true the cadaver was no cadaver. Rather was it a body in a state of suspended animation. An old wives' tale I dare say but it shows that no female in her right mind would ever place the least trust, dead or alive, in the organ of organs, as I once heard it called by the captious old midwife who first brought you into the world.

It was she who said that ninety-nine out of every hundred males should be castrated at birth and the one percent isolated but sumptuously cosseted solely for the purpose of perpetuating the human species, 'For,' said she, 'of all the attachments of the trunk it is the one which is to be trusted least.'

How wrongfully labelled have we penises always been. The old woman, for all her knowledge of the world, should have laid the blame for all my exploits fairly and squarely at your door.

I once heard an itinerant evangelist suggest at a street corner in the city of Dublin that there was nothing so profound as a common erection.

The truth is that there is nothing less profound for the pump in question, the pump of life, is the most uncomplicated adjunct of the entire human system, so whenever we hear a person say that he or she has read or heard something profound what it really means is that they are more mystified after experiencing this so-called profundity than they were before.

The point I would ram home – you'll find the expression endearing I'm sure! – is that I am simply your puppet and that I have no influence whatsoever over my destiny.

There are people who say that excessive drinking brings out the worst in me. What they should be saying is that it brings out the worst in you and that you are capable of submitting me to the most extreme excesses after a sustained bout of intemperance. You would place my very existence in jeopardy such is your lack of restraint and distortion of outlook after an alcoholic shaughraun.

You take the whip to conscience and oust him from his watchtower whenever it suits your vile purpose.

Conscience, poor creature, is a head-shaker and a tut-tutter rather than a dictator. It is you who dictates to and manipulates poor Mister Conscience until he is more of a yes-man than an honest witness for that which prosecutes on behalf of the Creator.

I remember just before your first fall cut you irretrievably adrift from lovely Lily Lieloly, you were at that manky stage in your debauch-filled career when a choice had to be made between your continuing virginity and your likely defilement.

I had fondly hoped that because Lily Lieloly was also a virgin you would preserve me for that glorious union when you and Lily would consummate your betrothal and bring everlasting joy to both your hearts.

Virginity is, unfortunately, something of a souvenir, often priceless to its owner but frequently worthless on the open market.

You held yours in so little regard that you unashamedly and heedlessly disposed of it at the first available opportunity. Even after that first disappointing encounter I had hoped that your unsatisfactory initiation into the sorry rite of illicit deflowering would signal your return to the road of righteousness.

It was not to be and in no time at all you had exhausted the last reserves of local harlots and accommodating amateurs. Soon you were to become a familiar figure in the iniquitous dens of nearby cities until you were rendered temporarily *hors de combat* by a four-feet-eleven masseuse who, for a few extra quid, provided you with what she termed the full treatment as advertised in the jargon of the trade, on a charge sheet which hung between framed photographs of the late John F. Kennedy and Pope John the twenty-third.

It was Sir Alexander Fleming, through the medium of his miraculous penicillin, who must be praised and thanked for your speedy recovery. You were to indulge your weakness at colossal expense of both the physical and financial kind before finally succumbing to the wiles and monies of the oldish and plainish heiress, Miss Penelope Fitzfeckid.

There followed several years of marital harmony, during which time Penelope presented you with two daughters and a bouncing boy.

Then one day you called me up unexpectedly for active service far from the home front. It was the evening of some rugby international at Twickenham.

There you were one minute carousing and chorusing with your cronies and the next in the rear seat of a taxi heading for one of those haunts where you once excelled yourself, or so you believed, in those rakish days before marriage.

You were recognised at once and rapturously received by the never-ageing Madame who, according to herself, had spent the intervening years wondering and worrying about your sustained exile from her buxom charges, all of who had now been replaced by younger and more agile exponents of the high and ancient art of copulation.

There were times during that long weekend when I feared for our survival but miraculously you managed to escape visitation from the wide variety of painful diseases which were then rampant in that particular parlour.

We were not to be so lucky on a later occasion which I will also never forget for another reason, this being that you put me to work when I was no longer capable and made me the butt of your paramour's vulgar wit – and not one word in defence out of you to whom I have given decades of incomparable service. Instead you laughed loud and long.

You once remarked to a crony that I had betrayed you. Your exact words were:

'I might have been a chap of infinite morality, a veritable paragon had I not been let down by the most contumacious pudenda!'

I heard you announce another time, in an effort to justify a short-lived affair with a local matron:

'What a wonderful fellow I would be but for this baggage of reproduction which demoralises my every thought and deed.'

Who knows better than yourself, my dear master, that it was nothing but your own interfemoral phantasising which was the paramount contribution in all our efforts. It has been said that I have no conscience and for once they speak the truth about me, for it is you who possesses the conscience and I can take some satisfaction from the fact that it keeps you awake nights.

However, it is true to say that your conscience takes leave of absence whenever I am called up to illicitly execute your iniquitous behests. Afterwards, when your conscience returns, I am sickened by the excess remorse in which you wallow, remorse, I might add, of little duration.

I will not cite other acts which I was obliged to perform on your behalf but I must mention your habit of urinating into your shoes whilst in your cups and indeed leaving your bed after a night consuming gallons of beer and advancing to the head of the stairs where you would set a minor cascade into motion. There must have been at least a hundred bed-wettings after your beer sessions. Indeed in your drunken stupors you have peed into purses, flowerpots, frying pans, pianos and wastepaper baskets, everywhere in fact but into the numerous chamber pots which your long-suffering spouse would so thoughtfully and strategically arrange at the precise places where you had emptied yourself before.

Often on your way home from pub crawls you would do it against dustbins and doorways, telephone and electricity poles, shop windows and sacrosanct monuments. No place was sacred when the urge beset you. Worst of all was that pre-wedding night when by some perverted mischance you located your mother's wedding bonnet and filled its upturned crown with a froth-covered outflow which would have done justice to a Shergar or a Nijinsky!

There was a time you did it through the keyhole of a watchful neighbour and very nearly deprived the poor creature of a vision already impaired from exposure to constant draughts and rain-squalls. There was the time you attempted to do it against the trousers of a custodian of the peace and had to exert all your influences to keep the matter out of the courts.

I will never forget the night you were caught red-handed doing it into a flowerpot in the window of the local bully boy. The kick which he implanted fairly and squarely on me and the remainder of your apparatus left me unwell for days. I have often asked myself how is it that man will persist in aiming knees, boots and fists at that part of the anatomy which has given him the most pleasure. It is one of the more intriguing aspects of man's mental infirmity.

If I were asked to recall the most outrageous statement you ever made I would suggest that it was that which referred to me as follows:

'A man with an enthusiastic penis,' you said, 'is the servant of a headstrong master!'

One of your cronies insisted that you deserved the title of philosopher after such a perceptive declaration whereas if the truth were told it was about as philosophical an inanity as the nocturnal braying of a wandering jackass. Too well you know that I was never your master. You and you alone are responsible for my every action and my survival for when you go I will have to go with you, and when you decay I will decay too. But for the miracle of penicillin I would have long since capitulated to the overpowering influences of your many silent and most unwelcome visitors, chief amongst whom are those age-old invaders – clap, syphilis and pox. Monday morning blues was your way of referring to the first of this terrible trio, and what a brave face you would put on when you would whisper to the discreet apothecary in his dispensary that you required a small jar of mercurial ointment often so unpharmaceutically referred to by the loathsome name of 'blue butter'. I refuse to recall the occasions and the wenches responsible for these visitations for I would not have it on my conscience that I scandalised the gentle reader with the more lurid details of your awesome sex life.

I am at a loss as to how I should conclude. Should I beg you to moderate your lifestyle, make representations to your better nature or ask you to turn to religion as a safeguard against eternal damnation? It would not matter one whit how I might address you since, as far as I am concerned, you have always seen to it that I will remain the most capricious of organs so that no trust whatsoever may be reposed in poor me!

Faithfully

Your Penis

The Nose Writes

Dear Brain

The only thing I can really say in your favour is that you never deliberately altered me. Altered I was by your headstrong foolishness. Would you had heeded the sage advice of the forgotten poet who wrote so wisely:

Those who in quarrels interpose
Must often wipe a bloody nose.

I recall that night in Forty-Second Street when you announced in a topless bar that Richard Nixon was a gentleman. If memory served me correctly you described him as the most misunderstood man in America.

I'll concede that you had no appraisal whatsoever of the coming blow but you might more profitably have kept your mouth shut especially since you were both inebriated and outnumbered. I was well and truly broken by the outsize fist of a squat Puerto Rican with no neck. Earlier you had told him in your own inimitable and cavalier way that he reminded you of John the Baptist with his head glued back on rather artlessly.

It was one of your more suicidal statements. However, we soon put all that behind us and after a botchy repair job by one of New York's most expensive quacks I was still a fairly prepossessing proboscis.

Then there was the time you all but exterminated yourself drinking whiskey. Your liver, however, is better qualified to speak about your whiskey period than I am but I must remind you, in case of a recurrence, that I doubled in size during that time and my colour was temporarily transformed from a natural pink to a vile puce.

But for the nasal sentiments of Cyrano de Bergerac so passionately and eloquently conveyed I must surely have become clogged and inoperable. Oh that was a great declamation!

'Let me inform you that I am proud of such an appendage since a big nose is the proper sign of a friendly, good, courteous, witty, liberal and brave man.'

When your doctor issued his ultimatum that your wife's widowhood was imminent unless you refrained at once from imbibing rotgut, you turned to beer. My size and hue were restored within weeks and tragedy was narrowly averted.

Apart from playing host to mucousness, liquid and congealed, I am also the harbourer of your sixth sense. You might say that we are one. I do not expect gratitude. It is part of my job to see to your survival and this is why I nurture and cosset this most valuable of all the senses although I will never know why such a lowly organ as I was chosen to be the repository of one so gifted.

I myself have no difficulty in smelling smoke, fumes and gases provided you are not drugged with alcohol but the sixth sense which I house is a smeller of pitfalls; just as I direct you towards appetising food so does the sixth sense upon smelling trouble direct you in the opposite direction.

The sixth sense is capable of detecting the approach of gracious in-laws and mendicant relations. The sixth sense, often confused with experience, determines from the volume and tempo of a simple knock on a door whether job or sorrow wishes to be admitted. The housing and maintenance of this priceless instinct is a most onerous responsibility and were I a boastful, trumpeting nose I should be blowing my coals all day long.

Vanity is not my long suit but I will tell you this for I know it to be Gospel. When you first met Lily Lieloly she did not look into your eyes nor at the ebony curls atop your young and imprudent head. She did not gasp as others did at the whiteness and uniformity of your dazzling teeth nor did she judge you by the manliness of your unwrinkled brow. No sir! She looked at me, your nose, the only truly classical feature of an otherwise lacklustre face. She looked at me and that look lingered longer than any look I have ever experienced before or since. Her full lips parted as though she would speak. No words came but I sensed that if she had spoken she would have said:

'Thou art the noblest Roman of them all.'

There was that awful period when you sported the moustache. You imagined you were being trendy whereas, in fact, all you did was to make yourself look ridiculous. Growing a moustache next to a nose is like pouring patented, bottled sauce over the mouth-watering creation of a world-class chef. I can stand on my own. The day you shaved off that bristling horror girls began to look at you again, particularly at that part of your dial where I hold sway.

There was the time you had your handkerchiefs mono-grammed. The subsequent damage to my tender tissue has not yet healed from the blowing you gave me. Every time you wanted to show off you whipped out that crudely-labelled cotton duster and trumpeted like a rogue elephant, so that all could hear and, hearing, take notice of your scribble-defiled snot-rag. You must never use me in that fashion again. I am attached to your face for the primary purpose of taking pressure off you. Granted I assist with your breathing but your mouth is big enough to cope amply with that. It is a good job that the same mouth forms such a substantial gulf between myself and the jaw which receives most of the credit for being the gritty, gutsy hardchaw of the face whereas I am extended far beyond his utmost extremity and

I am bloodied a hundred times more often than he is fractured or broken, bloodied so often by the probing nails of your index fingers as they scout my interior for recalcitrant snots that it's a wonder I'm not whittled away altogether.

I can never understand why I should be picked and eviscerated by unwelcome fingers, especially when I don't need picking. A high-quality, white, linen handkerchief discreetly and effectively used without resorting to excess is all that's required to see that my passageways are kept open. I am otherwise well able to maintain myself. Desist, therefore, from this vile practice before a nail-induced haemorrhage bleeds you to death.

You might also refrain from cocking your nose at people who are worse off materially than you are. I was created for better things. How often am I reminded of Dean Swift as you proceed upon your shallow pontifications about subjects where your ignorance is total.

> How haughtily he cocks his nose
> To tell what every schoolboy knows.

This is you down to the ground. Always remember that I am never haughty but that I am always noble. Please try to see further than me from now on. I am the most modest of appendages and I need not be. Three times in one short passage in *Romeo and Juliet*, the world's greatest tragedy, there is reference to me:

> Oh! then I see Queen Mab hath been with you...
> She is the fairies' midwife and she comes
> In shape no bigger than an agate stone
> On the forefinger of an alderman

Drawn by a team of little atomies
Athwart men's noses as they lie abed...
Sometimes she gallops o'er a courtier's nose
And sometimes comes she with a tithe-pig's tail
Tickling a parson's nose as he lies asleep.
Then dreams he of another benefice.

So you see, my friend, you are not being addressed by a common protuberance and if you must pick me make sure your nails are clean.

Finally, I would ask you to impose a more even tone over my snoring and try to avoid those fretful, fitful snorts that make for staggered snores which are anathema to me. An aborted snore is the most frustrating experience which may befall a nose. There is nothing a nose likes better than being snored through and I am no exception. Also, God bless me, I enjoy the occasional sneeze.

Sincerely

Your Nose

THE HEART WRITES

My dear Brain

You had better listen to me because for all your mastery of all the organs you cannot be aware of the number of beats which are left to me. I myself have a pretty fair idea but you give the impression you don't care.

You could, I dare say, devise a computer which when provided with the speed, strength and regularity of my thumping in relation to other complex factors would provide you with a rough idea of my maximum beat capacity.

The truth is, however, that while I may have a rough idea

of the number left I could be utterly wrong as so many other hearts have been in the past. Even specialists with brains superior to yours have been caught out repeatedly.

I am, of course, one with your soul which we are told is immortal. I am sure the soul exists and so are you. The soul it is which waits patiently for the end when it will assume our spiritual remains into itself for the flight to the hereafter and to God knows what. How's that Anne Hathaway's husband put it?

> *For in that sleep of death, what dreams may come*
> *When we have shuffled off this mortal coil*
> *Must give us pause!*

Pause is right, and if we were pausing all our days and doing nought other than pausing on this particular theme we would be as wise before as after. Therefore live, dear brain, reverse the day and the night you live in for it is all you may comprehend, and mark out a decent place in that land of no return by being decent here. Let us hear from Anne Hathaway's husband again:

> *The undiscovered country from whose bourne*
> *No traveller returns, puzzles the will.*

Puzzles the will indeed and will puzzle it until I cease beating. Therefore, be about your business for puzzlement begets fuddlement and your puniness, poor limited creature, might only be shown to be more pronounced.

We are as incapable of understanding God's designs for us and the concept of life after death as the beasts of the field are of comprehending the quantum theory of radiation. Indeed you would probably achieve a better result by putting a common jackass solely in charge of a human heart transplant than assembling the world's finest brains to solve the mystery of the hereafter.

The moral here is to know your limitations and have faith in your present state. Trust in the creator's plans for you. Trust in God and find peace of mind. How simple for those who can comply.

Alas, the imagination which you excite and ferment beyond its normal capacity complies with little save that in which it may indulge itself. I am your most faithful friend. I will be with you to the last when your soul will transport us to that realm which is beyond our ken.

How often, you ignoble wretch, have you implied in the everlasting tavern-wrangle which is the ultimate in human confusion, that there is no creator, no God, nothing at the end of all.

Like all alcoholically-stupefied brains you speak as though you had inside knowledge, as though you had just heard direct from the creator. I believe that God is omnipotent but sometimes I must be forgiven if I suspect that He is a little deaf, for if He heard only a little of the diabolical criticism to which He is subjected in public houses He would terminate the existence of the inane morons who flagellate Him.

Maybe I'm wrong and maybe it is how you provide Him with the laughter which is echoed in his thunder. 'There is no God!' I once heard you insist in a public house in Galway after your four kings were well and truly demolished by a straight flush of dubious origins in the biggest pot of the night. If you had kept your eyes open and watched the dealer you would only have had to contend with a very ordinary flush but you were too busy calling the barman's attention to your empty glass.

You doubt the hereafter and yet you instruct the ever-baffled mouth to pray for your deceased forebears and with your equally confused hands you disburse mass offerings for their eventual exit from purgatory and entry into the heaven in which you place no credence while sojourning on earth.

Sometimes it is as difficult for me to understand you as it is for you to understand the hereafter. It would seem that you endorse heaven with part of you and dismiss it with another. In your interminable tavern-agonising, fortified by overdoses of whiskey, you dismiss God's very existence and yet you pray in the dark or in times of trial for the same God's protection and forgiveness.

Your petty theological rantings have the same effect on God as the droppings of an underfed insect on the water levels of the Grand Coulee Dam.

How well I remember the countless times you would scoff at the idea that in the hereafter there would be an immediate judgement, where every last sin, venial and mortal, would be paraded before you, before God and before all the angels and saints and before all the happy souls who were granted access to the sight of God by virtue of their goodness during their stay here.

'How for Christ's sake,' you would ask, 'could anybody be aware of every last deed and every last thought of every last person who quits this mortal turmoil?'

It's a wonder you weren't rendered totally deaf by God's laughter, you heretical nonentity.

'How could any so-called divinity,' you went on, to the wonder and delight of your befuddled cronies, 'be capable of remembering the countless repetitive transgressions so wearisome and so inconsequential that they should really count for nothing at all and at the same time seem incapable of acknowledging cataclysmic occurrences where millions die?

'How does He manage to keep a mental record,' you queried

further, 'of every impure thought to assail the minds of honest men and women?'

The answer is simple, you poor benighted heathen. It is no strain whatsoever on God and His omniscient brain to store a record of all man's words, thoughts and deeds down to the most infinitesimal iota, from the beginning to the end of time. It is a God who provided man with the brain that devises computers which will one day soon be capable of revealing all of the world's knowledge and all of man's doings at the press of a button. Imagine the immensity of a brain which in its stride creates thousands of brains like yours every single day as a matter of course, and this among a million other wonderful creations among all the universes and galaxies ad infinitum.

You talk of cataclysmic happenings. Nature is God's brainchild just as man is, and He has given both the power to create and destroy at will thereby justly absolving himself but nevertheless dutifully recording all.

Alas, man's control of both himself and nature is limited in one vital respect. God has seen to that lest man endeavour to destroy God and thus destroy himself. That is God's charity at work and charity is the material which I house on your behalf together with love and compassion, beauty, truth and tenderness which temper the savagery that often runs berserk in you.

Only I, the heart, am capable of anointing you with love so that you do not instruct your limbs to run amok on murderous rampages.

Alas, I am powerless when your sensitive cess, fibres, layers and ineffable what-have-you are shocked and shattered by pressures and accidents, by traumas and tragedies.

Then I bleed for you as do the hearts of good folk everywhere. Here all truly human hearts extend themselves. Here they brim with concern.

So far you have escaped any serious damage which is truly miraculous when your alcoholic intake and propensity to disaster are taken into account. It is a miracle how your hundreds of all too impressionable components, from the central canal to the pyramidal tract, have withstood the sustained barrage to which you have subjected them since you first learned how to walk.

As far as our relationship goes I am always here supporting you, ever ready to heal and succour to the best of my ability, unendingly repaired to invoke all my human features so that they might operate for your benefit and for your salvation. Yet most of the time you take me for granted, except on those rare occasions when, through your self-indulgence, you force me to beat irregularly and even make me pause for breath or miss a beat on my perilous travail.

My workload is mighty but you never accord me a particle of the credit I deserve and yet in the body of Christ I am the sacred centrepiece, the well of compassion, the only divine dimension.

A million songs have been written about me. The loveliest and most everlasting of melodies have been composed on my behalf. Multitudes of jingles and rhymes are addressed to me every day. Wordsworth was only one of a hundred immortals who singled me out for particular mention:

Thanks to the human heart by which we live
Thanks for its tenderness, its joys and fears.

And what does elegant Tennyson say:

Tis only noble to be good
Kind hearts are more than coronets.

And how does humble Shadwell say it?

Words may be false and full of art
Sighs are the natural language of the heart.

And poor, great Goldsmith:

For other aims his heart had learned to prize
More skilled to raise the wretched than to rise.

All poets great and small have celebrated with me. When lesser organs and weary limbs clamour for the bugle of the brain to sound the retreat it is I who stands fast and bears the brunt. It is my courage that sees the body through. I am the rallier, the core. I have no boundaries. I am fathomless in my fearlessness, infinite in my mercy.

Even when you are transmitting demented demands for parley or submission I stand firm. I am the last redoubt. In the final analysis you are not the worst of brains, although by no means are you the best.

I give you some hope, however, out of my love for you. Let there be one good deed, one really unselfish act, one major contribution to the idea of goodness to show you possess the potential for a future which will be the opposite to your past. If this honest recital seems to you to be emotional and maudlin please to remember that it is

From

The Heart

The Right Ear Writes

Dear Brain

Please pay attention to your right ear. My comrade at the other side of the face wishes me to address you on its behalf as well. Indeed it would do so itself but for the fact that you once forgot to duck in a bar-room punch-up, resulting from a political imbroglio, and subjected it to the full impact of an outsize fist swung in the widest possible of arcs from the floor upwards, arriving ultimately with ever-increasing force dead smack on target and utterly destroying the entire area of that pitiful organ from helix to lobule.

Medical treatment, as the song said, failed o'er and o'er. The utricle and the auricle and the epitympanic recess, as well as the tympanic membrane and several other areas of its interior, were totally destroyed. It is now labelled a cauliflower and this it must remain until your time and ours draws to a close.

I believe I have served you well. Everything and anything from the lowliest buzz to the loftiest whine has been conveyed to you unerringly. Every message has been delivered. There is nothing within the range of human earshot that I have not faithfully conveyed to you, much of it distressfully and much of it joyfully, distressfully as when I conveyed news of your father's demise to you having been informed of the tragedy on your behalf by your tearful mother.

Perhaps the most moving and tenderest communication which I ever picked up was that which was delivered by your father when you were a wild young fellow. How's that Ledwidge puts it:

When will was all the Delphi you would heed,
Lost like a wind within a summer wood.

How well your father understood you. Of course, we must not forget that in his heart he was always young. He understood youth and he endeavoured all his life, as in your case, to cultivate it and cherish it.

How fondly I remember his mellifluous voice, never raised in anger but ever pleading, restrained and paternally sweet to me whose joyous task it was to deliver his lofty sentiments and sage advice tempered with good humour to your often inattentive self.

If you had received even one quarter of the warnings I transmitted to you you would be twice the man you are today. Oh the pearls of wisdom, the incomparably shrewd observations and the noble precepts which your father would have you treasure and which I handled with velvet gloves as I presented them to you. I believe, of all the sounds I processed, the dearest to me were your father's pronouncements.

The low, lapping sound of river water was another joy. So, too, was the loving whisper of a tender maid as was the monotone of the salt sea on a calm day. So too was sweet birdsong and the plaintive skirl of distant bagpipes, and how I loved the chiming of evening bells made heavenly by the holy singing of cloistered monks. I loved, too, the laughter of boys and girls, the rich, rare voices of mellow women, the far-off baying of hounds in the late watches, your mother's tender summons when you strayed by. And oh! the awful sorrow when I called you from sleep on her behalf to tell you that he had passed on before his time.

Of all the messages I was ever obliged to deliver that was the one I liked least. Even when your father was silent in your company it was a silence that emphasised his presence. His quiet breathings were like benedictions upon me and armed only with tranquillity he always imposed a balm on your troubled spirit. He knew when to speak and when not. Oh for those deep silences that only I can appreciate. True silence is no accident. It has to be created slowly. Hopkins was one of your father's great favourites:

> *Elected silence, sing to me*
> *And beat upon my whorled ear.*

If I could only choose the sounds I wished to hear. I am subject and must acknowledge ever the feeblest whisper, the faintest sigh, the lowliest croak, the most savage roar, the most rending tumult, the drums, the brasses and the deafening clamour. All must be received and converted by my complex apparati with the maximum accuracy and dispatched with pure articulation.

When a man says his hearing is deceiving him the ear must look to its machinery for, more often than not, omniparous nature must see to my needs. You never think about me. Always you take me for granted. Where would you be if I were cut off or damaged beyond repair because of your negligence! But let us return to your father and his rich humours. He put it well, God rest his impeccable soul, when he said that the heart had only so many beats.

A particular heart, of course, may exceed its allotted number through stimulation or suspension but, by and large, all hearts have fixed limitations.

I will recall, as you do, how your father called you aside one hazy summer's afternoon and invited you to take a seat in the small garden, sweetened, at the time, with the scents of herbs and flowers.

As a prelude to what he was about to convey to you he cleaned out the bowl of his pipe and began to pare paper-thin slivers from the plug of Bendigo tobacco which he had extracted from his waistcoat pocket.

Having pared a sufficiency he placed it in the palm of his left hand and ground it patiently with the base of his right until he brought it to the required consistency.

Those soft almost inaudible sounds were to me what honey is to the taste buds, what a girl's waist is to the lusty youth. How this simple paternal exercise of pipe-filling always fascinated you. I recall how he gently stuffed the pipe bowl with the shredded plug before thrusting the stem into his mouth. Then came the moment of fruition when he lighted the match which ignited the tobacco. Upwards spiralled the blue, fragrant smoke to be scudded and blown westwards before the temperate summer wind. It was a ritual which he used most of his life to impose a calming influence on delicate situations and the situation as it existed between you and he at that time was delicate in the extreme.

It was not long after the fateful evening when you substituted the local baggage for the lovely Lily Lieloly. After the baggage had come a sequence of similar involvements until you became so immersed in fornication that a concerned neighbour of the female gender felt constrained to put your most virtuous mother in the picture.

So horrified was that gracious lady by the inklings revealed that she could not lower herself to confront you. Your father, filling the role played by so many fathers from time immemorial, opened by informing you that it was not his intention to sermonize or condemn and mumbled in jumbled asides how well he understood such matters as the heyday in the blood and the sowing of wild oats and all that! Then he came to the point poor man.

'Tommy,' said he most paternally, 'it has come to my attention that you have been engaged in questionable pursuits with undesirable females. It saddens my heart to hear this and indeed your poor mother's heart is on the verge of breaking.'

You had the grace to bend your head and avert your furiously blushing face. It was then that your father, in his wisdom, rose to the occasion.

'The heart which beats in your young breast, Tommy,' he went on, 'has only so many beats and these beats increase in speed and volume whenever man allows himself to indulge in unchaste thoughts about the opposite sex. If mere thinking causes this acceleration of the human heart, what dizzy speeds are generated by physical contact with a buxom damsel of tartish disposition?'

He paused at this stage, if memory serves me correctly, and savoured a deep pull on his pipe. Instantly the tobacco in the bowl glowed red. Smoke issued from between the teeth at either side of the pipe-stem and from the now florid bowl several gossamer-thin trails of smoke were wafted upwards to breezy disintegration. Estimating that sufficient time had passed for his sentiments to sink in he resumed.

'Bad as physical contact such as kissing and embracing undoubtedly are,' said he solemnly, 'there is no known method of recording the astronomical velocity created by that most demanding and murderous act commonly known as copulation. Whilst even in moderation this heady exercise has been known to cause total physical collapse and subsequent mental derangement, can you imagine the risk to which a young and undeveloped heart is subjected when its equally immature proprietor exercises no restraint whatsoever but actually persists consistently with this suicidal practise until the heart is left without a single beat and there lies a ghastly corpse where once stood a handsome young man.'

Here your beloved father ended his loving admonition. Would that you had taken in his words. You cried salt tears when he had finished and vowed there and then to tread the straight and narrow.

In less than a week you were tripping the troublous trail of debauch once more, your father's words instantly forgotten the moment your senses were assailed by the perfumed swish of a prodigal skirt.

Would that you had one-twentieth the concern for your health that your father had. I might not now be counting your beats, wondering where the next one is coming from and fearful that there might not be a next one at all! I always listen apprehensively to that wayward heart of yours but you are what you are and I am only an ear, a servant as faithful as any but with infirmity beckoning more imperiously as time goes by.

Faithfully yours
The Right Ear

THE REAR APERTURE WRITES

Dear Master
No doubt you will be surprised to hear from me. I have unsuccessfully tried every other means of communication at my disposal. These are very often unacceptable to those who may avail themselves of orthodox means.

Up until this time, because of my extreme situation, I have had no choice but to express myself after the frowned-upon fashion of rear apertures everywhere. Few willingly listen to our protestations.

At the outset I must ask you to forgive the audacity of such a rotten stinker as I and to make allowance for my squalorous background and my undeserved reputation for underhand practices.

Do not, I implore you, be put off by my suspect address. Remember that many have achieved greatness in spite of their lowly origins. I know you love me the least of all your dominions and who, in truth, could love me for myself alone whose chief role is to channel the body's waste from its putrid confines to the world outside, a world visible to me only once in a blue moon when you are in dire need of a toilet in the great outdoors.

My secondary task is to convey and release the audible and inaudible, the fetid and the odourless gases of the dark interior. Sounds easy, but as one of your American cousins was once heard to remark:

'Try being an asshole the day after Saint Patrick's Day and see how you like it!'

Sometimes the anus is suddenly pressurised. I am not warned in advance and there is a foul-up. Nobody likes me for this although I am not to blame. Which of us has not endured this unhappy and embarrassing experience at least once in a lifetime!

It is I who refines and renders articulate all the explosive protestations of the anus. I am the ultimate processor of every sound that is allowed to escape from the behind. Only for me the disgusting bombast of these unsavoury revelations would be unbearably raucous.

It is I who conditions and musicalises these uncouth outbursts till they are often no more than prolonged plaints, inoffensive and sometimes amusing to the surprised listener.

Now and then there are renegades who surprise the system and who shock and confuse those of sensitive backgrounds who may happen to be in the vicinity, thus ensuring that my rating stays at zero. I can accept this. You might say I've grown up with it. What I cannot accept is the contemptible way you treat me, the absence of any sort of regard for my feelings, the never-ending workload, your insanitary attitude, your verminous, unwashed, pathogenic underclothes, your germ-infested, un-sterilised hands, your recklessness in choice of toilets, most notably the unflushed and obviously contaminated, where you will persist in irresponsibly depositing your buttocks for long periods while you futilely endeavour to make up your mind whether you are going to perform or not.

This is a most frustrating time for me. There I am, exposed to my natural enemies, willing and able to assist you in the discharge of your internal wastes while you persist with fitful piddling and misdirected pondering.

May God preserve rear apertures everywhere from the pensive and the pondering. Of all the scourges I have endured and in their entirety they would fill a book, the brooking defecator is easily the most despicable. He is a martyr to his own abstraction. He completely dispels from his mind the purpose which first brought him to the WC and indulges in wide-ranging flights of long-lasting fancy while the unprotected aperture is prey to the thousand contaminations for which privies are justly noted.

The longer I am allowed to remain exposed the greater the risk of infection and the less likelihood of any form of comprehensive cacation whereas with truly marathon sittings there is often the likelihood of no motion at all.

From my obstructed position I have no way of ascertaining what sort of expression dominates your visage during these extended sits and squats, whether it be rapture or sorrow, common contentment or simple suspension.

I dare say you might call me the blind eye of the anatomy but then anything is better than being called an asshole day in, day out. I suspect that while you sit fallow and functionless there is imposed upon your lineaments a trance-like expression which brooks neither interference or distraction.

You are at peace with yourself and the world and this is essential for man's well-being as long as it's not overdone. I have listened often while you rendered tedious soliloquies concerning your past, your present and the life of the world to come.

The real tragedy arises when you go on and on until you are so exhausted that the primary purpose of your visit has been supplanted by some other goal.

Fine if you submitted me to exposure in the open countryside where the air is pure and there is no likelihood of infection. This happens so rarely, however, that the experience might well be described as the annual holiday of the down-under cavity. Even when you do submit me to the benign influences of the rustic scene you are in such an almighty hurry that my holiday is over before it even starts.

When you fall asleep in the indoor toilet my nightmare begins for by so doing you extend an open invitation to every circumjacent creepy-crawly and parasite besides announcing to long-despairing germs that the time has at last come when they may assume bellicose roles once more.

The seismograph of my sensitive perimeter records the most shattering, devastating agitation while you are transported to the world of dreams forgetting the fearful dangers to which we are both exposed.

I recall with total horror the times you fell asleep on the seats of stinking WCs. I would listen to your drunken snoring while assorted insects mobilised themselves in lesser keys, using my vulnerable surrounds as landing bases for the later perpetration of outrages I dare not mention. Often you would sleep for hours, your grinding, grating snorts and intemperate skirls, oblivious to the frenzied pounding upon the privy door by legitimate aspirants to the vitreous throne which you so callously usurped.

Who could blame one of these demented claimants for wanting to implant the toe of a stout boot fairly and squarely upon your undeserving bull's-eye.

I wish, not for the first time, that there were some means by which I might detach myself from your stagnating posterior, to run away from home as it were, never to return or to be transplanted holus bolus to the rear of a more fastidious master.

If I were asked to recount the most trying period of our uneasy relationship I would plump for that miserable night when you unsuccessfully tried to launch yourself on a singing career. There I was, perilously suspended over the most abominable toilet bowl it had ever been my bitter experience to encounter, when you launched into the opening bars of 'South of the Border'. I had never heard you sing before. I had heard you humming tunelessly in the background while others joined in the refrain of a popular song but not until that night of the long sitting did you undertake the singing of a complete song.

I remember how I immediately expostulated through the only medium at my disposal. You totally ignored me as was your wont and went on to massacre a score of well-established ditties before exhausting yourself while you sat. You then mercifully submitted yourself to a deep sleep from which you did not wake until a neighbourhood rooster announced the arrival of the new day with a nerve-shattering sequence of cock-a-doodle-doos. I have searched fruitlessly in the hope that I might find something good to say about you before bringing this epistle to a close. There is, alas! nothing for which you might be commended.

Yours faithfully

Your Rear Aperture

THE INDEX FINGER OF THE RIGHT HAND WRITES

Dear Master

I'll grant you I am but one of ten but you may take it as a Gospel fact that I speak for all. Although you are left-legged you are right-handed and since it is universally accepted that the index finger of the dominant hand has sovereignty over all other fingers, from the thumb to the ludeen, I will take it upon myself, as a natural right, to address you on behalf of all.

The thumb is undoubtedly the bulkiest and the forefinger plays second fiddle to none in matter of length. The ring finger may be the most romantic and the ludeen or little finger the most lovable but it is I who must always point the way.

It is I who taps you on the head and jogs you my master for the resolvement of the prevailing pucker.

By historical and mythological right I am the finger of knowledge, not as an entity but as an instrument of your intent. I listen in respectful silence while the thumb and forefinger clack together for recognition. This is their right. I watch in understanding while the ring finger lights up with pride as the golden band of love is drawn past its knuckle. This is its entitlement. I comprehend when the ludeen or little finger is gently gnawed by your teeth as you reminisce or ponder. This is its role. They too accept that it is I who must point the way.

Each to his own place as the saying goes and all for the good of the whole. What could be more natural! *Naturam expellas furca tamen usque recorret!*

Alas and alack I digress! I wish that this were to be a paean of praise on your behalf but the truth is that I can recall little to offset my poor opinion of you, although there were those early days before you willingly submitted yourself to every conceivable form of debauch.

Those early days! I bet you cannot now recall the name of your first love, nay not your first love; rather should I have said your first sweetheart, that angelic sixteen-year-old Lily Lieloly. Oh for the sweet fragrance of her presence once more! Oh to hear her careless, innocent laughter, to savour her heavenly smile! How lovely, lithe and lissom she was, how pure and incorruptible! Whatever happens I shall never forget Lily Lieloly.

Moore captures my feelings in his song, 'Bendemeer Stream'.

> *No, the roses soon withered that hung o'er the wave*
> *But some blossoms were gathered while freshly they shone*
> *And a dew was distilled from their flowers that gave*
> *All the fragrance of summer when summer was gone.*
> *Thus memory draws from delight e'er it dies*
> *An essence that breathes of it many a year;*
> *Thus bright to my soul as 'twas then to my eyes*
> *Is the bower on the banks of the calm Bendemeer.*

Thus too is the memory of Lily Lieloly to me. Alas poor Moore, so often reviled by ungenerous upstarts because sentiment was his strong suit!

Where was I? It was by a stream, wasn't it, of a summer's evening, as the sun was sinking, as the birds were singing that Lily Lieloly and you sat in a glade near the riverside where the deep, mottled waters reflected the overhanging greenery of beech and sycamore. How could one ever dispel the memory of that sweet, sylvan scene!

That sublime occasion, my dear master, was my finest hour. I remember how a lone linnet took advantage of a lull in the evening chorus and used it to serenade his soulmate as she fluttered and flitted from bramble to bramble, from bower to bower. I recall the doubt in the hazel eyes and trembling lips of lovely Lily Lieloly as she looked unwaveringly into your face and asked if you loved her.

You straightaway cupped her sweet face in your hands and pressed your fingers, of which I was the privileged ringleader, against her silken cheeks. You made comparison of her melting eyes to the deepening cinnamon of the darkening stream, of her ash blonde hair to the silver beams of the strengthening moon and her bountiful lips to the purest rubies of distant, dusky Arabia.

In those days the poetry would surface in you like the chortling, churning waters of a richly-endowed spring.

'Do you love me, Tommy?' she asked secondly and with myself alone, your faithful index finger, you traced gentle patterns on her now moist lips.

'Love you?' you said, as you pressed me and the others once more to her face. 'I love you so much,' you whispered fiercely, 'that there is a hurt in me which will not heal, a hurt so awful that it pits itself against the very beating of my heart.'

You kissed her then but you did not have your way with her because the girl was pure as the morning dew, the evening star, the holy of holies!

That was long ago, Tom, before the pillaging years in their unstoppable succession reduced you to the sorry ould roué that you are today. You did not see Lily Lieloly after that. You allowed yourself to be waylaid by the neighbourhood baggage and so filled were you with shame that you could not look into the hazel eyes of Lily Lieloly ever again.

After that you went from worse to worse, starting off as a devotee of golf club teases and ending as an all-round libertine. Ah but then you married, not altogether for love, old boy, but for material possessions and the acquisition of a prime piece of shapely flesh. You fared only moderately in marriage and why should you fare better! You only withdraw what you deposit in the marriage stakes and your romantic deposits were few and far between.

You used me, my master, as you used your business acquaintances and those you called friends, solely for your own ends. You used me, who was clearly meant for better things, for such degrading chores as the evisceration of reluctant mucus securely secreted in the recesses of your puce-veined proboscis, directing me in your urgency to remove not only the recalcitrant snot but also the skin beneath, thereby causing sustained nosebleeds in both nostrils.

I might have been combined, under different circumstances, with my fellow fingers to wield an artist's brush and present the world with a masterpiece or to raise aloft the sword of truth and lead an army of knights against the forces of evil.

I might have, with the aid of your four faithful companions, placed a crown upon your head or if you had only opted for the priestly vows we might have, untimately, imposed pontifical blessings upon vast congregations and sent them forth across the world with messages of peace and goodwill.

In another age, with another master, I might have drawn your Colt .45 with lightning speed and dispatched to Boot Hill every last desperado on the streets of Larado!

Had you opted for refereeing I might have pointed goalwards imperiously for the last controversial penalty in the final of the World Cup. Instead I was called upon to scratch your already overscratched posterior.

I might have been the natural baton that conducted the Berlin Philharmonic or, if you had but entered politics, raised myself aloft after your election to the presidency, and confidently pointed the way forward to a better future.

I might have lifted myself to sway a dangerous mob and earned for us unprecedented applause as you silenced the fickle multitudes like a Demosthenes or a Marcus Antonius. But no! You preferred to ditheringly bite my nail when an important decision was called for or point the accusing finger safely at some unfortunate pariah already consigned to damnation.

You had me in every material pie when you might have impaled me on the consciences of the neo-Nazi and the perpetrators of apartheid.

You thrust me into your ear lest you hear whenever an anguished scream shattered the silence of the night. As well as demoting me to the lowly role of snot remover you also transformed me into a vomit inducer and sneeze suppressor.

Worst of all was when you deliberately bypassed grotto, shrine and sacred tabernacle as well as ignoring the last resting places of your forbears when you should have been directing me respectfully to your forehead where I might ceremoniously execute the Sign of the Cross in memory of all things good and holy.

Instead you would titter and scoff with your equally drunken companions when some brave soul dared to cross himself out of deference to the Blessed Trinity.

I'll conclude now in the cherished hope that this epistle will infuse in you a new determination to devise more edifying pursuits for

Your ever-faithful

Index Finger

THE EYES WRITE

Dear Brain

We can transmit images of every conceivable kind but our great regret is that we cannot look inward. We cannot be one with our parent, the mind's eye, thereby being in a position to observe on your behalf the wonders and beauties of the world. The mind's eye is your very self, of course, and we are but your servants. We cannot see beyond your mental limitations. We only see what you wish us to see.

This communication is long overdue by the way and we must say at the outset that it is our contention that our true capacity has never been realised, nor even partially realised chiefly because of your aesthetic shortcomings and your obsession with the carnal.

It became apparent to us at a very early stage that you were no Wordsworth and that your thoughts from youth onwards tended to descend rather than ascend.

You directed us to observe the bosoms and posteriors of golf club teases when we might have been gloriously surveying the beauties of nature. You had us savouring the sonsy swaggers of cheap tarts when we might have been beholding the willowy, fragile forms of delicate demoiselles, the serenity shining on their angel faces, their eyes cast shamefacedly downwards because of the obscene fashion in which you directed us to behold them.

We remember once of an April day you sat by the seashore pondering your future. At the time the world was your oyster and the pain after the rift with Lily was receding as the waves were receding before your very eyes which we have the honour to be.

Your normally turbulent mind had become somewhat becalmed by the gentle motions of the sea for it was a day without wind and the sweet, soothing monotone was a balm to your spirit. We had great hopes for you on that day.

The sky was blue without trace of cloud. On the horizon the smoke from a passing freighter stood like a slender plume in the still air. Seabirds crying joyfully drifted aimlessly overhead and then a curvaceous female appeared out of the waves close by. Without as much as a glance in your direction she unbuttoned the strap of her bathing cap and carelessly flicked her freshly-released curls with expertly-manicured hands.

We did not blame you when you rose from the stone where you had been sitting the better to view this luscious Aphrodite. Just then a soberly-dressed girl with a sweet and gentle face entered the scene. The whole situation was a classical example of your attitude to life and proof, if any was ever needed thereafter, that you were ever a slave to the meretricious.

Both girls were known to you, the bathing beauty casually but the soberly-dressed somewhat more since you had spoken to her and indeed danced with her in the days when you were still rebounding after your Lily Lieloly period.

Of the two we, the eyes, knew that the quality lay with the soberly-dressed and if you had given us our heads, as it were, and allowed us time to dwell on her we might have shown that she was a creature of true loveliness and convey to you the joyful tidings that under the brown costume which she wore was a body as lithe, lovely and desirable as any. Alas you became obsessed as always with the obvious, barely glancing at the clad creature but drooling uncontrollably after the other.

The girl in brown boasted short-cropped, light brown hair. Her eyes were as blue as the ocean serene which no longer occuped a place in your thoughts. Her smile, as she passed, was radiant and chaste. The two go hand in hand, you know.

The other was prettier on the surface with curling blonde hair, green eyes, rich pouting lips and a burgeoning body designed to infatuate easily-overcome libertines like yourself.

The scene was now set for the drawing back of the curtain. Old Nick must surely have been the stage manager. Possessed with that rare inside knowledge of human weakness and your own particular lack of godliness he rung the bell for the commencement of the play which has been presented on so many strands and beaches over so many years.

As she passed by the soberly-clad girl shortened her steps in the hope that a conversation might be forthcoming because for all your apparent weaknesses she obviously perceived in you some hitherto well-hidden qualities which might one day shape you into a worthwhile human being.

In normal circumstances, if the bikinied beauty was not present, you would have quickly engaged her costumed counterpart for she was a girl of rare and sensitive character. Even you, for all your faults, were aware of this.

Unfortunately you permitted her to pass by and concentrated your gaze on the creature who had emerged from the sea. The water droplets still glistened on her shapely shoulders and when she shook her hair free her body rippled and shivered, stressing her buxom shape and golden hue so that you immediately became sensually enraptured and a prisoner once more of your own inherent prurience. When she waved casually in your direction you bounded like a rutting stag through the shallow water until you found yourself by her side.

How old Nick must have smiled and how the forces of love and beauty despaired of ever making you see the light! We, your eyes, certainly could not but then you never presented us with the slightest opportunity of doing so.

The play, which was proceeding according to plan under the professional direction of Doctor Darkness, was no tragedy. Neither was it to be a comedy. We would suggest that we were about to witness a traditional farce. We were to be proved right. The vigorous, blooming creature by your side was possessed of a hollow metallic laugh which smote upon the sea's gentle cadences like a whiplash. Your crude jokes were finding their target.

There was no rebuff when your sweaty palm rested on her farthest hip. After all she was not without credentials or so it was believed. What poor girl is not when vile rumour runs unchecked from tongue to scurrilous tongue!

As you moved father away from the other strollers and bathers you cast us about seeking a place where you might lure her and be hidden from the prying eyes of the crowd.

Suddenly the girl stopped dead in her tracks. Her body trembled and shuddered. Her lips parted and her bosom rose and fell as though she had been seized by a sudden spasm.

What you could not have known, because of failing to employ us to the fullest, was that she had spotted in the distance a lusty young man for whom she entertained the most powerful romantic thoughts. Stupidly taking it for granted that she had succumbed inevitably to your manliness you thrust a hand deep down inside her wispy briefs. The play was coming to its climax. With a well-controlled shriek of disgust she administered a ringing slap to your face and pranced away from you with unconcealed dismay through the spray in the direction of the young man who had entered unexpectedly from the wings.

This commonplace farce was not yet ended however. All the pieces were not in place. You stood there in a state of shock for some time until the heady excitement to which you had earlier succumbed was replaced by a feeling of loss and remorse. The sheen which had earlier disported itself on the surface of the sea seemed to have lost its glitter. The seabirds now sang mournfully as though they were keening an irreplaceable loss. The ship had disappeared from the distant horizon and gathering there from the southwest were ramparts of murky clouds which would soon suffuse the shining heavens. You returned to the empty rock from which you had so ardently erupted a short while before, there to ponder life's cruelty before the stormy showers of April would send you scurrying like all the others for shelter.

The farce was about to play itself out in true fashion. All was set for the side-splitting finale which would bespeak the final curtain.

As you sat with your head in your hands, the tears forming in the wells of your eyes, the seabirds dived all about you and it seemed as though they were crying the name of Sheila.

'Sheila, Sheila!' they bleated as they circled immediately over your bent head. Hopefully you raised that same head and listened intently.

'Sheila, Sheila!' they mewed romantically and indeed that was, you imagined, the name of the costumed creature of the short-cropped hair and sensitive face who had passed by and was forsaken by you for the girl who had sallied out of the sea.

'Sheila, Sheila, Sheila!' the white birds called. How's that Gerald Griffin described the seagull:

White bird of the tempest oh beautiful thing!
With the bosom of snow and the motionless wing.

How often have we eyes marvelled at their elegant symmetry and now after delighting you with their fluent and silent flight they would remind you that all was not lost, that there were other fish in the sea. You should have looked before you leaped, however. That is precisely what we humble organs of visions are for, to measure the intervening paces between ourselves and the target and report what lies at the other end so that trouble may be avoided. Utilised thus we are of priceless assistance to our proprietor and will truthfully inform him of every hazard before age eventually curtails us.

In our prime there are no organs to match us. You did not apply us properly when you arose from your stone seat and stumbled crazily off in the direction taken by the costumed Sheila. At first she was nowhere to be seen. You were at a stage then after the stinging rebuff from the bikinied lovely where any form of consolation would suffice. Any port in a storm goes the old adage and thus it was with you as you now lumbered westwards into the sun calling out her name. When you came upon her she was in the arms of another, the first known sympathetic face she encountered after you had spurned her. He was a good-looking chap, lithe and blonde with a confident smile. They both laughed upon beholding your demented eyes and upon hearing the name Sheila repeatedly issuing from your dry lips. Her name it transpired was Mary Jane. Instantly you retraced your steps angered and shamed. The seagulls now ululated like banshees and then mewed derisively as they soared upward and outward. The rising breeze laughed at your plight and the freshly whipped breakers roared their appreciation of the farce which had just drawn to its close. It had been a great afternoon's theatre and how could it be otherwise with an actor of your stature playing the role he was born to play and the script ready made for your unique talents. All nature seemed in uproar, seas, winds, clouds and rain rendering encore after encore.

You slunk from that cheerless place a chastened wretch, a martyr to your baser instincts. We, the eyes, rallied to your aid, focusing our distracted elements on the outlines of distant mountains overhung by rich clusters of white cloud. We left the storm behind us and the next vista of interest to which we were exposed was the bar of the resort's only hotel.

On your behalf we surveyed the amber contents of whiskey bottles, the crystal clarity of gins and vodkas, the shining saffrons, the brighter tangerines and the pale gold of assorted sherries. The well-stocked shelves of better-class taverns and hotels are a source of constant delight to us. The colours of the rainbow reside in the array of cordials and intoxicants.

The shining bottles, freshly dusted, gleamed and tantalised as we took stock of every saleable beverage from the light chamois of tequila to the green savannah of créme de menthe. We, eyes, exult in presenting you with this challenging and luminous diversity of exciting colour. Nowhere else will one experience such an uplifting array. We would never object to spending long periods in such prismatic surroundings. We dallied for a period on the cardinal red of Campari and lingered yet again on the mustard of advocaat, flitted to the Russian red of raspberry and finally fixed ourselves on the old reliable amber of honest to God whiskey. The bubbles chortled in the optic as the measure filled. You always drank your whiskey neat but would chase the shorts faithfully with half pints of your favourite ale.

Is it any wonder that soon we were seeing sights that we had not seen before! Eventually we started to see double and the fat, unsmiling barmaid who had dispensed your first drink was now magically transformed into two of the most titillating and identical nymphs ever to stand behind the counter of a tavern. You ignored the printed caution behind the counter which stated:

'When our barmaids start to look beautiful it's time to go home.'

Then, of course, you were always a man who never went home when he should. As the barmaid was transformed once more into a single person her beauty decreased not a whit. You told her you loved her and could not live without her but it was a tale she had heard and digested calmly many a time and oft. When you proposed to her she laughed heartily and informed you that she was married already. Shortly after a second proposal and several further declarations of love our vision grew exceedingly blurred. Your hands trembled when you raised your glass. Consequently when you tumbled off the stool and fell into a heap on the floor it came as no surprise to any of the organs involved. The inevitable had happened.

Mercifully, as far as we were concerned, the orgy was ended. We were closed up for the night and would take no further part in the proceedings, nor would we see your mother arrive to collect your drunken remains, but we would open up for business as soon as you had slept it off and we would focus to the best of our impaired ability to see you through the morrow.

This interlude which we have recalled for you is to remind you that we are capable of infinitely loftier undertakings and that you have changed little in the years which have elapsed since that day by the seaside. Nevertheless, we will always be on the lookout for you but would be most appreciative if you could see your way to directing us towards scenes of natural beauty and rapture which abound for man's delight in the world which surrounds you. A time will come when we will be obliged to pull down the shutters forever! It would be a shame if we were not utilised more beneficially before that sad day arrives.

Sincerely

Your Eyes

The Guardian Angel Writes

Dear Brain

I am the echo of your breath. In quietude, before and after sleep, you may hear me if you are attentive. I should be a consolation, a guarantee that your application for admittance to heaven is still being considered.

I can be terrifying, however, especially when the conscience is justifiably restive after you have perpetrated an evil deed. Then I pulsate and become thunderous in your ears until the guilt drives you from your bed and you pine for instant forgiveness from the evil with which you have become besotted.

Your physical exertions may temporarily silence me but I am always there, always.

Drive me out and you are doomed. You cannot see me because I am not flesh and blood nor am I of the world. At my most visible I am a tiny haze that ups and downs in front of your eyes, that sometimes hangs suspended and moves only in unison with your eyes. Sometimes when you are spiritually pure and possessed of the grace of God, otherwise known as peace of mind, you will catch a glimpse of me in your eyes if you stand before a mirror. Settle for the glimpse for I am not at liberty to reveal myself in full.

I am what you would like to be but cannot because of your human shackles. You are in perpetual bondage to your appetites. I am there to leaven the natural evil which you have inherited. I am the antidote for despair. 'Ware these sins above all or I may be driven out; despair, pride and greed and scandalise not the little ones. Remember my friend that you are at this time of life but a russetting leaf. Your summer greenery is long blemished. You could drift downwards at any time. You would not survive a mortal storm and yet you still persist in bringing the winds of tumult upon your head. You flutter before the endearments of mild winds. Imagine your chances in a gale and yet you will persist in gambling with your destiny at this autumnal stage of your lifely proceedings. You would still sport and play beyond the confines of propriety as if there was no God. How often have you foolishly told yourself that things will be all right on the day, that the good you have done outweighs the evil. You foolish fellow. It is not you who will be holding the scales.

You are drifting towards the rocks and your barque is a fragile one, already partially decomposed from the buffeting to which you have exposed it over the years. I do what I can and will do what I can but you must improve if I am to be successful in my advocacy. I once heard you say in your devilishly logical way to another drunken companion:

'Why should we be isolated to outer darkness because our so-called saviour suffered for a few hours on a cross?'

He suffered all his life for you and your likes, you insignificant ingrate. Without His arrival the world would be in a state of darkness so terrible that it would be impossible to distinguish it from hell. There would be nothing sacred, nothing to which a man might cling. It is His spirit which maintains the light which is the repository of love, truth, beauty and compassion. Without His perpetual presence you would be less than a shadow.

How often have you denied God as a justification for your self-indulgence.

'There's no God,' comes the pitiable bleat from you and other apostles of despair and depravity. Remember that day by the sea when the white breakers foamed and thundered under a blue sky and a rising wind. Your breath was taken away as you gazed enraptured. I stood with you and rejoiced in the glory of God. Remember the old priest who knew you as a boy. He wandered past with his cane and dog.

'Isn't it lovely, Father!' you called out.

'It is indeed, Tommy,' he replied gravely. 'There is a God there after all.'

'What has God got to do with it?' You put the question silently to yourself but that old priest seemed to hear.

'Man didn't make this day,' said he. 'Nor did he make this scene and if it wasn't man it can't have been the Board of Works so it has to be somebody else, Tommy.'

When your face assumed a slightly mutinous look he spoke again.

'We don't have to call Him God, Tommy. What's in a name, lad?'

He passed by, a smile on his face. Later that day you were to argue in a hotel bar that God was too grave, that there was no humour in the Gospels, that they were the only books from which you never received a laugh. Point taken Tommy. Point taken. The Gospels are full of laughter, Tommy, because they are full of love and truth and these are the fathers and mothers of internal laughter, not the coarse, drunken guffaws which can be heard in public houses and lavatories. Have this laughter by all means but do not deny the existence of other other laughter.

Why do you think nuns go around smiling all the time? Why do so many priests and nuns and other people of God radiate so much laughter? It is because they rejoice in the glory and goodness of the Creator. You know me all your life, Tommy, and yet you do not know me at all because you have never taken the trouble to know me. That is why I now write to you, to beseech you not to dawdle in the mire of debauch while you might be uplifted by goodness and beauty. It is essential that we get to know each other soon so that we might resolve our differences so that I might contribute to the making of the good man you can still be and ought to be. Then would I salute you. Then would I say to the world:

'Come look at my pupil, at what he has made of himself, of what he is prepared to be. Come and behold the man who has come in from the darkness and now stands in the light.'

I do not expect you to stay in the light, Tom, old son. Just stay as near as you can. I accept your humanity for what it is, a continuing blight for which there is no permanent cure. All I want from you is an honest effort every so often and you will see that the sum of these efforts will pave the way for something outstanding between us, will bring us together as we were never together. It is my bounden duty to ensure that you are set on the road to true enlightenment. If I could accomplish this it would make me a very happy Guardian Angel. It would also make you into something special.

I wonder if you have ever noted certain priests and nuns and other sacred people who quietly yet elegantly shine their ways through a world which is darker than it is bright. Sometime it would be greatly to your benefit if you were to engage briefly in conversation with such people. You would see at once that they are God's people. God lets it be known that they are His people because He shines through them and He has given to their countenances a grace-filled radiance and a loveliness which can be inspiring.

You may if you wish catch glimpses of the Creator in the way these sanctified persons disport themselves, in the way they live and, indeed, in the way they die.

Look to them then and at them and absorb the tranquillity which they generate and you may come to know the true value of yourself. You will not be able to conceive of wrong while you are in their presence. They are to be found everywhere but mostly where there is need for them. They are the unselfish, the concerned, the compassionate, the forgiving. Those are the persons whose presences I always long to encounter.

I know, dear Tommy, that you may never be one of these but by talking to them and perhaps walking with them the meaning of earthly loveliness will be revealed to you. God visits every face but many faces are incapable of hosting Him for any length of time. Others are so steeped in evil that they turn from Him. I saw you turn, Tom, but your ensuing guilt gave me hope for you.

I wish I could precisely define my make-up for you. Firstly I am an angel, probably the most inferior form of an angel but an angel nevertheless. I am approved by heaven and I am composed of love and compassion. Also in me is the goodness of the people who went before you, your father, your grandparents, your uncles and aunts and relatives who have gone into heaven, your friends, and well-wishers who have followed. All of these are in my make-up and they have empowered me to look after you. In me there can be no evil although I may brush with evil on a daily basis. In me is total well-being for you from the angels and saints of the heavens and the almighty God who watches over all. My commission is to request you to be generous and caring towards your fellow-humans, to be considerate in your treatment of all people from the lowly to the highest and to let love of your fellow man and your God pervade your make-up to such a degree that evil cannot thrive there. Most important of all, of course, is that you should respect yourself.

I am different from the sixth sense in that I have a link with your Creator. The sixth sense is your physical custodian but I am your spiritual custodian. It is my function to preserve you and to present you whole and clean at the end of your days in order to justify my visitation with you and to ensure that you will have as good a chance of salvation as the next man. Nobody knows better than I the terrible burden you have to bear and the temptations that beset you from morning till night. However, you are spiritually well equipped to bear this burden and to resist temptation.

I am your alter ego except that I do not suffer from physical or moral contamination. Pollute me too much by your thoughts or deeds and you will render me ineffective. I am the sacred cocoon through which you would foolishly burst and vanish irretrievably were I not on guard for your sake and yours alone throughout my stay with you.

I will never desert you. If there is desertion you are the one who will do it. By my angelic nature I cannot and will not forsake you. Without me you have no armour against evil. You may escape your conscience from time to time. You may even escape permanently but you will never shrug me off. I will be there at the last day to stand up for you. I ask little in return, just one thing. Few people know, and you are not one of the few, that my feast day occurs on the second day of October. I would ask you to take yourself aside on that day and consider me. Do not pray for me. Rather pray to me. I have no need of prayer being an angel but it is my duty to foster prayer in you. May I say also that I would not be averse to having a few celebratory drinks with you on my feast day provided that you not over-indulge. Still I must concede that I would rather see you half-drunk on my behalf than to suffer the disappointment of your not remembering me at all.

You have never, once in your life, lifted a glass to me. I can accept this from people who do not indulge in intoxicating liquor but it is indefensible that men who drink for every known reason and often for no reason at all are not prepared to toast their Guardian Angel.

Remember my feast day then with prayers for yourself and your own and the salvation of those near and dear to you as well as the salvation of all well-meaning humans on the face of the globe. I am there all right; make no mistake about that. If you have a heart you must admit to a soul and if you have a soul you must admit to a conscience and if you have a conscience you must admit to having a Guardian Angel. All the spiritual aspects and all the physical aspects of the body resemble, in some ways, a deck of playing cards. Some have more value than others but it is the way the cards are played that shows their real importance in the game of life, which is the most bewildering and often most macabre game of all.

There was a night when you stopped to admire a particularly dazzling sky of stars. It was a frosty midnight in the month of December. You had just departed the lovely Lily Lieloly and your young heart was singing. Hearts have been known to sing when love is present and yours is no exception. You marvelled at the magnificence of the midnight sky. That was as close as you ever got to me, Tommy Scam. I was pleased with you that night. I gave you a spiritual pat on the head and endeavoured to infuse in you a greater love of God's creations. The moment passed all too quickly. The gentle images of the stars were driven from your mind by sinister and obscene thoughts of the heavenly creature to whom you had so recently bade goodbye.

I don't know what's to become of you at all. Should you be taken suddenly by a fatal seizure you would be poorly prepared for a confrontation with your maker and even I as a sympathetic go-between would be hard put to defend you. That is why I urgently entreat you to consider your position. Let us look at yesterday alone. There were no morning prayers before you undertook the business of the day. You failed to contribute a full day's work in return for the money you earned. You left your employers short but oh! what an outcry there would be if they left you short!

All through the day you entertained immoral thoughts about the new secretary who occupies a seat directly in front of you; difficult to blame you altogether for this. A young, short skirt and an old and dirty mind are important ingredients in the recipe for sexual debauch of the mental variety. You inflicted continuing harm on your much-abused stomach by substituting three whiskies for the soup and sandwiches which your body so desperately needed and once you get the taste of whiskey there is no holding you until total drunkeness sets in. What a way to end a day! Drunk and insensible, unable to eat the delightful meal which your wife prepared for you and nary a prayer from your sinful mouth before that intrepid and often fatal journey though the watches of the night.

You have always taken more out of the world than you can ever possibly put back into it. Still, as Paul says: 'I will be with you all the days even unto the consummation of the world,' but after that we may well find ourselves in a parlous puddle from which there may be no redemption.

There is still hope, however, as long as I am with you. You may still aspire and the lower a man has descended the easier it is for him to climb.

I am there to be emulated. Always remember that. With me as with God all things are possible and the best thing about God, because of the greatness of His love, is that He frequently allows Himself to be taken in by the last-minute repentances of lifelong reprobates as long as the sorrow is genuine and the firm resolve to sin no more is present.

Sincerely

Your Guardian Angel

The Sixth Sense Writes

Dear Brain

Nobody understands more than I the feelings of hopeless frustration festering in the minds of the unemployed millions who stalk the streets of our cities in search of gainful employment. There they are, willing and able to lend their considerable talents and skills to the advancement of the world and its peoples but must languish and despair forever in the awful knowledge that they will never make a meaningful contribution to life nor will they ever develop their natural potential to the full. Thus it is with me.

You, the brain, are my government and like the governments who have knuckled under to unemployment you have denied me my rightful say in your progression. If you had heeded me you might have won the hand of your first love, Lily. There are fateful moments in every man's life when only the sixth sense can direct him, and none more so than when he finds himself in the minefield of premarital miscalculation.

There you were, estimating your chances of an illicit relationship with that lovely and gentle girl when all the time the most inner of intimations were silently suggesting that you would be wise to be at your wariest.

I cautioned you that girls like Lily Lieloly do not come down in every shower, that she was pure of heart and angelic in temperament, that she was sweet and undefileable, but you persisted with your dastardly and foolhardy plot to seduce her.

I recall the setting well and I warned you with every fibre of my make-up that you were treading on dangerous ground. The sixth sense, alas, does not have a physical input to the body. Therefore, I could not seize you by the scruff of the neck as I would have liked and direct you from the wood's shady path to the bright glade.

The bright glade lay by a still stream traversed by hovering kingfishers and flitting water ouzels. Other birds sang sweetly in the surrounding blackthorn and insubstantial summer breezes set the leaves faintly fluttering as the dancing sun ascended the cloud-free heavens. What a setting for a gentle romantic dalliance, a place set aside for hand-holding and gentle kissing, for promises of lifelong love, promises true but no more, no more.

The shady wood path on the other hand took one away from the shining river and the greensward and lost itself in the shadows and there we stood, the three of us, your lustful self, your laughing-eyed Lily and your sixth sense, crestfallen, rejected and distracted.

You were, without knowing it dear Tom, at the very crossroads of your life and the path you would take on that glorious summer's day would decree the lifestyle that lay ahead of you.

All my components from insight to inspiration were unable to dissuade you from taking the wrong course. In one hand you carried a quart flagon of cider; in the other you lightly held Lily's graceful fingers. For a moment you stood silently, your gaze attracted alternately by light and shade. Lily, for her part, stood dreamy-eyed by your side, not caring which pathway you chose such was her faith in you.

From the very first moment she knew you she had placed her trust in you and now, with the aid of shadow, mossbank and cider you would endeavour to seduce her.

Earlier, in the town, she had protested when you had invested in O'Shonnessy's cider. She had insisted that you purchase a non-alcoholic beverage such as lemonade or orangeade but how airly you had dispelled the innocent girl's doubts as you held up the flagon of amber liquid to the light. Its bubbling, crystal clarity would advertise its harmlessness, protest its innocence and you, you sex-inspired knave, assured her that a body could drink a barrel of it without forfeiting a fragment of control.

O'Shonnessy's Sparkling Cider, and if one was to believe the label it was pressed out of mature and luscious fruit from the home orchard. The home orchard indeed! The world and his wife would swear that nothing but wild crab apples, windfallen and rotten, gathered for pittances by impecunious urchins were its chief if not its sole ingredients.

'My own mother drinks it,' you had lied outrageously, knowing that only once ever had she partaken of a small glass after hearing from a now disgraced quack that it had a mollifying effect on arthritis.

Upon hearing of your mother's partiality Lily's remaining doubts were dispelled and she tripped happily by your side till you found yourselves faced with a choice between glade and shade. Winsomely she danced by your side when you led her from the path of brightness.

You knew where you were going for already you had reconnoitred the river banks and their surrounds in search of a suitable spot for what you had in mind. I stayed with you all the time, alerting you and jolting you, vainly trying to remind you that another type of girl would have been far more suitable for the venture in which you would have Lily Lieloly participate. Indeed there are girls in a world of many girls who would require no stimulant such as cider or no secure surrounds for it is part of their nature to indulge such as you.

Lily was different as were most of the girls of your youth. You knew this and yet you gambled a lifetime in her presence for a lustful interlude.

You stopped at a dark pool over which hung the long green arm of a leafy chestnut. Alongside there grew a man-sized cushion of spring, spongy, whitegreen moss. Without more ado you uncorked the cider and held the jowel to the untainted lips of Lily Lieloly. Poor child she spluttered and choked but sport that she was she swallowed nevertheless. You drank copiously yourself and then you implanted a gentle kiss on the upturned face of your first love. You made her drink again and again as you did yourself until the bottle fell from your hand and rolled without a tinkle into the long grasses close by. Then you knelt and you drew Lily downwards also, cupping her heavenly face in your common hands as you drew her slender body close to your own and eventually side by side on the mossy bed. No birds sang in that loveless place and no breeze dared enter its clammy confines. The pool darkened as your body hardened and your desire took hold. Was there ever anything as lovely as Lily's blushing face before she realised for what evil business you had lured her into the shadows. You should have desisted from your purpose when that first faint flicker of alarm puckered her lovely brow and you should have begged her forgiveness when the initial shock became transformed into sheer terror. You should have released her, asked for her forgiveness and lain your lapse at the door of your unbridled manhood. She would have forgiven you. She was that kind of girl. But no, you forced your inflamed kisses on lips that now curled inward in disgust. You ripped her blouse apart and her beautiful breasts of the dun-dark nipples shivered and trembled from the unaccustomed exposure. She covered them with her shaking hands at which point you grasped her scantily-clad buttocks in your insensitive palms. She cried out asking you to restrain yourself but her pleas fell on deaf ears. How fortunate she was that you always had extreme difficulty in unbuttoning and unzipping the flaps of those cheap trousers of yours. She made good her escape as you tried frantically to rip the offending zip apart but it remained stuck. Knowing she had gone, your passion subsided as quickly as it had erupted. When the heinousness of what you had tried to do dawned on you you threw yourself on the mossy bed, face downwards, in a fit of remorse.

You might have had Lily Lieloly and her splendid, burgeoning breasts and her warm lips on yours and the silken subtlety of her white, pulsing body and all the incomparable intoxicating gifts which only a sweet, loving woman can bestow upon a man. You might have known heaven on earth if you had only heeded your sixth sense. I was and am one of the most priceless acquisitions a body can have. I must be heeded, however, if I am to remain sharp.

After that inglorious encounter with the girl you lost forever, I wilted somewhat and was for a long while the despair of the other senses who, capable as they are, cannot maintain the harmony of the human system without my presence. I am convinced that the sunless clearing where you contrived to trap her was not an evil place before you selected it for your dark deed. All it had before you polluted it was the potential for evil. I can tell because I have the means of pinpointing locations where evil may surface. After your departure from that place you left much of your innate wickedness behind you, that innate inheritance which is the scourge of every human. There it became absorbed into the bloomy surroundings, transforming them into a setting so accursed and malevolent that other sixth senses would be immediately alerted to its dangers thereafter. Places such as that unfortunate clearing are not evil in themselves. Only man has the capacity to generate evil into them and, in so doing, partially purifies himself.

After Lily you degenerated further, rallied briefly to a state of moderate goodness and later became for all time the very epitome of fallibility. You began to need me desperately after a while and you had the maturity to heed me.

There was the time of the bull. You walked through a morning field searching for mushrooms with your eldest daughter. Her happiness was reflected in you, in you who deserved nothing of that ilk, but she loved you. Then the good God in His mercy and generosity acknowledged that love and permitted the beauty of her young soul to temporarily shine on yours. As you both dallied now and then to pluck a mushroom from its loamy bed the dew flickered on the green grass and the cobwebs beaded with tiny drops glittered like diamond brooches in the sunlight.

It was a happy time and then, suddenly, as you straightened to add a mushroom to your store you sensed, through me, that danger had materialised behind you. Without me you would have been quite incapable of registering any such recognition. You stiffened but did not look round. This was the correct thing to do under the circumstances. Your other instincts wanted you to bolt, in fact insisted you quit the scene without wasting a thought on your defenceless daughter. Human love, however, which makes a mockery of terror and danger when it flowers to its fullest, spoke on your behalf:

'Run,' you whispered urgently. 'Run to the gate. Climb it and don't look behind. Off with you now.'

Dutiful daughter that she was she did as you bade. She would, without question, have walked over a clifftop had you commanded her. Behind you came the terrifying sound of scraws being uprooted. You knew then that you were being seriously considered for dispatch to eternity by Drumgooley's bull, a ferocious creature whose presence in the vicinity you should have taken into account before you risked you and your daughter's lives to satisfy your craving for mushrooms.

With soiled trousers and dyed hairs standing rigidly atop your head you tiptoed gatewards at what you hoped was a leisurely pace. Then came the bestial, earsplitting bellow which precipitated the charge. The race was on! The gate, only fifty yards away, seemed like miles. You were obliged to hold your paunch in your hands as you ran lest its downward plopping bring you to the ground and certain death. Your pursuer was in his prime. His rippling back spoke of his splendid condition but the bloodshot eyes were crazed and the brain tormented from the sapping services he had rendered to two score hederaceous cows and heifers from early summer. You panted as you ran. He snorted as he neared his victim. With the gate still yards away you stumbled but did not fall. Alas the distance between you and the bull was considerably shortened by this reverse. Only inches now divided you. Then you heard your daughter's voice:

'Come on, Daddy!' she screamed, and with a superhuman effort you managed to clamber over the gate, breaking your wrist as a result.

The bull, a lusty three-year-old of the Aberdeen Angus strain, pawed the ground inside the gate and lofted clay and sods over his powerful shoulders. Never did a daughter cling to a father with such fervent love. Never did so many warm tears rain on such a bristly face. Even you, perverted apology for a man that you are, were moved. Even I whose sole business is to issue warnings and cautions was prepared to concede at that moment that maybe you were not a full one hundred per cent bad.

You met another crossroads when taking the wrong turning could have cost you your life. As always I was vigilant. You stood outside the shoddy entrance to Madame Sin Su's Palace of Peking Pleasures in one of the seamier side streets of Soho. Madame Sin Su, Mistress of Euphemism. Who else but a Mancunian streetwalker could think up such a name! A short while before you had availed yourself of the services available behind the tottering facade that fronted the palace and now you stood undecided, not knowing whether to go left or right. The right seemed to be safer. The street was well-lit. There was a policeman standing at the end some distance away. This was the route for which you opted until I took a hand and imposed my restraining influences with all my might upon you. You heeded me and proceeded to the left. You may truly thank your sixth sense for having survived that night. The policeman was not what he seemed. Rather was he part of a gang of professional muggers who would cheerfully slit your throat for a sixpence. Knowing your penchant for preserving your finances you would most certainly have resisted or run off if that were possible. Either way would have been fatal.

There was the time you had the ink-wetted pen in your hand ready to sign on the dotted line of a contract which you believed would guarantee you vast profits. In a trice, at my bidding and without explanation to anybody, you had laid the pen down and refused to sign. Subsequently you learned that you would have lost all if you had added your signature. In spite of all I have done for you I doubt if you are even aware of my existence. I might not be visible or tangible but I am worth my weight in gold as any fair-minded man would admit. Please acknowledge.

Sincerely

Your Sixth Sense

THE CONSCIENCE WRITES TO THE BRAIN

Dear Brain

How about a little of your undivided attention? Up until this time, as far as I am concerned, your undivided attention has been scarcest of all identifiable commodities. You may well ask again as you have so often asked in the past in your own coarse fashion:

'Who the hell are you?'

I'll tell you who I am. I am that little inner voice which endeavours to tell you how to distinguish between right and wrong so that your whole being might come belatedly to know peace and tranquillity.

I am also the spirit of unrest and I will dog you to the end of your days. You have never been certain about my exact whereabouts and I have often heard you ask: 'Where the hell are you?' I am everywhere that you are but chiefly I reside in you although I have been known to make pilgrimages to your heart.

Often you have asked in frustration: What the hell are you?'

A religious person might call me the law of God written in the heart of every human. A layman might call me the judge and jury of human behaviour insofar as it relates to one person.

I know that I have caused you some anguish although not nearly enough because your spiritual hide is almost impervious to my proddings and prickings. I do unsettle you somewhat, however.

It's not that I wish to unhinge you altogether. That is not my function. Only you have the power to unhinge yourself and alas! how often has the disorganised brain ended life prematurely with bullet, poison, rope or water according to prevailing tastes or contiguity of one or other of this gruesome four! Conscience hath not made cowards of these poor demented creatures. Rather have we invested them with the lunatic courage to commit the unthinkable lest they commit the ultimate upon those they love and cause the greater folly.

Now to you! I have found you to be morally unconscious mostly in your self-induced sexual deliriums although aided and abetted by responsive partners.

I have found you to be frequently deaf in your responses to my queries regarding your financial dealings but I have found you at your most declamatory when others do unto you as you would unto them.

I have lived with you since you attained the use of reason which, in your case, was somewhat delayed beyond the normal maturing stage. As you developed into manhood you gradually tried to refine me to a state where I would be subject to your will and failing this made subtler bids in an effect to get me to work in the same harness as your will. Will and conscience can never be bedfellows, so your bid failed.

It was these failures which brought you to that inevitable state at which all humans arrive sooner or later when they cannot dominate me. Then comes the painful realisation that I must somehow be salved and placated.

An agreement between you and me became a necessity but in that pact you would continually try to deceive me although your need for total forgiveness was always paramount in your thinking. Without it you were ever on edge, sleepless, restive, incapable of self-consolation and self-forgiveness.

Self-forgiveness. There's a tricky one. Must man be shriven by outside agents or is the capacity to absolve himself within himself and is this legitimate in the sight of God? I am only the conscience and cannot say but it would make my work less complicated if there was an answer forthcoming.

I would be in favour of self-forgiveness where the brain, prompted by the heart, has already forgiven others. A man who has forgiven all those who have wronged him, however little or however mightily, should have the power to forgive himself.

It is not a power I would confer on all men, only on those whose natures are so forgiving that they would not even dream of withholding forgiveness from those who would ruin and destroy them.

The great question that arises here is my future in the event of your being consigned to damnation or hell or whatever. Being your conscience I am part of you, the most inbuilt part of you, the greatest single influence for good within the entire framework of your make-up. Am I, who has performed Trojan heroics in my efforts to guide you aright, to be dispatched to hell with you or am I to be segregated from the rest of the personality and sent aloft? Am I alone to be delivered, as it were, while my heart and my spirit and yourself and my all are consigned to everlasting and excruciating obscurity?

What becomes of consciences like me when you no longer function? Must I, who am not to blame, reside in hell with you or am I to be disposed to a limbo? If so you will be only partially in hell and I will be only partially in this new limbo or will I be received into heaven high and dry on my lonesome?

This in my estimation would constitute a forced breaking-up of the spiritual fundamentals, which I would hold to be illegitimate, and I must hereby advise you that it is your bounden duty to instruct your vocal cords so that they might express my views clearly and loudly to the responsible authorities and, thereby, avoid the reckless sundering of our very self.

Failing that, you might have your right hand address itself to notepaper where my views would be clearly set forth without embellishment; copies then to be made and dispatched to the more responsible newspapers in the hope that a sharp controversy might ensue which would eventually lead to badly-needed clarification on this vexatious topic.

Remember too that an act which might painfully prick one conscience often has no effect whatsoever on another so that you cannot expect to be guided by the complacency of another, so-called just man, after that person has perpetrated an evil act. The complacency does not reduce the abhorrence that should exist in you, dear brain.

There are consciences and consciences. There's the Christian conscience, the Catholic conscience, the Mohammedan conscience; the Atheistic, often the most tormenting of all; there is the Pagan conscience, the Greek Orthodox conscience and the Buddhist, and the whole shooting gallery of sects, factions and assorted conventicles, all making different and often lunatic demands upon their respective proprietors. However, in the final reckoning it is the individual conscience that matters.

You may be impressed or intimidated by local conscience, by national conscience and by international conscience but while these are fine in themselves and while they reform for the better and highlight ills and evils you are still left with me. There are also some comic aspects of conscience which may not seem in the least comic to their adherents.

In the western hemisphere a man may possess only one woman at a time while under the public eye but in parts of the East he may possess as many as he likes. I would like to suggest that occasional hell, frequent purgatory and too little heaven are the dominant features of a comprehensive human life so that the hereafter should provide a predominance of heaven for every Tom, Dick and Harry who has passed this hazardous way, who upon entry to this often godforsaken world is immediately impregnated with insurmountable prejudice, greed, intolerance, bigotry and all the other countless faults so rampant and ever-fermenting in you, the human brain.

As your conscience it is my duty to point out these things as it is your duty to acknowledge and weigh them against your more edifying activities. I ask you to ponder on all that I have conveyed to you, all for your future good I might add. Finally, I must inform you of one inescapable truth against which there can be no real argument, so take heed!

You may repent and recant privately and publicly until you are blue in the face. You may be publicly and privately forgiven of all that you have publicly and privately confessed but remember that it is with me you will have to contend at the end of the day, and if I don't give you the nod all your penitential posturings will count for naught.

As ever

Your Conscience